SEMI-SWEET ON YOU

HOT CAKES BOOK FOUR

ERIN NICHOLAS

ISBN: 978-1-952280-06-1

Editor: Lindsey Faber

Cover design: Angela Waters

Cover Photography: Lindee Robinson

Models: Christina Engel and Camden Grigsby

THE HOT CAKES SERIES

One small Iowa town.
Two rival baking companies.
A three-generation old family feud.
And five guys who are going to be heating up a lot more than the kitchen.

Books in the series:
Sugar Rush (prequel)
Sugarcoated
Forking Around
Making Whoopie
Semi-Sweet On You
Oh, Fudge
Gimme S'more

ABOUT SEMI-SWEET ON YOU

A slow burn, second-chance rom com!

She broke his heart ten years ago.

Now he's back -- and her new boss.

And she might still be semi in love with him.

But that's no problem, right? They can keep it professional.

Until her grandmother gets involved.

She's thrilled to think that Whitney and Cam are still in love. And invites him to move in with her...and Whitney.

Of course, Whitney can handle that too. Yeah, everything is fine. Just fine.

Until Cam makes it clear that he's all in.

Having him back is very sweet, but can she really have it all? Or will it all crumble around her?

1

——————

"I think my butt looks really weird in this. Can you come look?" Whitney called from inside the powder room in her office.

Piper was out at her desk in the reception area of the Hot Cakes executive suites and this dress was hers. Whitney did *not* think she was pulling it off. At all. The other woman wore the pinup-style dresses and looked like a million bucks. But Piper had the curves for it. And the attitude. She was confident, sassy, and sexy.

Whitney knew *she* didn't have the curves, and she was pretty sure she didn't have even half the attitude.

But she wanted it.

She really did.

She wanted a change, that was for sure, and her attitude was just part of it.

This dress might be a good start.

She turned in front of the mirror on the back of her powder room door. Or maybe it wasn't a good start.

She wasn't ready for a dress like this.

"Seriously, I don't have the curves for this," she called. Piper might be on the phone, but Whitney really needed a second opinion.

"I sincerely doubt I'd ever use the word 'weird' in regard to your ass."

Whitney swung around with a gasp. That was *not* Piper's voice.

"But I'm very happy to take a look."

Whitney sucked in a breath. Dammit. That was Cam.

Camden McCaffery.

One of the partners who owned Hot Cakes.

One of her new bosses.

Her ex.

Oh, and the guy who she was still sort of in love with.

Fuck.

She took another breath and then peeked around the edge of the door.

Cam was leaning against the doorjamb of her office door. Looking hot in a custom-tailored charcoal suit, the light blue shirt underneath unbuttoned at his throat. And cocky. As always. And amused.

"I thought Piper was out there," Whitney said. Which was obvious. But what the hell else was she supposed to say?

"That's who I came up to find too," Cam said, stepping into Whitney's office. "But she's gone."

"Gone?" Whitney asked. Piper knew she was in here trying on dresses.

Cam shrugged one big shoulder. "I guess."

Whitney swallowed, her eyes on that shoulder. He was so... yeah, big. Wide. Solid. He'd always been muscular, but now he was... big. He had definitely changed over the years. Grown. Filled out. Gone from cute to oh-my-God hot.

Which was really unfortunate for a girl who was trying to her damnedest to be over him.

She'd seen him here and there. It seemed every time he

was home to visit they ran into each other. Sometimes literally. Like the time she'd come around the big display of marshmallows at the end of aisle three at the grocery store and run directly into his chest. She'd jumped back, trying to avoid him touching her, and fallen right into that big stack of marshmallows. The entire store had come rushing to see what had happened.

And that wasn't even the most embarrassing time.

"So come on," he said, motioning her forward with his hand. "Let's see."

Her eyebrows shot up. "See what?"

"Your ass." His lips curled on one end. "Isn't that what you're worried about?"

"I can wait for Piper."

"Why?" He tucked his hands into his pockets. "I'm quite qualified to judge how a woman's ass looks. In dresses. In jeans. In shorts." He paused. "*Out of* all of those things."

He was an ass. She couldn't forget that. Of course, when he was an ass, it was on purpose. Especially when he was an ass to *her*. He was stubborn, had a quick temper, a deeply ingrained sense of justice and loyalty, and a pretty black and white view of how things should go, but he had never been an ass to her. He'd been downright sweet and protective and romantic and... sexy.

Until she'd broken his heart ten years ago.

So, yeah, she might deserve it a little. She knew that.

They'd been in love. He'd wanted her to go to college with him. When she'd said no, he'd wanted to stay in Appleby with her. So she'd broken up with him. No way could she have kept him here. But it had broken his heart.

And it certainly made working for him now a challenge. Hell, it made seeing him on Main Street a challenge.

He'd been poking at her for the past month. Ever since he'd come back to Appleby full time. Every time they were in a meeting together or had a conversation, he made comments that were meant to annoy her. She didn't know why, exactly. She could speculate, but she hadn't even let herself go there.

She just knew she had to hold her shit together. She couldn't lose her temper. She couldn't snap at him—or even glare at him, honestly. He was her boss. He was one of the reasons the company was still standing. That she had a job at all. That her family's name wasn't a curse word in this town.

She freaking *owed him*.

Which he was very aware of.

Maybe that was why he was poking. Because he knew she couldn't give it back. Or maybe because he was hoping to push her to the point where she would lose it and he could fire her.

Whatever the reason, she just had to breathe deeply, smile, let it roll off, and act professionally.

Good thing she'd been practicing all of those things for the past ten years working with her grandfather, father, and brother.

She was a fucking *pro* at letting male egos and snide remarks roll off.

It was why she drank wine. And kickboxed. And did yoga. More the kickboxing, but still.

Of course, Cam had started going to the morning yoga class *she* had always liked best, so she'd had to adjust her schedule because there was no way in hell she could be in a room with him for an hour watching him bend and stretch and flex.

"Come on, Whit. Let me see."

Fine. What she'd learned about the asshole men she'd been working with for the past ten years—yes, all her relatives—was that *not* letting them know they were getting to her was the most important thing.

She stepped out of the powder room, running her hands over her hips, smoothing the dress.

Cam's eyes widened as she came into full view.

Yeah, take that.

Hey, she didn't *say* the stuff out loud but that didn't mean she didn't think it. She schooled her features and just watched him taking her in.

His gaze tracked over her. Slowly. Twice.

Her whole damned body was tingling by the time he was done.

And if she didn't want him to know that his comments about being her boss and saving the company and how her family had nearly put three hundred and forty-seven people out of work got to her, she *sure as hell* wasn't going to let on that his biceps and tattoos and cocky smile got to her. And she was *not* going to react to him reacting to her.

Because he was. He really was.

His jaw was tight, he was standing straighter, and he looked as if he was putting every ounce of willpower into just standing there and not coming toward her.

She lied to people all day long. For years it had been to her dad and brother and grandfather. She told them she was fine and on top of things and thought things were going well. Those were all lies. She hadn't been fine, and she'd never felt like she was doing what she wanted to be doing, and no, she'd never liked how her family ran the business. She also lied to her grandmother, telling Didi that everything at Hot Cakes was great and she loved her job.

Didi Lancaster had started Hot Cakes and had worked in the business for the first five years or so but Dean, her husband, had convinced her that it just wasn't "right" for her to be working in their multimillion-dollar nationally renowned company. She was too good to be working in the factory, and she didn't know enough about business to work in the business offices or executive suites. That's where Dean and their son Eric —Whitney's dad—and later Whitney's brother, Wes, belonged. They let Whitney have an office too. Mostly because it had kept her under their thumbs.

Of course, she hadn't figured that out for about three years. But she'd known it for a long time now.

So yes, she was fully prepared to lie to Cam. And the rest of her bosses, for that matter. She was going to tell them that everything was great, that she thought they were doing a great job because working for them could not be worse than working for her own family.

She was also absolutely going to lie to Cam about how she felt about him.

It was just all for the best.

She had wine and kickboxing. It would all be okay.

Whitney said nothing as Cam continued to study her. It was probably really only about a minute, but it felt like she'd been standing there under his hot gaze for a week. Still, she stubbornly stood, waiting for his reaction. Because, by God, he was going to be the one to react first.

Finally he shifted his weight in a clear attempt to look more casual and lifted his gaze to hers. "You're gonna have to turn around if I'm gonna make a judgment about your ass."

She cocked an eyebrow. Camden McCaffery was full of himself. Always had been. He didn't care what people thought of him and he didn't really care for rules. Like sexual harassment guidelines at Hot Cakes. He just said whatever the fuck he wanted to. She knew how to handle him. He expected other people to say what they were thinking and feeling too. Without getting fired, of course.

Though she suspected she was *less* likely to get fired for speaking her mind with him than she would be if she lied.

If he knew she was lying anyway.

It was a good thing she was *very* good.

"But you think I look okay from the front?" she asked, propping a hand on her hip.

He shrugged. *Shrugged.* And her eyes narrowed.

"Your tits look amazing," he said. "But I'm not sure this dress is really right."

Yeah, bosses should not say things like *your tits look amazing* to employees. Guys should also not say things like that to their exes.

But if Cam thought that sexism and blatant disregard for her feelings was somehow going to give him the upper hand, he was very badly mistaken. She could deal with sexist assholes all day without even rolling her eyes. Visibly anyway.

It was so normal in her world, in fact, that dealing with his three partners—her other bosses, who were actually decent men who respected women and liked working with them—was a shock to her system. She found herself having to remind herself that they weren't being sarcastic when they asked what she thought.

But, yeah, she could handle Cam.

She smoothed the front of the dress again and looked down at her breasts. "Amazing, huh?"

That, of course, pulled his gaze back to her breasts. "Absolutely," he said simply, with a nod.

Yeah, she was a very accomplished, unapologetic liar. Except to herself.

She liked his reaction.

She was thinner now than when they'd dated. They'd been seventeen and eighteen when they'd been together but looking back, they'd been kids. She'd never been curvy but she'd been heavier than now. She was now more toned thanks to workouts to manage her stress. And now with Cam's eyes on her, she was really glad about every one of those sweaty sessions in her home gym and the yoga studio downtown.

"Well then, I'm thinking this dress might be just right."

He met her gaze. "Turn around."

She was also *very* grateful for ten years practicing schooling her reactions because *that*—the deep, gruff, firm command with the heat in his eyes—was *really* hard not to react to, even with all the experience she had.

She licked her lips, watched his eyes drop to her mouth, then turned—before she smiled.

She bent her knee, propping her hand on her cocked hip, and just stood, again letting him study her.

What did she have to lose? Her butt didn't look weird in it so much as *she* just looked weird in it. This was not her kind of dress. The dress was way too sassy for her. It was a wiggle dress —the hem narrower than the hips which caused the wearer to take shorter steps and added a little wiggle to the stride—and was bright red. She wore pencil skirts but they weren't this tapered, for one thing. They also didn't cling to her hips and butt like this. The material of the dress was a silky, stretchy fabric that hugged her body, giving the illusion of far curvier curves than were really there. The bodice was a halter style, cupping her breasts and dipping low between them, with the wide straps hooking behind her neck and leaving her upper back bare.

And she never wore red. She wore black and gray and navy blue. She had one forest green skirt too. But, yes, lots and lots of black.

It was another very, very long minute before Cam said anything.

He cleared his throat though.

And when he did, her stomach clenched. Or maybe what clenched was lower. It was an area that she hadn't felt clench in a while.

Probably since Christmas when Cam had nearly run her over in the crosswalk on Main and then had to come help her pick up her cookies and panties. She'd been carrying packages of both and had dropped them when he'd scared the ever-living shit out of her.

Watching him pick up the bright blue thong and scrap of a

bra—even brighter against the white snow and dark gray of the wet pavement they were lying on—and stare at them, had made her heart pound even harder than nearly being killed.

Then it had gotten worse. The cookies in the box she'd been carrying had been frosted sugar cookies that she'd secretly bought from Buttered Up, Cam's sister Zoe's bakery. She'd paid a little girl twenty bucks to go in and buy the cookies for her and then pass them to her behind the lingerie store. Whitney had slipped them into a plain bag so no one would know. The family feud between Buttered Up and Hot Cakes was three generations old and meant she couldn't freely shop in the bakery. Which sucked. It had always sucked.

Thankfully, Aiden, one of the new Hot Cakes owners, had fallen in love with Zoe and they were quickly obliterating all of the stupid tension between the two businesses. And maybe, just maybe, her working with the guys to build Hot Cakes back up and make it even better would heal the tension between the families.

Maybe.

Of course, she and Cam were a big part of that.

The feud had started with their grandmothers. But Cam's grandma, Letty, was gone and Whitney's, Didi, was in mental decline.

But those damned cookies and their icing had come back to bite Whitney. Some frosting had gotten on the thong that Cam held. And as she squatted there on Main Street—in one of her black pencil skirts with cold December Iowa air blowing up underneath—he'd swiped the frosting off the thong, lifted it to his mouth, and licked it off.

She hadn't felt one bit of cold air in that moment.

"Yeah, definitely not weird," he finally said, his voice huskier than before.

Whitney breathed out. He'd spoken first. She'd won that round of chicken.

She looked over her shoulder at him. "So I'm good to go in this one?"

"You can't wear this dress in Appleby," he said, shaking his head.

She frowned and turned. "Why not?"

"This dress is not you."

He was right.

She'd been dressing in conservative business attire because of her grandfather and dad. She'd been trying to be taken seriously for the past decade by the very men who should have been encouraging her to be involved in the company and proud of the things she'd tried to do. Not that the skirts and pants had worked. But this dress? No way would this have convinced her grandfather she should be introducing a new product to their line.

These guys though? Cam, Aiden, Ollie, and Grant? They were all in. They not only thought it was a great idea, they were very happy to have her leading the charge.

She couldn't wear this dress to the big dessert-baking competition and auction they were holding in the town square tomorrow. But she would love to hear Cam explain to her why.

It was too clingy. It was too *red*. It was too sexy. It was too... not Whitney Lancaster.

Which was why she loved it. She wanted to wear this dress. She wanted to have a man—she corrected that almost immediately—she wanted *Cam* looking at her in this dress exactly the way he was looking at her right now.

Like he was seriously considering how sturdy the desk behind her was and if they were really alone here.

Her pulse skittered under her skin.

They were alone. And that desk was very sturdy.

But, yeah, she suddenly wanted to hear Cam say all of that to her. Would he? Would he just put it out there?

She'd, of course, turn him down. She was not the sex-on-her-desk kind of girl. Either.

But she wanted to be that too...

Not with Cam, of course. That would be really, really, really stupid.

Whitney swallowed and worked on keeping her cool.

She was now thinking about sex on her desk. With Cam. Because of course she was.

He was looking at her like he was too.

And if she were being totally honest with herself—and she really did try to be that—Cam was the only one she could imagine having sex with. Period. Because he was one of three guys she'd had sex with. Ever. And she absolutely knew that it was pathetic and that was probably a huge part of why she was uptight and tense and kind of cool and bitchy at times.

But being Whitney Lancaster meant there weren't many guys in Appleby who were willing to approach her for dates, and she was not at all the type to go to another town. That would require girlfriends. And a desire to go to bars or clubs or... wherever people went to meet people.

Which meant she'd had sex two other times since her high school boyfriend. Both had been with men she'd met at business conferences. They had been single occurrences. And they hadn't been all that good.

Whereas having sex with Cam at age eighteen on blankets by the river and the back seats of cars and on the lumpy sofa in the basement at his house and in her bed when her parents were out for the night... had all been amazing.

Facing him now with that hot look in his eyes and her very sturdy desk behind them and her entire body suddenly humming with awareness was truly a test of that cool bitchiness she had going on.

She crossed her arms. "What's that mean?" she asked about the dress not being her.

But he just gave her a look that said he knew she knew what he meant. "There are no buttons."

She frowned slightly. "No buttons?"

"Hard to be buttoned-up without buttons."

Ah. Got it. Ha-ha. "Well, the idea of the contest and auction is that we're doing something new, right? New ownership, new product, new approach to the business?" She looked down at the dress. "Maybe I need a new look."

"You're going to cause heart attacks in that dress, Whit."

Whit. Ugh. He had to call her Whit? That nickname got to her. He wasn't the only person who called her that. The other guys did, too, from time to time. But that was the thing... only these guys called her that.

Her family didn't. Her friends... okay, she didn't have many friends, and the ones she did kind of have didn't call her Whit.

But these guys all did. Like friends. Or brothers. It was familiar and affectionate and it always made her feel warm.

But she knew they called her that because Cam did.

And when he had done it in the past, it had unquestionably been affectionate. And hot. It was now too. Probably because of the stupid dress, but right now when he said it, she could remember how he'd said it in those back seats and on those blankets by the river.

She lifted her chin. "Well, thanks."

He took a step forward. "I'm serious. You can't wear that to the auction. That's not a business dress."

"What kind of dress is it?"

"That's a sex dress."

Her eyes rounded. She'd poked but she was still surprised that he'd said it like that. "This is one of Piper's dresses."

"It's not a sex dress on Piper."

Whitney felt her mouth curving. "Piper looks amazing in all of her dresses."

Cam nodded. "Yeah."

"And she's got better breasts than I do. In every dress."

His gaze dropped to her breasts again and Whitney could only hope her bra would hide her nipples' reaction to his attention.

"I don't know if I'd say that," he said.

Her mouth was suddenly a little dry but she managed a little laugh. "Piper's breasts are bigger than mine, no matter what dress we wear, no matter what."

His gaze made it back to hers. "Bigger maybe. But you said better."

"You don't like big breasts?"

"I don't like any breasts as much as I like yours."

And there it was. Out loud. Hanging in the air between them. Needing addressing. And all her fault. She'd poked. She'd wanted this.

She swallowed, knowing that her cool and collected expression had finally wavered. Not only did she really like that he liked her breasts, but she also liked the insinuation that he'd never met another pair he liked more. "Thank you," she finally said.

Because what the hell was she supposed to say to that? She hadn't really thought that far ahead.

The corner of his mouth kicked up. "You're welcome."

She wet her lips again. So now what?

"Your ass too. While we're on the subject."

She pressed her lips together now.

"And your—"

"Let's *change* the subject," she said quickly. Her heart was hammering and she was very aware that she was three big steps away from her sturdy desk and about ten seconds away from becoming a sex-on-her-desk girl.

"Anyway," he said. "You can't wear a sex dress to the auction."

"It's not a sex dress," she said. "Piper wears this to work."

Then she frowned. "Do you think of sex when Piper wears this?"

She and Cam were talking about sex. This was really not how she'd imagined her night going.

"I do not," he said. "I..." He seemed to be thinking about how to explain something. "I notice her in this dress. This is a dress that's hard *not* to notice. And Piper is gorgeous and she wears the hell out of her dresses."

Whitney nodded, telling herself that the stab of jealousy she felt was really stupid. If Piper and Cam were going to get together, they would have by now. They'd known each other, worked together, for years.

For all she knew they *had* gotten together. She didn't know his history with other women because she very stubbornly refused to think about, wonder about, or *ask* about that.

She'd seen them flirt but Piper had this flirtatious air about her all the time. She treated all the guys like they were good friends she loved but who also drove her nuts. She took care of them. She gave them shit. She *called them* on their shit. She also bent over backward to help make things work and get them what they needed and wanted to make the company work.

Piper was amazing. As far as Whitney knew, there was nothing the woman couldn't do. She was easily five years younger than Dax and Ollie, who were the youngest of the partners, but she managed them as if she were an older sister. Or a mom some of the time.

She was undeniably gorgeous too. So maybe it just made sense that Cam thought so.

"But I think about sex when I see this dress on *you*."

Air rushed out of her lungs. Dammit. This was so bad. She and Cam could *not* talk about sex. They shouldn't talk about a number of things. Their past. Her family. Sex. Yeah, those were probably the top three. For sure. Though not necessarily in that order.

"You can't say things like that to an employee," she finally told him, her fingers digging into her arms.

He shrugged. "You have my boss's phone number."

She did. Though he didn't have a boss. But he had three partners and all three would care if she was feeling harassed. He also had a fourth best friend, Dax, who was a consultant for the company and who would also care how Cam was treating her.

And suddenly Whitney felt warmed by that. She had people on her side.

It was a very strange moment to realize that. It was a very strange moment to be touched by that. But it had been a long time since she'd felt like she had people who would have her back.

She'd told her father once that a business associate of his had hit on her at a big reception. He'd laughed and told her that was just how men treated beautiful young women and she should be flattered. She'd told her brother that a guy he'd gone to college with had propositioned her to secure a deal. He'd told her to stop being such a prude.

So yeah, it was really nice to know that she had people who would take Cam to task for this.

She also didn't miss the irony that Cam was the one guy she most wanted to talk about sex with.

He'd always been so sweetly dirty. He'd said things to her, even at age eighteen, that had been graphic and gruff and came completely from a place of emotion. It was like he hadn't been able to hold back. She'd loved it. But only because she knew that it was a sign of how much she affected him and how much he loved her.

Dirty talk as a sign of love? Yeah, well, that might sound strange to anyone who hadn't heard Camden McCaffery's dirty talk, but it was true. It had been one of the things missing with the other guys. Not the only thing, but clearly some of it.

No one had ever talked to her the way Cam had.

Even the first time he'd asked her out. He'd come up to her in the school hallway, said, "I can't stop thinking about you so you have to let me take you out."

She'd said, "I do?"

"You do. I have to either get over you. Or get you under me." He'd leaned in with a little smile and a look in his eyes she hadn't fully understood but that had made her feel hot and tingly.

She'd been seventeen. The rich, untouchable Lancaster princess, and the school bad boy had just said he wanted to get her under him. And she'd wanted that—him—instantly. He hadn't been intimidated. He hadn't been slick or flirty. He'd been straightforward.

She'd met his eyes and with her best haughty princess voice had said, "*That* won't help you get over anything."

She *still*, all these years later, couldn't believe she'd said that. She'd been a virgin. She'd been on two dates and she hadn't really thought they were worth repeating. She had nothing to back up her comment, but something about Cam's cockiness had brought her own out.

His cockiness had been all the more impressive because he'd been a McCaffery saying those things to a Lancaster. Their families would have flipped out to know that they were talking about even going to the movies not to mention flirting about sex.

Of course, that little thrill had made her even more willing to say yes.

They'd snuck around, had a lot of teenage sex, a lot of laughs, and fallen in love over the next year.

The best year of her life.

Still.

"So I probably also shouldn't say that I think of sex when I see you in a lot of things," he said, moving closer again.

Her heart tripped.

"You definitely shouldn't."

"Which means you probably won't tell me that you think about sex when you see me either."

Dammit. She shook her head. "No, I won't tell you that."

"Out loud anyway," he said.

"What?"

"You won't tell me that out loud."

"What's that mean?" But she was pretty sure she knew.

"It means that you tell me that in lots of ways, Whit," he said, his voice gruff. "Even if you don't say it out loud."

She took a deep breath. She had to be cool here. He could be bluffing. He could be trying to get a reaction. He could just be trying to get her to admit something he didn't know for sure. She might not actually be giving away how she felt every time she saw him.

"Some things never change," she said, lifting her chin, fighting for the detached air she wore like she wore her favorite perfume. Why was it so hard to find when Cam was around? "You're still completely full of yourself."

He actually gave a soft laugh. "Well, yeah."

That was another really appealing thing about this guy—he knew himself and he owned his flaws. Oh, he owned his accomplishments and talents too, but he owned his flaws.

She just wasn't sure he thought being full of himself was a flaw.

"You really like that dress?" he asked, his gaze tracking over her again.

She nodded. "I do. I think it's time I try a few new things."

She didn't like this dress. Well, she liked the dress. But she wasn't going to wear it. She wasn't... ready for a dress like this. She wanted to be. She wanted to feel confident and free of worrying about her image and prepared to just go with what felt good, but she'd spent twenty-nine years having to worry about what other people thought and how she presented herself and trying to prove herself. It was going to take some time to get to the point where this dress was a good fit. Metaphorically.

"Then I know exactly where you can wear it," Cam said.

"Oh?"

"Timothy's."

Timothy's was an expensive restaurant in Dubuque. White tablecloths, multiple forks, all of that. "Yeah, I guess this would work at Timothy's," she agreed.

"So let's go tomorrow night."

She froze. Slowly she lifted her eyes to his. "Us?"

"You and me."

"*Just* us?"

"Yes."

"Like a...business dinner? We'll talk about plans for—"

"No. Dinner, wine, dessert, me feeling you up under the table, walking downtown and talking, late drinks, then sex all night in a suite at the Hilton."

Whitney just stared at him. Her heart was thundering so loud that she almost couldn't hear anything else. This was the thing with Cam's straightforwardness—it was really hard to pretend that you misunderstood.

Okay, so her cool façade was going to waver a bit. So sue her.

"Not even a *pretense* of something else?" she finally asked.

"When have I ever been a pretense guy?"

He had a point. "So you actually want..." She trailed off and pressed her lips together, not sure she wanted him to fill that in.

He moved closer again. The air between them heated. At least *she* was feeling hotter.

"To look at you in that fucking dress all night long," he said. "Getting harder and hotter as the time goes on until we can't stand it any longer and I almost rip it off of you in the elevator on the way up to the room."

Well. Holy. Shit.

She'd asked.

And she'd wanted an answer like that.

But that answer was really the worst thing he could have possibly said.

How was she supposed to be completely professional and pretend she was over him when he said stuff like that?

He's just pushing your buttons, she told herself.

He didn't look like he was kidding. Or messing around. But she had to tell herself that was exactly what he was doing. Or she was going to grab him and strip him out of that hot suit and lick the tattoos that he'd added to since she'd last been able to lick them.

Daaaaaamit.

She took a breath. Then nodded. "Okay, so I guess my butt doesn't look weird in this dress, then."

He didn't seem surprised that was the only reaction she gave. "Definitely not."

"Okay, thanks for the input."

She stepped around him and headed for the bathroom.

2

He waited for her to change.

Of course he did.

He wasn't the type of guy to leave and let her catch her breath and gather her composure and see each other the next day as if he hadn't just confessed that he wanted to take her out.

And to a hotel. For sex.

He really hated beating around the bush, so he didn't. It made it so much easier when he knew that everyone knew exactly where he stood on things.

It was very important that Whitney Lancaster know where he stood on things.

That was why he was still here in her office, perusing the stuff on her shelves, playing with the stress ball he'd picked up from her desk, and thinking about the fact that she was at least semi-naked on the other side of the thin door of her private bathroom. And wondering what color panties she had on. Or if maybe it was a thong. Like the one he'd picked up from the snowy pavement a few months ago.

A gentleman wouldn't think about that. Or the last time he'd seen her in a thong. Or naked. Well, he assumed. He only knew maybe one and a half gentlemen and he didn't spend a ton of time with them.

A guy who was over her probably wouldn't think about any of that either.

Of course, he was neither of those things.

As evidenced by the things he'd said to her. And the fact that he was still here and planning to say more.

He squeezed the ball harder as he studied the framed photos that she had on the shelves of the massive cherrywood bookcase by her window.

The photos were of her with her family. Of course.

And wow, he really hated her grandfather and father.

He felt his chest tighten with bitterness and anger just looking at photos of them.

Dean and Eric Lancaster were the epitome of entitled, rich assholes who thought that they could do whatever they wanted to because they had money and power.

It was not a secret to anyone who knew Cam and his history with the Lancasters, or to himself—or the therapist that he'd seen for a while a few years ago—that a lot of his drive came from wanting to be a rich asshole too. He wanted to be at their level of wealth and success so that he could prove that they'd been wrong. About everything.

It absolutely wasn't mentally healthy, but it had worked out so far. He was rich and successful and he had surpassed them in both wealth and success. And he was asshole, but he was less of one than Dean and Eric were.

In fact, he now owned *their* business and was in the midst of helping build it into something that was bigger and better than anything they'd ever done.

The Lancaster family had run Hot Cakes for as long as it had existed. Up until about two months ago when Cam and his partners had bought it. Whitney's grandmother had started the company. After she'd stolen the first recipe from *his* grandmother. Him now owning the factory was fucking sweet. Pun totally intended.

Clenching and relaxing his fist around the lime-green stress ball, Cam leaned in to peer closer at the photo of Whitney and Dorothy—Didi to everyone who knew her—in front of the factory. Whitney had to have been about six or seven.

Even then she'd been cute. Long, dark hair, those big brown eyes that he'd always been a sucker for, that huge smile. She was wearing a red coat, grinning at the camera, while holding Didi's hand with one of hers, hoisting a Hot Cakes snack cake —it was too small in the photo to tell which one—in the air with the other.

It was strange, but it was the red coat that caught his attention.

Red.

She never wore red.

That was one of the reasons seeing her in Piper's dress had punched him in the chest. It was a bright, bold, happy color. She never wore bright, bold, happy colors.

But he hadn't realized it until he saw her in that fucking dress.

That was only one of the things about the dress that had sucked every molecule of oxygen out of his lungs and made him hard and stupid all at once.

Her tits really had looked amazing in that thing. And no, her ass had *not* looked weird.

But he could not get over that color.

She used to wear red.

Not just as a little girl, but in high school too. In the time he'd know her she'd worn red. And other bright colors.

Hell, he'd picked bright blue panties—well, it had technically been a thong, a detail he had *not* missed—up off the street at Christmas.

So she wore red *under* her black and gray and navy blue clothes that she wore to the office.

He hadn't put his finger on it until this very second, but that was why he hated her fucking clothes.

At first he'd thought it was because those pencil skirts did actually make her ass and legs look great and he figured he was just dealing with horniness and the whole wanting-what-he-couldn't-have that always simmered in the air when he was near Whitney.

Then he thought it was because they were very conservative, something he was *not*, and she paired them with those buttoned-up blouses that reminded him of what a good girl she'd always tried to be. Or the image of one that she'd tried to project at least. Which then reminded him of how naughty and fun that good girl could be when he got her to loosen up. Which led back to the horniness and the wanting-what-he-couldn't-fucking-have that plagued him.

But now he put his finger on it.

She wore those damned boring-assed colors that were *not* her and he would put a million dollars—and he could literally do that, thank you very fucking much—on the fact that she wore those because her grandfather or father had told her that's how she should dress to work for Hot Cakes.

He loved her in that red dress of Piper's.

Not just because she looked sexy as hell but because he would bet another million that *she* really liked that dress.

The door to the powder room opened behind him and he turned to face her.

She came up short when she saw that he was still there.

She was back in her silky light blue blouse and the dark gray skirt. He found it interesting they were wearing the same colors today.

But he really fucking hated her outfit.

He frowned and moved to her desk to return the stress ball

to its spot next to her plain black pencil holder. Damn, even the stress ball and pencil holder were boring. Dax had one that when you squeezed it the inner liquid squished out into multi-colored bubbles. Whitney needed one of those. Desperately. Literally and metaphorically.

"You're still here," she said.

"You didn't tell me if we're going to dinner tomorrow night or the next night," he said, tucking his hands into his pockets.

She tossed Piper's dress over the back of one of the chairs that faced her desk and regarded him with narrowed eyes.

"Neither. But you already knew that answer. So why are you really still here?"

Ah, see, that was the other reason he hated her clothes. When she dressed like this it was clear that she *felt* more buttoned up and cool. Not at all vulnerable and sexy.

"I'm really still here because I want to know when we're going out. We don't have to go to Timothy's. Hell, we don't have to go to dinner for that matter."

"Just straight to the hotel then?" she asked.

"Sure." He shrugged.

"Well, I guess it's a step up from the riverbank."

He lifted a brow and took a step closer to her. He didn't miss the way her breath caught for just a second. "You had *no* complaints on that riverbank, Whit." They'd been so damned hot together. Even as teenagers.

She wet her lips. "I was seventeen. What did I know?"

Yeah, well, at seventeen Miss Whitney Lancaster had been the best sex of his life. And that was still true ten years later. And he'd absolutely tried to erase that memory.

"You knew that you were madly in love with me and that nothing felt better than when we were naked together," he said.

She pressed her lips together, lifted her chin, and met his gaze directly.

He appreciated that. She was tough. She didn't want him to see that he affected her. That made this all so much more fun.

He took another step. Now he could reach her. He wasn't going to, but he could and she knew it.

"Go out with me."

"No."

"Let me put you up on your desk and convince you." Damn, he wanted to do that so fucking bad he almost had to reach down and adjust his cock. He did appreciate dress pants and the bit of give they had compared to denim. He was going to have to remember that if he was going to have these conversations with Whitney.

"No." But she swallowed hard after that one.

"Okay." He took one final step. Now she had to tip her head back to look up at him. "Let me bend you over your desk and convince you."

This time she had to swallow before she answered. "No."

He studied her face. Her pupils were wide and round, her cheeks pink, her pulse fluttered at the base of her throat. "You think I'm testing you," he said as he realized it.

"Are you?"

Well... He nodded. "Maybe a little. But not the way you think."

"You're not trying to find a reason to fire me?"

He was legitimately surprised that she thought that. "I don't want to fire you, Whit."

"No?" She looked skeptical.

"Oh, no," he said. "I want you right here, front row, center, watching me and my friends turn this company into so much more than your family ever did with it."

Emotions flickered in her eyes and he wasn't sure if he should brace for a fight or... what.

Finally she nodded. "Good. I want all of that to happen."

Yeah, he hadn't been expecting that. Not even a mild defense of her family?

"But," she said lifting her chin. "I want to... I *intend* to be a part of that. Not just sitting and watching."

She did, huh? "Because you're not really qualified to do anything else?" he asked, unable to resist the jab.

Hey, he wasn't *as big of* an asshole as the Lancaster men, but he would never deny that he could be one. Unmistakably. Unapologetically, too. Most of the time.

She took a breath. "I'm an asset to you and this company," she said instead of directly answering the question.

She was.

He nodded. "But you want to stay because you like that big old house you inherited from your grandma and you don't want to have to move and buy something on your own?"

Did it matter why she wanted to be here? As long as she was and she was a witness to the great work he and his friends were doing here? Yeah, it did matter. She needed to know where she stood with him, but he needed to know where he stood with her too.

And he had a feeling she was going to lay it all out. And that he already knew.

"I do like that house," she admitted. "This town is also my home. I don't want to live anywhere else. And I don't have a college degree to take to another company," she said, her chin up again, her gaze on his. "And I don't have any other experience except what my family gave me and I know exactly how that would look on a resume. But"—she took a breath—"what I really want is to take this company to levels my family never did. I want more markets, more products, and to double our bottom line. I want to expand the number of jobs here and to look at a second factory location. And I want to be a part of all of that." She crossed her arms and took a deep breath. "I want to be a partner."

He stared at her.

He hadn't been expecting any of that.

He really hadn't.

Whitney had always been sweet, dedicated to her family's company because that had been ingrained since she'd been born, believing that her grandfather and father could walk on water, willing to go along with whatever they wanted or needed from her. She'd been a part of the company up to this point. So why did this all sound like she'd been frustrated and was so determined to grab on to this change in ownership as an opportunity?

"I—" he started.

"Which is why I can't go out with you and I certainly can't sleep with you," she said.

Cam's eyebrows rose. "Hang on now."

"For one, it's ridiculous to even think we should go there," she told him. She dropped her arms, but she also moved behind her desk, putting the wide expanse of solid wood between them.

Cam knew that wasn't an accident.

"We broke up ten years ago," she said. "We are *exes* who haven't exactly been friends. Why would you think we should go out?"

"Well, first, *we* didn't break up. *You* broke up with *me*," he corrected, unable to help himself.

She just lifted her brows.

"And the fact we're exes and that you want to be more involved in the company is exactly why we should go out."

She gave him a *really?* look. "So if we sleep together you'll give me the partnership?"

"Girl, if you're even half as good as you were on that riverbank, I'll probably give you my shares too," he said. Again, unable to help himself.

She rolled her eyes.

He was probably lucky that she knew him well enough to know he was mostly just mouthing off. He really could end up with a sexual harassment suit against him with someone else. Of course, he'd never say that to anyone else. He did have *some* restraint and decorum. Besides, it wouldn't be true with anyone else.

No one else had ever rocked his world like Whitney had. It hadn't been because she had been experienced or even all that wild, she'd just been... he blew out a breath... madly fucking in love with him.

"But what I meant," he went on before he said anything else about sex. For now. "I think we *have* to date."

She frowned. "That makes no sense."

"Of course it does. We're not the only ones wondering about what's going on with us."

"Except that *we're* not wondering what's going on," she said. "We're not?"

That hand went back to her hip. "Are we?"

"I am," he admitted. "You're not?"

"We broke up." She held her hand up. "Fine. I broke up with you. *Ten years ago.* You've hated me for a decade, Cam. Now you own my family's company and you're my boss. *That* is what is going on."

He stalked to her desk, braced his hands on the top, and leaned in. "I do not hate you, Whitney."

Her eyes flickered with vulnerability for just a second. Then she did that annoying straighten-her-spine-lift-her-chin-smooth-her-features thing that made him want to swear. Loudly.

"I'm glad," she said coolly. "I really am. But the fact remains that we didn't work out and now—"

"I'm back."

"So?"

"So you sent me away. You broke up with me because you

thought I needed to leave Appleby. You thought I needed to go off to college and see what I could do outside of this town. And you thought you needed to stay. So we did that. I left. You stayed. And now I'm back."

"You're back for now," she said. "You're here to help Aiden and Grant and Ollie get Hot Cakes going."

"Why would I leave?"

"Your life is in Chicago."

"My best friends in the world are here now. Aiden and Dax and Grant are all staying," he said. They'd all fallen in love with Appleby girls. Girls who were happily tied here, girls who had no intentions of leaving. His sister and her best friends to be exact. "My family is here. My work is now here."

They'd headquartered their company, Fluke, Inc. in Chicago because that's where they'd all been when things had taken off. Grant was from there and he was the money guy. The rest of them hadn't had a preference for where their offices would be. But they'd sold *Warriors of Easton*, their online game, to a bigger gaming company several months ago. Dax and Ollie were still involved in creative and marketing tasks. Aiden consulted here and there. But Cam and Grant were mostly out of the loop now. That company had their own money guys and lawyers. Fluke could go in a number of directions now but right now their focus was Hot Cakes. Cam had no reason to go back to Chicago, honestly.

"You're staying?" Whitney said. "Really?"

He straightened. "Yes."

She pulled her bottom lip between her teeth. Obviously this was news to her.

"So we need to at least see if there's anything between us anymore," he said. "Everyone will be wondering." He sure as fuck was. He suspected there was plenty still between them, but he really did need to find out. He didn't know if what he was feeling was still all about the girl she'd been, the one who'd broken his heart, or if their past was something they could build on.

She was shaking her head now.

"Yes," he said firmly. "We need to go out. We need to give it a chance. If it doesn't work out, then we part as friends, and we can convince everyone that we gave it a fair shot, we both realize that we've changed and that we only want to be work partners now and everyone can finally exhale because the sexual tension will be gone and people won't have to walk on eggshells around us."

She frowned. "People aren't—"

"They are," he interrupted. "They don't know how to act around us because *we* don't know how to act. Are we friends? Are we more? Are we less? Are we just work associates? And are we both cool with that if so? Or is one of us uncomfortable or upset or horny? What if we're not together and we have a big company party and we bring other dates? How are we both going to act? Is anything going to get thrown and broken? Anyone going to get punched?"

She rolled her eyes at that.

Yeah, he'd punched a guy over her in high school. Twice.

Not the same guy. Two different occasions. One of them might have been an overreaction on his part though.

"We need to figure all of that out and get a handle on how we feel. We don't know because we haven't talked about it. We haven't explored it."

"Horny?" she repeated.

So she'd focused on that word. Interesting.

"Yeah, horny," he said. "My friends are wondering if I'm sitting in meetings thinking about fucking you on the conference table instead of actually listening to the details of the new proposal."

She blew out a breath. "You keep saying this stuff just to get a rise out of me."

"I'm saying it because it's true."

"Why would your friends be wondering that?"

"Because they know how I feel about you."

She wet her lips. "Which is... horny?"

"We can call it *intensely attracted* if that sounds classier to you."

"That would sound classier to anyone."

He just lifted a shoulder. Not many people would apply the word *classy* to him. Or any people.

She was watching him, her eyes slightly narrowed.

"What?"

"That all sounds very... mature."

He lifted a brow. "I've got my moments."

"Huh."

He couldn't help the half smile. He could admit that "mature" was another word that not many people had used to describe him in the past.

"We're ten years older, Whit. We've grown up. I went away and did other stuff. Now we have to find out what this is."

She took a deep breath, focused on the very boring black and silver lamp on her desk. "It's nothing, Cam." She met his eyes. "It can't be."

He felt his gut tighten. "I don't believe you."

She lifted a shoulder. "We'll just tell everyone we talked about it, decided to be friendly coworkers, that everything is fine and no one has to worry or wonder about anything."

He narrowed his eyes. "*I'm* wondering, Whitney."

She shook her head. "You're not. Not really. Not if you thought about it."

"What the hell does that mean?" He felt the back of his neck tightening with frustration. He really hated this uptight, cool side of her. Clearly she'd been perfecting this persona or whatever the fuck it was over the past ten years because it was pretty damned solid. Even when he was saying things about bending over her desk or fucking her on the conference room table. She was just facing it all. And still saying no.

"It means that the story hasn't changed. This is just chapter two."

He scowled. "What?"

"This company, Hot Cakes, has always been my priority," she said. She pulled in a deep breath. "It still is. Now even more than ever. Now I have a chance to really be a part of it in a way I haven't before. I'm not going to do *anything* that would keep me from showing my family that they were wrong to not put me in charge a long time ago."

Frustration slammed into him. *Fuck this company.* That was his first reaction. He was happy to be an owner now but—he had to stop even that train of thought. There was only one reason he was an owner. Aiden had asked him to be.

Aiden Anderson was his best friend. Had been since kindergarten. Aiden had wanted to come back to Appleby to be with Zoe and buying the factory had been a great investment and a way to save the town. That was right up Aiden's alley. Cam was with Aiden on anything his friend wanted to do.

It was a definite perk that this company had been the reason Whitney had dumped him and he now had the chance to build it up and show everyone that the minute a McCaffery got involved was the minute things got really good. But at the time Aiden had wanted to buy the company, Cam had not had a single thought about returning to Appleby on any kind of permanent basis.

That had changed over the past couple of months as he'd been home more helping the guys get the company going in the new direction. He'd loved seeing his family more. He'd loved being back in his hometown. He'd loved seeing his friends and partners excited about their new endeavor. And yeah, he'd loved being around Whitney again.

But any *happiness* about owning a chunk of Hot Cakes was

much less about the company itself and a lot more about lifting a middle finger to the Lancasters who hadn't thought he was good enough for Whitney.

Maybe a bit of a finger to Whitney too, since she'd gone along with that.

"And you think that being with me would jeopardize you being more involved with the company?"

"There's that risk," she said. "If we try dating again and it doesn't work out, there is no guarantee that we'll both be fine and be able to be friends and it will have no effect on the company."

"And you're not willing to take a chance?"

She crossed her arms. "No." She said it with her eyes on his, no hesitation, not even a blink.

"And what if one of us isn't okay with us *not* trying it and keeps wanting to and makes everything uncomfortable?" he asked.

"Well, I would hope the *maturity* we've both found over the past ten years would keep that from happening."

Yeah, that was probably how maturity worked.

He'd definitely done some growing up. He hadn't punched anyone in the face in years. He punched them in the face metaphorically now. In court. But that didn't happen as often as he'd like. One thing that came with their company's increased wealth and power had been a decrease in the number of people willing to tangle with them. He hadn't had a really good fight in a while.

Grant and Josie had gotten married a month ago so that she could have her gall bladder taken out and be covered on Grant's health insurance. Cam had been hoping the insurance company would fight him on that.

They hadn't. And he'd been annoyed.

He wasn't sure where his contrariness and love of a good fight came from but most people said he got it from his grandmother. The one who had held a grudge against Whitney's grandmother for half a century. That seemed to add up.

So he wasn't quite as inclined to think that he was grown up enough to just let this go.

He wanted to date his ex-girlfriend.

His hot, intelligent, creative, buttoned-up, cool and composed ex-girlfriend.

Yeah, that buttoned-up, cool, and composed bit was part of it. That wasn't the Whitney he remembered. The fact that he couldn't really rattle her was also absolutely part of it. He'd always been able to rattle her—in really good ways—before.

Maybe he was bored.

Maybe he was immature.

Maybe he was still in love with her.

But which of those this was, was exactly what he wanted to figure out.

"Okay," he said, he turned and started for her office door.

"Wait," she called after him.

He glanced back.

"Okay?" She frowned. "That's it?"

He shrugged. "For now."

That made her look worried.

Good.

He stopped in her doorway.

"For now?" she repeated.

"Yeah."

"So... you're not actually going to drop it?"

He gave her a slow grin. "Do you remember the last time you broke up with me?"

She *definitely* looked worried now. "Yes."

She probably wasn't thinking about him getting drunk and in a fight with her brother. Or the week of incessant phone calls. Or him getting drunk and in a fight with fucking Carter Jackson when he said he couldn't wait to take Whitney out. Or even how he'd broken her window by throwing a rock through it. He'd only meant to get her attention but he'd picked a rock that was too big. And he'd probably thrown in too hard.

Okay, he'd clearly thrown it too hard.

"You are *not* going to do that again," she said firmly. But she was nervous. For sure.

Yeah, she was thinking about how he'd kidnapped her.

It had only been for twelve hours and no one had even known she was gone. But it had been a kidnapping by the strictest definition, he supposed.

"I don't really drop things easily. As you know."

She sighed. "Come on, Cam."

"A few dates. That's all I want. I'm not proposing. I'm not asking to move in. We don't have to even let anyone know we're trying until we figure it out. All I want is a chance to see how things go. It can just be between the two of us."

She just looked at him, saying nothing, looking confused and concerned. Finally she shook her head. "Hot Cakes is too important. To both of us."

Now, see, that pissed him off.

It was a total flashback to the past. She'd chosen Hot Cakes over him before.

And when he got pissed, he wanted to dig in, wanted to fight, wanted to win.

He felt the surge of anticipation that he always got when he heard the words, "We're going to court."

He didn't punch people anymore. He wore them down with excellent arguments and being fucking *right*.

He gave her a big grin. "I'll see you tomorrow at the dessert auction."

Her eyes got round. Clearly, him grinning also made her nervous.

Good.

His gaze landed on the red dress draped over the back of

the chair in front of her desk. He crossed to it in four strides, swept it up, and then headed for the door.

"Hey!"

"You don't need this until the night of our first date," he told her.

He left her standing behind her perfectly neat and organized, boring as fuck, corporate desk in her damned gray pencil skirt, looking dazed.

3

"What do llamas have to do with cake?" Whitney turned to Piper as the other woman came up next to her. "Nothing," Whitney answered her own question. "That's what. Llamas have nothing to do with cake."

"I think those are actually alpacas," Piper said, looking toward the pen where the petting zoo was set up about fifty feet from the stage where the baking competition was about to begin.

Whitney felt her eyes widen. "That is not helpful."

Piper laughed, then looked at Whitney's face closer. She frowned. "You okay?"

Whitney took a deep breath—got a lungful of alpaca-scented air—and shook her head. "No, I am not okay." She turned her attention back to the stage that had been constructed four days ago in the center of the Appleby town square.

"Why not?" Piper looked around. "Everything seems great. Everyone is having so much fun."

Whitney sighed. "I have a baking competition happening on an *outdoor* stage as the temperature is inching past ninety.

There are bugs out here, the butter and cream cheese are melting, and I have no idea if our release forms cover if someone gets diarrhea from eating desserts made with eggs and cream that have been sitting out in ninety-two-degree weather."

Piper's eyes widened. "Oh."

"And there are not just llamas—or alpacas or whatever—in a petting zoo stinking the place up, but there are also goats, a potbellied pig, a miniature cow, and an *emu*."

Piper nodded. "I saw the emu."

"I didn't even know the Ryan boys had an emu," Whitney said. Drew Ryan and his brothers ran the alpaca farm outside of Appleby. Apparently, they had more than alpacas.

"Dave is cute."

"Dave?" Whitney asked.

"The emu's name is Dave," Piper said.

Of course it was. "I never should have let Oliver handle the petting zoo details," Whitney said, shaking her head. "But I was so busy with coordinating the baking competition and I was so happy that he'd let go of the idea of the Ferris wheel and actual circus tent that I figured a petting zoo would be harmless."

Piper nodded. "Well, in Oliver's defense, he's never put in charge of details. Of any kind. He probably didn't know what to do. He's not really the detail guy."

Piper would know. She was Oliver's executive assistant. Piper was actually the executive assistant to all five of the partners in Fluke, Inc., but it had taken Whitney only a few weeks around her new bosses to figure out that, while they all needed Piper, Oliver was the main reason for Piper's job. Ollie was... a dreamer. He was the visionary of the company, the big ideas guy. He was brilliant and creative and practically a genius. But he was also not into things like schedules and plans and rules.

"I should have known when he was so disappointed that we couldn't get actual acrobats to perform," Whitney said.

Piper just shrugged. "You really should have. Never put

Ollie in charge of something. Everything should go through Grant or Aiden," she said, naming the CFO and CEO of the company. "Or me," she said with a smile.

Piper really did handle Oliver. He listened to her in a way he didn't to anyone else. Piper had a way of communicating with him that seemed almost magical. She could anticipate most of his thoughts and needs. And Oliver could be hard to keep focused unless Piper was involved. She could absolutely get and hold his attention. It was fascinating.

Whitney blew out a breath. "That doesn't make this better now. Why didn't *you* stop him from having *goats* here?"

They were having a baking contest. On a stage. In the middle of the town square. Three handsome men were going to make three different desserts, cooking-show style, then the final judge was going to choose the winner. That winning recipe would become Hot Cakes' newest product.

This was Whitney's first big project for Hot Cakes since she'd gotten new bosses. The first big project she'd pitched to someone other than a family member. Ever.

The first big project that someone had said, "Wow. Yes. Let's do that." Ever.

And now she felt like she was going to throw up.

Hot Cakes had never added a new product. The products that made the company millions of dollars every year had been the same for over fifty years. But now with new owners it was the perfect time to launch something fresh.

Or so Whitney had told Aiden, Grant, Ollie, Dax, and Cam during her pitch last month.

And they'd bought it. They loved the idea. They thought it was brilliant. Well, four of them had anyway. Cam had seemed... determined to make her squirm.

She shifted her weight and shot a glance in his direction. He was standing off to the side of the stage with Ollie and one of the Hot Cakes employees, Max.

This was a terrible idea.

Cam had been making her squirm since he'd gotten back to Appleby and walked into that meeting last month and then volunteered himself as one of the bakers for this event.

But that had been nothing compared to the jumpy, jittery heat that had been plaguing her since last night and their little showdown in her office.

He wanted to date her? As in really *date* her? What? That made no sense.

Except that everything he'd laid out made a lot of sense.

Anyone who knew anything about their history—basically his four best friends and his entire family—would be wondering how things stood between them.

The only reason *her* family wasn't wondering was because all of them except Didi were now living in Dallas where their new company was based. Didi's dementia made it so that she would likely be unaware of Cam's involvement in Hot Cakes, and even if she did hear his name in connection, it would surely be difficult for her to put him together with Whitney's boyfriend from a decade ago.

But, yes, everyone who was aware of the fact that Cam now owned part of Hot Cakes and therefore worked with Whitney, would likely wonder how that was going.

Couldn't they just be friends?

Just then he tipped his head back and laughed at something Max had said and her stomach clenched. Hard.

No, they probably couldn't just be friends.

Not when she wanted to jump into his arms, wrap her arms and legs around him, and kiss him until he was squeezing her ass and groaning her name. Like she had done probably a hundred times in the past.

Ugh.

It had already been difficult to keep her composure around him, but now she knew he wanted her too. How was she supposed to ignore *that*? How was she supposed to walk into the conference room for a meeting and not immediately flush or stammer or trip over her feet?

Damn him for stirring all of that up. She wanted to be composed, totally professional, brilliant and organized and impressive and capable, so that the guys would offer her a partnership. Or so they would at least say yes when she asked to buy in.

But now she was going to have to deal with personal feelings for Cam the whole time? The composed part was out the window, probably. And if she couldn't handle working with him, why would the guys think she was partner material?

On top of that, she couldn't *quite* shake the idea that Cam had done it on purpose. *Was* he testing her? Maybe not to fire her. She believed his sincerity when he said he wanted her right there watching him and his friends make her family's company into a huge success. But maybe he was testing to see just how *not* over him she was and if he could get her to admit that she'd been wrong to let him go.

Well, the thing about that was... she hadn't been wrong.

He'd had an amazing college football career. He had a law degree. He'd met three of his four best friends who would be in his life forever. He was a freaking *millionaire*.

So, no, she hadn't been wrong to "let him go"... or force him to go. However he wanted to look at it. It had been the right thing and she wasn't sorry.

Did she miss him? Had she failed to find another guy who came even close to making her feel the way Cam had even as a teenager? Sure.

But she'd done the right thing *for him*.

"Do you believe me?"

She focused on Piper again. She'd forgotten the other woman. "Oh. Um..." She glanced around.

She was in the shade and still sweating as the aroma of

alpacas—and a pot-bellied pig, a bunch of goats, and an emu—drifted over the crowd that had gathered. And an hour-long dessert date with her ex-boyfriend, who she was still at least semi in love with, was about to be auctioned off to the highest bidder.

Nope. Not okay.

"I have *alpacas* at a baking event," Whitney said.

Piper nodded. "Yeah, and I told you that it wasn't Ollie's fault. But I don't think you heard me."

"It's not Ollie's fault?" Whitney looked over at the petting zoo.

That was *such* an Oliver thing. It was his partners, and friends who honed Ollie's ideas into manageable, doable proposals. For instance, Ollie would have said, *Let's have a petting zoo!* and someone else would have said, *Or we could have someone make balloon animals. Because balloons do go with cake. Whereas farm animals don't so much. And that way we don't have to deal with the smell.*

"Then who's fault is it?" Whitney asked as Piper chewed on her bottom lip.

"The alpacas are not a *terrible* idea," Piper said instead of answering directly. "We wanted to make this an event that would encourage people to come and get involved. The more activities and the more fun for people of all ages, the better."

Whitney regarded the other woman.

"So I have barnyard animals oinking and snorting in a pen fifty feet from the stage where we're going to be producing what we hope to be the biggest Hot Cakes product ever because *someone* thought that would draw more people down here?" Whitney asked.

"Alpacas kind of make this purring sound, actually. It's kind of like humming," Piper said.

Whitney narrowed her eyes. "Piper."

She'd really thought Piper was the one person immune to Ollie's craziness.

In fairness, even Whitney had *initially* thought Ollie's idea to literally turn this whole thing into a circus was funny and creative. But then she'd thought about how much liability insurance would cost for *acrobats*.

He'd been very disappointed, so she'd compromised by agreeing to a bounce house and food trucks—tacos, pizza, and pulled pork sandwiches—and a few carnival games. Snack cakes were, after all, fun. They were treats. Part of childhood. So associating them with fun and frivolity was okay, she supposed.

But she'd had to draw the line at knife throwers and people jumping through rings of fire.

And alpacas.

"Are you or are you not the reason I have alpacas stinking the place up as we speak?" Whitney asked Piper.

"Well..."

"*Piper.*"

"Drew Ryan is really cute."

Whitney blinked at her. Drew Ryan *was* really cute.

Whitney crossed her arms. "Ollie has a thing for Drew?" she asked, knowing that was not the situation at all.

"Um..."

"Oh my God, Piper! Drew talked *you* into having a petting zoo?"

"The petting zoo was totally Ollie's idea. At first," Piper protested. "But... I went with him to talk to Drew."

"And Ollie balked at the idea and you talked him into it?"

Piper winced. "Yeah."

"*You* have a thing for Drew?" Whitney asked.

"I don't know. Maybe I have a thing for Ollie being jealous of Drew," Piper said with a shrug. "Anyway, somehow we ended up deciding that alpacas would be a great idea. And then Drew added the other animals for free."

Whitney rubbed the middle of her forehead. She was *paying* for those alpacas.

"It's great," Piper reassured her, rubbing a hand up and down Whitney's back, comfortingly. "You're throwing the town a big party. It's a way to show Appleby that we appreciate them. It's just fun. It doesn't have to make perfect sense."

Whitney wasn't so sure of that. She took a deep breath—tinged with the scent of alpacas—and said, "Be honest. Do you *really* think we're pulling this off?"

Piper nodded. "Completely. You've done a fabulous job. I love how you organized this. Getting the Chamber of Commerce involved in narrowing down the top ten recipes was a great idea and having the town do the taste testing to choose the final three was brilliant."

The people of Appleby had been invited to a huge taste-testing event last weekend where they *had* set up tents. Gauzy white tents with twinkle lights, white tablecloths, music, and a champagne fountain as a matter of fact. It had been more like a classy, outdoor wedding venue than a circus, thank you very much.

Whitney looked around. "It does seem like people are having fun with this today."

Now those final three recipes were going to be baked live on stage by three hot, single, charming men with plenty of flirty baking innuendos and banter thrown around as they did it. Then the treats would be sampled by the Grand Dame of Hot Cakes herself, Didi Lancaster, and she would pick the winning recipe. As the company's founder, it was perfect that she be the one choosing the new product.

Of course, Whitney would be a lot less nervous about *that* if she wasn't Didi's granddaughter and didn't know Didi was in the early stages of Alzheimer's. At least no one else in town knew. *No one.*

Everyone thought Whitney was living with Didi simply because the older woman's house was enormous and it was silly for them to both live alone. But truthfully, Didi couldn't live by herself anymore. She wasn't safe in the kitchen, she would get lost driving, and she wasn't able to handle keeping track of her medications.

In another month, Didi would be moving into the gorgeous new wing of Sunny Orchard, the nursing home that Whitney's friend Dax Marshall had recently purchased and revamped. Didi was excited to move in and be closer to some people she'd known her whole life, and Whitney was beyond relieved that her grandmother was good with the move. She really wanted to get her relocated before the dementia made it harder for her to adjust to new surroundings and routines.

So far today had been a good day, and if Didi could hang in there until the final judging, everything would be fine. All she had to do was taste three desserts and say which she liked best. Dessert tasting was as familiar to Didi as anything, and Whitney really thought they could make it through this one event without letting on there was anything unusual going on with Didi.

Whitney could only focus on one nerve-wracking, headache-producing thing at a time though, so she looked at Piper.

"They are *totally* having fun," Piper assured her. "No one's even thinking about alpacas and cake not going together."

"Okay, so what do alpacas have to do with cake?" Jane Kemper asked as she and Zoe McCaffery came to stand with Whitney and Piper.

Whitney sighed. "Nothing," she said. "Absolutely nothing."

"It's *fun*," Piper said, giving Jane a look. "It's just one big fun time. That's all that matters."

Zoe looked at Piper and then slowly nodded as if catching on. "Right. That's right. Totally true. Big-time fun. It's great." She gave Whitney a huge grin.

Whitney knew that Jane and Zoe and Piper were just trying to make her feel better. But she appreciated it. Zoe was engaged to Aiden, one of Whitney's bosses and, maybe more importantly, she was a *McCaffery*. The McCafferys and Lancasters had long been rivals. It wasn't so much that Hot Cakes and Zoe's bakery, Buttered Up, were *actual* business competitors, but their grandmothers had been best friends at one time and when Whitney's grandmother, Didi, had split off to start Hot Cakes, it had ruined their friendship and started a family feud that had lasted for nearly three generations.

Then there was the little detail of Whitney breaking Zoe's brother's heart and... yeah, Zoe even pretending to try to make Whitney feel better about this event meant a lot.

Whitney blew out a breath. "Thanks, ladies."

"This is all a huge mess," Paige Asher said as she came walking up.

Whitney sighed.

"No, it's *great*," Piper said, trying the wide-eyed look at Paige that had worked on Zoe and Jane.

But Paige shook her head. "No, it's really not. I can't bid on Ollie."

Okay, that was *not* great. Whitney frowned. "You *have* to, Paige."

Piper nodded. "You do. You have to bid on him."

"Bid on him?" Zoe asked, frowning and looking between the three of them.

"The bachelor auction," Piper said.

"Wait, I thought it was a dessert auction," Jane said. "Ollie, Cam, and Max are going to bake the final three recipes on stage and then Didi is going to pick the winner. People are going to bid on those three desserts and the proceeds are going to the food bank." Jane looked from Piper to Paige to Whitney. "Right?"

"Yes," Whitney said. "Except that they're also bidding on an hour with the guy who baked the dessert. They get to have dessert *with* the baker."

Yep. Somehow this had also turned into a bachelor auction with three very hot men. One of whom was her ex.

Whitney rubbed her head again. Okay, that part had been totally her idea. Well, not the part about Cam being one of the bakers. She'd suggested it thinking Grant and Ollie would do it and they'd recruit a couple of other guys. But then Grant had gone and fallen in love with Josie and it didn't seem like he should be up for a dessert date auction. And then Cam had volunteered to be a part of it. Actually, he'd *insisted*. Whitney hadn't included him initially because he was still living in Chicago then. Well, and because she would have never thought to auction him off to another woman.

Yeah, there was that too.

Not that she'd admit that part.

The third bachelor baker was Max, one of the long-time factory workers who literally baked Hot Cakes every day.

The three were actually perfect for this. On paper. Two were owners of the company, the other a very long-term employee. Cam was a hometown boy who had donated a lot of money to the community in the past ten years. Ollie was used to being up on stage, entertaining and engaging an audience at Comic Con and other gaming cons because of *Warriors of Easton*. Max was well-liked in town and had been a part of the community for a long time. He was funny and charming and would have no trouble being up in front of everyone.

They were also all very good looking and single.

Whitney felt her stomach start to flutter with nerves again and she pressed a hand against it. She didn't have time to be nervous about the guys too.

The guy who was going to bid on Max was already planted in the audience. Max and Elliot had been exchanging texts and Snapchatting for the past month or so. Elliot worked for Fluke in Chicago as a programmer and Dax had introduced them. Elliot had enough money, thanks to Dax, to bid whatever it took to get that dessert date with Max.

The same was supposed to be true for Ollie. Oliver was... not the suave playboy the other guys of Fluke, Inc. were. He was good looking and rich and funny in his own way, but he was... a nerd. And Piper, who knew him best, had insisted that they plant a date for him as well.

Paige was a friend and she and Ollie had no chemistry, but Paige could talk to anyone for an hour. She'd agreed to bid on Ollie—with Whitney's money.

That left Cam. No one was planted to bid on Cam.

And that made Whitney's stomach tighten.

Every woman in town knew who he was. He was the bad boy who'd gone on to become rich and successful. He'd donated tons of money—into the millions of dollars—to the town in the form of a new sports complex, scholarships, a wing on the school, and new equipment for the medical clinic. And he'd helped save Hot Cakes and the three hundred and forty-seven jobs there... and the families who depended on those jobs. Truly, he'd helped save the *town*.

He was also gorgeous. Muscular, tattooed, short beard, piercing blue eyes, with a general brooding, rebellious air, and a naughty grin that would stop you in your tracks.

There were plenty of young, single women in Appleby who knew exactly what they were bidding on and would likely happily dip into their savings for a chance at dessert with Cam.

Whitney hated everything about this event suddenly. And, if she were honest, the alpacas were actually a very small part.

"This whole thing is *great*," Piper insisted again. "We're getting the town involved and interested. Everyone is coming down to bounce in the bounce house, eat tacos, pet alpacas, and then watch three hot guys make dessert. The auction will raise money. There is nothing *bad* about this plan."

Except Cam going on a date. That Whitney basically set him up on.

This was all so stupid.

He'd *certainly* dated other women. Camden McCaffery had *not* been sitting at home alone every night since Whitney had ended their relationship.

Hell, *she'd* been on dates too. That's what people did after they broke up. They were sad for a while, but then they moved on.

That would have *maybe* consoled her if he hadn't told her last night that he wanted another chance with her.

And now she was going to get to watch a townful of women *bid* on him right in front of her on a stage she'd literally helped construct for an event she'd come up with.

This was *not* great.

"Yeah, it's all great," Paige said to Piper. "But I just can't bid on Ollie. You'll have to get someone else."

"Why not?" Piper asked. She was frowning at Paige. "You promised."

"Yeah, well, that was before Elliot brought Christopher with him."

Piper's frown deepened. "What?"

Paige leaned to the side. "Do you see Elliot?"

Piper peered over her shoulder and Whitney turned as well. The programmer was standing near the far end of the stage talking to a tall guy with dark hair and glasses. He looked like all of the other guys milling around in t-shirts and jeans and tennis shoes or work boots. He held a glass of lemonade and seemed to be just hanging out, enjoying the day. Whitney knew everyone in Appleby. That guy was not from here.

"Yeah," Piper said. "That's Chris. He's another of our designers. He works with Dax." She focused on Paige again. "Wait, you know Chris?"

Paige sighed. "Yeah."

"What's going on?" Whitney asked. "How do you know one of Fluke's designers?"

"Well, I didn't *know* that I knew one of Fluke's designers. But I flirted with *that* guy at Granny's the other night," she said, referring to the bar in town that specialized in, of course, hard ciders.

"Okay. So?" Piper asked.

"So we made out. Heavily." She tipped her head. "Then I told him I was a real estate agent in Kansas City and gave him a fake number. And that my name was Kara."

"But... why didn't you want him to know who you were?" Piper asked. "Chris is a great guy."

"Because I wanted to have a couple of drinks and make out with him and that's *all* I wanted to have with him," Paige said. "Which means, now that he's *here*, I need to avoid him until he leaves. So obviously, I can't call attention to myself by bidding on Ollie."

"But—" Piper started to protest.

"Sorry. Thanks for understanding," Paige said. Then she smiled and turned and slipped through the crowd.

Headed in the opposite direction of where Chris was standing.

Piper turned to Whitney. "Things just got less great."

4

——————

Whitney signed. "You think?"

"Now what?" Piper asked.

"*You'll* have to bid on Ollie," Whitney said.

"No way."

"Why not?"

"I can't. I... work for him."

Whitney laughed. "So?"

"I just can't."

Whitney didn't understand that, but she honestly didn't have the time or energy to devote to *another* complication.

She glanced at Jane and Zoe but they were out. They were both spoken for.

Whitney sighed. "Then I guess we'll just let the ladies of Appleby bid without knowing who the winner will be."

"I... don't know." Piper didn't seem thrilled with that either.

"I don't think you have to worry," Jane said, nodding to the crowd.

The baking show was going to start in about five minutes. The crowd was gathering closer to the stage and, yes, there were a lot more young women than men. Or older women. Or kids. The crowd was predominantly women about Cam and Max and Ollie's age. Most of the women in Appleby knew that Max was gay, so it was safe to assume that Ollie and Cam were the draw here.

Whitney pressed her hand against her stomach.

Could she disappear during the baking show and auction? Dax was going to MC the whole thing. Piper was here and on top of things. Aiden and Grant were both here somewhere. Surely Whitney wouldn't have to *watch* Cam strut out on stage in the blue jeans and tight black t-shirt Piper had decided he should wear to show off his tattoos and muscles. She wouldn't have to watch him bake. Something he was actually quite good at. He was a McCaffery after all. He'd grown up in Buttered Up bakery. He'd been baking since he was old enough to hold a mixer. She was *well* aware that women found that sexy. And *surely* she didn't have to watch him get bid on by the beautiful women who would be vying for a date with him.

She probably needed to go check on... the alpacas. Or something.

"*That* is why we can't just leave Ollie up there to be auctioned off," Piper said.

"Because a ton of women in Appleby have noticed that he's good looking and know he's a rich genius?" Jane asked. "Come on. Why can't Ollie have some fun?"

Fun. Yeah. They might have fun on these dates.

Whitney glanced toward the side of the stage where Cam and Ollie and Max were waiting to take their places at the mini-kitchen stations they'd built into the stage for the contest.

He looked *good*. That black t-shirt did very nice things for his shoulders, chest, and huge biceps. But it was the smile he was wearing that really made her heart flutter. Dammit.

Being over him was a lot easier when he wasn't *here*.

When he was here in Appleby, in the same office, working on the same projects, and showing up to this event as one of the baking bachelors looking gorgeous, it was really hard to ignore that she'd been madly in love with him when he'd left Appleby. And that she'd never had a reason to get over that.

Then she'd found out that as Grant's attorney, Cam was supposed to draw up divorce papers for Grant and Josie after they'd gotten married temporarily so Josie would have health insurance coverage, but he hadn't done it. He'd faked the paperwork, somehow knowing that Grant and Josie should stay married.

That was damned romantic. Hopeful. Sweet even.

Did Cam still believe in love? Had she *not* totally ruined that for him forever? She'd like to think so.

But she did not want to watch him find someone to date and possibly fall in love with right in front of her on stage in the center of Appleby.

She also didn't want to date him herself.

Well... she didn't think she *should* date him herself.

She did want to. Or maybe she just wanted to have sex with him again.

"Ollie isn't really casual-dating, bachelor auction material," Piper said, pulling Whitney back to the conversation at hand.

"Oh?" Zoe asked. "Why's that?"

Piper chewed her bottom lip.

"From what I understand from the way the guys talk, Ollie gets plenty of attention at all the conferences he goes to," Jane said. Ollie went to those conference with Dax. Jane had probably heard a ton of stories.

"Those are gaming conferences," Piper said.

"So?" Jane asked.

"So those women are into *Warriors of Easton*."

"So?"

"So he can talk *Warriors* all day," Piper admitted. "And—" She drew in a deep breath. "I'm not sure how much they all *talk*. I think those women know who Ollie is and they're fans and they flirt a bit and then... they don't go out to dinner or shows or have *conversations*, if you know what I mean."

Whitney did know what she meant. Ollie had casual flings and one-night stands with women who thought he was amazing because of the video game. But Piper looked annoyed, and a little sick, talking about it.

She knew exactly how Piper was feeling. She didn't want to watch Cam be bid on either, but there was nothing she could do about that.

"Oh, there's Dax," Jane said. "I'm going to go give him a pep talk before he gets up there to MC." She grinned and headed in her boyfriend's direction.

Whitney shook her head. Dax Marshall needed a pep talk about getting up on stage and being fun and charming like Whitney needed... another alpaca.

"I'm going to go find Aiden too," Zoe said. "And then I need to head back to the bakery."

"You're not going to stay for the show and auction?" Whitney asked.

Zoe shook her head. "No offense but, I don't really care what new product you guys roll out. Aiden loves what you're doing, and if he's happy, I'm happy."

Whitney felt a little warmth spread in her chest at hearing that Aiden was happy with what she was doing. If he was happy enough about it to talk about it at home, that was something.

"And," Zoe said. "If I'm honest—which is probably pretty important in this new friendship we're forging after years of hating each other because our grandmas told us to—there's a tiny bit of me that's hoping it flops." She grinned. "I do know that you're not really my competition, but it's been so ingrained that I can't help it sometimes. I'm working on it."

Whitney had to laugh. Their grandmothers had truly taken grudge-holding to a new level. They'd been best friends and had started out at Buttered Up, Zoe's bakery, together. But when Didi had wanted to try new things and Letty had shut her down, Didi had gone off on her own. As things picked up, Didi had gone back to Letty and offered her another chance to do it together. "They're selling like hot cakes, Letty!" Didi had told her. Letty had still said no. So Didi had named her new company Hot Cakes and had painted those words in huge block letters on the side of the building.

"Well, sorry." Whitney couldn't help but tease Zoe. "With Aiden working on this, I really doubt it's going to flop."

Zoe gave her a smile that was full of love. "Yeah, you have a point." She sighed, pretending to be put out. "I guess I'll just have to get used to us *both* being successful."

Whitney smiled and nodded. "Guess so." Lord, she hoped so.

Zoe moved off to find her fiancé too and Whitney looked at Piper.

Okay, she couldn't keep Cam from being bid on, but she could help Piper out.

"I think I can fix this," she said.

Piper gave her an interested look. "*You're* going to bid on Ollie?"

Whitney actually laughed at that. "That's a terrible idea. Ollie and I alone for an hour? We'll end up with alpacas walking on tight ropes through circles of fire. Or something."

She absolutely loved brainstorming with Ollie. He never said no, he never shut things down, he never didn't at least consider everything she said. The creativity just flowed out of her and she couldn't believe how *good* that felt. She'd spent ten years having ideas and then having those ideas ignored or even flat-out mocked. These guys never did that. Even when Aiden or Grant put a little common sense and practicality to the plans, they never ever made her feel silly or irrelevant.

Piper nodded. "True. We should probably keep the two of you apart unless you have a chaperone."

Whitney smiled at that. "I have a better idea about who should spend an hour with Ollie. Come on."

She started across the grass toward a group of boys. One of them was Henry McCaffery, Zoe and Cam's younger brother. He was the biggest *Warriors of Easton* fan in the world. Aiden was practically like a brother to him as well so Henry absolutely had an inside track to news and behind-the-scenes about the game. He was a bit of a local celebrity himself, being so close to two of the guys behind the game. But Aiden was the CEO and Cam was the company attorney. Neither of them had created the game. They weren't designers. The game—the story, the characters, the graphics—those all came from Dax and Oliver.

Who better to spend an hour with Oliver, talking about the thing he knew best in the world, than three eleven-year-old boys who thought he was basically a god?

"Hey, why aren't you wearing the red dress?" Piper asked, apparently just noticing.

Whitney sighed. She was in one of her pencil skirts. A black one, which was *not* helping with the heat out here, and a pale green sleeveless blouse. And, yes, one-inch black heels.

She knew it was boring and made her look uptight. Well, *now* she did. She'd thought—hoped—that her work clothes made her look put together and professional. But last night with Cam, changing from the red dress back into her gray pencil skirt, had been like magic. She'd gone from feeling exposed and mixed up to feeling cool and like she could face him. Sure, inside, everything had still been a riot of emotions. But she was used to that.

Her skirts and blouses were like armor. She *looked* like a put-together corporate executive, so she felt like one facing her grandfather, father, and brother. When she was wearing a sexy red dress, she looked like a woman who was ready for a hot date and hoped that dress would end up on her date's bedroom floor. And that's how she'd felt facing Cam while wearing it.

His reaction to the dress hadn't helped.

But his reaction to her skirt and blouse had. He'd clearly thought she seemed uptight in that outfit. Which was fine. Uptight was better than vulnerable.

"I, um, thought this was better for today," she told Piper.

Piper waved a hand at her face. "A short sundress or shorts and a tank would be better for today," she said. Piper herself was dressed in a bright yellow dress with a halter top that cinched at the waist with a neon blue belt and flared from her hips, ending just above her knees. Her long hair was piled on top of her head and wrapped with a yellow scarf with blue polka dots, and she wore bright blue sunglasses. She managed to look like a fashion icon while still being cool. Whitney was very impressed. While she sweat through her polyester and silk.

"Yeah, you're right," Whitney said. She wore sundresses and shorts and capris around home.

"So where is the red dress?" Piper asked.

Cam had it. He'd taken it because she, supposedly, didn't need it until their date. The date they were not going on. But she definitely felt a shiver at the memory of how he'd looked at her in that dress.

"I was wondering if I could keep it for a bit?" Whitney asked. "I really like it. I'd love to find a reason to wear it."

"Of course," Piper said. "Red is a great color for you."

"Hey," Whitney said, stopping and turning to face her new friend. "Where were you last night anyway? You left me in my office trying on that dress alone."

"I had to run down and get something from the break room," Piper said. "But I passed Cam on his way up. I figured he could tell you how you looked in it." She had a sly look in her eye now.

"Oh."

"And did he?" Piper asked.

"Did he what?"

"Tell you how you looked in it?"

Whitney studied Piper. How much did the other woman know and what was she fishing for?

"I didn't even see Cam last night," Whitney said, just to gauge Piper's reaction.

The other woman laughed. "Liar. I saw him when he came back out. A *long* time later. Carrying my red dress. That he informed me *he* was keeping for a while."

Whitney's eyes widened and her mouth dropped open. "No he didn't."

Piper was grinning. "He totally did. So... I'm cool with that. As long as I get details *after* you wear that dress."

"I'm..." Whitney shook her head. "I'm not wearing it for him."

"Yeah, that is *not* what his expression or tone of voice said," Piper told her, still grinning.

"Well, he can think whatever he wants, but..." She took a deep breath. "It's not a good idea."

"Be that as it may," Piper said. "It's a *Cam* idea."

"What's that mean?" Whitney felt trepidation slip down her spine.

"It means it will happen. One way or another," Piper said, lifting a shoulder.

"He always gets his way?"

"Pretty much. By the time Cam's involved with an idea, he's thought it all through, he's looked at all the angles, he's done the research. He knows all the possible outcomes and has a plan B, C, and D. And once he's in on something, he's all in. He'll give it his all. He just..." Piper seemed to be thinking for a moment. "He doesn't take on fights he isn't sure he can win," she finally finished.

Yeah, that shiver of trepidation was a full-on wave now.

Combined with a stupid mix of anticipation. How hard would he try to convince her that giving them another try was a great idea? How hard would he have to try before she gave in?

Hard. No question.

But she wasn't stupid enough to think that she could resist him forever. He'd have to pull out the big guns but... that could be fun.

She swallowed hard.

Piper read her expression accurately. "Don't be scared," she said with a grin. "You know him, right? Nothing to worry about."

"I do know him," Whitney said. "Which makes me *more* worried. He might..."

Could she admit this to Piper? She didn't know the other woman *that* well. But who could she admit this to? She didn't really have girlfriends. She worked a lot and... she sighed. Her family members weren't great at cultivating relationships that weren't work related and she'd inherited that, she supposed. She didn't relax and just sit around and talk about nothing. She felt like things should have a purpose and she was drawn to people who felt the same way. People who worked fourteen hour days, seven days a week.

Plus, she'd never really had nonwork friendships modeled for her. She'd seen her mother host teas with other executives' wives. She'd seen her dad golf with men he had professional relationships with. She'd seen her parents and grandparents and their "friends" at dinner parties and holiday parties at their homes. But the social events always also functioned as business events.

She had never seen her father or grandfather drink more

than a single glass of scotch. That made you lose control and Lancasters *never* lost control.

She'd never seen her mother in ponytail and sweatpants or her grandmother reclining on the couch watching a movie. That would indicate relaxation, and Lancasters also never relaxed. Not fully. Until recently. Didi had clearly relaxed since the rest of the family had moved to Dallas.

"You're even *more* worried because Cam might what?" Piper prompted.

"He might want a little revenge."

"Revenge?" Piper asked.

"I broke his heart. He might... I don't know... want to mess with me a little. Make me fall for him and then be the one to walk away?" Whitney suggested.

Piper didn't respond right away. She was clearly considering all of that. Finally, she nodded. "I see what you mean."

Whitney felt her heart fall. She didn't want it to be true. She could admit that to herself, anyway. She wanted him to really want her.

What she would do with that was another question, but she wanted to have that problem.

"But I know Cam too," Piper said. "And I guess, maybe I've known him better over these past few years, right?"

Whitney nodded. That had to be true. Piper saw him every day. And she saw him with the guys. The five guys—Aiden, Dax, Grant, Ollie, and Cam—were so natural together. It was clear that they could fully be themselves when they were a group and they appreciated and loved each other and *wanted* the others to be who they were. It was so fun to watch them.

And it made her want the same thing. She wanted a group that she could belong to like that. But you couldn't make things like that happen. They just did. Fate. Kismet. Karma. Magic. Whatever it was, it wasn't something you could *make* happen.

"So I can tell you, for sure, that when he comes back to

Chicago after being here visiting, and running into you, he's a mess," Piper said.

Whitney felt a little bad about it, but she perked up at that. Her heart thumped a little harder. "Really?"

"He gets super drunk the night after he sees you and then he's a hungover mess the next day at the office," Piper said with a nod. "I've gotten really good with the hangover cures."

Whitney hadn't known that. She knew *she* was always shook up after seeing him, but he'd always acted cool when they'd run into each other. He even seemed angry at times. Like seeing her was a huge, annoying inconvenience.

"So," Piper said. "I don't think that he's wanting revenge. I think he's still got feelings and now that he's here, he's probably thinking that he wants to see where things stand."

That had been, essentially, what he'd said. But wow, hearing someone else say it made it feel really real.

"The question now is, what do *you* want?" Piper asked.

To *not* mess up this chance to make Hot Cakes great and to be a part of that. To earn the respect and trust of the men who had come in and saved the company, and her family's reputation. To have a job because she was good at it and not just because her grandmother told her grandfather and father that they had to make a place for her in the company.

And Cam.

But she couldn't have it all.

Thankfully, before she had to answer, Dax took the stage. He had been one of the partners in Hot Cakes, but then he'd met Jane. She had refused to date one of her bosses. She didn't like how that looked. Whitney should talk to Jane. Jane would surely see her side with this whole Cam thing.

But Dax being, well, Dax and the master of the grand gesture, had simply sold his shares so Jane would say yes to a date. She had said yes. And they were now madly in love and planning to get married next summer.

Would Cam be willing to give Hot Cakes up to be with her? Maybe. Cam was known for bucking convention. But she didn't want that either.

She was a businesswoman, whether her family saw it or not, and she understood the importance of having talent. Cam was not only a great attorney, but he cared about Hot Cakes more than any other attorney they'd ever be able to hire. He would protect the company from any threat because he was protecting Aiden, Grant, and Ollie too.

"Welcome everyone!" Dax said into the microphone with one of his incredibly charming grins. "We are so excited to have the town of Appleby, Hot Cakes' home, as a part of this process," Dax said.

Dax might not have a financial interest in Hot Cakes, but he had an emotional interest in it. Because of Jane and because of the four men who were like brothers to him. It made sense that he would use the term *we*. He'd weighed in with advice and ideas throughout the rebuilding of Hot Cakes.

"Come on," Whitney said to Piper. "Let's go convince Henry and his friends to bid on Ollie before things get really going."

They made their way toward Henry and his group.

"Hey, Henry," Whitney greeted.

"Hi."

Henry knew her. He had been born their senior year of high school. She hadn't spent time with Cam's family. Their romance had been a huge secret from everyone but Aiden. The McCafferys wouldn't have been any happier about their relationship than the Lancasters had been when they found out. But Appleby was a small town and Henry at least knew who Whitney was.

"I have a treat for you," she said.

Henry looked interested and his friends turned to pay attention as well.

"How would you all like to spend an hour tonight with Ollie Caprinelli?"

Henry's jaw dropped open.

They *of course* knew who Ollie was. In their world, he was a god. And someone they watched on YouTube regularly. He and Dax were celebrities in Henry's corner of the world.

"*Really*?" one of his friends, Hunter, asked. "We could do that?"

The truth was, Henry could get an hour with Ollie any time. His big brother and the man who was practically a brother were Ollie's best friends. She was shocked Ollie hadn't been invited over for dinner at the McCafferys'. Aiden had already been a regular guest, dating back to even before his mom had died and Maggie McCaffery had become his surrogate mother. Zoe's two best friends were regulars around that table as well.

But Whitney wondered if maybe the McCafferys had told Henry that he couldn't have his own friends over when the *Warriors of Easton* guys were there. That could have become chaotic.

This was a chance for Henry to be a big shot with his friends.

"Yep." Whitney pointed at the stage. "He's going to make one of the desserts and then people are going to bid on eating that dessert with him. You get a whole hour."

"But it's like a date, right?" Jack, another of Henry's friends asked.

"Nope," Whitney said. "It's just an hour of time. With dessert. Anyone can bid and the highest bid is the winner."

"But a bid takes money," Henry said.

"Right." Whitney had to swallow hard as she met Henry's gaze.

He had Cam's eyes.

Or they both had their mother or father's eyes.

But she definitely saw Cam in Henry's face and she was

struck by a twinge of sadness that she hadn't gotten to know Henry. She'd love to see Cam as a big brother. She'd never really seen him with any of his family except from a distance. When they'd been at school events or social events around town, she'd had to stay away and pretend they were nothing more than classmates. But it had been clear that the McCaf-ferys were close and that Cam loved his family deeply. He'd been loyal to his family's legacy with Buttered Up and had stubbornly believed every bit of the story about how Didi had stolen the first Hot Cakes recipe from Letty.

They'd argued about it only once. Then they'd agreed to not talk about it.

But the feud between their families had still kept them from being a couple in public. From spending Christmas together. From getting to know the people that were important in each other's lives.

That's why it had been such a big deal when he'd told her he was willing to stay home, skip college, and come to work for Hot Cakes so he could stay in Appleby with her.

And it had been one of the reasons she had pushed him away.

"We don't have enough money," Henry told her.

"I've got ten dollars," Hunter said.

"I can ask my mom," Jack added.

Whitney shook off the thoughts of young Cam and all the things they'd missed out on back then. And since.

She grinned. "That's the even better news. *I've* got the money."

Henry, Hunter, and Jack's eyes all grew round.

"You would *give* us money to use?" Henry asked.

"Yep." Whitney gestured to Piper. "This is Piper. She's the only one that will take care of the money if you win."

"So what do we do?" Hunter asked.

"You get up there toward the front, and when it's Ollie's

turn, you raise your hand," Whitney said. "You keep raising your hand until they say you won."

Henry looked downright amazed. "Wow. That sounds easy."

"Super easy," Whitney agreed.

"I'll even go up there with you," Piper said. "To help you with what you should do."

Whitney smiled at that. Piper was very used to herding and taking care of a group of guys. Honestly, these boys being eleven wouldn't faze her a bit—the Hot Cakes guys were sometimes very much eleven-year-olds in their behaviors.

"I'm going to go... check on the llamas," Whitney said.

She for sure couldn't be right up front for this. Watching Cam baking would be hard enough, but no way was she going to watch him get auctioned off.

Piper gave her a knowing look.

"They're actually alpacas," Henry told her.

With a surprised laugh, Whitney nodded, "Right. Alpacas."

"Let's go, guys. You want to be right down front," Piper said, nudging them in the direction of the stage.

Whitney watched them weave through the crowd and took a second to appreciate that there *was* a crowd.

Then her eyes wandered to where Cam was standing on stage. He was behind the middle cooking station. He was wearing a bright yellow apron over his fitted black t-shirt now —a not-really-that-subtle nod to his family's bakery which was all yellow and white from their décor to their take-out boxes to, yes, their aprons—but his tattoos and muscles and the black stud earring he wore in his left ear and his this-is-gonna-be-fun grin were all still on full display.

His eyes met hers, and even from the distance she felt the jolt of awareness.

"When we decided to introduce a new product, for the first time in the company's history, we knew it had to be something special," Dax was saying, having just explained how the baking competition and auction were going to work. "We wanted to make a big deal out of it, because it *is* a big deal. The new product represents the new directions and plans that we have for Hot Cakes. But it has to fit in with the Hot Cakes history and story. And who knows that better than the people of this town who have been a part of it?"

Whitney felt her throat tighten unexpectedly. She hadn't known what Dax was going to say but that was so... nice.

It was no small thing that *her* family had owned Hot Cakes for the past three generations. And that it was *her* father who hadn't cared about the business and as soon as her grandfather passed away had been ready to let it fold.

Her family had almost caused three hundred and forty-seven people to have to find new jobs and, in most cases, uproot their families and move. Appleby was a very small town. There were only so many jobs. Those people would have all had to seek employment elsewhere. In some cases it would have meant taking their entire family away from Appleby. Many of those people had grown up here, had raised their families here. This was their home. Leaving because the factory closed would have been huge.

Of course, it would have affected the town in general too. All of those people leaving would have meant many would have taken spouses with them. That would have caused Appleby to lose teachers and nurses and business owners, daycare providers, community volunteers. The entire community would have felt it.

"And just so you all know," Dax continued from the stage. "The guys up here have a bet as to who will go for the highest amount."

The crowd laughed and Whitney had to smile. That sounded just like them. Max, who wasn't an owner, but a Hot Cakes employee, was just as cocky and fun-loving as the other guys. According to Aiden, he was thrilled to be included and was ready to ham it up for the crowd.

"And whatever that highest bid is, Hot Cakes is going to match it," Dax said. "That means our local food bank is going to get an even bigger check. So be very generous. These guys will earn it."

She really liked them all. Whitney took a deep breath. She really did. She liked the guys who'd taken over for so many reasons, and she particularly liked them all together. She loved sitting in the meetings and just watching them interact.

She really liked Cam.

That was why she would love to be his friend. Be someone he joked with and teased like he did Piper. Someone he could laugh with and brainstorm with and even argue with like he did the rest of the guys. They all butted heads at times but it never affected their relationship and it was always with the ultimate goal in mind. They all were also pretty good at admitting when someone else had a better idea. They encouraged each other even as they sometimes disagreed.

She wanted that. She wanted to work with a group of friends that she respected and knew respected her. She wanted to be proud of their accomplishments individually as much as she was with her own. She wanted to share a common purpose with people who were as passionate as she was, yet always wanted to do the right thing and really *cared*.

Whitney had pleaded with her father to let her take over operations if he was no longer interested, but he'd blown off her suggestion—as he had practically every other suggestion she'd ever made in relation to the business—and declared that he was tired of being tied down in Iowa and was heading to Dallas.

But now, thanks to these guys, she had the chance to be important.

She was grateful to Aiden, and Dax, and Grant, and Ollie,

and Cam. Maybe especially Cam. He could have probably shut the whole thing down. He could have said fuck no to saving Hot Cakes and the Lancasters' reputation. But he hadn't. She was undeniably grateful for that.

Now that the Lancasters were no longer in control of Hot Cakes, she wanted Appleby to feel secure and happy about having Hot Cakes here and to know that it was going to be here for a very long time. She wanted to help the guys make this business venture wildly successful. They'd taken a chance on all of it and she was going to make them glad they had.

That meant she and Cam had to keep from breaking each other's hearts. Period. And the only way to do that was to stay away from each other. Personally anyway.

That meant no sexy red dresses, no private time in her office, *no* dating.

They were going to be business associates and maybe, eventually, hopefully, friends.

So being an adult woman fully in control of her emotions, she turned on her heel and headed for the alpaca pen.

5

Well, there was no way he was going to be able to be just coworkers or even friends with Whitney.

At least not until he tried to be more.

Cam was grateful that he could bake and flirt on autopilot —one of the perks to growing up in a bakery and having lots of practice. At both.

He was somehow pulling off the chocolate coconut bars while entertaining the audience by giving Ollie and Max shit about their own baking, while thinking about Whitney.

And how hot she looked in that stupid, ugly pencil skirt she was wearing today.

It was ninety-two degrees on a bright, sunny summer day in the town square. The event was casual and fun and *outside*. What was she wearing that stupid skirt and blouse and *heels* for? She should be in a sundress and sandals. Showing lots of creamy skin. And she should have her hair up in a ponytail. At least until he pulled it down to run his hands through it as he kissed her.

She should look like a small-town girl at a town event. Not a corporate shark trying to sell stuff to people.

Cam worked on not scowling as he melted the chocolate over a low flame on the built-in stove top in his mini kitchen. He didn't care about the auction except he'd be damned if he'd lose the top bid designation to Ollie or Max.

They both had date plants in the audience anyway. And surely that came with a budget.

Cam was on his own in upping his bid amount.

But he wasn't worried.

He was from here and knew all twelve of the ladies in the front row. He also had a reputation. And the best recipe.

He wasn't worried about fetching a big price.

He did wonder how Whitney felt about that though.

She'd gone off toward the petting zoo several minutes ago. Which was annoying. How was he going to impress her with his baking and flirting if she wasn't even here?

Not that he should have to impress her with either thing. He'd baked for her before. And he'd flirted her right out of her panties on numerous occasions. Including last night in her office. Okay, he hadn't quite gotten her panties off, but he'd proven she wasn't immune. That's all he'd really needed to know.

She'd never been immune to him. Even in high school, when their families were stubbornly feuding with one another and both of their grandmothers would have lost their minds if they'd known he and Whit were dating, it had only taken a dozen homemade chocolate chip cookies and a whispered, "sneak down to the park with me and I'll give you something even sweeter" to get her to say yes to him.

And now she was off looking at alpacas instead of watching this baking-auction thing? That had been *her* idea?

He realized that he'd been whipping the melting chocolate way too hard, and he made himself take a breath and slow down.

He glanced up at the girls in the front row. They were definitely still watching him. At least the whisking had made his arm muscles bulge. He almost laughed. He wasn't really the flex-for-it type of guy. Except when he was giving his friends shit about his muscles and tats giving him an edge with the ladies. But hey, you had to use what you had when you were in competition. Mostly it was his intellect and stubbornness that he flexed in his job, but Piper had insisted on the t-shirt to show off his arms, so he was going to assume that was his greatest asset today. And his cookies. The literal ones.

"So once everything has heated up and is nice and firm," Max was saying to Cam's left. "That's when you know it's time to pour on the sticky stuff."

Cam almost snorted. But they were all wearing mics so that everyone could hear their "baking" instructions. He had to admit, Max was good at the innuendo. It was partly the tone of voice he was using. And the way he was looking at Elliot, his date plant—and one of Fluke, Inc.'s best programmers—right down front.

But Max was a big, burly guy who also had muscles and tats and a beard, along with a very deep voice, and with the way he said some of the things he said, like "sticky stuff," even the girls in the crowd who knew he was gay were watching him with interest.

"You have to be sure that everything is soft and warm and ready," Cam agreed. "But you also don't want to go too fast when it comes to the sticky stuff." He removed his saucepan of chocolate from the burner and turned to the cookie crust he'd made a few minutes ago. "It's okay to take it slow," he said, letting his voice drop as well as he poured the chocolate over the crust. "There's no need to rush. The firm parts and the soft parts need to come together easy."

Max, on the other hand, did snort, the sound loud in his mic. The crowd laughed.

"I'm with you," Max said. "Sometimes slow is the way to go.

But if you get things firm enough before you even start the sticky stuff, you don't have to be overly gentle." He winked at the crowd. "Of course I mean the crust of this caramel crunch bar. You want that crust firm enough so it doesn't fall apart when you're... eating it." That little pause before "eating it" definitely made those two words sound very dirty.

Cam loved it. Max was a ton of fun.

Cam nodded with a grin. "Though, honestly, things... coming apart..." He used that same pause and tone. "Once I get my hands on them isn't that unusual."

"So you... make a mess?" Max asked. "When you're baking?" He said baking with a tone that clearly conveyed I-do-not-mean-baking.

"Hey, as long as the good stuff gets to my mouth, I'm absolutely okay with a little mess," Cam returned with a grin.

Max gave him a nod. "I'm with you on that, brother."

The crowd was completely with them. Grinning and laughing and nudging each other and whispering. Cam and Max were doing everything Whitney had asked—baking while making it fun and a little sexy but still family-appropriate since the innuendo would go over kids' heads.

He glanced around again, trying to not seem obvious. Where the hell was she? She was missing all the fun. And why did he get the impression that was pretty usual for her?

He spotted her, and her ugly skirt, over by the alpaca pen.

She was choosing alpacas over watching him be funny and charming and kick ass at baking?

Well, she could run, but she couldn't hide. Their conversation about getting back together—okay, *he'd* been the only one talking about that, but she'd been there—was not over.

"This doesn't look right."

Cam and Max glanced over at Ollie. Ollie wasn't doing as well with the sexy innuendo and bro-banter. He had been far too preoccupied with following the recipe he'd been given.

Piper had assured them that Ollie had practiced it prior, but he was clearly *not* a natural in the kitchen.

That made some sense. Ollie was a big-picture guy, much less concerned with details. Like the difference between a quarter tsp and a half tsp.

That was because the rest of them, including Piper, took care of that stuff for him.

So Ollie baking, in front of the whole town, was kind of a bad idea.

But very entertaining.

"What do you mean?" Cam asked, peering over at Ollie's kitchen center.

Cam was in the middle—as he should be, in his opinion—and could see that the filling for the lemon bars Ollie was supposed to be putting together did, indeed, look odd.

As in, it was brown and not yellow. For one thing.

Ollie scooped up a spoonful of the brown liquid and then let it dribble back into the pan.

Yeah, that wasn't right. It was the consistency of soup.

"Well, someone has to be the loser," Max said, lifting one huge shoulder. "Better you than me."

Ollie looked over at him. He was wearing his black rimmed glasses and a t-shirt that said *I paused my game to be here.* He didn't always wear glasses, but Piper and Whitney had decided that Ollie should play up the "hot nerd" role—definitely their words, not Cam's. Ollie was a nerd. In some ways, anyway. But Cam had always gotten the impression that women were drawn to his creativity and adventurous side more than his intellect. Or his glasses. Ollie was brilliant and very interesting, as long as you were talking about things he was interested in. He had the attention span of a fifth grader. But he was a hell of a lot of fun. And he *always* wanted to try new things, do more, go places. That was probably part of that short-attention-span thing, but he was always the one saying "let's see what happens" and "no reason not to try it."

He wasn't quite as over the top as Dax. He also wasn't the goofball that loved to make people laugh. He didn't jump out of airplanes, buy a racehorse, or fly to Japan on a whim for the story or the YouTube video like Dax did. Ollie did the things he did for the experience of it.

Fortunately he'd found Dax to be there beside him so he wasn't wandering in foreign countries alone. Or maybe unfortunately. Ollie had never had an idea that Dax hadn't said, "hell yes, I'm in" too.

"Can we fix this?" Ollie asked Cam.

He seemed oblivious to the audience watching them.

Cam took pity on his friend though. "I think you just need to start over. You have to stir it the whole time." Clearly the sugar had burned.

Ollie sighed. "The *whole* time?"

"Yep." Cam tried not to grin.

Ollie turned to the audience. "I'll give someone a hundred bucks to come up here and stir this for me."

Cam rolled his eyes. He even had to make *stirring* a big deal?

There was a small shift in the front row toward the stage, but Aiden stepped forward and turned to face the crowd.

"That's against the rules," he said. "The guys each have to do all of their own baking."

Now see? Shouldn't *Whitney* be over here enforcing the rules?

Cam glanced toward the alpacas again. She was now petting one of their noses. Surely she could hear what was going on over here though. At least the stuff he and Max and Ollie were saying into the mics. Like that Ollie was trying to cheat.

"Yep, do it yourself, Caprinelli," Cam said, focusing on toasting his coconut.

Whitney is kind of toasting my coconut right now, he thought to himself.

"If you want anyone bidding on you, you better get going too," Max said, folding the "crunch" part of the caramel crunch bars into his own melted chocolate.

"I'll still bid on you, Ollie!" a female voice called from the crowd.

"I don't need cookies! Just you!" another woman called.

"Yeah, I can get cookies anywhere!" someone else added.

Cam glanced over at his friend with a grin. Ollie pushed his glasses up his nose and looked out at the crowd.

"Well, in that case..." he started.

"Just make your stupid bars!" another woman called.

This voice Cam knew though. It was Piper.

He found her standing a few people back. She was easy to spot. She was wearing bright yellow today. As always, she stood out. In a very good way. Piper Barry wasn't like the other girls in Appleby. She was funny and smart and blunt as well as incredibly capable and organized, keeping them all in line with barely an effort. Seemingly, anyway. Yet she had this high-maintenance way of putting herself together and an I-know-who-I-am-and-what-I-want air about her that kept her *just* shy of being completely down to earth.

Right now, her hands were propped on her hips and she was frowning at Ollie.

Cam and the rest of the guys suspected Piper had feelings for Ollie that went beyond employer-employee, but their friend was oblivious. Even while Ollie found himself jealous over Piper at times. For instance, he really didn't like Drew Ryan, the alpaca farmer. And *everyone* liked Drew. But Drew flirted unabashedly with Piper, in front of Ollie, and that apparently rubbed the genius the wrong way. He just wasn't genius enough to figure out *why*.

Ollie sighed. "I guess I'm making these bars," he said dryly.

"Though calling them stupid probably doesn't help from a marketing perspective."

The crowd laughed.

Piper's eye roll was big enough to be seen from several feet away.

Ollie took his pan, dumped the contents into the sink, and sighed loudly into his mic. He turned back to the crowd and put on a truly excellent "sweet puppy" expression. "I will remake the bars, but I'm just going to warn whoever bids on me... you might have to do the baking. I, however, can bring plenty of other... talents... to our time together."

There was a collective *oooh* from the front row and Cam shook his head with a grin. Ollie could bring the flirty-sexy when he had to. Nice.

Ollie went back to the top of his recipe and Cam and Max continued to banter as they finished theirs. But Cam couldn't stop looking in Whitney's direction.

She had now moved down the fence and was talking to another alpaca. No one was that into alpacas. She was plainly avoiding. He just didn't know if it was the entire spectacle over here—which had all been her idea to start with—or him in particular.

Unfortunately, there wasn't a timer on this event so he couldn't stomp over to the alpaca pen and demand to know what Whitney was thinking.

The no-time-limit thing was good for Ollie though, who was mixing and muttering into his mic. Whenever they were all finished, the auction would commence, and then Didi Lancaster would sample each dessert and determine the winner. Then they'd meet up with their date for the evening and head to their preselected location.

Max was going to take his date—who would certainly be Elliot—to the picnic area on the other side of the park.

Ollie was going to be bid on by Paige Asher and Cam wasn't

even sure if they were actually going to go on their "date." Paige was a set up so that Ollie didn't have to deal with an actual date. The guy got plenty of women, but most of them were hot, fun, very short-term hookups. He didn't really do relationships. Mostly because Ollie sucked at things like remembering birthdays, or even showing up for dinner sometimes. Ollie was a great guy and a good friend, but he was also fortunate that he'd met the four men that were his best friends and partners. None of them ever took it personally that he forgot things like one of them having their appendix removed or one of their birthday parties.

Women, on the other hand, would get tired quickly of having their birthdays forgotten or him not showing up at the hospital. In his defense, he never would have been offended if they'd blown off *his* birthday or hadn't brought him balloons to the hospital either.

Last year, Piper had reminded Ollie it was his birthday, in fact.

So it was better that he hang out with women who wanted to talk about *Warriors of Easton*—yes, their fanbase included women—and were happy with a one-night stand with one of the creators.

Their groupies were kind of like the girls who wanted to hook up with a member of their favorite rock band just to say they'd done it. The *Warriors of Easton* groupies just happened to often dress up as elves and stuff.

Cam had decided to take his date to Buttered Up. Well, outside of Buttered Up. His sister's bakery had little tables set up in front of the huge windows in a sidewalk-café style. The dessert they'd be eating wasn't from Buttered Up, but he'd get coffee from inside and he wanted the people who would be following the date on social media to remember that he was a McCaffery and that Buttered Up was his family's business.

He would have taken his date inside but Zoe had forbidden

it. Even after he'd pointed out what great publicity this would be showing how the McCafferys were now heading up all of the major dessert making in Appleby and that the two businesses, that were long-time rivals, were now coming together.

She'd said that if he brought a Hot Cakes product, even a future one, into her store, she'd cut him off from all Buttered Up desserts for six months.

The whole we're-not-rivals-anymore thing was a work in progress.

Cam also suspected that Aiden had brought Hot Cakes products into her bakery on at least a couple of occasions, but also figured they had been used in ways that Cam didn't want to associate with his sister and best friend, so he hadn't pointed that out.

Aiden could likely get away with a lot of things Cam couldn't.

That was probably as it should be.

When you fell in love with someone, you gave them more slack.

Again, he glanced over at Whitney. Her back was to the entire baking-show-slash-auction setup. If she was avoiding him, why? Because he'd made her uncomfortable last night? Or because she couldn't stop thinking about last night? Or because she wanted everything he'd offered last night but she really did think it was a bad idea and avoiding him was easier than facing it?

He hadn't made her uncomfortable. He knew her. She had been surprised, and turned on—which also might have surprised her—but she hadn't been upset or nervous.

He liked the idea that she had been thinking about it nonstop. He certainly had. He also liked the idea that she wanted it, but thought she shouldn't, and the only way to avoid giving in to everything was to avoid *him*.

She couldn't avoid him indefinitely.

And they *were* going to figure this out.

Their history and their feelings for one another now was a huge-assed elephant in the room any time they were, well, in a room together. If she wasn't on board with outright dating and figuring it out, there were other ways for him to spend time with her, get to know her again, see how she reacted to him. They saw each other every day at work. Obviously, he could find some alone time with her.

And he already liked the reaction from her to that alone time.

Seeing her outside of the office might take some doing. Apparently, her high school friends had moved away and she wasn't very social now. This came from Jane and Piper. Yes, he'd asked. He had no qualms about getting his friends and coworkers involved in this.

She lived with her grandmother, Didi, now, so he couldn't just show up at her house and say, "Hey, I want to date your granddaughter again. But it's okay because it probably won't work out."

Because, one, Didi hated his family and had likely been a part of Whitney breaking up with him before. And two, because he wasn't so sure it wouldn't work out.

That's what he needed to find out.

He needed to know if they were going to be friends or more. At this point, those two things were the only options. He didn't hate her. The past ten years might have been easier on him if he had. He could have just moved on. But he hadn't. And he thought he might still be in love with her.

The only way to get over *that* was to get to know her.

He was in love with the Whitney from ten years ago. He needed to know *this* Whitney to figure out how he felt. And she needed to know him.

Finally, Ollie was finished and his bars looked a lot more

like lemon bars this time. Cam wasn't so sure he'd be willing to take a big bite of one though.

Dax took center stage again and kicked off the auction portion of the event.

"Okay, here we go, everybody! You've had a chance to see what the guys have to offer—"

"*Part* of what we have to offer," Max interjected.

Dax grinned. "Right. Of course." He turned back to the crowd. "You've seen *some* of their talents and you know what happens when they get their hands on some... sweet ingredients—"

Could a crowd collectively giggle? Because this one just had.

"And that they're not afraid to get a little... sticky," Dax went on.

Dax could certainly bring the innuendo as well.

There was more laughter and the front row moved closer to the stage, almost as one. Cam braced his hands on the countertop in front of him and just watched his friend with a grin. Dax loved the spotlight and loved helping people have a good time.

"And then you add a little *heat,* and, well, I'm guessing some of you can't wait to get your mouths full of some of the stuff up here on this stage."

Cam laughed along with everyone else.

"So without further ado, let's get this auction started," Dax said.

The crowd cheered and Cam shot Max a grin. Max was enjoying this.

On his other side, Ollie looked resigned. At best. That made Cam grin too. Paige would be fine. She could talk to anyone. Maybe she'd take him over to meet the cats at the yoga studio. It was also a cat café. It was also an adoption center. Except that the forms and interview process Paige put people through was intense and very few people passed it. So it was, actually, just a way for Paige to collect cats and not have anyone call her a crazy cat lady. To her face anyway.

"Okay, first up, Max!" Dax gestured toward the big guy with the caramel crunch bars.

Max played it up even though he knew Elliot was there and Max very much wanted the date with Elliot.

The bidding actually climbed past three-hundred dollars while Max watched amused and surprised. Elliot was bidding, but so was another guy... and three girls.

"Hey ladies," Max interrupted at one point. "I'm flattered, but you do know that caramel crunch bars are the most I've got to offer you, right?"

One of them called out, "And lots of laughs and a ride on your motorcycle, right?"

Max grinned and nodded. "Can do."

"I just need a selfie with you to send to my ex," another called. "He'll be totally scared of you."

Max nodded again but added, "You need me to make a phone call or a visit to someone's apartment with a warning?"

Cam's eyebrows lifted. Having Max show up to tell some creepy ex-boyfriend to back-off might be something they should talk about having him do regardless of the auction.

"Nah, the photo will be enough," the cute brunette told him.

"Let's do that anyway, then," Max told her.

Cam liked Max. They thought alike.

"Great," the girl gave him a big smile. "And maybe a ride on your motorcycle?"

Max laughed. "Sure."

"I'm totally in this for a ride on your... motorcycle," the other guy said, moving in next to the girls right in front of the stage.

Max lifted a brow. "That right? You from out of town?"

"Yep."

Max glanced at Elliot. "Huh."

Elliot held up a wad of cash. "One thousand dollars."

There was a beat of silence, then the three other bidders turned toward Elliot.

"Seriously?" one of the girls demanded.

"Dammit," the other said. But she was going to get the selfie and maybe a ride anyway.

"One thousand and one dol—" the guy started.

But Elliot pulled more money out of his pocket. "Fifteen hundred."

Max's laugh boomed over the mic. "He came all the way from Chicago for this... motorcycle ride," he said to the guy.

The guy frowned at Elliot and then turned to Max. "Well, how about my two hundred bucks for your number. For after "Chicago" here goes home."

Elliot had pushed his way to the front of the stage now too. "Two thousand for the dessert date *and* for you to not give him your number."

Max looked over at Cam, clearly feeling cocky now. "Hot Cakes is matching this bid, right?"

"If it's the highest," Cam told him mildly.

Max laughed. "You think you'll go for more?"

Cam lifted a shoulder. "I think we should find out."

Dax pointed at the guy next to Elliot. "You going higher than two thousand?"

The guy sighed. "No."

Dax looked at the girls. "How about you?"

The brunette shook her head. "We even talked about putting our money together and... nope."

"Selfie right after this though," Max told her.

"Okay." She gave him a grateful smile.

"Okay then, the caramel crunch bars and an hour with Max

go to Elliot Even!" Dax pointed toward Piper. "You can settle up with Piper."

The crowd applauded, Elliot grinned widely, and turned toward Piper.

"Now it's Oliver's turn," Dax said. "Lemon bars and an hour with the brilliant creator of *Warriors of Easton* and one of the new owners of our beloved Hot Cakes!"

The group of women down front moved closer to the stage. Seemed it didn't matter that his lemon bars probably tasted like shit. Cam grinned and turned, settling his hip against his kitchen station, to watch.

"Who will start the bidding at fifty dollars?" Dax asked.

Ten hands, nine females and the one guy who had lost Max to Elliot, went up.

Dax looked surprised. And amused. "You're in again?" he asked the guy.

The guy shrugged. "Love *Warriors of Easton*."

"Free game tokens for a year if you take these lemon bars and let me go home," Ollie told him.

The guy opened his mouth, but Dax cut him off. "Not how this works, Oliver."

Ollie rolled his eyes.

Cam laughed.

"How about free game tokens for a year, a selfie for my social media, and *you* give me Max's phone number?" the guy asked.

Everyone laughed. Ollie looked at Max. "Well..."

"You have to *bid*," Dax said. "How much you want to put up?"

"Two hundred," the guy answered.

Several of the girls in front of him turned on him with scowls.

"Ladies?" Dax asked. "Anyone going higher than two hundred?"

Cam scanned the crowd but didn't see Paige anywhere. He frowned and glanced over toward Whitney again. She should be over here making sure this went according to plan, shouldn't she?

Of course, Piper was here. And she didn't seem concerned that Paige wasn't one of the bidders. Maybe something had come up and they'd planted someone else. But whoever it was wasn't bidding against this guy.

"Two hundred and fifty," one of the women finally said.

Dax nodded. "Anyone got two hundred and sixty?"

"Two hundred and sixty!" one called.

"Two hundred and sixty-five," the guy said.

"Two hundred and sixty-six," the first woman called.

"Four thousand dollars!"

Everyone turned toward the voice a couple of rows behind the bidders. Cam's eyes widened. He knew that voice. That was his little brother.

Henry and his friends pushed to the front of the crowd.

"Four *thousand*?" Dax asked him.

"No, not four thousand." This came from Piper who moved in behind the boys. She leaned down and said something in Henry's ear.

"Four *hundred*," Henry amended.

Dax laughed. "Okay. You sure?"

"Yep!"

Cam frowned. Where the hell had Henry gotten four hundred dollars? He scanned the crowd for Zoe. Maybe she'd had something to do with it. But he didn't see her.

"Dude, where'd you get that?" Cam finally asked.

Everyone in the crowd—or at least most of them—knew Henry was Cam's younger brother.

"No, no," Ollie said. "You can't talk him out of this now."

It made sense that Ollie liked the idea of an hour with three eleven-year-olds better than with any of the women. Ollie talked to eleven-year-olds all the time, both at cons and online. That was their target demographic. Even though their fans ranged anywhere from about eight to forty and were both male and female, their core was truly boys from about ten to twenty.

"Well, he can't use Monopoly money or something," Cam said.

"Sure he can," Ollie said. "I'll trade you your fake money for real."

"It's real," Henry said. Then he looked up at Piper. "Right?"

She nodded. "Right."

"*You're* giving him the money?" Cam asked. Yes, he still had his mic on and, yes, everyone could hear this. But it was all for fun. And charity. No one would actually care if Piper was giving money to kids to bid on time with Ollie, right?

"Hey, he's bidding for his mom? Does *she* get to go on the date too?" one of the women asked. "That's not fair."

Okay, maybe someone would care.

"I'm not his mom!" Piper said.

"Much older sister?" the woman asked, then turned to Dax. "Just because he's a cute kid, doesn't mean I'm just going to let him have this. Four fifty."

Cam looked at Ollie. He did *not* look happy.

"She's not his sister," Dax said. "Just a friend."

"Still, if *he's* bidding then he's the one that goes on the date. She doesn't get to go along," the woman insisted.

"Well, I don't *want* to go along," Piper said. "If I want to eat lemon bars with Ollie, I can do that anytime."

"Oh really?" the woman said. "Well, maybe not after he's spent an hour with *me*."

Piper's mouth dropped open. Then she turned to Dax. "Three thousand dollars."

6

The woman's eyes went round. "Hey!"

Piper looked at her. "What? Anyone can bid."

"I thought you didn't want to go on the date."

"Turns out I want *you* to go on the date even less."

Cam looked over at Ollie. He was watching Piper with an expression that was impossible to read.

Dax was clearly hiding a smile. He looked at the other woman. "You want to go higher than three thousand?"

The woman was clearly appalled by the whole thing. "No. Of course not. I don't have that kind of money!"

Dax shrugged. "Then it's going, going, gone." He pointed at Piper. "Lemon bars with Oliver Caprinelli to the lady in yellow."

Piper looked incredibly smug. She looked down at Henry. "You have a dollar?"

He nodded and held one up. She plucked it from his fingers. "And now *you've* bought the lemon bars with Ollie from me." She looked up at Dax and then glanced at Ollie, then back down to Henry. "Have fun."

Cam covered his mic and leaned toward Ollie. "You paying her back that three thousand for savin' you?"

Ollie shook his head, still watching Piper. "We didn't plan that."

"She's digging into her savings for you?"

Ollie finally looked over and gave Cam a little smile. "Well, I did offer her three thousand dollars to make me some of her sweet and sour meatballs yesterday."

Cam laughed. "Did you get the meatballs yet?"

"Guessing I'll have them tomorrow."

Cam shook his head, grinning.

"And last but not least, Camden McCaffery," Dax announced, pulling Cam's attention back to the center of the stage.

Cam straightened and gave the crowd a big grin, even as he stupidly wished Whitney was over here.

Wouldn't it be a nice twist if she came walking over and bid a couple thousand on him to take everyone immediately out of the running the way Piper had for Ollie?

Better yet, Whitney could bid a cool five grand and make him the big winner, while she was at it.

"Five thousand dollars!" a voice called out.

But it was *not* Whitney's.

Everyone, including Dax and, of course, Cam, turned toward the voice.

It was Didi Lancaster. Whitney's grandmother. The ex-owner of Hot Cakes. The founder. Cam's grandmother's ex-best friend and nemesis for the past half century.

She was being helped up the steps that led to the chair they'd designated for her as the final judge. A place of honor, really.

"Didi?" Dax asked, casting a glance in Cam's direction. "Are you... what did you say?"

She got to the top of the steps and let go of the young man

who'd helped her up. She straightened the hat on her head that reminded Cam of the hats the Queen of England wore. It was a carnation pink that was the exact color of the lighter pink in the Hot Cakes logo and it matched the skirt and jacket she wore over a buttoned-up white blouse.

Cam had a flash of *this is where Whitney gets it* but he shook it off. Kind of. Whitney looked very much like her grandmother and he couldn't help but think he was looking at Whitney at age seventy-two. Put together. Classy. Beautiful. Mildly intimidating.

"I *said*," Didi said, "that I'm bidding five thousand dollars."

The crowd was completely silent.

Dax gave Cam a *what the hell?* look.

Yeah, Cam had no fucking idea.

"You're bidding five thousand dollars for what?" Dax asked.

"To have dessert with Camden, of course," Didi said, giving Dax a look that clearly said she thought he was a cupcake short of a dozen.

"Ooookay," Dax said.

Cam looked out over the crowd. But there was no one who had more than five thousand dollars. For one thing. For another, no one was going to tangle with Didi Lancaster.

"Looks like I just brought in the highest bid," Cam said. What the hell was he supposed to say? He wasn't going to decline time with the woman in front of the entire town. And she was feisty, but she wasn't exactly *scary*.

He was a little curious about what she had in mind here, honestly.

He'd spoken to Didi maybe twice in his entire life. But she'd grown up as his grandmother's best friend. She'd helped start the bakery where he'd grown up and where his mom had worked and that his sister now owned.

And she was Whitney's grandmother.

He wasn't going to disrespect her, and having a conversation

—and some chocolate coconut bars—with her for an hour or so could be interesting.

"Looks like you have," Dax agreed, following Cam's lead. "So... going... going... gone!" he said. He pointed at Didi. "You're the winner."

She smoothed the front of her jacket. "I'm ready to go. I certainly hope you're going to drive the Roadster."

The 1960 MGA Roadster was actually Dax's car but Cam looked at his friend and Dax nodded.

It was a helluva nice car and Cam wouldn't turn down the chance to drive it. He was surprised Didi knew the car even existed, but hey, she'd just agreed to pay five thousand dollars to eat cookies with him. He'd drive her in whatever she wanted.

"I guess I'm ready too," Cam said, pulling the apron off over his head. He wasn't sure how this part was supposed to go.

"Well, hang on there," Dax said quickly. "We need Didi to pick the winning recipe first."

Piper was suddenly up on the stage next to Didi.

So she hadn't gone far. Cam grinned. He should have known she wouldn't let them too far out of her sight.

Piper handed Didi a pink plastic fork. "Let's get you a taste of each," she said.

She led Didi to Ollie's station first. Ollie slid his pan of lemon bars closer to the two women. With Piper's hand on Didi's elbow, Didi took a forkful from one corner. She lifted the bite to her mouth. After a moment, she frowned. Then her nose wrinkled. Then she shook her head. "Too much lemon," she announced, setting her fork down.

Ollie's eyes went wide. "But they don't suck?"

Didi gave him a reproachful look. "You seem like an intelligent young man."

"Thank you."

"Isn't there another word you could use to express what you mean?"

Ollie thought about that for a moment, not looking even the tiniest bit ashamed. "Probably," he finally told her. "But *suck* communicates clearly so I don't see a reason to find another word."

Didi studied him for another moment. "It's a little crude."

"So was the taste of my first batch," Ollie told her.

Ollie wasn't being impolite. He said what he meant. Often without a filter, but with pure honesty. It was one of Cam's favorite things about him.

Didi finally nodded. "All right, then. No, they don't suck. But you can do better."

"Don't know that I'm cut out for baking," Ollie said.

"What are you cut out for?" Didi asked.

Cam glanced at Max and then at Dax. They hadn't expected Didi to have a conversation with each of them.

"I'm the lead of our creative team," Ollie told her.

"And what's that mean?" Didi asked.

That seemed to stump Ollie for a moment.

"It means I come up with the ideas."

"What kind of ideas?"

"Ideas for our video game," Ollie said. "I write the stories, create the characters. Then Dax designs them."

Didi nodded, considering this. "What about Hot Cakes?"

"I helped with ideas for this event," Ollie said.

"Like what?" Didi wanted to know.

Ollie glanced toward the alpacas. "The petting zoo."

Didi looked in that direction as well. "Well, what do alpacas have to do with cake?"

Ollie just blinked at her.

"So you don't *do* anything?" Didi asked him. "You don't get your hands on the things you do? You don't *make* anything?"

"I, um... surround myself with people who have talents far beyond mine for those things," Ollie said.

Didi didn't roll her eyes. That seemed like it might have

been beneath her. But she gave every impression that she was rolling her eyes internally.

"You might be pleasantly surprised by how rewarding it is to be directly responsible for something that makes someone else happy," Didi told him.

Then she turned and headed for Cam.

She actually left Piper a few steps behind.

Everyone on stage was stunned.

The only person who challenged Ollie, really, was Piper, but she didn't really *question* him. She pointed out when he was being a pain in the ass or when one of his ideas was just way too crazy to work out, but she didn't really make him explain himself. None of them told him to do something himself rather than making them do it. They all just accepted that Ollie would say and do some big, crazy things and that their jobs were to mitigate it. They didn't really ask him why.

Speaking of stunned, Cam noticed Whitney had finally joined the crowd. She was at the back, on the very edge, closest to the alpacas, but clearly her grandmother's voice had drawn her over.

She looked like she wasn't sure if she should come intervene with Didi. Or disappear entirely.

He wondered if Whitney had caught the detail about Didi bidding on him. Well, she would find out soon enough.

"Camden," Didi greeted him as she came to stand directly in front of his cooking station.

"Hello, Mrs. Lancaster," he said.

A faint smile curled the side of her mouth. "I already know that your bars will be good."

"Why is that?"

"Your grandmother was the best baker I've ever known."

It was a fact that Letty Lancaster had been the best in the eastern part of Iowa if not the entire state. But hearing her ex-best friend, the woman she'd feuded with for most of her life, say so struck him as particularly complimentary.

"Is baking talent genetic?" he asked with his own smile.

"Fabulous baking is fifty percent about practice," Didi said. "And I know you've been in the kitchen since you were a little boy."

He nodded. Buttered Up had been a second home to his whole family. He knew every inch of the bakery.

"The other fifty percent is about love," Didi said. "And I know that you were taught to put love into the things you make."

That also hit him hard. Directly in the chest. Letty had been proud of her bakery. Stubbornly so, in fact. She'd never changed her menu in all the years she'd owned the place. All of the recipes were original and were as familiar to the people who bought them as the goods that came from their own grandmother's kitchens. There were families in Appleby that had never had a pie or a cake that *hadn't* come from Buttered Up.

But a lot of Letty's emotion about the bakery after she and Didi had parted ways had been about proving that she was better than Didi and didn't need Didi to be successful. He'd always had the impression that there was as much resentment there as there was love. It had always made him sad for his grandmother, actually, and he'd hated that she'd passed it on to his sister.

Thankfully, Zoe had changed her mind and was looking at it differently now that the guys had taken Hot Cakes over. Aiden had had his work cut out for him though. It had definitely helped that Zoe was in love with him before the guys had bought the business. Even if she hadn't realized it.

"I was taught to do everything I do with an eye toward being the best," he finally said.

That wasn't saying that it *wasn't* about love. He did love the company and product that he and the guys had created together, but he knew that it was more that he loved having created it with the four men who were like brothers to him. He wasn't sure he was quite *in love* with Hot Cakes or those products. Yet. Maybe it would come.

His gaze found Whitney over Didi's shoulder.

She loved the company.

That made him want to at least like it.

And he should probably examine that more closely later.

"You undoubtedly got that from your grandmother too," Didi said. "She always wanted to be the best."

He nodded. He was aware that a portion of the town that was here was witnessing this conversation. That could be important. Listening to Didi Lancaster, founder of Hot Cakes, say nice things about his family could show that things were good between their families and would make everyone feel more secure about him being one of the new owners.

He and Aiden felt strongly about keeping Hot Cakes open and solid because it did matter to their hometown. It was important the factory stay here.

But, yes, Cam wanted it to be even better than it had been under the Lancasters. Not just a bigger operation but a better place to work and with better products.

"It's too bad she was a stubborn ass," Didi finally said. "We could have made something great together."

Cam huffed out a surprised laugh. It wasn't often you heard women referring to other women as asses, and certainly not older women wearing pearls.

"She was a bit hard-headed," he finally had to agree.

Didi nodded. "The Hot Cakes cakes could have been better with her on my team."

He lifted a brow. It was probably not a great marketing move to have the original baker and founder of the company saying that their products weren't the best they could have been. But he couldn't help but love that she was complimenting his grandmother in front of the town they'd split with their feud.

"You think so?" he asked.

"No question. She was always the better baker of the two of us," she said. "But Dean had the big business ideas." She glanced at Ollie as she referred to her late husband, the man who had made Hot Cakes the huge multistate company that it was today. "It's wonderful to have ideas. You just need to have the goods to back it up. Otherwise it's just a lot of hot air, and sooner or later, people catch on."

Cam looked over at Ollie. Didi seemed intent on teaching his friend some lesson. He wondered why, exactly, but if Didi saw something in Ollie that she wanted to nurture then...what the hell?

Ollie hadn't had a lot of nurturing. He was an only child and his parents were similarly brilliant people who were pretty detached. It had taken years for him to get *truly* comfortable joking around with the guys. But he was still puzzled by things like family dinners at Cam's mom's house once a week that also included Zoe's two best friends and now, their significant others. The idea of big family gatherings and friends-that-turned-into-family seemed foreign to Oliver, even after a decade of being close to the four men who were his business partners.

"I've got the goods," Cam said, pulling Didi's attention back to him.

She smiled. "You sound like a typical McCaffery."

Fair enough. He tipped his head in acknowledgment.

"The problem there is that you're not as open to being taught or changing," she said.

That was also fair. The McCafferys were well-known for being stubborn as hell. But he wondered if Didi had an under-lying meaning or lesson for him as well. It wasn't as if the

McCafferys were the only ones in the family feud. The Lancasters had been just as stubborn. Hell, it had been Didi who had taken the recipe for Butter Sticks from Letty and turned them into her own business.

"If you think there's a way to improve this, you let me know," he told her.

She dipped her fork into the edge of his pan of chocolate coconut bars. Her nose was already wrinkled by the time she lifted the fork. "Well, the first way to improve them is to take the coconut out."

He laughed. "They're chocolate coconut bars."

"Yeah. So they already"—she looked at Ollie—"suck."

Ollie grinned. Cam laughed.

"You're not a fan of coconut?" he asked.

"You didn't wonder why none of the Hot Cakes have coconut in them already?" she asked.

He sighed, pretending to be hurt. "So I've lost before you even taste it?"

"Yes," she said simply. "But you still get to have dessert with me," she added. "So that's a win. We're just going to have to go to your sister's bakery for something good to eat."

Cam was again pleasantly surprised by Didi's public compliment of something to do with his family. "I can arrange that," he told her.

Didi handed her fork to Piper. "But I also want to be fair. Here. What do you think?"

Piper tasted the chocolate coconut bar. She nodded. "Delicious actually."

"Do you want to taste the lemon too?" Didi asked her.

Piper glanced at Ollie. "No. Oliver never adds enough sweetness to anything."

Cam coughed to cover his laugh. She was annoyed with Ollie today, clearly. He looked at Ollie. He had his arms crossed and was watching Piper as if he was equally annoyed, but also confused as to what he'd done wrong.

"So I guess that means I win," Max said from the end of the stage.

Didi looked at him. "Well, it *is* possible that I won't choose any of these."

Piper frowned. "I don't know. We do need to have a new product to launch." She glanced toward the crowd, probably looking for Whitney.

Cam looked for her as well. She was still standing at the back, chewing on her right thumbnail. That was the sure sign she was nervous about this. Well, she needed to get her sweet ass down to the front, or better yet, up here on stage, and take control.

He lifted a brow as she caught his eye.

She didn't move.

"I'm not going to choose a subpar product for Hot Cakes," Didi said, lifting her chin slightly.

The move was so familiar to Cam that he had to shake his head. Whitney's stubborn, don't-mess-with-me expression was an exact replica of her grandmother's.

"The town helped choose these," Piper said. "We had nearly a hundred entries. I promise these are not subpar."

"Well, we'll see," Didi said, moving toward Max.

Piper handed her another fork.

Max held his pan out.

Didi lifted a forkful of caramel crunch bar to her mouth and tasted it. She chewed. She swallowed. She thought for a moment. But there was no nose wrinkling.

"These are delightful," she finally said.

Max's mouth spread into a huge grin. "Thank you."

"Very good," she said, nodding and setting her fork down. "But—"

Everyone froze. Piper actually groaned.

"You shouldn't let other people tell you how to express yourself," she told Max. "I would have expected more from you. Something bolder. Something with more... flavor. Cinnamon and cayenne," she said. "Or maybe raspberry and dark chocolate."

Max lifted a brow. "Because I'm gay?"

Didi looked surprised. "You're gay?"

"I am."

"Huh." She seemed to think about that. "No, I meant because you're a big, bold personality," she said. She studied him for a moment. "But if you wanted to put rainbow chips in something I suppose that would—"

"Grandma!"

Finally Whitney arrived in front of the stage.

Didi looked down at her. "What?"

"That's... enough." Whitney's cheeks were bright pink.

"I'm being *supportive*," Didi said. "If Max wants to express his sexuality—"

"He is a *baker*. Not everything has to be about his *sexuality*," Whitney said. She cast an apologetic look at Max. "I'm sorry."

Max shrugged one big shoulder. "It's okay, Whit. This is how people learn."

Whitney visibly sighed. "Grandma, let's just focus on the baking."

Didi put her hands on her hips. "Listen up," she said. "Talking *is* how people learn. So I'm going to teach you something about baking. Baking because it *matters* to you is when it's the best. If you're making caramel crunch bars because they are your favorite, or because they were what your favorite uncle always brought on road trips, or because they were what your mom tucked into your lunch box, then that's one thing. But if you're doing it because other people told you to, they are going to lack something. If you want to make something with rainbow chips because it makes you happy because rainbows are beautiful representations of gay love and you want to help people see that in their everyday life, then that's wonderful. Or if you want to make a dark chocolate raspberry cake because, dammit, people might need something more than chocolate and vanilla and strawberry cake with vanilla icing!"

Everyone, including Whitney, was completely quiet, staring at Didi.

"Buttered Up bakery does better baked goods," Didi said. "They are made from scratch and are made with care and love. But Hot Cakes are a part of everyday life and little moments that people don't even think about until later. They are just the cake that your dad pulled out when you were out fishing or the cakes that your mom put out on the little plates in your tea set when you had picnics in your backyard. Until one day you've outgrown those fishing trips and picnics, or your dad or mom is gone, and then you'll pull out one of those cakes and suddenly it *means* something. So Hot Cakes have the potential to be important too and *that's* something you better keep in mind as you're going forward adding to the list of cakes we... I mean *you*... offer."

Didi sniffed, lifted her chin, and then started for the steps on the end of the stage opposite of where she'd ascended.

After a stunned moment, Whitney seemed to shake herself and hurried after her to help Didi down the wooden steps.

Didi paused at the top and looked back. "And the caramel crunch bars win," she said. Then she looked at Cam. "I'll meet you beside the Roadster. I'm actually in the mood for pie."

Then she descended the steps regally.

Piper turned wide eyes to Cam. "Um, wow."

"Yeah," Cam agreed. But he was already covering his pan of bars with the aluminum foil provided.

"So..." Piper said, clearly expecting Cam to fill in some blanks.

But he had no idea how to do that. Didi Lancaster was a

force and it seemed that giving up Hot Cakes wasn't something she was blasé about. He had to admit, the idea of spending a little time talking with the woman was intriguing. He'd never had a one-on-one conversation with her and she surely had some interesting stories.

Dax finally turned to the crowd. "Well, that's that. The new Hot Cakes snack cake will be a caramel crunch bar!"

The crowd applauded on cue.

"Thank you all so much for joining us for this important event," Dax went on. "We hope that you had some fun and that you know how much it means to us to be a part of the Appleby community," he said. "We hope to be here for many, many years to come."

More applause.

"Be looking out for the name announcement for the new snack cake and our big kick-off event for that!" Dax said. "You all, of course, will be the first to get a taste!"

Cam lifted a brow. They hadn't talked about next steps. But now it looked like they'd be having a kick-off event. Well, okay, then.

But Cam was going to put his foot down about having alpacas at *that* event.

7

"I promise that I tried to talk her out of it."

"Why'd you do that?" Cam asked Whitney as he helped Didi into the passenger seat of Dax's Roadster.

"Because this is crazy," Whitney said. She was standing by the front bumper of the car, watching them with a very worried expression.

Cam shut the door and turned to his ex-girlfriend. "Crazy because she's your grandma? Crazy because she was my grandma's nemesis? Crazy because she's paying five thousand dollars for a conversation she could have had just by asking me?"

Whitney studied him for a moment, then said, "Yes."

He chuckled and walked toward her, stopping right in front of her. "Maybe those are all the best reasons for us to have this conversation," he said.

Whitney frowned. "What do you mean?"

He shrugged. "I think I need to explain to her that she could have just asked to talk if she wanted to. I'm sick of this feud, Whit. I think everyone is. Zoe and Aiden have started the healing process and I can do my part."

The wrinkle between her eyebrows got deeper. "Because

you think Appleby needs it to be over?"

"Because I need *you* to be over it," he told her honestly.

She looked surprised. "You do?"

"You're going to be *a lot* more amenable to the idea of us dating if you know that our families don't hate each other and that we don't have to sneak around this time and that the town isn't whispering about us."

Her eyes were wide. "I told you I'm not going to date you."

"You did. And I'm working on convincing you otherwise. One way to do that is to remove as many barriers as possible. Like the fifty-two year feud between our families."

"That's not why I said no," she told him.

He didn't even think twice about lifting a hand to Whitney's face. He smoothed the pad of his thumb over the crease above her nose. "Then you have nothing to worry about with me taking your grandma out for dessert."

Whitney's breath caught as he touched her, and she stared at him even after he slid his hand down her cheek and then dropped it.

"The business is more important to me than a relationship," she said. It was clear she was warning him. "If I have to choose, I choose Hot Cakes. Why would you set yourself up to be hurt again by that?"

He gave her a slow smile. "Because you don't have to choose."

She swallowed hard. But it was clear from the look in her eyes that she didn't believe that.

Well, he'd have to deal with that later. Because he had another woman waiting in the car for a date with him at the moment.

"I'll have her home by curfew," he said, stepping back and grinning. He pulled the keys from his pocket and started to turn away.

He was startled to feel Whitney's hand on his arm. "Cam."

He looked back. "Yeah?"

"She's..." Whitney pressed her lips together and glanced at her grandmother through the windshield. She smiled affectionately, then looked up at him. "Her memory is not great. And she sometimes loses track of what's going on. She might get a little lost while you talk."

He nodded. "Okay."

She wet her lips. "Really?"

"It's going to be fine. We'll talk for a little bit, we'll have some pie, and I'll bring her home."

"Okay." She still looked unsure. "Call me if you need anything. If anything gets... weird."

He smiled. "There are things I need from you, Whit, and I'm going to take you up on that offer to call you. But it won't be about your grandma."

She looked startled, and with that promise hanging between them, he took the chance to get in the car and start the engine. He was not going to let Whitney believe anything was settled between them, and the more she had to think and wonder about the things he said, the better. He wanted to be on her mind.

Cam looked over at Didi rather than watching Whitney watch them with that slightly dazed, slightly worried look on her face.

"So you need some pie, huh?" he asked.

Didi gave him a big smile. "Thank you for loving my grand-daughter."

Okay, so speaking of startled...

Cam tipped his head. "You think I love her?"

"You've always loved her," Didi said with a nod, looking at Whitney through the windshield. "Even when that made things really hard on you."

Cam thought about what Whitney had said about Didi getting lost on details. "You knew about us being together?"

They'd done their damnedest to keep their relationship from their families. He knew that Zoe had known about them. She'd caught them up in Cam's bedroom once and another time in the basement. But Zoe had kept the secret. So had Aiden. But Cam wasn't sure who had known about them on Whitney's side. He'd always figured no one. She'd had a couple of girlfriends in high school, but he knew they hadn't been people she trusted implicitly. He'd always thought it was really sad she didn't have people she knew had her back no matter what.

He knew for a fact that her dad and brother hadn't known about them because they'd never confronted him. And they would have.

So to think that Didi had known made him curious.

"I knew that she was in love for a long time before I figured out who it was," Didi said.

"How?"

"You gonna take me somewhere there's pie or not?" she asked.

Cam laughed and nodded. Right. They had a whole hour "date" ahead of them. "Sure. Of course. I know just the place." He put the car into drive and headed for Buttered Up.

And, yes, Whitney stood in the parking lot and watched them drive away. He gave her a little wave.

She didn't return it.

Okay, well, he'd just bring her grandma home safe and sound and she'd see everything was fine.

They pulled up in front of Buttered Up a few minutes later. Everything in Appleby was only a few minutes away from everything else. He helped Didi out of the car and into the bakery.

Zoe and Josie were expecting them and apparently there were several other people in town who were curious enough about this date to show up to witness it themselves. The bakery was full. Every one of the little round white tables that dotted his sister's bakery had people at it, except one. They'd left one open. The one right in the center of the room.

He shook his head but escorted Didi to the table that was clearly for them, smiling and nodding at people as they went. What else was he going to do?

Zoe was behind the counter and she gave him a look that said *well, this is weird*, but it was Josie that came out to wait on them.

"Hi," she greeted. "How are you?"

"In desperate need of pie," Didi told her. "I would like peach, with the cinnamon whipped topping, and a cup of coffee with cream on the side."

Josie looked at her. "Cinnamon whipped topping?"

It was an extra thing that only those "in the know" were aware of. His grandmother had always added cinnamon to her whipped cream topping for peach and apple pies. Those were the only things she put it on and she'd only done it at home. Not in the bakery.

Cam leaned in. "Did you have cinnamon whipped topping with my grandma?"

Didi looked like that was an extremely stupid question. "Well, of course."

"They don't do that here," Cam said. "That was something she only did at home when she made pies."

"Well, *that's* ridiculous," Didi said. "Tell her to do it now. I've been looking forward to having that topping on my pie again ever since Dean died."

Dean, her husband, had passed away about a year ago. Cam blinked at her. "Why haven't you come in before this?"

"I've been very busy with the funeral preparations," Didi said.

Cam nodded. "I suppose so. When was the funeral again?"

He knew when it had been. He'd thought about coming

home for it. For Whitney. But his friends had talked him out of it.

But it had killed him to know that Whitney might be sad and hurting. He'd finally sent flowers. To her directly. With only, *I wish I could meet you at the bridge* on the card. She would know it was from him. *Meet me at the bridge* was the note he'd slip into her locker or leave on the dash of her car.

"Last week," Didi answered. "It was lovely."

She thought Dean's funeral had been just last week? Cam glanced at Josie, who just lifted a brow. She was clearly letting him take the lead here. "Do you think... the kitchen... could make something special?" he asked.

Josie *was* the kitchen here. Along with Zoe, of course, but Josie was the more creative cook of the two.

"I think we can manage it," Josie said with a bemused smile.

"Thanks. I'll have the same," Cam told her.

Josie nodded and moved off.

"Dean wouldn't have wanted you having Letty's whipped topping?" Cam asked Didi. If Didi thought the funeral was just last week, that was something much different from her just getting a date mixed up from a year ago.

"Oh goodness no," Didi said. "Dean didn't like anything having to do with Charlotte."

Very few people called his grandmother Charlotte, but it seemed that Didi was one of them. "Did she call you Dorothy?" he asked, very curious about their relationship. He had been at various times over the years, but Letty hadn't liked talking about Didi so he didn't know much. He liked the idea of getting more history about them from Didi.

"She does," Didi told him, referring to Letty in the present tense. His grandmother had also passed away.

"Dean didn't like you to have anything to do with my grandma then?" Cam asked.

"Oh, no. I couldn't even make any of her recipes. He knew

which ones were hers and he wouldn't eat anything I'd learned from her."

Cam felt his eyes go wide. "Wow. Really. How did he know which ones were hers?"

Didi smiled at him. "Because she cooked for him all the time when they were dating."

Cam stared at her for several seconds. She was a little confused, obviously, thinking Dean had died last week and that Letty was still alive. But *this* was interesting.

"They dated?" he asked. "I didn't know that."

In fact, he wondered who did know that. He wasn't sure his mom and dad even knew that. If they did, it was a well-kept secret. The Lancasters and McCafferys had hated each other Cam's entire life. It had always been understood that it was because Didi stole Letty's recipe for the now famous Butter Sticks that had launched Hot Cakes.

But damn, there might be even more scandal behind it all.

"Oh, yes." Didi leaned back in her chair, folding her hands on her lap. "She turned down his proposal and he never got over it."

Cam swallowed hard. "Dean Lancaster *proposed* to my grandmother?"

"Of course. She was a catch," Didi said. "Beautiful, independent, smart, sassy."

Yep, that was his grandmother.

"Why did she say no?"

"Because Dean was an ass."

Again Cam was speechless for a moment. "But... *you* married him."

Didi nodded. "Horrible mistake. Except, of course, I have Whitney because of him."

Her granddaughter. Not her two sons, not her three grandsons. Didi only named Whitney.

And Cam had to agree that Dean had been an ass. Along

with their son, Eric, and their grandsons, Whitney's brothers Wes and Will and her cousin Brent.

Cam leaned in. Didi seemed in the mood to share and he was going to take advantage. Maybe she was always like this, but in case she wasn't, he wanted as much of the story as he could get.

"So tell me what happened," he said.

Didi shrugged. "He and Charlotte dated for a few months. He fell in love, she didn't. He proposed, she said no. He never got over that. Though part of it was his ego and the fact that people didn't say no to him. After Charlotte and I split up and I was on my own, Dean asked me out. He was very handsome and charming and I was feeling very alone. I said yes. He romanced me and I got pregnant." Didi lifted a shoulder again. "And that's that. He took over the business and made me a very rich woman."

Cam was happy that Josie delivered the pie and coffee just then. He had to process all of that. There was nothing about the story that was familiar to him at all. Other than that part where she and Letty split up.

"Let me know what you think of the topping," Josie told Didi, setting her plate down.

"Oh, it will be perfect," Didi said, sitting forward and picking up a fork. She seemed genuinely eager. "Charlotte's concoctions are always perfect."

Again with the present tense reference to his grandmother. Cam and Josie shared another look. He didn't know much about Alzheimer's. Letty had been sharp until her very last day when her heart had given out. Should he correct Didi or let her go on thinking Letty was still around?

That was a good question for Whitney. He could text her.

Or he could wait and talk to her after he dropped Didi off at home.

He grinned, picking his fork up as well. That was a great

reason to linger at Whitney's after this date.

Josie went back to the kitchen and Cam and Didi ate without talking for a few minutes.

Didi seemed completely immersed in enjoying the pie.

Letty hadn't made it but it was her recipe and the girls never strayed from Letty's recipes by even a half a teaspoon. Letty's desserts really were the best he'd ever tasted and as he'd traveled extensively over the past few years with Fluke, Inc. he'd made a point of trying various desserts in all the places he visited. He'd never found better than his grandmother's.

It was a damned travesty that Didi had gone without Letty's desserts for fifty-two years.

"How long were you and Dean married?" Cam asked after a few bites.

"Fifty-one years," Didi replied after taking a sip of coffee.

"So you and Dean started dating shortly after you started Hot Cakes."

She nodded. "It wasn't even officially Hot Cakes then. Dean was the one who pushed to make it grow. I got to name it. That was about it." She said it with a tone that clearly said what she thought of that.

Cam knew the basic story. Letty and Didi had worked at Buttered Up together. Some of the local men wanted to take cake and pie in their lunches to the local factories and farms. Didi tried to talk Letty into individually packaging some of their best sellers. Letty had refused. Didi had done it on the side just so she could prove to Letty that it was a good idea. Letty had been furious. They'd broken up and Didi had gone on to open her own business individually packaging treats and selling them out of her house to start.

"Of course, the business was *why* he asked me out," Didi said, taking another tiny bite of pie.

"What do you mean?"

"He saw the potential in what I was doing. He knew he

could make it into something big. And he wanted to hurt Charlotte that way." Didi met Cam's gaze. "That's why I had to stay away from Charlotte completely after Dean got involved. He said we couldn't risk having a legal battle, but I know he knew that I would have kept asking Charlotte to be involved. He didn't want the complication of working together with the woman he was in love with and the woman he'd married."

Cam was almost speechless over this whole story. Almost. He *really* wanted to know more. "You think he was still in love with my grandma?"

"Oh yes. At least a little. And he wanted revenge. He wanted to show her that she'd made a mistake not marrying him."

"That didn't bother you?" Cam would have never imagined having this conversation with Didi Lancaster or pushing her for personal details about her marriage, but she seemed willing to talk. She could always tell him to fuck off. In a very sophisticated way, of course.

"Well, I was naïve for a long time and didn't realize it," she said. "And when I did, we'd been married for nearly eight years. We had children. We had a business. I would have had to let Dean have Hot Cakes and everything that went with it if I left him. He wasn't a *bad* husband, he just wasn't that good at it. And I did, of course, enjoy the privileges that went along with the money and status." She looked sad for a moment. "I liked that too much for too long. That doesn't last." She looked up at Cam. "When I realized that Dean was preparing the boys to follow him into the business and to continue to push it and make it bigger, I started to have regrets."

"Like what?"

"Charlotte," Didi said, her voice softer. "And Dean making my sons selfish, shallow men motivated by money."

Cam wasn't sure what to say to that. She seemed truly sad and he wasn't sure how to comfort her. Besides, he thought she probably should regret those things, at least a little.

"And, of course, what almost happened with you and Whitney."

He jerked his head up and met Didi's eyes. What had *almost* happened? "What do you mean?"

"I know Whitney felt she had to choose us or you."

Cam swallowed hard. He hadn't realized that anyone knew about that. He didn't know how the conversation had gone with Whitney and her family. He didn't know who she'd said what to. He didn't know if she'd announced she was running off with him and they'd forbid it or if they'd somehow found out she'd been seeing him and they'd told her she had to break it off or if she'd asked for a job for him and they'd refused. All of those scenarios and a few others had gone through his mind over the years when he'd let himself think and wonder about it—usually after he'd been to Appleby for a visit and gotten incredibly drunk.

But mostly he'd told himself that it didn't matter and he didn't care.

It *didn't* matter. The end result was the same no matter who had said what to who.

He still wondered.

"That was a long time ago," he finally said.

"I'm so glad you stayed together anyway," she said.

He blinked at her. "Um—"

"The company was so important to Whitney. But I'm just so, so glad that you stayed together even if you had to keep it a secret. Love—true love—is worth whatever it takes." Didi was staring off into the distance. "You don't want to get to be seventy-two years old and realize that you completely missed it."

Cam felt his chest tighten. Didi hadn't been in love with Dean. She'd missed out on true love and she was realizing it now, late in life. That was incredibly sad.

But she thought that he and Whitney had stayed together.

"The way you look at her is the way every woman should be looked at by the man she's sharing her life with," Didi told him. She sat forward and took the last bite of pie from her plate.

Cam didn't know what to think. Didi seemed so resolute about so many things, but she was clearly confused about a few things. A few important things. Like how long ago her husband had died. And Cam and Whitney's entire relationship.

"I'm not sure Whitney is convinced this is forever," he finally said. That was true enough.

Didi looked shocked. "Why not?"

"The business is still very important to her," he said. "She thinks us working together could make that complicated."

"No." Didi frowned and leaned in, grabbing Cam's hand. "No. You have to show her that's not true. That business... it's done some good things. It's important to Appleby. But it can *not* be the reason that another couple spends their life without love."

Whoa. That was intense. Cam squeezed her hand. "I want to convince her we belong together."

That was his mission even before this.

Didi's eyes filled with tears and she squeezed him back. "You *must*. Whitney deserves love. She hasn't had nearly enough of that. Her father was also completely involved in that company. I think he loves his wife, but he did not show that little girl enough love when she was growing up and he hasn't respected her since she's been a part of the company."

Cam's chest got tighter. He'd suspected that Whitney had been working to gain her father's approval and that Eric had been a workaholic at best and a neglectful father at worst. But hearing Didi say it, about her own son, made Cam want to punch Eric Lancaster. And made him want to go straight to Whitney, wrap her up in his arms, and convince her—however he had to—that she could have it all. She did not have to choose between Hot Cakes and love.

"I will do whatever I can to show Whitney that this can work," he said.

Didi drew in a long breath and let him go, sitting back. "What are you doing each day between one and four p.m.?" she asked.

"I'm... at work."

"But you're one of the bosses, right?" she said.

"Yes."

"And I'll bet that you work until nine at night or on Sundays if needed."

He nodded. "Yes."

"So you can take a few hours off each day."

He could. Of course. His work wasn't really eight-to-five work. Sometimes it was twenty-hours a day for several days in a row. Sometimes it was just a couple of intense days. Some days were very routine. Others, he had almost nothing to do.

"What do you have in mind?" he asked.

"Whitney has a woman come over each day. She makes our dinner, does some light housekeeping, runs errands for us."

"Okay."

"I want you to do all of that."

He waited for her to go on, but she didn't. She simply finished her coffee.

"You want me to come make dinner for you?" He could do that. It would give him a reason to see Whitney outside of the office. And he was a great cook.

"I want you to come babysit me each afternoon."

Okay, that wasn't what he'd been expecting. "Babysit you?"

She nodded. "Whitney feels like I shouldn't be alone for more than an hour or so at a time."

"Why's that?"

"I set the kitchen on fire."

That was a good reason. He lifted a brow. "On accident or on purpose?"

Didi laughed at that. "I *accidentally* set a kitchen *towel* on fire by setting it on the stove. But to hear Whitney tell it, it was a five-alarm blaze."

"It could have turned into a five-alarm blaze," Cam said. A fire, of any kind, wasn't nothing.

"That's what she said," Didi agreed. "She was especially mad that I called her instead of the fire department."

Cam's eyes got wider. "Yeah. 9-1-1 is always first."

Didi nodded. "I remembered that after Whitney told me."

After the fire was started and she'd wasted time calling Whitney. Yeah, that wasn't good.

"Maybe you shouldn't use the stove when you're there alone," Cam suggested.

"She reminded me of that rule after the fire too," Didi said. "And then she had Katherine start coming over."

"That doesn't seem like a bad idea. If it's hard for you to remember things," Cam said carefully.

"I suppose. But she's annoying."

"Katherine is annoying?"

Didi nodded. "She wants me to exercise and she always wants to watch me do things like make my coffee and start the washing machine. She treats me like a child."

"Have you talked to Whitney about it?"

"It makes her anxious. She wants it to all be good. She wants me to be safe and happy. That's why I'm moving into Sunny Orchard," Didi said. "It will be easier for Whitney to relax and concentrate at work once I'm living there."

Cam frowned. "You're moving into the nursing home to make things easier on Whitney?"

"Of course." Didi dabbed at her mouth with her napkin. "But it's fine. It's a lovely place. I'll have a new suite. And I know a lot of people who live there. I like to play cards and things." She gave Cam a smile. "It's a great solution. But my new apartment won't be ready for another month. I can't tolerate

Katherine for another week not to mention a month. And this is the perfect chance for you to show Whitney what it would be like to live together and make a real life together. You can show her what being married to you will be like."

Cam was glad he was done eating. His throat was suddenly tight and there was no way he could have swallowed anything.

Didi was simplifying this, of course. You didn't just move in with a woman and her grandmother and start making dinner and entertaining that grandmother in the afternoons when that woman was still unsure how she felt about you.

But that was the part that made him pause.

He wasn't so sure that Whitney didn't know how she felt about it. He was pretty sure she knew exactly how she felt but knew that could be complicated.

So he needed to show her it wasn't complicated. Having him around could actually make things so much easier. She could have it all. Hot Cakes, him, *and* her grandmother safe and happy.

Hot Cakes was important to her? She wanted to prove that she belonged there? That she could contribute to the company's growth and success? She wanted a chance to be a kickass corporate tycoon? Fine. What did she need to make that happen? A partner. Not in business but in life.

He wanted to know if they could still fit. He wanted to know who Whitney was now, ten years later, and how he felt about that woman. He wanted to know if they could have a relationship now. He needed to be *with* her to do that. They needed to spend time together for that.

This was just about the most perfect setup for them both.

"You've got a deal," he finally said to Didi. "But I have to warn you... I'm not going to let you win at checkers or cards or whatever we're going to be doing all day."

Didi lifted her chin. "I would be insulted if you did."

"Good." He grinned at her.

"And you'll have to move into the house."

"Why's that?" he asked. He wasn't opposed to that at all. Didi's house was huge. He was sure there were at least six bedrooms. He was currently staying in one of the rooms at Zoe's house. But so was Aiden. Well, Aiden was staying in *Zoe's* room with her.

He was happy for his sister and his best friend, but it was a little weird being there with them when they were cuddling on the couch, or flirting in the kitchen, or coming out of the bathroom at the same time, wrapped only in towels.

"I'm a night owl," Didi said. "I always have been. But Whitney feels strange about going to bed before I do. So she sits up with me. Then gets up so early for work. She's sleep deprived." Didi frowned. "And grumpy because of it. It would be great if someone else could sit up with me. You can sleep in until noon if you need to. I do."

Cam thought about that. He didn't mind staying up late at all. He wasn't an early morning person. Thankfully, the Fluke guys all liked to get a later start in the morning so their team meetings were certainly not first thing in the day.

And this was for a month. Just until Didi moved to Sunny Orchard. He could flex his hours for a month. Or work from Didi's house. The Hot Cakes offices were a five-minute drive. If he needed to go in he could pop over there, not leaving Didi alone for too long. Or he could take her with him.

"You have an extra room for me?" he asked.

"I have five extra rooms."

"How many bedrooms does your house have?"

"Seven."

"Good Lord."

"I know."

He grinned at her. "When do I start?"

"Tonight." Didi slid her chair back and stood.

"Oh." He got to his feet as well and dug his wallet out.

Josie was there a minute later. "Don't you dare try to pay for this," she said, gathering up their plates and cups.

"Oh, I'm not paying," he said. "I'm tipping." He slipped a one hundred dollar bill into the pocket of her apron.

She lifted a brow. "You realize I'm in love with and living with one of your partners, right?"

Yes, Grant had as much money as Cam did. He grinned and nodded. "Be sure to tell him I tipped you a hundred bucks. That will annoy the hell out of him."

She shook her head, but laughed. "Of course."

Annoying Grant Lorre was entirely too much fun and since he'd met and fallen for Josie, he'd gotten a bit more laid back, making it harder to rile him up.

"Tell him I said you look hot in that apron too," he added. *That* would irritate Grant.

Didi slapped his arm. "If you're going to marry my grand-daughter you need to cool it with the flirting with other women."

Josie gave him a wide-eyed questioning look.

Cam simply nodded. "That's a good point." He took Didi's hand and tucked it into the crook of his arm. "At least when her grandmother is around."

Didi smacked his arm again, but she chuckled.

Josie looked very interested.

"Tell Zoe I'll see her later. And we'll see you all at dinner at mom's tomorrow night."

"We?" Josie asked.

Cam looked down at Didi. "Yep. We." He was going to take Didi and Whitney to dinner at his mom's house.

That was really weird.

He couldn't wait.

8

———————

Whitney couldn't believe she was actually pacing the foyer of her house waiting for her grandmother to get home from her *date*.

With Cam.

Where were they? They'd been gone for far longer than an hour. The auction had clearly been for an *hour* of time.

Of course, she was sure that Elliot and Max were spending more than an hour together, and if Henry and his friends got Ollie going on *Warriors of Easton,* they could easily hang out the rest of the evening. Ollie might even come to the office with a bunch of new ideas for the game tomorrow.

But Didi and Cam? What were they possibly doing for this long?

She heard a car in the circle drive in front of the house and sucked in a quick breath. She started for the door. Then she stopped. She couldn't meet them at the door. That would make it seem like she'd been waiting for them. And possibly pacing.

Whitney bolted for the couch in the sitting room off to the side of the foyer and grabbed for the first thing on the coffee table just as the front door opened.

Cam and her grandmother were laughing as they stepped into the house together.

For a moment, Whitney felt her heart flip at the sound of her grandma's laughter. Didi and Whitney used to laugh like that together when they played dolls or had tea parties or were reading books inside her princess tent.

Didi had always been the one to play with Whitney. Everyone else had been too busy or not even home much of the time. But Whitney hadn't missed anyone. Not until she was older and realized just how little time her parents actually spent with her. She'd always had Didi to go to the park with and to play dress-up with and to bake with.

She felt her eyes stinging as she thought about how long it had been since they'd spent time like that—just silly, fun time enjoying something together. They hadn't baked together in years probably.

She blinked the water in her eyes away as Cam and Didi came around the corner. Whitney looked up as if she'd just heard them and smiled. "Welcome home."

"Hello, darling."

Whitney had to take a second look at her grandma. She realized Didi was glowing. Actually glowing. She looked happier than Whitney had seen her look in far too long. It made her seem younger.

Whitney couldn't help but look at Cam then. He was smiling too, looking genuinely happy, and the way he had Didi's hand on his arm was very sweet and gallant.

Cam had made her grandmother look like that. Wow. He hadn't just put up with the crazy date idea and taken her out for a quick piece of pie. They'd been out for nearly two hours and they both genuinely looked like they'd had a great time.

Dammit, that didn't make it any easier to *not* think about kissing him.

Whitney had to take a deep breath before she said or did

anything.

She stood from the couch, trying hard to look as if she'd been lounging and reading, hardly aware of the time.

"Why are you sitting in here?" Didi asked, blowing Whitney's nonchalant cover immediately however.

"I just... thought I'd read for a bit until you got home." Whitney waved the book she'd picked up from the coffee table.

"In here?" Didi asked, looking around as if confused.

It made sense that she'd be confused about that.

This room was for looks only. Didi and Dean had occasionally sat in here with someone who had just dropped by. Usually someone wanting a donation to some cause or fundraiser or campaign. This room was for entertaining uninvited guests. For short periods. This room at the front was very pretty. And entirely uncomfortable.

Invited guests and family used the living room and the even less formal family room at the back of the house.

Whitney sighed and set the book she held back on the table. She glanced at the front. It was a coffee table book about neckties.

Neckties. Who put together books about neckties? More, who bought and displayed a book like that?

Dax Marshall would. Whitney actually smiled at the thought. Dax loved crazy ties and had a whole collection.

"You're reading in here?" Didi asked.

Whitney nodded. "I was thinking about giving this book of grandpa's to Dax."

Didi looked at it and smiled. "I like Dax. Yes, give him the book."

"Great." Whitney picked it up again and handed it to Cam. "Are you going to see him tonight?"

Cam shook his head. "Actually no." He glanced at Didi, then back to Whitney. "You can give it to him tomorrow."

"Okay." She looked at him for a long moment. "So thanks

for bringing Grandma home."

"Of course."

There was another long pause where it seemed everyone was waiting for someone else to do something.

"I'm going to make tea," Didi announced, turning toward the kitchen. "Whitney, take Cam upstairs."

Whitney blinked. Then frowned. Then blinked again. Her grandmother was not as clearheaded as she used to be and she'd undeniably lost some of her filter. But she wanted Whitney and Cam to go upstairs together?

"Excuse me?" she asked.

"He's going to pick a bedroom," Didi said, as if it was the most obvious thing. "Show him the way. He didn't sneak into *this* house to see you, so he doesn't know his way around."

Whitney heard the little surprised squeak that came from her own throat.

Cam, on the other hand, laughed. "Are you guessing, Didi? You think we're going to give up secrets?"

"You *didn't* sneak into her bedroom? Not even once? What kind of teenage love story was that?" Didi asked.

Whitney opened her mouth but was only able to squeak again.

Cam looked a little offended even as he smiled at Didi. "Of course I snuck into her bedroom. More than once."

"I figured," Didi said.

Cam chuckled. "Should I take that as a compliment?"

"Of course." Didi glanced at Whitney. "Every woman deserves a man who will scale buildings for her."

Whitney felt her eyes widen and she looked at Cam. He didn't seem shocked. In fact, he was nodding. And looking at Whitney.

"You're absolutely right, Didi."

"Anyway, I don't want you falling and breaking your neck," Didi said, turning toward the kitchen again. "You can now use the front door and the stairs. Whitney will get you a key tomorrow."

Didi headed down the hallway.

When she was out of view, and earshot, Whitney swung to face Cam. She was going to get him a *key* tomorrow? "What is going on?"

He gestured to something behind him and Whitney moved closer so she could see. But she only got as close to him as was absolutely necessary.

"I need to take my stuff up to my room."

There was a suitcase sitting in the foyer.

A *suitcase.*

Whitney propped her hands on her hips. "I leave you alone with my grandmother for two hours and now you're best friends and moving in here?"

He was watching her with one corner of his mouth curled. "Pretty much."

"Cam, *what* is going on?"

"Your grandmother doesn't like Katherine. She asked me to come and stay and keep her company during the day while you're at work."

Whitney stared at him. None of that made any sense.

Well, she knew that Didi didn't really like Katherine. She'd told Whitney that a number of times. But the truth was that Katherine just made Didi do some things she didn't like but that were important. Their daily walk for instance. And eating something other than cereal. And not spending the day watching *Golden Girls* reruns.

Okay, so Didi wanted a replacement for Katherine. But *Cam?*

"How, exactly, did that come up and why in the world would you agree to that?"

He took a step closer and Whitney had to fight the urge to back up. She didn't actually want to get away from him. On the contrary, she wanted to get a lot closer. But she couldn't. That would complicate things enormously.

A lot like having him hanging out here every day and being sweet to her grandmother.

Not to mention him *moving in*.

"It came up in our conversation," he said with a shrug as if he didn't remember exactly how. "And she and I have a common goal, and me being here a lot helps us toward that goal."

Whitney narrowed her eyes. "What's the goal?"

"Making you happy."

That wasn't exactly what she'd been expecting him to say so it took her a second to really process it.

"You think you being here with my grandma is going to make me happy?"

He nodded. "You want to focus on Hot Cakes and being a part of the team and showing your new bosses that you're dedicated and valuable. But your grandma being here and needing company is distracting and causes you to need to leave work in the middle of projects sometimes. Like when she sets things on fire." The corner of his mouth curled again as if Didi starting things on fire was amusing. "If I'm here, Didi is happy and you're free to concentrate on work."

Whitney swallowed. She really did need someone to help with Didi if she was going to put in the time and concentration she needed at work. Her father's departure and the guys coming in and taking over had been a blessing in a lot of ways. Whitney was starting fresh with the guys. Even slightly ahead. They valued her experience with the company over the past ten years.

But the changes and increased demands on Whitney's time and attention were coinciding with a crucial time with Didi. It was another month before Didi could move into Sunny Orchard where she would have more activities and supervision.

Her meals would be provided—and would include vegetables —and she wouldn't have to use a stove at all.

Whitney had really been hoping that Didi could tolerate Katherine for another thirty days. Surely it wasn't *that* bad with Katherine.

"Why would *you* do this? Really?" she asked. "Why do you care if Didi is happy with Katherine?"

He took a moment to answer. He took another step closer and tucked his hands into his pockets. The movement drew her attention to his arms. He'd always been muscular and solid, but he definitely had the arms—and shoulders and chest and abs —of a man now. The last time his arms had been around her, making her feel comforted and loved and sexy, he'd been a boy. She couldn't help but wonder how they would feel around her now.

She shook that off quickly though. *That* was even more complicated than having him getting along with her grand-mother. It was one thing for them to see each other regularly and to have something in common with Hot Cakes. It would be a lot more convoluted between them if he was a part of her personal life as well. But if there was a physical connection too, she wasn't sure she'd be strong enough not to just fall headfirst in love with him. Again.

"I've been really clear about what I want, Whit," he finally said. "I want a chance to see what, if anything, is between us now. It's been ten years but I wouldn't say we had a lot of closure. If we spend time together and decide to be friends, great. If we can only manage to be coworkers at Hot Cakes, then, fine. I guess. But if we can be more, then I absolutely want to know that."

"So you're using my grandmother to get closer to me?" she asked, crossing her arms, feeling suddenly raw and jumpy.

Her life had been easier when Cam had lived in another city and only came home occasionally. It had always hurt to see him. She'd always wanted more than the few minutes of inter-action. She'd wanted more than acting as if they were just acquaintances, like she did with any of the other guys she'd gone to high school with who were home for the holidays and passed her on the street.

It had never felt right with Cam. It had never been *enough*.

But then he'd leave and she'd forget about him again. Or at least push him to the back of her mind.

Until she heard a song that reminded her of him. Or passed his family's bakery. Or passed the house where he'd grown up. Or passed the road to the river where they'd spent lots of time in his back seat. Or... any of the other dozens of places in Appleby that reminded her of him and their past together.

Which was almost every day.

Yeah, it was *incredibly* difficult to forget about an ex-boyfriend in a tiny town where you'd spent a year in love with him.

Especially when you hadn't really ever gotten over him.

And you hadn't found a guy who could replace him in any way.

Him moving into her house and becoming a co-caregiver to her favorite person in the world was *really* not the way to move past any of that.

"I think *she's* using *me* to get out of doing crosswords with Katherine," he said, lifting a shoulder. "But I'm not going to turn down a chance to be around you more, Whit."

"I don't think this is a good idea." She pressed her arms into her stomach.

"Why not?"

He knew. He *knew* why it was a bad idea in her mind. It was because it was going to be hard for her to hold herself back from him. But he wanted her to say it out loud.

"You have a job."

He gave a short laugh. "I own the company. I'm best friends

with—and have dirt on—all of the other owners. I can do a lot of my work from here. And if I need to be in the office, it's a five-minute drive."

"So you would leave her alone," Whitney said. "I can't have you—"

"I would never do anything that wouldn't be completely safe for her," he broke in, looking annoyed that she'd even suggest that. "I will handle this."

"How?"

"You don't need to worry about it," he said. "That's what's so great about this. I'm taking this off your plate."

"To get on my good side."

"Yes."

He didn't even try to hedge.

Now she wanted to hear *him* admit something. He was trying to get her into bed. And he was willing to use her grand-mother to do it. Gross.

Though it didn't *really* feel gross. It felt... good. Someone wanting to be with her so badly that he'd pull out all the stops? She honestly wasn't used to people wanting to be with her as much as Cam seemed to.

And it was Cam. There was just nothing gross about him. Period.

"Why?"

"Because I care about you."

That made her stomach flip in spite of how tightly she had her arms crossed.

"And because you want to—"

"She cried, Whit."

Whitney stopped and frowned. "What?"

"She cried." He sighed. "She regrets so many things that happened with my grandma. With your grandpa. With the business. But she's so glad that *we* stayed together. I didn't have the heart to do anything but agree with her."

Whitney's frown deepened. "You told her we stayed together?"

"No. But I didn't correct her, either." The way he lifted one brow was almost as if he was daring her to tell him he'd been wrong to placate her.

Whitney pulled in a breath. She wasn't going to tell him he was wrong. Grandma tears were the worst. If he'd been able to resist feeling bad and doing whatever it took to make Didi feel better, he would be a bad guy.

And Camden McCaffery was definitely not a bad guy.

"She believes it though," he went on. "She thinks that we stayed together and have kept the relationship hidden all this time."

Whitney pulled in a deep breath, then nodded. "She also probably thinks it's only been a year or so since you left town."

That made her heart ache. She didn't want to lose Didi. Her grandmother was her only family left here in Appleby. But, in many ways, Didi had always been her only family. At least in the make-her-feel-supported-and-comforted way families were supposed to function. Didi was the one Whitney had her best childhood memories with. Now she was slowly losing the bright, funny, sweet woman who had been her advocate and had always believed in her.

Whitney was going to be on her own soon. Maybe the Alzheimer's would take a few years to steal Didi completely, but already her grandmother was changing. Their relationship was changing. Eventually Whitney would be alone. And there was nothing she could do about it. She felt like there was a sharp, hot poker jabbing her just below her ribs when she thought about that.

She needed her work. She needed to secure her place at Hot Cakes. She needed to be vital there. That was all she had and she needed to be a *part* of something. Her family was gone, the family business was gone, her grandmother would be gone. Hot Cakes was the one place she could belong.

Of course, even Hot Cakes had changed on her, but she was still there and she had a better chance now at being truly essential to the business. It was the only thing she could control. She could control her work and her performance. Everything else involved other people, and, as she knew too well, other people were out of her control completely.

"Even if that is what she thinks," Cam said about Didi's poor perception of time. "It makes her happy. Really happy. She wants us to be together. She wants to know that someone is loving you and taking care of you."

His words made Whitney's stomach swoop and then dive. She felt the air between them heat. This was different than how he'd talked to her in her office last night but it affected her similarly. Being loved and taken care of by Cam was absolutely as tempting as being seduced by him. Honestly, with Cam, all of that had always gone together.

"So you're going to lie to her?" Whitney asked.

That was so stupid. She wanted to hear him say it wasn't a lie. She wanted to hear him say that he did love her and wanted to take care of her. But what if he said that? That would make all of this so much harder. She had to resist. Hot Cakes was her focus. She couldn't do anything to jeopardize her position there.

"It's a month," he said after a long pause. "Right? A month until she can move into her new apartment."

Well, he certainly hadn't said, "Let me be your knight in shining armor."

And she was *glad* he hadn't said that. That would have been ridiculous. He couldn't love her. He didn't really know her anymore.

Which was the point he was trying to make when he said they needed to date and figure things out.

Whitney pressed her lips together, telling herself to stop being ridiculous. She finally nodded. "Right. A month."

"A month should be enough time to figure out what we are."

"What we are?" she repeated.

"Coworkers, friends, or..."

Whitney felt that she was holding her breath waiting for him to fill in that last word.

"Or?" she prompted when he just stood watching her.

"Everything," he said.

Her breath caught again. They were going to find out if they were coworkers, friends, or everything.

"I feel like I'm not getting much say in this," she managed, noting that her voice sounded scratchy.

She knew that Cam heard it too when he stepped forward one more time. Now they were only inches apart. Close enough to reach out and touch. Close enough that if they *didn't* touch, it would be very obvious they were making that choice.

"You can say no to anything I suggest," he said. "But that doesn't mean I won't make the suggestions."

She wet her lips. "Suggestions like?"

"Like that we should sit on the front porch with a couple of beers and talk. Like that we should sit on the couch and watch old movies. Like that we should go for a midnight swim in the pool out back."

Those all sounded relatively safe. And tempting as hell. Which made them *not* safe.

"And like we should make chocolate chip cookie dough," he went on.

Okay she could maybe do this. Chocolate chip cookie dough and playing in the pool. Maybe they could end up being friends. That was a nice, safe compromise between coworkers and... she swallowed hard... everything.

"And you should let me lick it off your nipples."

9

W hitney sucked in a sharp breath and her eyes flew to his as he turned the sweet, date-like ideas into sexy and oh-my-God-yes in a blink.

Her nipples definitely liked the idea. They tingled as if he was already covering them with cookie dough and tightened in anticipation of the licking.

He reached up and cupped her face. "Let me stay."

She had to clear her throat before she could answer. She also noted that she didn't pull back away from his touch. She probably should. In a second.

"I didn't realize I was in a position to *let* you stay... or not," she said.

"I'm not staying if you're completely against it," he said, brushing his thumb over her cheek.

"What if I'm a little bit against it?" she asked.

He gave her a half smile. "That I can work with."

They just stood staring at each other for several heartbeats. His touch felt hot against her cheek, but she also wanted more. More of her body getting hot from him touching.

"We need to figure this out. You have to realize that," he

finally said. "I don't know if this is all just left over from ten years ago or if it's real now."

She knew exactly what he was talking about. The chemistry. The wanting to be closer. The wondering about his life and what he was like now.

She did want to know.

She was just scared.

Because she was pretty sure that she would like all of it. A lot.

"Okay," she finally said softly.

She did want her grandma to be safe and happy and she wanted to let Didi make as many decisions for herself as possible as long as she could. If Didi wanted Cam around, then Whitney shouldn't be against it.

She'd be at work all day anyway. She'd be here, with Cam, only a few hours a day. And Didi would be there with them. How intimate could it be?

And maybe if he was here all the time, in her space, in her way, she'd realize that she was over him. That she didn't want him around all the time. That they didn't match up anymore. That they'd outgrown each other.

Yeah.

Maybe.

"You know those suggestions I'm going to be making and you're going to have the chance to say no to?" he asked huskily.

She nodded.

"Here's one."

He leaned in, close enough that she could feel his breath on her lips when he said, "Let me kiss you."

Oh damn. She wanted that. She wanted it so much. She was weak. Some of it was that she simply didn't feel wanted very much. Not just in the man-woman-naked-bodies way but just in general. That *sounded* pathetic, she knew, but it wasn't so much that it made her sad, it was just what she was used to. She wasn't sad about not being wanted. It was more that she was surprised to *be* wanted.

No one sought her out for her opinions, no one gave her big, important tasks. People always took her no answers seriously. If she was invited to a function and she declined, that was it. No one pressed. If someone asked her out and she said no, the guy always let it go. She knew it came from being a Lancaster. The Lancasters had power in Appleby and she knew that people were, in general, intimidated by them. Her grandfather and father had put a lot of effort into making sure that people believed the Lancasters were better than everyone else.

So to have Cam pressing to be with her, to get closer, was new. And felt good.

Plus, it was Cam.

She'd never stopped wanting him.

"I—" she started.

"The tea is getting cold!" Didi bellowed from the kitchen.

Whitney and Cam stilled. Then she felt him sigh. But he didn't pull back. "You going to let me do this or not?"

He was already practically kissing her. When his lips moved as he spoke, they brushed hers ever so lightly. His body heat surrounded her. She swore she could feel his heartbeat pounding. Or maybe that was hers.

She found it funny that they were standing so close, almost kissing, talking about kissing, but not really doing anything. It still felt incredibly intimate. They were very much in each other's personal space. They both clearly wanted this. She certainly wasn't pushing him away or stepping back. But the only actual connection was his hand on her face. And their mingling breaths.

Clearly he was going to *insist* that she make this decision. He wasn't going to just sweep her up and kiss the hell out of her before she could protest and then let the chemistry take over.

That also seemed intimate. Him coming as close as he

could but then wanting actual acquiescence from her. Verbal acknowledgment that she was agreeing.

"Whit," he said, his voice low and rough. "Push me back or pull me closer."

She slid her hands up to his chest, not sure until the last moment if she was going to fist his shirt and pull him in or push him away.

Cam, however, didn't look surprised when she pushed.

He let go and stepped back though. He didn't seem angry or even frustrated. It seemed that he'd been expecting her reaction actually.

"Okay," he finally said.

She wet her lips. "Thanks," she said, hoarsely. And she meant it. She appreciated that he was giving her these choices. Kind of.

It would be *a lot* easier to just climb him like a tree and give in to everything zipping between them if he'd just back her up against the wall, seal his mouth over hers, and start running his big hands over her body. Then she could pretend she was just caught up in the moment and enjoy the hell out of it without actually admitting she wanted any of that.

Which he knew.

She could see it.

He knew that she *wanted* him, but that she didn't want to admit it.

So, of course, he was going to make her confess before he did anything more.

"In case you've forgotten, I'm very stubborn," he said.

Whitney gave him a nod. "I remember."

"And something you should know about me and the past ten years," he said, holding her gaze steadily, "I've also gotten very used to winning. "

That actually made her heart trip and her inner muscles clench.

See, she should really feel trepidation at that implied promise from him. But she didn't. Right along with liking the feel of being wanted was a flutter of excitement over being *pursued*. No one came after her. Outside of invitations to fundraisers or, again, the occasional dinner date that she almost always said no to, she wasn't asked for much. And no one ever asked more than once.

"I'll keep that in mind," she said, trying desperately not to act *excited* about the idea of him trying again and again to get close to her.

He looked at her for a long moment and a thought flickered through her mind—*he knows*.

It was possible. Cam knew her well. Or he *had known* her well. But back in high school she'd been a lot more sought after. People had wanted her on school committees and projects. She'd been a cheerleader, runner-up for Homecoming Queen, invited to parties. She'd been popular. Wanted.

For stupid things like picking a winter dance theme or helping girlfriends do their hair for pool parties.

But she'd absolutely been wanted by Cam back then. He'd wanted everything then. He'd planned on them getting married. He'd planned for them to spend their lives together.

But now, no one wanted her for important things.

Until Aiden and the guys had taken over Hot Cakes.

Until Cam had decided he wanted to date her again.

She blew out a breath. It was crazy how important both of those things were to her.

She shouldn't lead Cam on. She shouldn't tease him and make him think there was a chance if there wasn't.

But maybe it was okay to relish being wanted for a little while.

And for sure Camden McCaffery could handle being teased. He might even enjoy it.

"You gonna show me to my new room?" he asked, his tone

changing to a more playful note. His eyes told her that he was onto her.

"I'm sure you can find your way," she said, feeling a jolt of... something. Playful and teasing could be fun. It was clear that Cam was going to let her call some of the shots. That made her feel less jittery about everything. "Third door on the left is probably the best choice." She moved to step around him, planning to join Didi while he headed upstairs. She didn't need to show him the way. She *shouldn't* show him the way. They might not make it back down here.

"Why is that?"

"It's one of the bigger rooms," she said. "It has its own bathroom."

"And how many doors are there between that one and yours?"

Her belly flipped and she felt warmth rush over her. She glanced over her shoulder feeling something she hadn't felt in a *very* long time. Sassy.

"A couple. And several squeaky floorboards," she tossed back to him. She paused. "But it's not like Didi can hear squeaky floorboards when her hearing aids are out."

Then she turned and headed down the hall before he could say—or do—anything else.

———

I t wasn't as if he'd never been mixed up and wound up because of Whitney Lancaster before.

She was the only woman who had ever actually *confused* him. But he knew why. She was the only woman he'd ever cared enough about to try to figure out. He was sure that had he ever tried to figure another woman out, he would have been confused then too.

But as he took his suitcase up to his new temporary

bedroom, he was trying to figure out what was going through Whitney's mind for sure.

She'd given in on him staying here with Didi far easier than he'd expected. It *was* a little crazy when he first thought it or said it out loud. But when he was talking to Didi about it, or explaining it to Whitney, it actually made sense.

Bottom line, he wanted to be here, Didi wanted Katherine to *not* to be here, and Whitney needed someone to be here with Didi.

Win-win-win.

Whitney had agreed, if reluctantly. Then she'd let him almost kiss her. Sure, in the end, she'd pushed him back, but she hadn't done it with any feeling. She'd seemed reluctant about that too.

He meant it when he said he was stubborn and used to winning.

The question really was, what was he trying to win?

He'd gone into this with Whitney thinking that they just needed to figure out what they were going to be going forward. They needed to see what was still there and what was real now.

It had taken less than twenty-four hours for him to shift to wanting her. Period. Not just physically—though that was as strong as ever, if not stronger—but just her. He wanted to be the one she leaned on when she needed help. He wanted to be the one coming home to her as he'd done tonight. He wanted to be the one she came home to.

He was shocked by how quickly that shift had happened and how strong those wants were.

They still needed to get to know each other again. They still needed time to go over the past ten years. And for what the next ten would look like.

He was still going to have to come to terms with how important Hot Cakes was to her. He was willing to help her do what she wanted at work. He wanted to support her. He wanted her to feel included and valued the way her family apparently hadn't included or valued her.

But he also wanted to show her there was more to life than that company.

He felt a ball of frustration tighten in his gut thinking about how much she'd given the company and how determined she was now to make it the most important thing in her life.

He knew many strong, independent women. He'd been raised by two, was the older brother to one, got to work with one—Piper—every day. He loved strong women. He wanted Whitney to be one.

But his grandmother, mom, sister, and friend knew there was more to life than work.

Whitney didn't seem to.

He wanted to show her that as well.

And, yes, he wanted to be one of those things that mattered more to her than work.

This was complicated.

But complicated was something he was used to. It was something he was good at. He was the lead attorney for a multi-million-dollar company. He loved a good fight. He loved going toe to toe with people who could stand there and argue back and make him work at it.

That was Whitney.

She knew what she wanted. She'd fight him on it. He just needed to have his arguments ready.

Feeling better about everything, he tucked his clothes into the drawers in the dresser in the bedroom. He checked out the bathroom, felt the mattress, and looked at his view out the window.

It was all nice. Very nice. Five-star hotel-level nice.

He still really mostly cared about where Whitney's bedroom was from here.

He left the room, heading back for the kitchen. He thought

for one second—maybe two—about opening doors along the hallway to find her room.

But he didn't.

He wanted to be invited into that room. He wanted her opening that door for him.

And she would.

Eventually.

Probably.

———

Cam slipped back inside from the back patio. He'd given Aiden a call to let him and Zoe know he wouldn't be home tonight. He'd left a message, feeling a little relieved that Aiden hadn't picked up. He wasn't sure what his best friend's reaction would be to him *living* with Whitney and he wasn't sure he wanted to hear about what a dumb idea it was at the moment. There would be time for that later.

There was a single light glowing over the sink. The rest of the first floor was dark. And quiet.

Uh-huh. Whitney had taken advantage of him being outside to slip upstairs.

Cam had cooked. Pasta primavera with grilled chicken. They'd had a nice meal, during which Didi had told stories about her and Letty growing up. Stories he'd never heard before and loved. They'd been like sisters from the time they'd met as little girls. He and Aiden had been like that.

He'd snuck glances at Whitney as they talked. She'd seemed happy. Didi had been downright delighted. Maybe it was because she had a bigger audience than usual for her stories. Or maybe the two women didn't actually spend their mealtimes talking and sharing stories. He could imagine Whitney reading files or working on her laptop while she ate.

Well, that ended now. If he had anything to say about it.

Which he probably didn't.

At least he could listen to Didi's stories. He enjoyed hearing about his grandmother as a little girl.

But he couldn't help but wonder if Whitney had a friend like he and Aiden had been or like Didi and Letty had been? She'd had friends in high school, but they hadn't been close like he and Aiden had. She'd been amazed by how close he and Aiden were and often commented on how nice it would be to have someone like that. What about now? Did she have people —even one—that she could truly confide in and be herself with?

Well, she did now.

He was going to be that friend. Even if that's all she would let him be.

Of course, she had to stay up past 9 p.m. if they were going to talk and share and get to know each other.

He debated his move here. He didn't know which room was hers and he wasn't about to go knocking on doors when one of them was Didi's. Also, he should give Whitney space. He knew that spending time together on more neutral territory—where there weren't beds a few feet away or a tub big enough for two —was probably a good idea.

Then again, he thought maybe just kissing the hell out of her, getting her naked, and showing her some other ways he'd gotten better over the past ten years might not be a terrible idea. They could talk after. After he made her face, very directly and intimately, the chemistry that was still alive and well.

Or he could play it cool. Be patient. Do what he'd come here to do, hang out with Didi, make Whitney's life easier and wait for her to come to him.

He wanted to do that.

But he was really afraid that the kissing the hell out of her and getting her naked part would take a lot longer with that approach. And he wasn't sure how long he could wait on that.

He'd liked talking dirty to her that first night. He'd loved watching her respond.

He pulled out his phone and texted her.

I'm making chocolate chip cookie dough. You should come down.

He set the phone on the counter and moved around the kitchen, checking the cabinets and pulling out ingredients. He was a great baker, taught by one of the best ever. But chocolate chip cookies were his specialty. He knew that the sound of that didn't impress most people. How special could chocolate chip cookies really be anyway? But that's because they'd never had his. He was the best. Even better than his grandmother.

And, yes, she'd even admitted it to him. Though only to him. And only when they were alone.

It was several minutes later, but finally Whitney replied.

I'm already in bed.

Cam grinned. That was almost too easy. *Okay, I'll bring it up to you. The horizontal surfaces up there are probably softer than the ones down here.*

He started measuring and mixing, knowing that it would be a bit before she responded again.

But he'd only gotten the flour and baking powder combined before his phone chimed.

He looked over, wiping a hand on a dish towel.

I don't want to have to shower tonight. I'm a morning showerer.

He grinned. Yes, this had the potential to get sticky.

I promise to be sure to remove all traces of cookie dough from your nipples. And elsewhere. I'll be very thorough.

He waited, just in case she got right back to him.

She didn't.

He went back to mixing. He got everything but the chocolate chips mixed in before he heard anything from her.

"You've *got* to be kidding me. That was a jerk move, Cam."

He turned toward the kitchen doorway.

And nearly dropped the bowl he was holding.

10

She'd apparently come straight down, without bothering to change her clothes.

Her hair was up in a high ponytail on the top of her head, the long strands falling around her freshly washed face. She had a bed sheet wrapped around her body and tucked under her arms but he could see the spaghetti straps of the pale green nightgown she wore underneath. He *really* wanted to know how far down that nightgown hit on her thighs. And if she was wearing panties.

She looked just-out-of-bed, adorably mussed, and... a little pissed. Her cheeks were flushed and she was *not* smiling.

Still, he couldn't stop staring. Not even when the one, very tiny, part of his brain told him that this was *not* playing it cool.

Of course, texting her about licking cookie dough off her nipples wasn't really *cool* either.

Speaking of her nipples... Surely she wasn't wearing a bra underneath that nightgown either. Women didn't wear bras to bed. He knew that much. His entire body reacted to the thought, the way the sheet molded to her breasts and the smooth pale bare skin of her shoulders.

She didn't cross her arms. She didn't move closer so that the breakfast bar on the other side of the kitchen island would block his view. She didn't even fidget. She just let him look.

So he did. He drank her in.

This was not the pretty, thin, young innocent girl whose virginity he'd taken down by the river.

This was a gorgeous, trim, curved-in-all-the-right-places confident woman.

Who was calling his bluff by showing up in the kitchen after the texts he'd sent.

His gaze found its way back to hers and he could see the challenge there.

"I never kid about nipple licking," he finally said.

She sucked in a quick breath but it was hard to tell if it was surprise or lust. "You have to stop."

"Why?"

"You can't tease me. And flirt. And get... dirty. Not when you're *living* here. That is all kinds of inappropriate."

Inappropriate. Maybe. With anyone else it would be. But it did not feel inappropriate with them.

Cam reached for the bag of dark chocolate chunks and dumped them into the bowl. He folded them into the dough, then set the bowl down, and tossed the spoon into the sink.

He braced his hands on the counter and met her eyes.

"I know I should say I'm sorry. I'm not."

She took a breath and let it out. "Cam, I understand that you're teasing. But I have to be able to be comfortable here in my own home."

"I make you uncomfortable?" He frowned. He didn't quite believe it, but he hated the idea that might be true.

"You... could very easily make it difficult to sleep," she said.

Oh, well that was different. He grinned. "Dirty dreams never hurt anybody."

She lifted her chin in that sexy, stubborn way that he didn't remember but kind of loved and kind of hated at the same time. "They will if they keep me from being fresh and sharp at work tomorrow."

He shouldn't like the idea of getting her so wound up she couldn't sleep.

"What are you thinking?" she asked, clearly noticing the small grin he was trying to hide.

"I shouldn't say. It would be inappropriate."

She narrowed her eyes. "Is it something about helping me work off the pent-up energy and play out the dreams so I can sleep peacefully?"

He let the grin go. "Yep."

She sighed. "Cam, this isn't going to work."

He straightened. "It will. I promise. I'll be good."

It was clear that she didn't believe that, but she didn't *quite* roll her eyes. She drew herself straighter and wet her lips, then said, "You're my boss. And my ex. Having you here is weird. Having you sexting me is even weirder. We have to have some rules."

"First, that wasn't sexting." That wasn't even close to the things he'd say and ask her to do if they were sexting. "Second, having me here shouldn't be weird, Whit."

"But it is. Because..."

He lifted a brow. "Because?"

Her eyes dipped to the bowl of cookie dough then back to his. "Because it's all tempting."

Damn right it was. "Well, good."

"*No*," she said it with force and with a frown. Then she pulled in a breath and said more calmly, "I'm sorry, but I think that if you're living here we need to work on the friends part of this whole... situation."

Their relationship was a situation? And why did she keep taking those breaths and changing her tone of voice while they were talking? "I told you that I want more than that. That's partly why I'm here."

"You're pushing."

He gave her a nod. "A little. I need to push with you."

She frowned. "I don't like that."

"I think you do." He crossed his arms. "I think that you don't like that you like it. But I think you do like that I'm pursuing you and seducing you."

"You're not *seducing* me."

"Talking about putting cookie dough on your nipples?" he asked.

She shifted her weight and dropped her gaze to the bowl again and he wondered what sensations were going through her body. Was she tingling and hot? Were her nipples hard? Because he was hot and hard, for sure.

"You have to respect what I'm feeling," she finally said, meeting his gaze again. "This complicates things in a way that concerns me."

He studied her. She seemed to be holding back. Which was interesting. Whitney had always been happy and sweet and confident. The girl he'd dated ten years ago had been accommodating and roll-with-it and always up for whatever he wanted.

"You're the one who pointed out the doors and squeaky floor boards between your room and mine," he said.

She nodded. "Momentary lapse of judgment."

"Can we have a few more of those?"

She didn't smile at that either. She shook her head. "No. I shouldn't have said that." She sighed and her shoulders slumped slightly. "It's fun to flirt and tease with you. But it's a bad idea. It's distracting, and with you here all the time now"—she frowned at that—"I think it could be very easy to go... offtrack."

"The track being Hot Cakes?" he asked.

She nodded. Then bit her bottom lip.

Them being together was offtrack? That was not how it felt to him. At all.

But they were, evidently on very different tracks. He had accomplished what he wanted with work. Hot Cakes was great. He wanted it to be successful too. Absolutely. But his huge accomplishment had been Fluke, Inc. and *Warriors of Easton*.

He'd absolutely been focused and determined when it had come to building the company and making it a fucking *phenomenon*.

Whitney hadn't had a huge business accomplishment yet.

He got where she was coming from. But it *was* possible to have that *and* a personal life.

Probably.

He didn't really know. He hadn't had a *relationship* when they'd been getting Fluke off the ground. Hell, he hadn't had a *relationship* since Whitney.

But she was trying to be successful with Hot Cakes. She wasn't doing it alone. But she didn't believe that. Or she didn't know what that really meant. Yet.

"I don't think I can keep from flirting with you," he finally confessed. "Especially when you come down here at night in your nightgown looking..." He almost said *totally fuckable*. But that would likely go on her inappropriate list. "...so sexy."

Then he cringed slightly. That was a little better, but he probably should have said "beautiful." Or maybe not have said anything at all about how she looked.

He shrugged before she could say anything. "It's going to be impossible for me to not notice how you look, Whit."

She blew out a breath. "Which is another reason this is a bad idea."

"Because it tempts you?"

Her eyes flashed. "Because I should get to come down to *my* kitchen in whatever I want to wear and not worry about getting hit on." Then she took another breath. "I'm not used to having guests."

He didn't want her to think of him as a guest. That was for fucking sure. And he wasn't *hitting on* her. That sounded like they were two strangers meeting for the first time in a bar or something.

They were hardly strangers.

Aren't you? a tiny voice whispered at the back of his mind. Yeah, maybe they were. They'd been apart for years. And a lot had happened to them both in that time.

There was something else niggling at him. The way she kept seeming to calm herself. She'd never had a temper. Not that he'd seen anyway. She'd never snapped at him. Hell, he wasn't sure they'd ever fought. They might have disagreed a few times, but they'd never had an actual argument. He'd never made her cry. He'd never laid awake at night regretting something he'd said. They'd never raised their voices.

Not until the end. They'd fought the night she'd broken up with him. She'd cried. He'd laid awake that night. He'd regretted more than a few things from that night.

But the idea of an angry Whitney was intriguing. If he could talk about bending her over her desk and licking cookie dough off her nipples, then she could certainly tell him if she thought he was being an asshole.

Not this "inappropriate" or "uncomfortable" stuff. Those words made him itchy. They weren't right between them. But she could definitely be angry or frustrated.

"Are you actually uncomfortable around me?" he finally asked. He didn't think it was true but he needed *her* to know it wasn't true.

He couldn't quite name the emotion that flickered across her face with that. It was surprise maybe, mixed with confusion. And maybe relief?

"Not exactly."

"We still have chemistry."

She swallowed hard. "Yes."

"But you don't want it. You're afraid of it."

Her eyes narrowed. "I don't know if I'd say that."

"You do want it?" He knew that wasn't what she meant.

"I'm not *afraid* of it."

Good. That was really fucking good. "You just want to ignore it."

"Yes."

"But I'm pushing you on it, making you feel it and face it."

She shifted her weight again and her hand tightened on the sheet where she was holding it between her breasts. "Yes," she finally said.

"And that doesn't make you *uncomfortable*. It makes you mad."

She met his eyes. "Yes," she said after a moment.

"Then tell me that," he said.

She just pressed her lips together.

"Don't try to make it polite and business-like," he said. "Tell me how you *really* feel."

"You're my boss," she said.

For fuck's sake. "Not in this house, I'm not," he said, letting his own exasperation show.

Her eyes widened. "You're my boss no matter where we are."

He shoved a hand through his hair. "No. I'm not even really your boss at Hot Cakes and you know that."

"Do I?"

"Of course you do. You know I'm not going to fire you. Even if I wanted to, which I don't because I'm not a fucking idiot, the guys would never let me do it."

Again emotion flickered over her face. It looked like she really wanted to believe him but didn't quite.

"I don't want to give you all *any* reason to think I'm not up to the job."

"Your job is safe." He was trying hard not to grit his teeth. She'd never been this obstinate before.

She's not the same girl, that annoying voice whispered.

Yeah, yeah.

"Even if I *don't* sleep with you?" she asked.

For just a second, the obstinate, contrary part of *him* reared its head and he wanted to tell her that she was absolutely required to be in his bed every single night. The job was that important to her? Then fine, he'd use that to his advantage.

But, of course, he didn't say that. He would never say that.

"What happens outside of the office has nothing to do with your job," he said.

Though that was maybe not entirely true either. Because the more he was around her, the more he wanted to be sure she stayed working for them so that he could see her every day.

"What about if something happens *at* the office?" she asked.

"If you do finally let me bend you over your desk and hike up one of those ugly skirts, then no, that will have nothing to do with your job," he said, unable to hold back.

Her eyes narrowed at that. "I meant what if I tell you one of your ideas is terrible or tell you that you're being an asshole in the office sometime?"

His brows rose. "Your job would still be safe," he said. "In fact, if I do have a terrible idea or I'm acting like an asshole then you *better* tell me."

She didn't look entirely convinced but she didn't say that she didn't believe him either.

"Tell me that right now," he challenged.

She chewed on her bottom lip.

He moved around the edge of the kitchen island, closer to her. "Whitney. Tell me right now what you're feeling."

"This is a terrible idea," she said softly.

He nodded. "Okay."

For a second she looked a little sad. Then she lifted her chin again. "And it's an asshole thing to do to text me about cookie dough and nipples when I'm trying to go to sleep."

He stopped moving but not truly outside of her personal space. He could reach out and touch her easily.

"So I should do it earlier in the evening going forward?" he asked.

She shook her head but there was a ghost of a smile on her lips. "Not what I meant."

"*Tell me* what you mean," he said.

She swallowed. "Fine. I want you. I know that doesn't surprise you and I know it's just going to make your ego even bigger but, yes, I want you. Yes, there's chemistry. But I want to do a great job at Hot Cakes too. Maybe more." She didn't seem entirely sure of that, however. "Even if it doesn't affect my actual job, even if you wouldn't fire me if we had a fight at home or whatever, it affects my performance because it distracts me and makes me jumpy and makes it hard to concentrate on work. I want to do a good job for *me* too, Cam. I haven't had a chance to prove myself to others before, but at the same time I haven't had a chance to prove myself to me either. Because I've never been able to really implement my ideas or projects, I don't actually know if they're good. I think they are. They seem to be. But..." She pressed her lips together. "Ollie thinks my ideas are good."

"Of course he does," Cam said.

"But Ollie also thought having a petting zoo at the cake tasting was a good idea," she said.

Cam couldn't help his grin. "Everyone loved the petting zoo."

She rolled her eyes. "Well, implementing ideas, actually *doing* the things I think up, is new to me. I have no idea if I'm actually good at any of this."

"You are."

"You have *no* idea if that's true," she said. "And you have to stop saying it until you do. Don't placate me. Don't compliment me because you want in my pants. Just let me do my job and do it the best I can and let's see how it turns out."

She had a point.

Dammit.

He figured she was good at it, but honestly, if she hadn't had much to do with Hot Cakes other than having her name associated because of her family then… well, maybe she *wasn't* good at it. He didn't believe that, really, but she had a point about wanting to prove it. To them and to herself.

This was important to her for *her* too.

"Fine," he finally conceded. "No more compliments on your work until you prove yourself."

She nodded. "Thank you."

"But I can still say that you look hot as hell wrapped in a sheet with your hair up like that?"

Heat flickered in her eyes. The only sign that he wasn't way off base here.

Still, she shook her head. "No, you can't say that."

"Because it makes you uncomfortable?" he asked.

She hesitated, then said, "Because it makes me think about how hot *you* would look wrapped in only a sheet."

That hit him with heat but also satisfaction. She wasn't uncomfortable with their chemistry. She was distracted. That was okay.

"I would look really good wrapped in only a sheet. Down low. Around my waist."

She pulled in a long breath. "Stop it."

He grinned. "Okay."

Her gaze tracked over his torso, then she sighed. "Asshole thing to do before I go back upstairs."

She could take that thought with her when she went back upstairs to bed. He wasn't apologetic about the idea of keeping her awake for a bit.

"Not sorry."

"I know."

Then she narrowed her eyes again. Though this time it seemed she was just thinking about something. "So I can do whatever I want? Say whatever I want? No consequences? No issues?"

He hesitated for some reason, but then nodded, mostly curious. He wanted her to be totally honest with him. He wanted her to feel free to feel and think anything and to tell him. "Yep."

"Okay." She stepped close, took the front of his shirt in her fist, rose on tiptoe and kissed him.

It was the first time their lips had been against the others in a decade. Far, far too long. Which had to be why it took him a good three seconds to respond. Just as he was lifting his hand to cup the back of her head and deepen the contact, she pulled back, smiled up at him, and then turned and left the kitchen.

He stood staring at the doorway for a good minute, his hand suspended in the air.

She'd tasted like toothpaste. She'd smelled like soap. Not a specific aroma, just soap. Clean and fresh and sweet.

But mostly she'd *felt* like... home.

He had never forgotten what it felt like to hold her, to kiss her, to make her laugh, to taste her—all over—and it all slammed into him in those moments after she left him in the kitchen.

It was like when memories came flooding back when he heard a song from the past or tasted one of his mom's recipes he hadn't had in a long time or when he saw one of the photos that hung on the wall on the way up the stairs to his childhood bedroom.

It was as real as if it had just happened and yet seemed a little like a dream.

Holy hell.

He wanted more of that. A lot more.

Yeah, moving in with Whitney and her grandmother on a whim had to be the best idea he'd ever had.

Grinning and feeling pretty fucking good about everything, he wrapped and stored the cookie dough in the fridge for baking tomorrow and cleaned up.

A few minutes later, he clicked the light off and started down the hall to the staircase.

He heard footsteps coming down as he got to the foyer. His heart kicked against his ribs. Had Whitney changed her mind about leaving him with just one kiss?

"Whit?" he asked softly.

"No," came the answering not-quite-a-whisper.

He smiled into the darkness. "Hey, Didi."

"Hi, honey."

"You okay?"

"Sure."

He heard a step creak as she came down further.

"What are you doing?"

"My show is on."

It was eleven at night. He doubted her show, whatever it was, was on. But Whitney had mentioned that Didi was up at odd hours.

"Which show?"

"*Magnum, P.I.*"

Cam grinned. Okay, so maybe there were reruns on. "The old one or the new?"

"There's a new one?" she asked.

"Yeah. They remade it."

Didi stopped on the third step up and he could now see her with the light spilling in through the tall windows on either side of the front door from the lamps on the porch.

"Why in the world would they remake it? Tom Selleck can't be replaced."

He had kind of figured she'd feel that way. His mother did. "The new guy is pretty handsome," Cam told her. "According to my sources."

"Hmph," Didi said. "I'm not interested."

"You don't even want to check it out? Dark hair. Lots of muscles. Really nice cars."

She hesitated. "Well…"

He grinned. "It won't hurt to watch an episode or two."

"I suppose."

"And I assume you like Tom Selleck's new show then? *Blue Bloods*?" he asked.

"Tom Selleck has a new show?"

"He does. Pretty popular."

"Can you find that one too?"

"I absolutely can." If Whitney didn't already have all the streaming services needed, Cam could fix that in about two minutes.

"I knew having you move in was the right thing to do," Didi said. She came the rest of the way down the steps.

"Oh… now?" he asked. "How about we watch tomorrow?"

"Don't be silly," she said, moving past him to head down the hall to the family room. "We're both awake, we might as well do it now."

Cam heard another creak on the steps and he glanced up. Now that his eyes had adjusted to the dark, he could see more clearly. Though obviously it was Whitney. There was no one else in the house.

"She wants to watch *Magnum, P.I.*?" Whitney asked.

"Yeah. Is that the usual routine?"

"Yeah. She's seen all the episodes a dozen times but…" She sighed. "She doesn't remember them so they're all new to her."

He smiled slightly. "That's kind of great. I'd love to see some of my favorite shows and movies for the first time again."

"Yeah, well, *I've* also seen them all a dozen times now. It's not so great."

He gave a small laugh. "Then it really *is* great that I'm here. I've never seen a single episode of *Magnum, P.I.* Old or new."

"She'll be up until three a.m., Cam." Whitney sounded exhausted just thinking about it.

"But then she sleeps in late tomorrow right?" he asked.

"She'll sleep past ten. Probably. Though…"

He could see that she was chewing on her bottom lip. "What?"

"This will sound bad."

"Come on, Whit. Tell me."

"Okay, I put a bell on her doorknob when she goes to bed so I can hear her when she gets up."

"Seems like a good idea. Why do you think that sounds bad?"

"It's something people do for little kids. I feel bad that sometimes I use techniques like that."

Cam moved to stand directly at the bottom of the steps. Whitney was five steps up but this way he could see her fully. And she could see him. "You're doing it to keep her safe," he said. "You're not harming her in any way. And it probably helps you sleep more soundly because you're not worrying about what she's getting up to."

She nodded.

"So stop feeling bad. It's all good. And now tonight you can put some earplugs in or put some music on or something and sleep like a baby. I've got this."

"You don't have to do this."

"Does it make you like me a little more? Make you a little softer toward me? Make you a tiny bit closer to wanting to take your clothes off with me?" he asked lightly.

He could see her fighting her smile even from five steps away. "The first two things, yes."

"Not the naked thing?" he asked, lifting a brow.

"Well, I already want to take my clothes off with you, so this doesn't necessarily have anything to do with that."

Okay, he had not been expecting that. But he liked it. *A lot.* He grinned. "Of course you would say that when there's a sweet little lady wide awake and wanting to watch TV—"

Just then the clatter of a tea kettle hitting the floor broke the relative quiet of the house.

"And needing some assistance in the kitchen," he finished with a little grimace.

Whitney laughed. "If you think I wasn't completely aware of the situation when I made that confession, you're crazy."

"I'm not going to forget it," he told her, his voice husky.

There was just a beat and then she said, "I know."

She turned and headed back upstairs.

Cam appreciated that she was going to let him do this—stay up and take care of Didi. That was why he was here, of course. Well, one reason. But, while she'd resisted at first, once they got over all her arguments, she was now letting it go.

She was either totally trusting him—or she was really exhausted.

He couldn't imagine staying up until 3 a.m. every day and then getting to the office by eight. It was possible that before the guys had taken over Hot Cakes that she'd come in later, but she was always there well before he strolled in at nine. She was trying to impress them. She didn't know that early birds weren't the guys' style. Though Aiden had been showing up earlier at the office since he'd been with Zoe. Grant probably would be too now that he was living with Josie. The girls went into the bakery at 6 a.m.

Still, no one judged anyone else for what time they got to work. Well, not beyond the usual ribbing about what—or who —had kept the guy up late the night before and had him guzzling coffee the next morning.

Of course, that had all changed a lot too. Three of the guys were now in serious relationships and Cam did *not* want to hear about what Aiden and Zoe had been up to late at night.

He heard another clatter from the kitchen and he headed in that direction before the sounds changed from the sound a tea kettle against the ceramic tile to something more like a tea *cup* hitting the floor.

"Let me get that," he said, taking the kettle from Didi where she was filling it with water. "I assume you like chocolate chip cookies?"

She gave him a wide-eyed look. "Who doesn't like chocolate chip cookies?"

He nodded. "Weirdos."

"Exactly. Never trust someone who doesn't like cookies."

"Sage advice." He filled the kettle and set it on the stove.

He could have made her tea from the Keurig sitting on the counter about a foot away from the stove, but he figured Didi was a lot like Letty had been.

His grandmother always maintained that cutting corners was for things like shopping for pants and dusting bookshelves. She said when you found pants you liked, you bought two pairs in every color and were done with it for a good long while. She also kept her books at the front edge of the shelf so she only had to dust the tops of the books. As she said, no one ever looked *behind* the books.

But cutting corners was never for food preparation. That included tea.

He got Didi settled in front of the TV. He started *Magnum, P.I.* at season one, episode one. If she didn't remember them anyway and he was going to be watching with her, he might as well see it from the beginning.

He could see her and the TV from the kitchen with the open-concept design of the less formal rooms at the back of the massive house. He put the cookies in the oven as the first episode rolled. Didi sat on one end of the sofa with a blanket covering her lap and her tea cup cradled between her hands. She looked completely content and Cam smiled. It was late at night, but otherwise there was nothing wrong with this. And Lord knew he'd spent plenty of nights up late reading briefs or writing proposals or exchanging snarky emails with the attorneys for other companies who put in similar long hours when needed.

"I'm so glad Whitney finally has someone to appreciate her," Didi commented as he joined her on the couch. "Besides me, of course."

"I absolutely do," Cam said sincerely.

"Good. Fuck her father and brothers."

Cam snorted. Didi's words made him feel amused, for sure. But also... protective. No one was going to treat Whitney the way her father and brothers had any more. Yeah, fuck her dad and brothers.

He smiled at Didi and she returned the grin. Then she looked back at the TV. "Okay, shh... Tom Selleck is on."

Yeah, he and Didi were going to be fine.

11

"What if we make them in the shape of alpacas?" Ollie asked.

Whitney looked at him. She still wasn't entirely sure how to tell when Ollie was being serious. Though she was starting to learn that he was always about half serious. He threw ideas out and left it to his partners to decide which ones would stick and which ones were ridiculous. But he never said things he didn't mean at least a little.

"You think we should make the new bars in the shape of alpacas?" Grant asked.

"Why not?" Ollie asked. But when he asked the question he sincerely wanted to know the reasons why that might be a bad idea. "Everyone loves alpacas."

"I do *not* think that's true," Aiden said.

"Okay, *most* people like alpacas," Ollie countered.

"The petting zoo was a huge success," Piper said, handing Grant a folder.

She wasn't officially part of the meeting but she never hesitated to give her input. And her input was always excellent. Whitney couldn't figure out why the guys hadn't made Piper a business partner yet. Of course, they needed her in the role she held, keeping track of everything and everyone. Maybe that was it. They certainly paid her well for it. Whitney had seen her employee file. She saw all the employee files. But over the past few months it had been clear that Piper earned every single penny.

"I don't know if it was *huge*," Ollie said with a little frown.

Aiden nodded. "Oh, it was."

Piper gave Ollie a smug smile.

Now that Whitney knew the petting zoo had been Piper's idea and had stemmed mostly from the fact that she thought Drew Ryan was cute—and she liked making Ollie jealous—Whitney rolled her eyes.

"These are the caramel crunch bars we're talking about, right?" Dax asked.

Whitney was glad Dax still came in for the 9 a.m. meeting. He was fun to have around, had great ideas, and she'd noticed that when all five guys were together, they were much more creative and relaxed.

Of course, they were missing Cam today. Again. This was day three of Cam living with her and Didi. And missing the morning meeting at Hot Cakes. Because of her.

Well, because of Didi. Actually because of *him*. He was the one who had decided to insert himself into their situation. So she didn't feel guilty exactly. But as someone who wanted Hot Cakes to be the very best it could be, she was aware that they were missing a piece of their puzzle.

Ollie nodded. "Yeah, the new bars."

"So they'll be brown—because of the chocolate," Dax said. "And a little lumpy because of the crispy-crunchy pieces."

Ollie shrugged. "Yeah."

"And then you want to make them look like an animal."

Ollie frowned. "What are you getting at?"

"Alpaca poop," Dax said. "That's what I'm getting at. They could remind people of alpaca poop."

"I thought you liked alpacas," Ollie said.

"Love them."

"So..."

"But they poop, Ollie." Dax shrugged.

"But they'll be *shaped* like alpacas," Ollie said. "Not like poop."

"Sure. But the color and texture could be reminiscent of poop. Add in the animal shape and it might put that thought in people's heads," Dax said.

"It might just be you," Ollie told him.

"No, I think he has a point," Piper said, picking up plates that had held muffins from Buttered Up.

It was a really good thing that they'd smoothed over the tension between the two businesses if for nothing else than because it meant they could have breakfast pastries at morning meetings now. Zoe's muffins and scones were amazing.

"You're just saying that because you're being contrary," Ollie said.

Piper gave him a look with one arched brow. "I am?"

"You are," he said with a frown. "You're disagreeing with everything I've said lately."

"Maybe you've been wrong a lot lately," Piper said.

"I figured you would love the alpaca idea," Ollie replied. "What with your new fascination with the Ryan farm and all."

"That's sweet of you to think of me," Piper said with a big—totally fake—smile. "But my *fascination* with the farm isn't really about the alpacas."

Ollie's frown deepened. "Should we just make the new bars look like Drew Ryan then?"

"Don't be ridiculous," Piper said.

Ollie relaxed slightly. Whitney was probably the only one who noticed, but she'd been watching him carefully. He was jealous of Drew. She just wondered if he realized *why*. Did he know that he had feelings for Piper? Oliver Caprinelli was brilliant but he seemed oblivious to everything having to do with Piper and *her* feelings for *him,* and, for some reason, Whitney wouldn't be surprised to find out that Ollie didn't even realize that he was annoyed by Drew because *Ollie* was in love with Piper himself.

"If we were going to make Drew into a snack cake it would be *devil's food* with a *sweet, smooth, creamy,* filling." She paused. "And it would have to be *jumbo* sized."

Whitney pressed her lips together to keep from laughing and Grant, Aiden, and Dax all swung to look at Ollie.

Clearly those guys realized that Ollie had some feelings besides appreciation or admiration for his assistant.

"We already have chocolate cake with cream filling," Ollie finally said.

It was not a great comeback. But it was very funny. To everyone else.

Piper just nodded. "Yes, we do." She looked at Aiden and pointed at his computer. "By the way, Cam is joining via video."

Aiden opened his laptop and clicked a few buttons. "Hey, man," he greeted a moment later.

"Hey," Cam's voice returned. "Sorry I'm late."

"No problem. We're discussing the shape of the new snack bars."

When it was said like that, it sounded stupid, Whitney had to admit.

Aiden turned the computer to face the rest of the table.

"We should give Cam a chance to weigh in on the shape," Ollie said. Though he didn't look like he actually cared what Cam thought. He was watching Piper as she moved around the room. "What do you think of alpacas?"

"Um," Cam said.

"No," Grant said. "Dax has a good point about the poop."

"The poop?" Cam echoed.

Aiden sighed. "Yeah, maybe you did miss a few things."

"Alpacas," Ollie said, his eyes still on Piper. "The new bars—"

"That will look like poop," Dax interjected.

"Should be shaped like alpacas," Ollie finished.

Piper faced him with a hand on her hip. "I thought that we'd already—"

"It will be far more cost effective to keep them squares or rectangles," Whitney said quickly.

Everyone stopped talking and looked at her.

"We're already set up to do squares and rectangles. And circles, of course," she said.

Grant nodded. "Good point."

"Squares and rectangles are boring," Dax said. "No offense," he added to Whitney.

She smiled. "None taken." It wasn't as if she'd been the one to decide the shapes of their snack cakes. Then again, she doubted much thought had been given to it at all. Back when her grandparents had started Hot Cakes there probably hadn't been a lot of shape options in the big machines they'd installed to make their cakes. "But it really will cost less to keep doing the shapes we've already got. No need to reconfigure the machines that way."

Grant and Aiden both nodded. Looking slightly relieved if she wasn't mistaken.

"How quickly can we get the new bars into production?" Aiden asked. "If we stick with common shapes?"

The question was directed to Whitney. Of course it was. None of the other people in the room knew as much about snack cake production as she did.

She nodded. "Keeping with the common shapes will cut that time down dramatically as well. A couple of weeks," she said. "It's less about making the snack cakes themselves—we have the base recipe and can pretty easily adjust it for mass production and shelf life—but it's about the process of transitioning machines." She looked around the table. They all seemed interested, and as if they weren't sure what she was talking about.

No one else said anything.

So she went on. Trying very hard not to fidget. Or look at Aiden's computer. Too much. She felt Cam's eyes on her though, even through that screen. It was all made stranger because he was sitting in her kitchen at the breakfast bar. Where he'd offered to lick her nipples...

"Whitney? You were saying something about the Cinnamon Curls?" Grant asked.

See? *This* was why it was a problem for her to be involved with Cam. She'd get distracted in the middle of explaining that the Cinnamon Curls were their lowest selling cakes so that machine could possibly be used part-time for the new bars, but that because the new bars were chocolate and the Cinnamon Curls were not it would be a bigger transition than using a machine that already used chocolate.

She blew out a breath. She was *not* going to think about Cam and her breakfast bar and that he probably *really* hated what she was wearing today. It was all gray.

"Right. As I was saying..."

She explained how adding this new product would affect their production line. It could mean decreased production of other cakes, that they needed a plan to transition existing machinery, that it might mean increased shifts for workers and the need to hire additional employees, that they might need new equipment entirely, and even an addition to the factory. No matter what or how they did it, it would mean more man-power and money.

Grant was nodding as she finished, and Aiden sat forward in his chair.

"That all makes sense to me," Aiden said.

"Do you think we can draw up some projections?" Grant asked.

She nodded. "Of course."

"Great," Aiden said. "Just let us know where we should start."

Whitney lifted her brows. He was just going with it? She felt a moment of panic. They were just going to trust her completely? They didn't have any questions? No concerns? No alternatives to offer?

"Unless I'm missing something," she said.

She wasn't. She'd sat in on meetings about production dozens of times. They'd never launched a new snack cake but they'd upped production on most of the cakes in their product line. They'd expanded to new markets and needed to meet that increased demand.

She'd always found the meetings pretty boring and wouldn't have believed that she'd absorbed much knowledge from them, but it had all made sense. If you needed more cakes, for whatever reason, you needed to be sure you had the machines for it and the people to run those machines.

"I don't think you're missing anything," Aiden told her. "We need a machine to produce the new cakes and we need more people. Seems easiest to use what we already have until we see what the demand is like."

She nodded. It did. It was pretty straightforward.

"And I don't think hiring will be a problem," she said, not sure why she felt the need to throw that out there. "Everyone here is talking about the great changes you've already made to benefits and work shifts and such. We've had more applications coming in than usual."

The men all smiled at that and she realized why she'd said it. It really mattered to these guys that their employees were happy and that they had a reputation as good guys to work for. She liked that about them so much.

Dax looked especially pleased. "Awesome."

She also liked how much it mattered to him even though he was no longer one of their bosses. He'd been a huge part of the changes they'd made for their employees from benefits to work environment.

"We should offer a couple dollars more an hour for the later shift, of course. We can have a job fair. But—" Then she hesitated.

These were big decisions. She did *not* want to get too far ahead or in too deep in case things didn't work.

"But?" Aiden prompted.

Whitney took a breath. She'd known Aiden for a long time. He was Cam's best friend. He'd been one of the few people who had known about her and Cam in high school. He'd kept their secret for a very long time. He had Cam's back whether he agreed with every decision or not. He was a great friend.

She wanted him to be her friend.

The thought seemed to come from out of the blue. It seemed misplaced in the midst of a business meeting. But these meetings always showcased how these people fit together. They each had strengths and weaknesses and they balanced each other almost perfectly. They'd found each other and together had created not just a wildly successful business partnership but an enviable friendship.

And she wanted to be a part of it. She wanted to fit somewhere the way they all did.

Aiden had come back to Appleby for Zoe. He'd bought Hot Cakes as part of his new life. And the rest of them had come with him. To help him. To support him. To back him up. But also because they probably couldn't imagine being in Chicago without him.

She didn't have anyone following her. She didn't have

anyone staying for her. Hell, her family—the people she'd given *her* dedication to—had left to go to Dallas, leaving her here.

She supposed she could have gone with them. But they hadn't asked her to.

"But what, Whit?" Aiden asked.

She did *not* want to screw this up. They were trusting her to know how they should move forward with this new product. What she knew came from listening in and observing. She'd never actually *done* it. She'd never really done anything. She'd led a few meetings, met with a few accounts, gone to a few conferences, but she hadn't really led anything important. Certainly not launching an entirely new product including everything from the recipe to the labor needed.

This whole new-snack-cake thing had been her idea.

And they'd ended up with alpacas at the taste-testing event.

She swallowed. "I just think we should start small," she said. "Maybe we can transition one of the machines for a night shift three nights a week. We'll offer overtime and hire a small crew and let them know it's temporary work for now. I don't want them to think they're coming on full time if it doesn't take off the way we'd like."

Aiden watched her for several seconds. Then he nodded. "Whatever you think."

She felt her gut tighten. That might have been the worst thing he could have said.

Grant glanced from Aiden to Whitney then back before he nodded. "We'll follow your lead, Whitney."

Her gut tightened even further and she felt a little sick.

Whitney forced herself to take a deep breath. She needed to relax. This was how a new product launched. Probably. They had to actually *launch* the product to see how it went. It couldn't be successful if they didn't put it out there.

She never should have pitched the idea of a new snack

cake to the guys. Or she should have gotten all of this together before she did. Why hadn't *they* asked about all of this before they put together a big event to choose what kind of snack cake they'd be adding? Obviously they needed machines to *make* whatever it was. And packaging. And a name for it.

She felt her heart racing.

They hadn't asked because they didn't know how to do this. They'd been trusting her to do it. They'd been following her lead. *She* was the one who should have known the proper steps to take and what all they needed to do.

Fuck.

"Cam!" A voice called on the computer. A voice Whitney knew very well. "I need the food processor!"

Cam met Whitney's eyes through the computer screen. "She does *not* need the food processor."

Whitney felt a little tension leave her shoulders as she smiled. "No, no she does not."

"I can't make guacamole without it!" Didi called.

"You most certainly can!" he called back. "Hand mashed guac is the way to go. As we discussed this morning."

"So you *hid* the food processor from me? In my own house?" Didi demanded.

"Yes. But I'm not sure I needed to," he told her, "since you're looking for it in the bathroom!"

"Are you making fun of me having memory problems?" Didi asked.

He grinned. "Of course not." He turned back to the group. "I need to go." He disconnected without waiting for anyone to say anything.

Whitney wasn't sure if she should laugh, or hide under the table, or head straight home.

The guys all laughed as Aiden closed his laptop.

"I so fucking love that he's being kept on his toes all day and that it's a seventy-something-year-old woman doing it," Dax said, shaking his head.

"Cam and Didi Lancaster," Aiden said. "I did not see that one coming." His gaze landed on Whitney. "This is... an interesting development."

"Talk about grand gestures," Dax agreed.

Whitney suddenly found herself ready to tell everyone what was going on. That was weird. She recognized it was very unlike her—or anyone in her family—to tell personal details, especially to work acquaintances. But she still heard herself saying, "My grandmother is in the early stages of Alzheimer's. She needs someone with her for all but very short periods. She didn't like the woman I hired, so during their dessert date she talked Cam into being her companion until she moves into Sunny Orchard."

They all took a moment to process that.

Aiden was the first to speak. "I'm sorry, Whit."

"Thanks. It's been hard," she admitted. "But I know it's going to get worse. I'm grateful she's excited about Sunny Orchard," she said to Dax. "That will be better for her. But we're just in this in-between stage right now since my family went to Dallas." She frowned. It wasn't as if her family had been a ton of help when they'd been here, honestly. A lot of it had still fallen to Whitney and she and Didi had both preferred it that way. But Whitney had been left out of so much at Hot Cakes that she never felt that she was missing anything at the office by not being there.

"You're okay with Cam being there?" Aiden asked.

She glanced up, refocusing on the men around the table. She wasn't missing out now. In fact, they were all looking to her to lead them through this next stage.

She should have kept her mouth shut about a new product until Didi was settled at Sunny Orchard. She'd just gotten caught up in excitement and things had snowballed with the brainstorming with Ollie and... she hadn't expected them to listen to her, honestly. She'd tossed it out there the way she had a dozen other ideas over the years with her family, but she was so used to those ideas barely making a blip on anyone's radar that she hadn't been prepared for anyone to actually say, "Let's do it!"

"What do you mean?" she asked Aiden. Now that she was really looking at him, she saw there was something in his expression that looked almost like concern.

"Cam can be damned pushy and stubborn as fuck," Aiden said bluntly, sitting forward.

Whitney straightened.

"If you don't want him there, we'll get him out," Aiden told her. He looked at Grant.

Grant nodded. "Just say the word. We can deal with him."

Whitney's eyes widened. She felt a strange surge of an emotion that was hard to name. They were... protecting her? Coming to her defense? Willing to "deal with" one of their best friends for her? That felt good in a weird way. She really didn't have people taking care of her. Other than Didi. And even then there had been a lot of "pick your battles" advice from her grandmother. The idea that these guys would be on her side rather than Cam's was surprising and really nice.

But there were no sides here. That was the truth. She just did not want these men to get into a conflict with Cam. There was no need. She wasn't upset with Cam. Now.

"No. It's... okay."

Aiden shook his head. "I'm not sure it is."

Whitney felt her head shaking as well. "No. Honestly it is."

Even before the kiss, it had gotten okay. But since the kiss... well, she wanted him to stick around. It hadn't even been a *kiss*. She wanted a *kiss* now. Which was really stupid and a pretty great way to ensure that she made a really big mistake—an even bigger mistake than kissing him in the first place. But she was sure of one thing...she didn't want him to leave.

"When he first told me about helping with Didi, I thought he was crazy, I'll admit. But you should hear him explain it." She gave them a grin.

Aiden didn't smile back. "Cam can convince most people of most things. It makes him an amazing attorney."

She lifted a brow. "You think he somehow tricked me into this?"

"When Cam wants something, he gets it," Dax said. He said it in a very matter-of-fact way.

"So he wants to help my grandmother out," Whitney said.

Dax gave her a look. "I don't think that's all he wants."

"Oh, Cam will be great with Didi." Piper swept back into the room. She proceeded to set cold bottles of water in front of each of them.

None of them had asked for water, but three of the four men reached for the bottles right away. Whitney smiled, amazed by the dynamic. Either Piper could *sense* when the guys were thirsty even from fifty feet away, or the guys just assumed they were thirsty if Piper was giving them water.

"You think so?" Ollie asked. "Cam doesn't seem like the... nurturing type."

Piper shrugged. "Exactly."

"What do you mean?" Ollie asked.

"I'm guessing a woman who started her own company and helped grow it into a multimillion dollar company isn't the type to want nurturing," Piper said. "If she's in the early stages, then she's probably aware of the fact that she's forgetting things or that usual tasks are more difficult now. The last thing she'll want is to be *taken care of*. She'll understand that she needs to be safe and she needs some help. So why not choose a hot guy who's funny and who can be sweet, but who won't coddle her, to spend time with if she has the chance?"

"Cam can be sweet?" Ollie asked. "I haven't really noticed that."

"He can be very sweet," Piper confirmed.

"Give me three examples."

"He sent a plant to Conner Daniels when his father passed away."

Ollie looked surprised. "He did? Or *you* did?"

"He did. He asked me for a florist but he even made the call."

"Isn't Conner the lawyer who sued us over the use of the name Vandragon Dungeons?" Dax asked.

Whitney could have kissed Dax. On the cheek of course. But she was so glad he'd clarified who Conner was so *she* wouldn't ask. She knew she should *not* be, or act, interested in Cam and details like who he was sending plants to, but dammit, she was.

"Tried to," Grant said with a nod. "Cam won. Of course. But yeah, he and Conner were absolutely *not* friends."

"See?" Piper said to Ollie. "That was sweet. They were on opposite sides in business and Cam kicked his ass, but he still sent his condolences over a personal issue."

Ollie narrowed his eyes. "Fine. Two more."

"The donations he makes to Appleby."

"You mean the donations he makes that get his name in big block letters on the side of things?" Aiden asked with a smile.

Okay, Whitney knew about those. He'd donated money to build the youth sports complex, and that did, indeed, have his name—his last name anyway—on the side of it. He'd also donated to various projects around town when the community needed something but had trouble coming up with the funds.

"Those," Piper said. "But also the scholarships, the medical bills, the service dog training."

Whitney glanced around the table and saw that Cam's friends looked as surprised as she felt.

"The what?" Aiden finally asked.

Piper nodded. "He has a foundation where people can apply for funds for all kinds of things. Help paying medical bills or help buying a handicapped accessible van or anything like that." She looked smug. "He never makes a big deal about that."

Clearly. Whitney had never heard about any of that.

"He knows that the people needing the funds don't want to make their needs public and he's fine just helping out behind the scenes. Believe it or not," she added with a little smile.

"Huh," Ollie finally said.

"Sweet, right?" Piper asked. Her eyes met Whitney's.

Dammit, that was sweet.

"Fine," Ollie conceded. "One more."

"You think he gets stupid drunk after seeing Whitney every time he comes home because he's emotionless and cold-hearted?" Piper asked.

Whitney felt her chest tighten.

"Only a guy who's *sweet*, down deep anyway, would still have get-drunk feelings for a girl ten years later," Piper said.

Now Whitney's throat tightened too.

She didn't get drunk after she'd seen him, but she knew exactly how he felt.

"Fine," Ollie said. "I guess *maybe* he has a sweet side." He rolled his eyes.

Piper laughed. "He does. But he'll be good with Didi. He won't baby her and he won't let her get away with anything that's not safe."

Ollie laughed. "Yeah, Cam is *not* the type to baby someone."

Piper nodded. "He'll make her behave."

"How will she take that?" Dax asked Whitney.

"Well." Whitney shrugged. "My grandpa was pretty domineering."

"Oh?"

"Yeah. But..." Whitney started actually thinking about the question. "Grandma kind of did whatever the hell she wanted anyway, honestly."

"That sounds like Letty," Aiden said with a small smile.

Whitney returned the smile. Aiden hadn't been Letty's grandson by blood, but he'd still been her grandson in the ways that counted. His mom and Cam's had been best friends and the boys had grown up together. After Aiden's mom had passed away when he was fourteen, he'd more or less moved in with the McCafferys. He'd spent as much time at the bakery and with Letty as Cam had, truly.

Whitney nodded. "Her motto was always *it's easier to get forgiven than get permission*. She embezzled money from the company forever."

All the eyebrows in the room went up. "What?" Grant asked. "How? It was *her* company."

"Okay, it wasn't really embezzlement," Whitney said. "But she took money from the company that my grandfather and father never knew about. My grandfather took the business over early on, figuring he was better at the 'money stuff' than she was. He let her be in charge of the recipes and overseeing the bakers and production lines for the most part, but he was in charge of all the money and marketing. But she had employee loyalty and the company accountant paid money into a private account that was Didi's alone, that my grandfather never knew about."

They all laughed and shook their heads.

Ollie finally said, "Cam might have his hands full."

Whitney nodded. "Seriously."

"That's awesome," Dax said with a huge grin.

"Is it?" she asked. She wasn't so sure. Not if she wanted him to stick around.

Then again, if she wanted him to leave her alone, this was maybe the perfect solution.

It did not feel like a good solution. Because she didn't want him to leave her alone.

"Yeah, it's awesome," Ollie agreed. "Cam is pretty used to getting his way with beautiful women. I think having a couple he has to work a little harder with is perfect."

A couple. Ollie had said a couple. That meant someone other than Didi.

Whitney did *not* ask him who else he meant.

12
<hr/>

The doorbell rang and Cam jogged to the front door. His mom was bringing some of her homemade cleaning solutions over. He needed something to get the upstairs tubs clean and he hadn't been able to find anything good in the closets and cupboards at Whitney's. He suspected she had a cleaning service come in or that Katherine had done the cleaning and had taken the supplies with her.

He hoped Maggie included some furniture polish too.

He pulled the door open with a big smile.

But it wasn't Maggie.

He sighed.

Dax, Aiden, and Grant were on the front step. Grinning like dumbasses.

Aiden held up a plastic grocery bag. "Special delivery from Maggie."

"She asked *you* to bring it over?" Cam asked.

"No. We *totally* volunteered when we heard where she was going," Dax said. He took in Cam's appearance from head to toe, including the yellow Buttered Up apron Maggie had dropped off to him yesterday and the rubber spatula he held in his left hand. "You have a little something..." Dax pointed at his right cheek.

Cam wiped at his cheek, his hand coming away with powdered sugar. He sighed.

Dax grinned. He turned to Grant. "Yes. This was definitely a good idea."

Grant nodded. "Oh, yeah, this makes me very happy."

"You're all jerks," Cam told them, turning on his heel and heading back into the house. "Come on. I've got cookies in the oven. I don't want them to burn."

His friends followed with laughter.

"Hey, Henry!" Aiden called as they all stepped into the kitchen.

Henry waved absently over his shoulder. He and Didi were on the couch in the family room playing *Warriors of Easton*.

"Maggie said to bring him home if he's bored or driving you nuts," Aiden said.

"He's fine." Cam grinned at the back of his little brother's head. "He's been kicking her ass, of course, for two hours, but he's telling her she's winning and she's delighted."

Aiden grinned as he set the plastic bag of bottles and jars on the counter. "Henry would probably let her win but I'm not sure he knows *how* to lose at *Warriors*."

Cam chuckled. "Exactly."

He pulled on an oven mitt and crossed to the oven, taking a dozen perfectly browned lemon cookies from the rack. He set them to the side and slid another pan in, setting the timer, then pulling the mitt off and tossing it to the side.

He turned to find his friends watching him, clearly amused.

"This is very... domestic," Dax said.

Cam lifted an eyebrow and planted his hands on his hips. "And?"

Dax nodded. "I would never have guessed you'd be house-husband material."

Cam shrugged. That didn't bother him at all. "I'm good at *everything* I do."

Dax laughed. "Touché."

"I asked Maggie if we should bring some food over. Or dessert," Grant said. "But she said you and Didi have been over for dinner every night and that you leave before dessert because you've been making stuff here."

"I have." Cam gave him a challenging look. "My stuff is better than my mom's."

Dax's eyes grew wide. "That better not be true, McCaffery."

"Why's that?"

"Because that means you've been depriving me of your goods for ten years? I might never forgive you."

"I've been giving you plenty of my goods," Cam told him. "Just not the baked kind."

"You're a bastard," Dax said.

Cam grinned. "Wow, news flash."

"I don't know." Aiden had come around the breakfast bar and was now lifting a cookie from the cooling rack. "Zoe thinks all of this"—he gestured, encompassing the kitchen and Didi and Henry and everything—"is really sweet." He lifted the cookie to his mouth.

Cam plucked it from his fingers before he could bite into it. "It *is* really sweet," he said, putting the cookie back with the rest.

"Hey."

"What? You don't need those cookies. You're living with and practically married to someone who *owns a bakery*. Those are for Didi and Henry."

"And Whitney?" Dax asked, wiggling his eyebrows.

Cam grinned. Whitney never ate the desserts he made in front of him, but there were always at least a couple missing by the time he checked on them the next day. He already knew that she especially liked anything with chocolate and caramel. But he'd bet there would be some lemon cookies missing tomorrow too.

"Whitney too," he said with a nod.

"And is the toilet bowl cleaner and dusting solution for Didi or Whitney?" Aiden asked. He swiped another cookie and quickly got it to his mouth before Cam could grab it back.

"Both," Cam said. But then he shrugged. "Mostly Whit, I guess. I mean, she'd be the one doing it, or paying to have it done, if I didn't."

Aiden chewed and swallowed. "Damn, man, you *are* good at that."

Cam smirked. Then tossed cookies to Dax and Grant too.

"So you're seducing a woman by cleaning toilets," Dax said. "I can *totally* relate to that."

"I'm *helping* a *friend* out with some things," Cam said.

But damn, he wanted to seduce this woman. Not with toilets. Or furniture polish for that matter.

But, yeah, maybe with cookies.

"About that," Aiden said.

"It's great," Cam told him. "We've got a routine. Didi and I start our day after Whitney's already left for work. We hang out. We go to Mom's for dinner. I bring leftovers home for Whit. She works late, so we're already upstairs by the time she gets home. She's in bed by the time Didi is up to watch *Magnum, P.I.* We stay up with cookies and reruns until two or three and then sleep in. It's working."

For now.

He hated not seeing Whitney more. That part wasn't really going according to plan. But he was fine keeping things running at home and, it was clearly allowing Whitney to do some pretty awesome things at Hot Cakes.

And he couldn't get over the look on her face during that meeting.

She'd looked worried. Almost scared. As if she was suddenly realizing she was in over her head and was panicking a little.

It was true the guys were giving her full lead on... well, everything. And, from what he'd gleaned from both Whitney and Didi, she hadn't had that before.

So he was doing what he could to make work all she needed to focus on.

Even if that meant there was no time or attention for him, either.

"Oh, hot damn!" Didi crowed from the room off the kitchen.

"You're really good at this," Henry said.

The men all laughed, assuming he was just trying to make her feel good.

"I was always a fast runner," Didi said. "Way faster than your grandma. But she was a better climber."

"He has to keep pausing it," Cam told the others. "She wants to keep telling him stories about when she and Letty were kids. I just overheard about the first time they baked cookies for a tea party and burned them but were determined to make them seem delicious so their mothers wouldn't tell them they couldn't bake anymore so they ate them all anyway."

Cam had felt a strange urge to yell into the living room to wait for him. He wanted to hear stories about his grandmother as a little girl.

"Like the other night at dinner," Aiden said with a grin.

"I couldn't believe when Jane and Josie and Zoe followed Didi and Henry into the living room after dinner instead of heading out to the patio," Dax said, his smile affectionate.

Usually the girls went out to the back patio with spiked lemonade or wine while the guys cleaned up after dinner.

Instead, Zoe, Josie, and Jane had followed Didi and Henry into the family room where they were going to resume the *Warriors of Easton* game they'd started before dinner.

Didi had talked almost nonstop through dinner, telling stories about her and Letty, stories about the early days in the bakery, and even stories about the origins of Hot Cakes. She'd laughed and smiled through it all, seeming lost in her memories and very nostalgic about Letty. Even the chicken had reminded her of her old friend.

It had instantly endeared her to all of the McCafferys and their friends, and within minutes any awkwardness was gone. And having the woman they'd all spent years believing was their family's nemesis passing the chicken and potatoes around Maggie's dining room table seemed completely normal.

"She reminds me so much of my grandma," Cam agreed. He looked at Aiden. "Her sense of humor is almost identical. And she is a handful."

Aiden nodded. Letty had been his adopted grandma just as Maggie and Steve had been fill-in parents after his mom had died and his dad had disappeared into his work and his bottle of liquor. He grinned. "She kept you on your toes today?"

She most certainly had. "The crash you heard on the phone earlier wasn't her dropping anything," Cam said. "It was her *throwing* stuff. She was trying to find something in the cupboards. She nearly gave me a heart attack when I walked into the kitchen and found her *standing on the counter* and rummaging through the cupboards. She was just tossing the pots and pans out of her way." Cam paused in his dish rinsing. "Ask me what she was looking for."

Aiden lifted both eyebrows. "What was she looking for?"

"Tequila."

Aiden, Grant, and Dax all snorted.

"It was nine thirty a.m.," Aiden said.

Cam nodded. He was aware. "She said it was time for margaritas."

"What did you do?" Dax asked.

"Made her margaritas."

They all looked surprised.

"Orange margaritas. With no tequila in them," Cam clarified. He'd blended orange juice with ice and a bit of lime juice and poured it into a margarita glass and served it to her by the pool. "She said it was the most delicious margarita she'd ever had."

"You lied to her," Grant said.

"Yes, I did." Cam didn't feel even a flicker of guilt over that. "It made her happy and kept her safe."

They all nodded. He hadn't really expected any of them to give him a hard time.

"Were you able to get any work done today?" Dax asked, seeming amused.

Cam lifted a shoulder. "A bit." He reached for a towel and dried his hands. "I took the laptop out to the patio while she sunbathed with her margarita and answered some emails on my phone while she was watching her Spanish soap opera."

"Didi speaks Spanish?" Dax asked.

"No. She said that makes it better because she can pretend they're saying whatever she wants them to."

Dax laughed. "Well, if you need to come into the office, bring her with you. Some of the girls watch soap operas in the break room and there's a couple of Spanish ones. Didi could hang out with them."

Cam grinned. "I might do that. I took her to yoga yesterday."

"No way," Aiden chuckled. "How'd that go?"

"It was perfect. She laid down to do the deep breathing, a kitten crawled up onto her chest and started purring, and within two minutes they were both asleep."

"She just took a nap during yoga?"

"Yep." Cam shook his head. "So I went through a few of the moves and... two hours later, Paige woke me up because her pregnant mom's class was coming in and they were a little louder and she didn't think I'd be able to sleep through it."

The guys all paused a beat and then started laughing. "You napped at Paige's?"

Cam grinned. "Yeah. There was no class after ours, and then there was one for older gals and they all decided I must need the sleep." He pushed a hand through his hair. "Which I did. Didi had me up watching *Magnum, P.I.* 'til the wee hours."

Aiden pushed away from the counter. "This is going to be interesting."

Cam glanced toward the family room. "But good, I think. It's kind of nice already."

Aiden nodded. "Henry misses Letty."

"We all miss her," Cam said. His chest felt a little tight.

He'd come home fairly often for a guy who lived in another city and had a demanding job, but Letty had passed away quickly. He had regrets about not being there more and only barely getting home before she died. Having Letty in his life was something he'd always taken for granted and he was sorry about that now. Henry wasn't the only one who was enjoying having someone around who reminded him so much of his grandmother.

Aiden clapped him on the shoulder. "Yes, we do," he agreed. "And it seems that Didi is really enjoying this."

Cam nodded. "Maybe Whitney isn't the only one that the Lancasters didn't pay a lot of attention to."

Grant's and Dax's eyebrows rose but Aiden actually nodded. "And speaking of Whitney..."

"We already talked about Whitney."

"We need to talk about her some more."

Cam had known this was coming. "Whitney and I are fine."

"Are you?"

This actually came from Grant rather than Aiden.

All three of his friends faced him fully. Grant folded his arms, Dax put his hands on his hips and Aiden braced a hand on the counter beside him, which blocked Cam's escape from the kitchen.

Cam sighed. They were feeling protective of Whitney. He'd been expecting his. His friends were all protective types, in one way or another. Dax the lesser of the three, but he was still not about to let one of his friends mess with a woman that he liked and respected. Well, *any* woman really, but it was clear they all liked Whitney and that meant Cam wasn't going to get away with so much as looking at Whitney wrong.

Good thing he didn't want to look at Whitney wrong at all.

"We need her," Aiden said firmly. "We knew it before, but she has absolutely confirmed it now. She has to lead us in... most of the things we have coming up."

Cam knew that. It had been obvious during the meeting, even over his computer screen. "Of course we do."

He wanted Hot Cakes to be successful, of course. But not because of his own bank account, and less and less because of wanting to throw it back in the faces of the Lancasters. It was about his friends. This was important to Aiden. And Grant now that he was staying in Appleby with Josie. It was also important to Whitney.

That was the ultimate reason Cam wanted this to all go forward and be huge. Aiden and Grant could make it work, somehow. They'd probably have to hire some more people. Consultants and shit. But they'd figure it out. Eventually. Possibly not on the timeline they'd laid out that morning though.

But they were both already millionaires, for fuck's sake. And they were also entrepreneurs who had previously built a business from the ground up. They'd find something else if Hot Cakes flopped.

This was a lot bigger deal to Whitney. It was all she had.

So yeah, he was going to be her friend. So that she would feel she could confide in him so he could help her. But also because she'd made it clear that was what she wanted. She hadn't bullshitted him or taken her panties off to try to get her way—which definitely would have worked. She'd been clear about what she wanted.

Now, she needed help. And he and his friends were, obviously, the best ones to give it to her.

"So don't piss her off," Aiden said. "Or turn her off about working for us."

Cam frowned. "Which is why she and I are going to be just friends."

"And boss-employee with no extra shit," Grant said, almost as if he hadn't heard Cam. "You can't be making her uncomfortable or to feel like she has to worry about—"

"I know," Cam said. "I think we should offer her a partnership."

All the other men were quiet, clearly surprised.

"She's doing more to move things forward than the rest of us," Cam said. "She deserves it. That will help her feel like she's truly an equal part. That we trust her. And that she doesn't have to prove anything to us."

"So you can sleep with her then without it being weird?" Dax asked. He'd given up his share in the company so he could date Jane, an employee.

"No." Cam sighed. "I'm trying to be mature here."

"Sorry," Dax said with a grin. "Mature isn't really something I'm used to. Hard to recognize it."

Cam nodded. "Fair enough. Especially with me. When it pertains to Whitney."

They were good enough friends to not confirm they agreed with that. At least out loud.

"I'm trying to be a good guy," Cam said.

"This is a one-eighty in five days," Aiden commented.

"It is," Cam agreed.

Aiden shook his head. "I really expected fireworks from you two."

Cam nodded. "Me too."

"But you're *not* at each other's throats?" Aiden asked. "It's not tense or awkward?"

He hardly saw her, really, so no it wasn't either of those things. But honestly, it wasn't tense or awkward anyway. He'd expected them to fight. Or at least bicker. But... it didn't feel right. She made him feel protective and hell, proud. Yeah, *proud* over the things she was doing at Hot Cakes. Of all the crazy things.

Laughter from the family room made him smile and he said, "Whitney and I have bigger things going on than a breakup from ten years ago."

Aiden gave him a little frown. "You sure?"

"We were kids. We're both different people now." Cam took a breath and looked at the other men. They were his best friends. They knew him better than anyone. They had his back. "She and I haven't talked, not really, in years. We haven't spent time together. When I think of her, I think of the girl I knew. I'm just getting to know the woman who is now my business partner for all intents and purposes. How can I be angry with her? Or hurt by her? Or... in love with her? I've just met her in a lot of ways."

The guys just looked at him. Dax looked confused, Grant looked skeptical, and Aiden looked worried.

Cam shrugged. She might physically want him. They did have chemistry. And a history. But she didn't want *him*. Not as a boyfriend. Not as someone she confided in. Not as someone she turned to for help.

Not as a friend.

She might let him kiss her. Maybe even strip her naked and smear cookie dough all over her. But when it came to brainstorming at work, she clearly loved doing that with Ollie and Dax. Obviously she respected and admired Grant and Aiden because it was important to her to impress them. She'd rather work late than come home and hang out with him and Didi.

He wanted to be important to her somehow. Someone she needed. And it was clear that what she needed most was a friend.

"I might be a different guy than I was ten years ago, but there's something that just makes me want to be what she needs."

"And she needs an ally right now," Grant said.

Cam looked at him. "Yeah."

Grant nodded. "I noticed she seemed nervous, or worried, during the meeting the other day."

Cam didn't like that the other man could read Whitney like that. But then again, maybe her discomfort had been *really* obvious.

"She was," he said. "I saw it too. She wants to impress us, show us that she can be valuable to us."

"She *is* valuable to us," Aiden said.

"I know. But she has to prove it. She doesn't just want words. She needs to pull this project off, make it successful."

Aiden took a breath. "So we just back off? Tread carefully? Be sure to, what? Praise her a lot or something?"

"Nope," Cam said. "You guys don't treat her any differently. Treat her like a colleague. Ask her opinions, question what she's telling you. Nothing different than how you've treated her in the past. When she pulls this off, she'll know it's because she really did it. There won't be a question about if you were easy on her or anything." He paused. "*I'm* the one who's going to treat her differently than I have in the past."

After a moment, Aiden nodded and clapped him on the back.

Cam was expecting to hear, "Good job, buddy. Proud of you."

Instead Aiden said, "Good luck."

To which Grant and Dax simply nodded.

Cam blew out a breath. Yeah. He was going to need it.

13

Whitney hadn't been killing time at the office. Exactly. She'd wanted to dive into the huge to-do list she'd ended up with after the meeting two days ago. But it had been really nice to think that she *could* stay late. She didn't need to rush home. She'd never *had* to rush home. Katherine had been there with Didi. But Didi had been grumpy when she'd gotten home too late and left her with *that woman*. Tonight Didi was with Cam.

And this had been Didi's idea. Whitney felt a lot less compelled to get home and "rescue" Didi if she didn't like how things were going.

Of course, Didi would have to remember that the whole thing had been her idea.

Didi was delightful. She really was. But she had always been a high-energy person and that hadn't diminished at all with her cognitive decline. In fact, she now got her time mixed up and got bored more easily which made her boundless energy harder on family, friends, and caregivers. She liked to be entertained and, like getting up around midnight to watch *Magnum, P.I.*, she didn't follow the clock that others did. She just did what felt good in the moment. At times, when she wasn't sleep deprived or watching an episode of *Magnum, P.I.* for the seventh time, Whitney actually envied that about her grandmother. Whitney would love to just do whatever felt good when it felt good.

Didi might be in the mood for a burger at seven in the morning or pancakes at seven at night. She might want to go to bed at 10 a.m. and sleep for eight hours or she might want to go for a swim at ten at night.

It was all harmless, for the most part, but Katherine had wanted to try to keep her on a "normal schedule" and they'd butted heads. In Katherine's defense, it was a little tough for a caregiver to adjust to things like sleeping the day away and staying up all night, but Whitney had been torn between understanding where Katherine was coming from and wondering why the hell you couldn't just have a burger at 7 a.m. Or 3 a.m.

Whitney had tried to just roll with Didi's schedule and her family had been lenient... okay, that wasn't true. Her family hadn't noticed when Whitney came and went from the office. Because she was never considered vital and was never in charge of anything important. If she wasn't at a meeting, it didn't make a difference. She didn't have deadlines. So she could sleep late with Didi after being up grilling burgers by the pool at 3 a.m. and watching *Ferris Bueller's Day Off*—one of Didi's favorites— on a huge movie projector from their chaise lounge chairs until five.

Now she couldn't do that. Not only would the guys notice— something she actually appreciated—but she now *did* have work to do. Work she *wanted* to do. Work she wanted to do well.

Work she couldn't do while a little hung over from 3 a.m. hard root beers that Didi insisted went with the burgers—she wasn't wrong—or the heartburn that went with eating the french fries dipped in spicy aioli—that Didi also insisted went with the burgers and that she also wasn't wrong about—at 3 a.m.

Whitney let herself into the house, wondering what shenanigans Didi had been up to today and how Cam had handled it. Because Whitney was sure there had been shenanigans. Of course, the way Didi had talked him into this crazy plan of moving in here in the first place had Whitney pretty sure that Didi was getting her way with Camden McCaffery. The big, tough bad-boy lawyer was probably wrapped around Didi's little finger.

Then again, Didi had a thing for muscles and tattoos—something Whitney had found out watching movies with her grandmother and hadn't particularly needed or wanted to know. So Whitney wouldn't be surprised to find out Cam had charmed Didi into doing whatever he told her to do.

Either way, honestly, it had been nice to not feel the need to rush home and to be able to focus at work until she got through what she'd determined to be the top things on her to-do list.

The house was quiet. Surprisingly so.

Lights were on and she heard the sounds of water running and a hand mixer from the kitchen. She glanced up the stairs. The upper hallway light was on, as it was once Didi went to bed so that when she inevitably got up in the night, she wouldn't stumble in the dark.

It was likely Cam in the kitchen.

Whitney's heart thumped at the realization. She also realized she'd been anticipating seeing him.

She shouldn't.

She shouldn't get used to him being here. She shouldn't *like* him being here. It was nice that he was here helping if Didi really did want him here. Whitney definitely wanted her grandmother to be happy, of course. And it was only for the month. That made it not one-hundred percent crazy. Maybe only eighty percent.

But the strongest emotion Whitney should feel was gratitude. Gratitude that she could work late. And that Didi was happy. And that her house hadn't been on fire at any point in the hours since she'd left it that morning.

As far as she knew.

If there had been a fire, it had been taken care of and the house was still standing. That was fine in Whitney's book. As long as *she* didn't have to deal with it.

She stopped in the doorway to the kitchen.

Cam was at the stove, his back to her. He was stirring something in a bowl on the counter next to the stove. There was a pan of something *on* the stove and she noticed a cake pan next to him as well. It smelled heavenly. Chocolatey. Rich.

He was wearing one of her grandmother's aprons too. Over a dark gray t-shirt and a pair of jeans. The t-shirt fit snugly to his shoulders and back which tapered to his waist and tight ass. His muscles bunched as he stirred, drawing her attention, as always, to his tattoos.

Yeah, her grandma wasn't the only one who liked muscles and tattoos.

Whitney sighed.

Gratitude was not the only thing she felt about him being here.

She felt hot and like there were bees buzzing around in her stomach. Not butterflies. Nothing as gentle and sweet as that. The sensation was a lot more insistent and absolutely not sweet.

She also felt conflicted.

So Cam wasn't really her boss in the way that she might have to worry if she was the VP of Marketing and Sales in any other company. The owners of the company, including Cam, trusted her and needed her. They didn't treat her like a subordinate. She didn't actually think they'd fire her if she and Cam slept together. Even if it ended badly and she threw one of Zoe's muffins at him during a meeting. Or something.

In fact, she had the impression that she might even have the other guys on her side if she threw a muffin at Cam. Provided she had a good reason. Which she would. Of course.

If they were to try to have a relationship and he left dirty socks all over the bedroom rather than putting them in the hamper or something, she'd just throw muffins at him at home. She'd save work muffin throwing for work-related issues.

Not that she and Cam were going to try to have a relationship.

At least not one that involved his socks on her bedroom floor.

They were going to be... something that had nothing to do with socks. She supposed they had a relationship in the strictest sense of the word. The way she had a relationship with Aiden. There was history, sure, but she had history with Aiden too. Hers and Cam's was more complicated and involved but she was now as involved with Cam as she was with Aiden.

Though Aiden wasn't in her kitchen right now. With chocolate. Making her think about how chocolate sauce would be far better for nipple-licking than cookie dough.

She really wanted to go into that kitchen right now.

So instead she turned and headed upstairs to check on Didi.

Didi was in bed but not asleep. She had her favorite pink nightgown on and was sitting up, propped against her headboard, reading. Whitney smiled as she stepped into the room. She'd listened to so many stories sitting on that very bed in that same position with Didi.

They'd started with the usual childhood bedtime stories and nursery rhymes but they'd quickly gotten to *Little Women*, *Alice in Wonderland*, *A Little Princess*, *The Chronicles of Narnia*, *Little House on the Prairie* and *Nancy Drew*. They'd read *The*

Diary of Anne Frank together, a first for both of them, and gone on to read other classics that Didi hadn't read before, discussing them under the down comforter in their own little world. It had been their own tiny book club and Whitney would always be grateful to Didi for her love of reading.

"What are you reading?" she asked, moving into the room.

Didi looked up and smiled. She turned the book so Whitney could see the front. "I've had this book forever, but I don't think I've read it."

It was *Anne of Green Gables*. Whitney kicked her shoes off, making sure they landed over near Didi's armchair and out of the path Didi would take from the bed to the door when she got up in the night. Whitney pulled her blouse from the waistband of her skirt as she joined Didi on the bed, sliding in next to her, and cuddling close. "You have. We read it together." They'd read it three times, actually.

Didi laughed softly. "Well, it's like reading it for the first time. Which is actually lovely."

Whitney put her head on Didi's shoulder and took her hand, cradling Didi's between her own. "I would love to be able to read some of my favorites again for the first time. You're lucky." She meant that. There were so many unfair things about Alzheimer's and she dreaded most of them, but she'd take the few silver linings she could find.

Didi kissed the top of her head. "I think so too. I'm very lucky to have you and Cam taking care of me."

Whitney smiled. Of course Didi already loved Cam. "You had a good day?"

"Oh we've had a lovely few weeks," Didi said. "He's so funny and kind. Yoga is fun, the kittens are so cute. I'm so good at the east warriors. I had four purple diamonds and killed three trolls just today. I've never met a man who can make good mashed potatoes. And the margaritas are the best I've ever had. He didn't even get mad about the dented pot."

Whitney repeated all of that silently, trying to figure each thing out. Okay, yoga and kittens did actually go together in Appleby. Had they gone to Paige's? It was possible. Cam did go to yoga at Paige's studio. It was why Whitney had changed the class time *she* attended. Watching Cam stretch and bend and flex the one time they'd been in class together had been too much for her. Apparently, it had been too much for several women because, according to Piper, who also attended regularly, Paige had asked Cam to move to the back of the room for future classes.

But Whitney had never thought about taking Didi to yoga. She'd assumed Didi would be bored after just a few minutes and they wouldn't make it through a whole class. She hadn't wanted to disrupt class for everyone else and, if she were being honest, *she* wanted to have a full class. She loved yoga.

As for the east warriors, she assumed that was something about *Warriors of Easton*, the guys' video game, but she'd had no idea that Didi knew how to play, not to mention being good enough to win. Then again, Whitney knew nothing about the game. She'd stubbornly ignored learning anything about it over the years because, while she was happy for Cam and happy to have been proven right, it was also a reminder that she had, in fact, been right about him being better off without her.

Moving on from that, Whitney thought about the rest of what Didi had said.

It was possible that Cam had made her grandmother mashed potatoes and margaritas today.

But Didi also thought Cam had been here for a few weeks.

"He's such a good man, Whitney."

Whitney tipped her head to look up at her grandmother. Didi might not know what day it was for sure or how many she'd spent with Cam, but Whitney could see that she was perfectly aware of what she was saying right now.

And she was right. Cam *was* a good man. "I know."

"Different than what we're used to."

Whitney felt her chest tighten. He was that too. So different. She and her grandmother had never specifically talked about the sexism and neglect in their family. It would have been like discussing ugly furniture. Why mention it when it was right there and so obvious and they both clearly saw it and hated it? But it had bonded them. Didi's support of her had always meant so much and it was why Whitney really wanted Hot Cakes to be the company it *should* be—a company that Didi could be proud of, run the way she would have run it.

"He's definitely very different," she agreed.

Didi's hand squeezed hers. "I'm so glad. You deserve that. He sees what you're worth. And he'll help you see it too."

Whitney felt her eyes prickling with tears. She sniffed. "You've always helped me see what I'm worth."

"I'm glad." Didi leaned over and kissed the top of her head. "But you can never be loved too much. And I think Camden is going to love you like you've never been loved."

Whitney felt her breath catch in her lungs and she had to force herself to breathe out.

Wow. That was... a lot. A lot that she really couldn't deal with right now.

How many margaritas had Didi had today? Maybe that explained some of this.

Well, there was one person who would know for sure. She should probably go talk to Cam. About the margaritas. And how Didi's day had been from *his* perspective. Yes, that made sense. She should for sure check in with him. About the margaritas.

"I love you, Grandma," she said, lifting Didi's hand to her lips and pressing a kiss there.

"I love you too, my darling."

"I'm going to go say goodnight to Cam and then head to

bed." Whitney pushed herself up to the edge of the bed. "Are you good? Need anything?"

"I'm fine, darling," Didi said with a wave of her hand. "Go spend time with your man. Give him a big kiss for me."

She winked. Didi actually *winked* at her.

Whitney was torn. She really should correct Didi about Cam being her man and him loving her and everything being wonderful now going forward. But then again, it was harmless, right? Just like letting her eat burgers at 3 a.m. Okay, it might be a gray area. Just like the middle-of-the-night burgers were. But Cam staying here was temporary and Didi would, unfortunately, eventually forget about it. Just like, eventually, she wouldn't be able to eat those burgers anymore. At 3 a.m. or otherwise.

Whitney felt her eyes stinging as she headed down the stairs. For as long as she could, she was going to do things that made her grandmother happy. Even if it involved Cam and spicy aioli.

She stepped into the kitchen and found Cam apron-less with the most decadent-looking chocolate bars on the counter in front of him.

As if she needed anything else to make him tempting.

"Hey, you're home," he greeted.

"Yeah. A little bit ago. I was just up with Grandma."

He nodded and stretched plastic wrap over the top of the pan. "She settled down?"

"For now."

"She had a big day so I'm wondering if she'll be up a little later than usual."

Whitney crossed until she was on the opposite side of the island from him. That was closer to him, which she wanted to be, but with a barrier between them. Not that she thought she needed it because of *him*. She was feeling like *she* was the one who was on the verge of doing something stupid. Something naked... but stupid.

She was surrounded by the smell of chocolate and he had a smear of it on his left biceps. As if she didn't want to lick the swirling tattoo there already.

"I wouldn't bet on it. But tell me about this big day." She eyed the bars. That were now covered.

"Let's see. It started with margaritas by the pool."

Whitney lifted her brows. "So that was real."

"She told you?"

"Yeah. But she also thinks you've been here for a few weeks already, so I wasn't sure."

He laughed lightly. He seemed to be in a great mood. And didn't seem tired. She always felt tired this time of night.

"Well, they were real in that we had drinks in margarita glasses out by the pool, but I didn't put any tequila in them."

"Oh, really? I always..." Maybe she shouldn't admit that she let her seventy-six-year-old grandmother drink whatever and whenever she wanted to.

"You always?" Cam asked, bracing his hands on the counter across from her and leaning in.

She was distracted for a moment by the way his triceps bunched and how big his hands were.

"I, um..." She winced but said, "I let her drink whenever. She gets her time mixed up and I figured it wasn't the worst thing. It's not like she's driving anywhere or going to work with a couple of martinis in her."

"She likes martinis too?" Cam asked.

Whitney laughed. "She likes all of it. Any of it. I don't always know what inspires her to want certain drinks. I mean, she wants the hard root beer with burgers and usually saves the margaritas for fajitas or nachos, but she likes martinis and pina coladas and fuzzy navels almost any time. Oh, and Kahlua and cream. She loves Kahlua and cream."

"I'll keep that in mind."

Whitney just stared at his smile. She couldn't remember when she and Cam had just smiled at each other over a minor shared amusement. That was stupid.

"You think it's okay I let her drink?" she asked.

He looked surprised for a moment. "I have no idea. I didn't let her drink because I didn't know if it was okay and was going to ask you. I didn't know if it would interact with medications or anything."

It probably was surprising that she was asking him if something was okay for Didi. Wasn't *she* supposed to be the one who knew that stuff?

She shook her head. "It's not a problem with medications. She's very healthy. Other than the... Alzheimer's." Dammit, she always tripped over that word. Whitney took a breath. "She's always been very healthy. She's also always been a big personality. A little..."

"A little what?" he asked when she trailed off.

"I was going to say kooky. That's what my dad and grandpa called it." She met Cam's eyes. "But that's not right. She was fun. That's what it was. It was just that they were allergic to fun. Or just incredibly unfamiliar." She sighed. "That made me sad when I realized it. I think my dad must have thought she was fun when he was growing up, right? At some point when he was little? But my grandpa convinced him it was weird and he got serious and took after his dad instead."

She sniffed, then lifted her chin. "Anyway, that's why it took so long to realize something was going on with her mentally. She was always fun and liked to do off-the-wall things. If it wasn't for her not remembering TV shows and books and how to do basic things, I wouldn't know now that anything was really wrong."

"Well," Cam said after a moment, his voice a little gruff.

"For what it's worth, I think you can stop using the word *was*. She *is* fun. We had a great day."

Whitney felt her heart melt a little at that. Yes, Didi was fun now too. She got a little confused and the fun happened at strange times of day, but it was definitely still entertaining.

Whitney gave him a smile she was sure looked wobbly. It felt wobbly. "I'm glad you think so."

He simply nodded. He was looking at her but the smile was gone. Now he was *watching* her.

She drew in a deep breath. "So the margaritas were real. Mostly. What about the trolls? She said she killed three."

He nodded. "Also true."

"*Warriors of Easton*?"

He nodded again.

"Did you let her win or is she a natural?"

"Henry just told her she was winning and she believed him. He would have let her but it's hard to do that."

Whitney felt her eyes go round. "Henry? Your brother was here?"

"Yes. Though the first time they played was at Mom's."

"Your mom's? You took Didi to your mom's house?"

"After yoga. We went for dinner."

Whitney straightened away from the counter, staring at him. "The mashed potatoes were your mother's?"

He smiled slightly at that. "Didi ate *a lot* of mashed potatoes."

"She said you made them."

"I peeled them." He lifted a shoulder. "She was in the living room with Henry killing trolls. I was in the kitchen. I don't mind her thinking I made the best mashed potatoes of her life though. Goes along with the margaritas."

Whitney stared at him. "You took *my grandmother* to *your mother's* house for dinner." She was still processing that. Clearly.

"We've eaten there every night," he said. "We all have dinner at Mom's once a week anyway. Sometimes I'm there more often. Mostly because I'm staying with Zoe and Aiden and they get disgustingly romantic. But yeah, we've been there each night this week."

"Who's *we all*?" For some reason Whitney felt very tense suddenly.

It had never occurred to her that Cam might take Didi to his mother's house. Why would that have ever occurred to her? Their families had been sworn enemies forever. At least for all of *their* lives. Actually, for all of their parents' lives too. The fallout between Didi and Letty had happened before either woman had been married or had children.

"My sister, Aiden, Dax and Jane, Josie and Grant." Cam shrugged. "Everyone."

Whitney felt her stomach clench. Wow. That really was everyone. Didi had not just gone into the lion's den, but the lions had invited a few tigers and panthers over too.

Okay, that wasn't fair. It was a huge overreaction as a matter of fact. Didi was clearly fine. She was in great spirits. And the mashed potatoes had practically rocked her world.

But she'd spent the evening with the *McCafferys*? That was bizzare. A few days with Cam and already everything was turned all around.

If Whitney's family were still in town...

But they weren't. And even if they were, it would have been easy enough to hide this from them. They never paid much attention to what Whitney and Didi did.

Still, this felt very strange.

She frowned at Cam. "I don't love this."

He frowned back. "Why not?"

"Because her cognitive issues are private," Whitney said. "The fact that she needs help is private. We don't want the entire town to know."

He narrowed his eyes. "You had help coming in."

"We had Katherine sign a nondisclosure. Everyone thought she was just cooking and cleaning. And she was doing those things, so it wasn't a total lie."

"And what are people going to think about me being here?"

"That we're dating," Whitney said. "Isn't that the story? That's what you and Didi came up with at the bakery, I thought. I thought she thought that we've been together all this time and now that you're back in town and my family is gone, we're no longer keeping it a secret."

His jaw ticked for a moment, but then he nodded. "That's what she thinks. At least sometimes."

"So the rest of the town can think that."

"You're fine with that?"

"Better that than them thinking she's got dementia."

"So us being together is at least better than a horrible, progressive neurologic disease," he said. "Got it."

Whitney pulled a breath in through her nose. "Now that Hot Cakes is in new hands, speculation about the business and what might happen is less of an issue. It never would have actually been an issue, but people didn't know that my family didn't let Didi have much to do with the company after the first few years. Didi was always the face of the company. People might have worried about what would happen if she was sick. Now that's not a problem. But her condition is private. I'd like to keep it private and preserve her dignity as long as possible."

"There's nothing to be ashamed of," Cam said, scowling. "It's not her fault, or yours, that this is happening. Alzheimer's is a terrible, unfair condition that is indiscriminate in who it affects. In fact, it might be a great thing if people knew she had it. Show others who are going through it that no matter how much status and money you have, this disease can still hit. We could use it to increase awareness. Do some fund-raising for—"

"No." Whitney crossed her arms, her chest tight. "No, Cam. We've donated money to research. We've donated money to Sunny Orchard. We've done all of that. We don't need to make it public."

"Then just to show some solidarity with other families who are going through shit," he said. "Jane's dad has a neurologic condition that has him living at Sunny Orchard. You and Jane could talk about how it feels to watch a loved one go through something like that."

"No." Whitney shook her head adamantly.

Jane Kemper was a strong, smart, no-bullshit person. Whitney liked Jane. But they had nothing in common. Jane was, frankly, more than a little intimidating.

"This is private," Whitney went on. "Didi has always been someone who kept to herself, who kept things within our family, and I don't think she's in a state where she can make a decision about going public now. And we can't make that decision for her."

Cam's jaw tightened again and he took a breath. "Did she keep to herself or did your grandpa keep her to herself?"

The tightness in her chest increased and she had to swallow twice before she said, "That's none of your business."

"Isn't it?" he moved around the edge of the counter.

Whitney felt her heart rate increase as he got closer. It wasn't fear. Her brain recognized that. But that was what the surge of adrenaline felt like.

"Fine. It's one thing for you to know what's going on with her," Whitney said. "You're my boss."

His frown was deep and swift. "Stop fucking saying that."

She lifted her chin. "It's true. And, yes, eventually you'll all have to know because things will deteriorate with her health and I might have to miss work and might have to adjust deadlines. But that's all the more reason for me to get things in place and going well before that happens."

"Things in place," he repeated. His voice was low and almost angry sounding. "At work, you mean."

"Yes. This new product launch and everything," she said. "And, of course, there will always be more going on but I'm hoping that we'll be past all of this newness and we'll be working well together and you'll all know what I can do and will be able to trust that I can handle my part even if I'm away from the office more at times."

Cam's eyes glittered and he *looked* a little angry now. "That's what you're thinking about when you're working late? How to get ahead now for the eventuality of when your grandma gets sicker and you need to be gone? So we trust that you can handle things and, what, don't fire you while you're taking care of your grandma?"

"Yes."

"Jesus, Whit." He shoved a hand through his hair. "You think we're that big of assholes?"

She swallowed. "Of course not. But it's only fair that I plan ahead." She could feel the tension coming off of him. He seemed... not angry, actually. Annoyed. And frustrated. That seemed more accurate.

"And for now," she went on. "I would really appreciate if you could keep my family's personal business *personal*. You came into this situation because you and Didi got together and she got a wild hair. You weren't really invited. Not by anyone who knows every piece of this. But you're here now. Because *Didi* wants you to be. But that doesn't give you permission to bring a bunch of other people into it."

She saw that he'd noticed her emphasis on *Didi* when she'd said who wanted him here. His eyes narrowed again. "And you think my family is a bunch of assholes too."

She sighed. "Cam..." She shook her head. "I don't know your family. I know what my family felt about your family. I've had it ingrained that your family doesn't like us and wants us to fail."

"You know *me*. You fell in love with me."

She flinched as he put that out there so bluntly.

"You think assholes would have raised a guy you could fall in love with?"

He was closer again. How did he keep doing that without her noticing him moving?

Then she realized that it was *her* who had moved. Closer to him. Into his personal space. Close enough to feel his heat. To see the gold flakes in his green eyes. To feel his warm breath on her cheek. And lips.

But he didn't move back.

"You think that you could fall in love with a guy who had friends who were assholes who would blab all over town about your grandma's situation?" he asked.

But his voice was softer now. Huskier. And his eyes dropped to her lips.

"I think that this is complicated and it's temporary. Can't you just keep this between us for a few weeks?"

"No."

He didn't even hesitate. He didn't even think about it for a second. He didn't even pretend to consider what she said.

She frowned. "No? Just no?"

"No. Your grandma has had several great days. My family and friends have enjoyed having her around. I've had a good time. There's no reason to not have other people involved, Whit. They can make things better."

"You don't know what you're talking about!" she exclaimed. "You've been here for a few *days*! Maybe they've been particularly good days but it's still new. Tomorrow might be bad. Eventually it *will* be bad. You can't bring all these people in."

"Whitney."

"People who don't know her," she went on without pause.

"People who don't know about her condition. They won't know how to handle things if they go bad."

"Whit—"

But she was on a roll. "What if she gets confused or scared? What if she gets angry? What if she can't figure out why she's suddenly surrounded by people she's always believed hated her? What if—"

Suddenly Cam took her chin between his thumb and first finger and brought her mouth to his, cutting off her words. And her air supply. And every thought other than *Cam's kissing me.*

She had no idea what she'd been saying. She vaguely recalled her heart beating hard a few seconds ago, but it was drumming against her rib cage now and the reason for that completely consumed her.

Cam was kissing her.

For about two seconds his lips had simply pressed against hers, as if to only stop hers from moving. But then *he* moved. Both his body—up against hers, his other hand going to her lower back and pressing her close—and his mouth, tipping slightly to make the contact more complete, and opening.

His mouth was hot and insistent. The hand that had held her chin, slid along her jaw and into her hair, cupping the back of her head. He tipped her head too, taking the kiss even deeper.

His tongue stroked over her bottom lip and she went on tiptoe to get closer to all of that while opening her mouth. He groaned, the hand on her lower back gripping her silky shirt now. The silky red shirt she'd paired with the dark gray skirt that he surely hated since it was one of her work skirts.

She gripped the front of his shirt similarly, pulling him closer or using it to pull herself closer to him—she wasn't sure. It didn't matter. She was as against him as she could get with the height difference and her heels still up in Didi's room. Damn, she should have left those on.

Then Cam helped her out. He turned her and, without breaking their lip-to-lip contact, boosted her up onto one of the high-backed chairs that faced the breakfast bar. He tried to step between her knees, but the skirt was too fitted for that.

"Hate these," he muttered. But his big hands dropped to her thighs and before she realized what he was doing, he'd slid the skirt up so she could part her knees. Which he also helped with.

He moved her knees apart as he stepped in and before she could so much as gasp, he took her face in both hands and put his mouth on hers again.

Now she was at the perfect height. She really had no choice but to kiss him back, sliding her arms around his neck and wiggling to the edge of the stool so she could get as close as possible. That made her skirt slide even higher until her silk panties were against the seat of the stool. And Cam's denim-covered erection was against the front of those panties.

They both groaned and Whitney swore her leg lifted itself to wrap around Cam's thigh. He felt so good. Right. There. She hadn't had anything so good right there in far too long.

"Whit," Cam said gruffly, dragging his mouth from her lips to her ear.

"Yes." She didn't know what she was saying yes to exactly. But she was pretty sure it didn't matter. Any idea he had tonight, in this room, seemed like it would be great. There was kissing and cake. As far as she was concerned, Cam was two for two in this kitchen tonight.

But he didn't really ask her a question. Maybe he'd been kind of asking permission though, because his hands dropped to the front of her blouse and started unbuttoning.

Great idea. Her hands went to the bottom of his t-shirt and pulled it up, putting her palms against the hot bare skin that covered his ribs.

He groaned against her ear as she explored the contours of

his abs. He pushed her blouse off her shoulders and she dropped her hands only long enough to let it slide to the floor.

Then he was kissing her neck and across the top of one shoulder. He cupped that opposite breast in one big hand and Whitney sucked in a quick breath. He kneaded the flesh through the silk cup and ran his thumb over her hardened nipple, while pulling the bra strap out of the way of his mouth. The strap slid down her arm, making the cup of her bra fall partially away from her breast.

He gave a low growl as he looked down, then teased her nipple with his fingers, plucking and rolling.

Hot shocks of sensation jolted through her and she tightened her knees, squeezing him.

"Oh, I like that," he told her roughly, pulling on her nipple again.

"*Cam.* Please."

"I've got you." He dipped his knees, putting his mouth to her nipple and sucking.

It was relief and torture at the same time. It eased the ache there but started a new one pulsing between her legs.

"*Cam!*" She was louder this time.

His tongue licked over her hard tip as his hand squeezed her hip. He kissed his way up her chest and over her shoulder to her neck where he sucked lightly before he dragged his mouth to hers again.

Her fingers bumped down his abs to the front of his jeans as he kissed her. His tongue slid along hers and she worked the button on his jeans loose, then the zipper. She had to touch him. She slipped her hand past the denim and cotton a second later, gliding along the hard, hot length of his cock.

His breath hissed out as he ripped his mouth from hers. He pressed into her hand even as his hot gaze collided with hers.

"Whit."

His voice was tight. He sounded like he didn't have enough air to even say the word.

"I've missed you," she said, wrapping her fingers around his shaft and squeezing.

"*Jesus*," he groaned.

He put his hands on her shoulders, tipped his head back and dragged in air. Then he dropped his hands to her wrists and pulled her hand from his body.

"Wha—" But she didn't need to finish the question. She saw it in his face. He'd changed his mind.

"We need to stop," he told her gruffly.

"No." She pulled out of his grasp and grabbed the bottom of his shirt attempting to pull him in again. If she could get her mouth on his *she* could keep *him* from talking.

For some reason she sensed that she should keep him from talking.

He wrapped a hand around her wrist and held her. "Yes. Stop."

He reached for the bra strap he'd slid from her shoulder and pulled it back into place.

"What? Why?" She demanded as he stepped back.

He wasn't out of reach, but his body language was saying clearly that he didn't want her to reach out.

"We need to just be friends."

14

Whitney blinked at him.

He waited for a few beats, giving her a chance to respond, she assumed. But then he said, "Whit? Just friends."

She nodded. "I heard you."

"So that's okay, right? That's good? What you want?"

She wet her lips, looked down at herself—her skirt hiked up, her blouse on the floor—then at him and the very obvious erection behind his open fly.

"No, not good," she said.

He blew out a breath and rezipped his pants. Then he tucked his hands into his back pockets. To keep from reaching for her maybe? "Why not?" he asked. "You were the one who was against the idea of us dating again."

She nodded. "I'm against *dating*, yes. But I can honestly say I would very much rather have sex in this kitchen than talk about my grandmother's Alzheimer's in this kitchen. If being friends means talking about that, or my family being a bunch of assholes, or how you think my personal and professional priorities are all screwed up then... no. Not really interested."

She pushed him back and slid to the floor, smoothing her

skirt down as she went. She bent to retrieve her blouse and slipped it on, buttoning only the two buttons between her breasts just to keep it closed until she could get upstairs.

She faced him again. "Also," she said as she ran a hand through her hair, knowing it was mussed from Cam's fingers, and really wishing his fingers were there again, "If you *don't* want to have sex with me, then no more kissing."

Cam winced slightly. "I did that to shut—stop you from talking."

Her eyebrows rose.

"You wouldn't stop, and raising my voice might have woken Didi up and putting my hand over your mouth seemed unnecessarily aggressive."

She rolled her eyes. "Yeah, yelling and hands over mouths are definitely aggressive."

"It was just an impulsive reaction."

She nodded and took a deep breath. Okay, so he hadn't been planning to kiss her. That was maybe good.

"So why *your* sudden change of heart on us dating?" Whitney asked.

"Because I saw your face on the video call the other morning."

She frowned. "What does that mean?"

"You're nervous about the project."

Her heart thumped hard in her chest and she took a moment to answer. He'd seen that in her face? Via *video call*?

She wet her lips. "I didn't hide that very well, huh?"

"But I don't think you're just worried about impressing us. You need to impress yourself."

She just nodded. There was no sense in arguing with him about that, considering he had read her expression correctly.

"I've never had a big project like this."

He nodded. "And it's important to you."

"Yes."

"So I'd say that means you need a friend more than you need a date."

She studied his face. Wow, that was sweet. Insightful. *Nice.* Finally she nodded. "You're right."

"And we've never been friends," he said. "We were nemeses because of our families. And classmates. Then boyfriend-girl-friend. Then..."

"Exes," she said with a shrug. She'd never considered him an *enemy* exactly, but they hadn't stayed friends after their breakup, either. And no, they hadn't really been friends before they'd started sneaking around.

"Yeah. Exes. So maybe we should try the friend thing. Hot Cakes needs you and I have a vested interest in things going well there. And you need help with Didi to make that project happen."

She nodded. Her throat was tight. This was nice. Almost a relief. Having someone realize that she was nervous without her having to confess it was nice. Having someone say, "let me help" was nice. Having it be someone who was making her grandmother happy was nice.

"Okay. Friends."

"And you have to stop putting work *between* us," he said. "We're on the same team. That's going to take us some getting used to, I know. But it's true. You're not doing *all* of this yourself. You're doing the stuff that the rest of us can't do. For now, the ball is in your court. When you've got your part done, then the rest of us will take our pieces and do our stuff."

That also sounded really nice. A team. She hadn't had that before.

"Okay," she agreed.

"And if you don't want Didi with my family then, say it. But don't make this about boss-employee-work bullshit."

She lifted a brow. "Okay. I don't want Didi with your family."

She wasn't sure she really meant that. But she was curious about his reaction to her saying it.

He gave her a nod. Then said, "Too bad."

"What?"

"Didi will be going to my mom's with me for dinner whenever you work late."

Whitney's eyes widened, then narrowed. "Is that just a ploy to get me to not work late or—?" She glanced at the cake. "Do you bake but not cook?"

He shrugged. "You can take it however you want."

That wasn't a no. Did Cam want her here for dinner some nights? And if so, why? The friend thing?

"But it's silly to cook when my mom is already doing it and wants us there," he added. "And Henry wants to see Didi again. And everyone loves hearing her stories, especially the ones about my grandma."

Whitney felt her heart flip again, but it was a softer feeling this time. "She might be in a mood one night and tell them *bad* stories, you know."

He smiled. "Maybe. But Letty told us plenty of bad stories about Didi. It's probably only fair that we hear a few from the other point of view."

"Your grandma told you bad stories about my grandma?"

"Of course. They were archenemies, remember?"

No one in Appleby could forget.

"It's actually even more likely that you'll hear the same stories over and over," Whitney said. "She probably won't remember what she's already told you."

He shrugged. "We don't mind. Letty did that too."

There was a sadness mixed with affection in his expression.

"You miss her," Whitney said.

"A lot," he agreed with a nod. "I came home to visit, but the last few years I wasn't around as much and I missed out on a lot."

"And Didi makes everyone happy because she reminds them of Letty?"

"Yeah. And Letty never played *Warriors* with Henry so he thinks Didi is especially awesome."

"Didi *is* especially awesome," Whitney said softly.

It was nice to think that her grandmother could fill in some gaps for a family who had just lost someone they loved. And she suspected Didi liked Henry a lot. Her own grandsons would have never thought to have her play video games with them. Whitney would have, but not her brothers. Maybe Henry would let Didi read some of her and Whitney's favorite books to him. He was eleven, but if he was missing his grandma, cuddling up with Didi for a story or two might be exactly what he needed.

But she wasn't going to let Cam off the hook quite that easily.

"So when you said that if I didn't want her spending time with your family to just say so... you didn't mean that it would matter. But I could feel free to say it."

He smiled. "Exactly. You can always tell me how you really feel or think about something, even if it's something that's my idea."

"But you won't listen," she pointed out.

"I'll *listen*," he said. "But that doesn't mean I'll always agree with you."

She sighed. "Ditto."

He nodded. "I know. But *friends* can be honest with each other."

"Okay. Well, *honestly*, this is all really weird. All of it." From them kissing to Henry and Didi becoming buddies.

"Yeah," Cam acknowledged. "But if the way things were before was 'normal' I think I'm in favor of weird."

He might have a point. It did feel better to think their families could get along rather than thinking she and Cam needed to keep the three-generation-old family feud going.

She sighed. "So you totally know what you're doing?"

"No. Do you?" he countered.

"No," she admitted.

Not with work. She'd never led a project before. And not with Didi. Alzheimer's was a strange disease. There were commonalities among patients, of course, but no two people were alike. Whitney didn't know for certain if she was doing something right or wrong when she let Didi drink margaritas in the middle of the night or when she said okay to Didi hanging out with the McCafferys. Or anything else, honestly.

"The main thing I've learned about having a group of friends who really care about me and my happiness is that if I fuck something up, I've got people who can help fix it," Cam said. He paused, watching her. "Have you ever felt like you could screw something up and it would still be okay?"

Whitney shook her head slowly without even thinking about it. She had definitely never felt that way. Not with her friends in high school. Not with the acquaintances she had now. Not with her family.

"So that's what you need most," he said. His voice was a little gruff, but he seemed determined. "You need real friends. You need to have people who have your back."

Whitney actually felt her eyes stinging slightly. That sounded amazing. She'd been watching these men together for the past couple of months and completely envying their relationships. She envied how comfortable Piper was with them as well. It was clear that even when they disagreed, they cared about one another. And when it came to Hot Cakes, they were all working toward the same goal and trusted and respected one another.

She wanted that.

All of it.

A lot.

Cam was right. Maybe it was because he knew her. Maybe it was because he was really paying attention. Maybe it was because she was not good at hiding her feelings and vulnerabilities after all. But, yes, she wanted all of that. Trust and respect and a team and friends.

"It's pretty pathetic that I don't have any friends at age twenty-nine, isn't it?" she asked softly. "And it should feel uncomfortable to admit to you that I didn't have a good relationship with my dad and grandpa and brothers."

Cam's jaw tightened and his eyes flickered with emotion. "Does it?" he asked, his voice rough.

Did it feel uncomfortable or pathetic? Strangely, no.

"Not really."

He gave a single nod. "Good."

"I understand why you want me to feel comfortable at work," she said. "That benefits Hot Cakes, and you. But why do you care if I have friends?"

He pulled in a breath and wet his lips. "Because I want to be the one who gives you what you need."

His words were husky and they hit her in the gut. Heat spread and she sucked in a breath. That sounded very protective. Almost possessive. Yet, comforting at the same time.

"Really?" she asked. "You think I need this?"

He met her eyes directly. "Yes."

"You could feel smug about that," she said. "You could be happy that I've been pretty lonely and unhappy all this time."

Again, his jaw ticked. "I guess. But I don't. Not a bit. It makes me crazy knowing that you haven't had what you wanted and needed."

She stared at him. Wow. This was all so unexpected. Everything about Cam being back had been unexpected. From the chemistry still between them to how he'd just rolled with everything going on with Didi to... this.

"You wanted me to be happy without you?" she asked, her voice a little husky now too.

"No." He blew out a breath. "I don't know. No, I didn't want you to be happy without me, exactly, but it makes me nuts that you've been alone and feeling... not good enough and not valued and not fulfilled. It's... confusing as fuck."

She laughed softly. "Actually, I get it," she said, realizing that she really did.

"Yeah?"

"I've been really happy that *you* have been so successful. I watched your football career and, of course, everything that's happened with Fluke and I've been proud and happy about how that all turned out. Even though I really missed you and it made me sad to be without you."

His eyes flashed at that and Whitney had the definite impression that he wanted to reach out and pull her in close.

"And," she went on. "When I watch you with the guys, and with Piper, I'm so, so happy that you have them. Even while I'm jealous of how well they know you and all the memories they have with you."

She saw him ball his hand into a fist, as if fighting that urge to reach out.

"So," she said. "I get what you're feeling a little, I think. I care about you enough to want you to be happy but I also care enough to be a little sad that I'm not a part of it."

He nodded. "I definitely hate that you haven't been happy. And I definitely want to be a part of making you happy. And I'm pretty thrilled that what you need is friends, because I have some of the best and I'm happy to share. That is, at least, something I can give you."

She smiled even as her throat tightened. Being friends with him and him realizing how important this Hot Cakes project was to her was amazing. She didn't have to worry about hurting him or choosing work over him and ruining everything.

And the intense desire to step forward and wrap her arms around him and beg him to cover her in chocolate sauce was just a product of that relief and gratitude.

Probably.

"For the record, it's also nice to have a friend helping with Didi. I'm kind of winging it there too."

He smiled. "When I first came back to town, if someone had told me this"—he looked around the kitchen—"is where you and I would be, I never would have believed them."

She nodded. "I know." It seemed crazy on the surface that the person who knew about Didi and was helping her with the caregiving was Camden McCaffery. Yet... it didn't feel crazy. "And I—" She took a breath. "I trust you. If you think her playing video games with Henry is good, then... it's good. I don't know what I'm doing." Whitney shrugged. "My philosophy is pretty simple—when I'm her age and I know I'm running out of time to remember the fun and the people that matter, then I'm going to do what I want, when I want. If I want burgers at three a.m. with my granddaughter or margaritas by the pool at nine a.m. with my granddaughter's ex-boyfriend, then, yeah, I'm going to do that. And pray I've got people around me who will let me, while keeping me safe."

Cam just looked at her for a few beats. Then he nodded. "So you *do* know what you're doing."

That surprised her. She laughed lightly. "I don't think so."

"You're making her happy and doing it out of love. That's what you should be doing."

Whitney stared at him.

"You okay?" he asked.

"Just... thank you."

"I mean it."

"I believe you. It means a lot from you."

"Because I've been an ass to you for ten years over other decisions you've made?"

She snorted. "Something like that."

He tipped his head in acknowledgment. "Well, it's come to my attention that I was angry at someone who... isn't real."

She felt her eyes widen.

"I thought I knew you, Whit. But I'm learning that I don't. I knew the eighteen-year-old you. And I'm not sure I even knew her that well."

He was right, of course. It had been a long time since they'd known each other and how well did two eighteen-year-olds really know one another? Or themselves for that matter? Especially when at least half of their time had been spent making out. They'd had to sneak around because of their families' animosity toward one another, so she'd never seen him with his grandmother or gone to the movies with him or... anything else. Their time together had always been alone and it had been stolen, hidden time.

"You have a point," she said. "We're just getting to know each other. Like new acquaintances."

"Well..." He gave her a slow smile. "We know *a few* things about each other. I mean... I do know that you're ticklish behind your left knee and that tequila and Jason Aldean songs make you horny and you love when I kiss your—"

She stepped forward, slapping her hand over his mouth.

He lifted a brow and she felt his mouth curve behind her palm.

"If I was taller, I would have kissed you to shut you up too because, yeah, the hand over the mouth is a little aggressive."

He nodded.

She let her hand drop away. "But yeah, you need to shut up. That's not stuff *friends* talk about." The heat was still swirling through her body and she could hear Jason Aldean's "Crazy Town" playing in her head.

He held up a hand. "You're right. Sorry."

She nodded. "Okay. So... friends."

"Friends."

She glanced at the cake pan on the counter. "And you didn't make those bars to use the way you'd suggested using the cookie dough the other night then?"

He cleared his throat. "Um, no. They're for Didi actually."

"You made my grandmother bars?"

"Letty's recipe. Something she never made for the bakery. Only family and close friends ever got those bars. Didi mentioned to me that she missed Letty's baking and cooking all these years. Thought she'd enjoy tasting some of it again."

Wow. That was pretty sweet. Nice even.

"What?" he asked when she didn't react.

"You're doing all of this, with my grandma and the bars and the support at work, and you're actually insisting that we *not* sleep together."

He cleared his throat again. "Right."

"Huh." She believed him. And that actually did make her relax a little. "Well, save me a bar? To eat."

"Sure."

She gave him a smile and turned to head upstairs.

"Hey, Whit?"

She turned back. "Yeah?"

"Just out of curiosity... if I *had* made the bars for that purpose..."

She grinned and her eyes went to the stool where she'd been very happily shirtless and *he'd* been the one to pull back. "Totally would have worked."

He grinned. "Good to know."

And even though they were talking about putting chocolate cookie dough on nipples, she felt a warm surge of happiness. Friendliness even.

Friends. Just friends. With Camden McCaffery.

Well, stranger things had happened.

Probably.

15

She was so fucking gorgeous.

Cam had always enjoyed the morning meetings of Fluke, Inc., but he'd never been hard and aching in the middle of one.

He was sure his friends and partners would be glad to know that.

But he was stunned by what a turn on it was to watch Whitney during the meeting a week later.

She was freaking glowing.

He knew he was staring at her like a lovesick idiot. He also knew that Aiden, Dax, and Grant had noticed. They kept casting glances in his direction. He felt their eyes on him. But he wasn't looking at them.

He was looking at Whitney. The way her eyes were sparkling, the faint flush to her cheeks, the smile that was so easy and genuine. He was even appreciating the way she looked in the boring-as-hell navy-blue pencil skirt and ivory blouse she wore. Hot. She looked hot. He still hated those skirts, but today the damned thing made her look hot. Of course, she could have been wearing a sack and he would have thought she looked hot, because it wasn't about the skirt. It was about how she was standing there, excited, confident, and she hadn't once lifted her chin in the way she did when she was gathering her fake confidence and meeting his eyes directly even though she didn't want to.

Today she was meeting his eyes directly. She was meeting everyone's eyes directly.

And the way she looked in that pencil skirt wasn't about the skirt at all. It never had been. He'd hated those skirts because she'd worn them to make herself feel like the corporate executive that she wanted to be.

Today she *was* that corporate executive. With or without that skirt.

Cam shifted on his chair as he thought about how much he'd love to see that skirt crumpled on the floor of her office next to her desk—while he checked out what kind of panties she wore underneath those stupid skirts.

Which was a completely inappropriate way for him to be thinking of his *coworker* and *friend*.

"Our focus group thinks this has huge potential," she was saying. "It's also a focus on younger customers. Kids are already a part of our demographic, of course, but we've never focused on them before."

"But they're still squares," Ollie pointed out.

"Yes," Whitney agreed. "But doing it this way won't require a massive overhaul to our equipment." She hit a button on her laptop to display the next slide. "Your suggestion to make them in the shape of alpacas got me thinking," she told Ollie. "But this way will be not only more cost effective for us, but will make more sense," she added with a smile. She pointed to the images on the screen. "Each bar will have an animal *footprint* stamped into it. It will look a lot like the footprint would look if a kid saw it out in nature, in the dirt or mud."

"So instead of poop, people will think of mud when they see these bars," Dax said with a grin. "Great."

Whitney laughed. "I'm not worried. The focus group didn't bring that up at all." She turned back to the presentation. "We'll start with five different animal footprints. They will all be wild animals native to Iowa. White-tailed deer, fox, jackrabbit, coyote, and a beaver."

"No alpacas?" Ollie asked.

"Alpacas aren't native to Iowa. Kids aren't likely to see those in nature around here," Whitney told him."

Ollie frowned. "Shouldn't we do interesting animals?"

"I think fox and coyotes are interesting," Cam said, giving Ollie a knock-it-off look.

Ollie rolled his eyes.

"We can add to the collection," Whitney said. "If it takes off. The idea is that kids will want to collect all the footprints, so they'll keep going back to the store for more Critter Tracks."

"But they'll be eating the footprints," Ollie said. "Right?" He looked around. "We don't want them sticking these things under their beds, do we?"

"They each come with a collectible card," Whitney said, clicking to the next slide. "The card has a colorful photo of the track as well as a photo and facts about the animal it belongs to."

Ollie's eyebrow went up. Cam grinned. Just like that, his friend was in.

Dax sat forward. "You know, it would be easy to set up a website to go along with this. Kids could get codes from the collectible cards. They could go to the site to learn more. We could have a little virtual world where they could follow the animals around, learn about their natural habitats, that kind of thing."

Cam's grin grew. Dax was in now too.

He caught Whitney's eye. She clearly realized it too. She was positively glowing.

"Maybe the kids could become one of the animals," Ollie added. "And interact in the world that way."

Dax was nodding.

"This is a lot more than anything Hot Cakes has ever done before," Grant said to no one in particular.

But Whitney nodded. "It's a way for us to go above and beyond with our customer base. Be more than just a factory." She smiled at Ollie and Dax. "To tap into the talents we have here rather than just sitting in offices and looking at spreadsheets."

Her eyes widened and she looked at Grant quickly.

"Not that there's anything wrong with paying attention to the spreadsheets and bottom line. That's important too. Of course."

Cam coughed and lifted his coffee cup to hide his smile.

Aiden didn't even try to hide his. "No offense taken," he said. "Everyone here understands that profitability will be an important factor. But it's not the only factor. Especially when we're talking about branching out and growing the brand."

Whitney nodded, but she was still watching Grant for his agreement.

Grant just looked at Whitney for a long moment. Cam could see that Whitney was holding her breath. Cam was too. He knew that Grant and Aiden's approval mattered to her. Ollie's and Dax's did too, but frankly theirs was easier to get. They were always up for something new and different. It was Grant and Aiden she'd have to convince the new idea was worth the money and investment of resources. And risk.

Finally Grant nodded. "I like it."

Whitney let her breath out and her smile grew. "And..." She clicked to the next slide. "If things go well, we could reach out to groups that do animal education to see if they would want to include our treats as a part of their program. Zoos, of course. And the Department of Natural Resources does some educational programs. We could even do some specialized things. Maybe, for a group that does a lot with, say, penguins. We could do treats with penguin footprints."

Cam looked at Ollie. Ollie's eyes were bright and Cam could see his friend's wheels turning.

"Fundraising," Ollie said. "We could offer a portion of the proceeds to a program for penguin preservation or something."

Whitney's eyes brightened as well and she turned more fully toward Ollie. "*Yes.* There must be an awareness day for penguins. There are awareness days for everything. We could do something to coincide with that."

"We could have various habitats on the website," Dax said. "They could click a tab to interact with animals in the prairies and then another tab to interact with penguins and polar bears."

"But penguins and polar bears don't actually live together, right?" Ollie said. "They're commonly put together in commercials and things, but they live on opposite poles."

Dax frowned at him. "Are you sure?"

"I'm pretty sure."

"But... the snow."

"Polar bears live in the arctic and penguins live in the Antarctic," Piper said, breezing into the room with a new carafe of coffee.

"Oh." Dax seemed disappointed.

"You could still do different habitats," Piper said, patting his arm. "Just have to put them on two different tabs."

"I guess that's true."

"Maybe Drew would want to do alpaca treats," Piper said, leaning over Ollie's shoulder to refill his cup.

Ollie's bright expression pulled into a frown. "Why would

the alpaca farmer want treats? Nobody goes out there. Except you."

Piper gave him a big smile as she moved to Cam. He held his cup up for her to fill.

"He and his brothers are talking about opening up the farm to some tours for kids. Day cares and preschools and things like that. Making it a full-time petting zoo so that kids can learn about the animals up close and personal. I was going to talk with him about teaching the kids about some of these wild animals too. Maybe looking around their property for jackrabbit and fox tracks. Drew and his brothers are real outdoorsy types."

Typically Cam would have exchanged a what's-going-on look with Aiden or Grant as Piper poked at Ollie—a not outdoorsy type at all. But he found himself looking at Whitney instead. She was watching him too. She gave him an arched eyebrow and he shrugged. But he also grinned. He liked sharing that little nonverbal communication with her.

Ollie scowled. "Kids will like Dax's animals better, I guarantee."

"I'm sure Dax can make it a lot of fun, but learning about *real* animals in the *real world* could be good." Piper's smile had faded. "You spend a lot of time in virtual worlds. Maybe some time in the real world where you don't get to call *all* the shots would be good."

Ollie swiveled in his chair and pinned her with a stare. "I call *all* the shots?"

She propped a hand on her hip. "You try to."

"And then you go ahead and do whatever you want to anyway."

"You mean, I fix the things that won't work your way or that you mess up by forgetting that the real world doesn't follow your rules all the time like Easton does," she said, referring to the magical land in their video game.

"Piper," Ollie said, his voice low and firm and far more serious than any of them were used to hearing. "Enough."

Piper didn't look intimidated. Or impressed. She looked pissed.

Cam felt his brows lift. Dax sat up straighter. Grant leaned forward in his chair. Aiden actually got to his feet.

"Okay. Let's get back to Whitney and the presentation," Aiden said in his best knock-it-the-fuck-off voice. "Piper," he added, his tone gentler. "We can talk later."

She stared at Ollie as she took a breath, then she looked at Aiden. "I'm fine. Everything is fine."

Yeah, even Cam knew that when a woman said she was fine the way Piper had just said she was fine, she was most definitely *not* fine.

Whitney spoke up. "Piper."

Their executive assistant looked at her.

"*We* can talk later," Whitney said.

Piper nodded. "Great."

Aiden looked at Cam. Cam grinned at his friend. Then they both looked at Grant. Who also smiled. Then they all looked at Ollie. Who was frowning. But not in a confused, what's-going-on way, rather in a oh-shit-this-isn't-good way.

On the contrary, Cam thought this was actually very good.

Piper had been putting up with the Fluke guys and the stupid levels of testosterone in their conference rooms for years now. It was time for there to be more estrogen balancing things out.

Piper and Whitney could be good for one another.

He loved everything about this.

"Whitney," Aiden said. "Is there anything else we should know at this point about the new product?"

She shook her head. "I'll send an email summarizing everything. If you're all okay with where we're at, I'll move ahead with getting the stamping equipment and talking to our accounts about the new bars."

"Great," Aiden said. He glanced around the table. "Anyone have anything?"

"Good to move forward in my mind," Grant said. He met Whitney's eyes. "Great job. You've pulled this together quickly and you've got all the I's dotted."

It had only been two weeks since she'd first presented about how they needed to change up their machines and think about hiring more staff. It really had been fast. Then again, she'd been working until ten almost every night.

Cam shook that off. It was fine. It was what she needed to do and he'd said he was in full support of it.

Whitney smiled at Grant, clearly pleased. "Thank you."

"I fucking love it," Dax told her, shoving his chair back and standing. "I'm going to do some website brainstorming this afternoon."

"Don't you have a meeting with the Alzheimer's Association people today?" Whitney asked with a frown.

"He does," Piper confirmed. She turned to Dax. "They'll be in your office at one."

His office at Sunny Orchard, not here at Hot Cakes.

"Right," he muttered.

Whitney chewed on her bottom lip and Cam felt his shoulders tightening as he watched her worry.

"He'll be able to do both," Aiden assured her, pushing the papers in front of him into a stack and then rising. "Honestly, Dax is best when he's got a million things going on in his head."

She nodded. "Okay."

Aiden paused and reached out, squeezing her shoulder. "Seriously. Piper will be sure he stays on track. Sunny Orchard is a priority."

Cam didn't say anything, but he felt himself frowning. Sunny Orchard and the Alzheimer's programming better fucking be a priority for Dax. Aiden was right. Dax was a master multitasker and really did do best when he was juggling several balls. Cam had never been concerned about his partners getting their stuff done, and done well, before. One of the reasons Fluke worked well was because the guys all did their thing and trusted the others to do theirs.

For the first time, Cam was going to follow up with one of his partners on something that wasn't a legal matter and something that he didn't really know much about at all. Just to be sure Dax was doing it. Hell, Dax wasn't even a partner in Hot Cakes. If he did the website stuff for their new product, he'd be doing it as an outside consultant.

But yeah, Cam was going to check in. He never did that.

"Hey, guys, hang out for a minute," Cam said, coming to his feet.

Dax paused on his way to the door, looking back.

Grant kept his seat and Aiden dropped his hand from Whitney's shoulder and faced Cam.

"Everything okay?" his friend asked.

"Sure." He was going to make *sure* everything was okay. "Just need to follow up on a couple of things," Cam said. His eyes went to Whitney. "Thanks for the presentation."

She looked flustered suddenly, but she nodded.

He didn't like her flustered, but right now he needed to deal with the guys.

"Of course," she said as she gathered her things. She shut her computer and stacked her folder and notebook on top. She lifted them, wrapping her arms around it all. Then she took a breath and looked at him again. "I'll... talk to you... later."

"At home," he confirmed.

He liked how that sounded. He also liked how it made her cheeks get pinker. Surely she knew that everyone in the room was aware of where he was sleeping. And why. But yeah, it sounded intimate and he liked it. He liked the idea of going home to her, with her, at the end of a workday.

"I'll go check on Didi," Whitney said.

Cam wasn't sure if she said it to inform him of where she would be when he was done meeting with his partners, or, possibly to remind him that Didi was waiting for *him*.

He nodded. "I'm sure she's happy with Max. They were drinking cappuccino and watching the Game Show Network when I left them."

By now they were probably playing Ping-Pong on one of the tables Dax had brought in when he'd self-appointed himself in charge of employee morale. Before he'd sold his shares in Hot Cakes. They'd kept the break room with all of Dax's touches though. He really did know how to make a place one-hundred times more fun.

"I'll go get her when I'm done here," he told her. "I'll take her home and see you later."

Whitney lifted her chin. In that fucking way she did when she was gathering her resolve.

"Stop by my office before you go get her," Whitney said.

He gave her a nod. "Okay."

She nodded in return, then gave the rest of the men a smile. But this smile was forced. Cam felt his eyes narrow.

"I'll see you all later," she said. "Thank you for your time this morning."

Then she stepped around the edge of the conference table and left the room. Her chin still up.

"What the hell was that?" Aiden asked as the door shut behind her and Piper.

Cam turned and realized Aiden was speaking to him. "What do you mean?"

"You were pretty cool with Whitney there at the end. Basically dismissing her like that."

Cam lifted a brow. "I didn't dismiss her."

"You did," Grant said, sitting back in his chair and smoothing his tie. "You said you needed to speak to us, making it clear that you didn't want her to stay."

Cam opened his mouth, then shut it. Well, fuck. "I didn't want her to stay," he said after a second.

"Why not?" Aiden took his seat again.

"Because I wanted to talk to you all. About her."

Aiden gave Grant a look.

"Knock it off," Cam snapped, scowling at them.

"What?" Aiden asked.

"Looking at each other like you know what's going on in my head."

"Okay," Grant said, in the very annoying I-already-know-what-you're-going-to-say tone he used. Often.

Which was a lot like the look that said he knew what was going on in Cam's head.

"Why don't you tell us what's going on in your head?" Grant asked.

Fine. He wasn't going to waste time and breath telling Grant he was being a condescending ass. Grant was doing it on purpose. And Cam needed to get down to Didi and get her home so they could get to yoga on time.

"You need to stop being stoic when Whitney's talking to you about ideas," Cam said to Grant.

"I don't know what you mean."

"You do. You do it to all of us all the time," Cam said. He planted his hands on his hips. "You sit there, your face completely devoid of emotion or reaction so that none of us know what you're thinking until you're good and ready to let us know. The thing is, it doesn't matter with us. We know that's how you are. But Whitney... she..." He sighed. "She wants your approval. She wants you to like her ideas. You can't just sit there like... you."

Grant lifted a brow. "I told her I liked the idea."

"After you made her sweat. I don't like that. You have to let her see you engaging with her ideas." He shook his head. "She had dealt with enough of that bullshit where people she cared about withheld their thoughts and feelings and left her out. She's not going to get that here from us."

Grant gave him an indecipherable look, but, to Cam's surprise, nodded. "I hear you. I'll work on that."

Cam straightened. "You will?"

"Yeah. I know what you mean. I know how I feel when Jocelyn is proud of her work. I'll do better with Whitney."

Cam wasn't sure what to say. "Okay. Thanks."

"My pleasure."

"What about with us?" Ollie asked Grant. "Will you be nicer to us when we bring you new ideas too?"

Grant shook his head. "I doubt it."

Ollie just sighed.

Cam looked at Dax. "And you—"

"What I'd do?"

"You better fucking pay attention to what's happening at Sunny Orchard," Cam said.

"Wow," Dax said. "Relax."

"I'm not going to *relax*," Cam told him. "This is important."

"You're overreacting. I know that Whitney isn't just some employee, but you don't have to come to her defense here. There's no enemy here."

"That's not what I'm doing," Cam said. Defensively.

"You glared at me twice for *coughing* during her presentation," Dax said. "Like you were pissed I was interrupting her or something."

"I was pissed you were making it hard for everyone else to hear. And that you might miss what she was saying," Cam said.

Dax nodded. "That's not an overreaction at all."

Cam shook his head. "You can't be spacing out in your office, thinking about little video foxes and rabbits running around instead of getting that Alzheimer's program going, Dax. That's a big deal."

Dax looked genuinely surprised. "I wouldn't space out *that* far. Of course that's a big deal."

"You forgot you even had that meeting today," Cam pointed out.

"For two seconds," Dax protested. "I've got it. I can do both things."

"He's *best* when he's not focused on just one thing," Ollie defended Dax. "He's great at juggling lots of balls."

Dax gave his friend a grateful smile. "Thanks. I make a point of taking care of my balls."

"And you don't get worked up about how we all do stuff," Ollie said to Cam. "What the hell? We all do our shit, our way, get it done. You don't have to babysit us."

"Yeah, well, Dax's balls had never been this important to me before." Cam winced as he said that out loud. He scowled as Ollie grinned. "I mean it. Now that Dax brought up the website, now Whitney's thinking about it too. So now he needs to pull that off. But the programs at the nursing home matter because of Didi. So now he has to do it all. Well. *Very* well." He frowned at Dax. "You drop any of those balls and you'll have to answer to me."

Dax didn't look impressed, but he held up his hands. "It's all good. I care about those things too, you know."

Cam believed that he did. Just not as much as Cam did. Or as much as Whitney did.

"And you need to get your shit together too," Cam said, pointing at Ollie.

"Me? I'm easily Whitney's favorite person here."

Cam felt a very stupid, very juvenile surge of jealousy at that. He shook his head. "No. You're not."

"Well, I'm her favorite when it comes to business ideas," Ollie said, with a shit-eating grin. "I'm always up for anything. *I* never tell her no."

Cam debated just letting that go. He knew he should definitely let that go. "What are you talking about?" he asked instead.

"I'm just saying, I don't know how you do it," Ollie said with a shrug, sitting back in his chair and propping one ankle on his opposite knee.

"Do what?" Cam asked.

"Say no to that girl. She's gorgeous when she gets excited about work ideas. I can only imagine how she looks when she's... just excited."

Cam gritted his teeth. Ollie was messing with him. Oliver wasn't usually the one to give the rest of them crap like that. That line right there was more of a Dax line. Or, honestly, a Cam line. He'd very much enjoyed saying stuff like that to Grant in the time between Grant meeting Josie and realizing that he was just going to fall in love with her and there wasn't anything he could do about it.

"How do you know I say no to her?" Cam asked.

"You have definitely not said *yes* to her," Ollie said. "Not *yes* yes anyway."

Cam narrowed his eyes. "What the fuck does that mean?"

"That." Ollie pointed at Cam. "You're too wound up to have said *yes* to Whitney. Though I don't know how you're helping it."

Cam took a breath. Okay, Ollie was assuming he and Whitney hadn't slept together because *Cam* needed to get laid. That was fair. Kind of. "Maybe *she's* said no to *me*."

She had. Basically. Once. But he'd been the one to pull back from their kiss the other night. The kiss where her skirt had been hiked up and her shirt had been on the floor and her breast had been in his hand...

Ollie shook his head. "She doesn't look at you like she said no to you."

"She doesn't?" Dammit. He didn't need to act interested in that.

Dax was the one to answer that though. "Definitely not. She looks at you like *you* said no to *her*." He tipped his head to the side. "Like maybe you started something you didn't finish?"

"You can *not* read all of that from me," Cam said. Dammit. These guys knew him well, but there was no way they knew him that well.

"Jane looks at me like that," Dax said. "When I start something in my office just before we have to go somewhere. The whole rest of the time we're with other people she gives me these looks that are part I-want-to-smother-you-with-a-pillow and part I-want-to-tear-your-clothes-off." He grinned. "It's worth doin' once in a while just because the anticipation makes it so great later."

Awesome. Now Cam was going to get to think about *that* for the rest of the day. Was Whitney thinking about their kiss? Had she realized she was grateful he'd pulled back or was she thinking about repeating it sometime? Picking up where they'd left off?

She'd made a lot of progress on the project. Surely, she was feeling more secure here. Surely, she was feeling more comfortable and a part of the team and confident in her ability to pull this all off. He'd given her space and time to get the work done as well as all the resources she needed. Piper had even been assigned to be her right-hand person for the duration of the project. She'd been given full latitude to do whatever needed done with staffing and the machinery and the supplies. She was fully in charge.

And she was rising to every bit of the challenge.

But maybe, once this was wrapped up and she'd realized she belonged here, she was valued here, and could pull all of this off—she'd relax and would be able to think about something else.

Cam shook his head. "Stop distracting me. Whitney is fully focused on this project. As she should be. We should all be thrilled about that. As you noticed from the presentation today," he said, looking at each of them pointedly. "She's doing an amazing job. She's completely pulling this off. She doesn't have time to be messing around."

Ollie nodded. "So you're *not* messing around. That's why you're so grumpy."

"I'm *grumpy*," Cam said, "because you need to stop giving Piper a hard time."

Ollie scowled. "Me and Piper are fine."

"Look, man, I don't know what's going on there but if Whitney wants to put alpaca prints on those damned bars, then we're going to do that. Even if it means that you have to think about Drew Ryan's handsome face every time you see one of them," Cam told him.

Ollie blew out a breath. "Whatever. I don't give a fuck about Drew Ryan."

Yeah. That was definitely *not* true.

"Whitney is doing a great job," Aiden said. "And we get that you're one hundred percent in her corner."

"We should *all* be one hundred percent in her corner," Cam said.

"Yeah, well, maybe not the way you are," Aiden told him.

"What does that mean?"

"You were watching her during the presentation like you were proud and awed and imagining bending her over the conference table all at once," Aiden replied bluntly.

Cam opened his mouth, but no words came out.

"I know how it feels to watch a woman and think all of that..." Aiden trailed off and cleared his throat.

Yeah, the woman he was talking about was Cam's *sister*. They didn't really need to delve into that too deeply. "Great," Cam said. "I appreciate your commiseration."

"It's just that I get how you can get knotted up when you want her to be successful, but she needs to figure it out on her own," Aiden said. "Just... lighten up. We're on your side. Her side too."

Cam took a deep breath.

Okay, yeah, he was being hard on these guys. His friends realized that Whitney was important here and they were treating her with respect and including her in these decisions. Hell, they were letting her lead the way.

"Fine," he relented. "Just... pay attention and do your shit. And... be nice."

They all grinned.

Yeah, okay, *they* were usually the ones telling *Cam* to be nice.

Everything was different now. Because of Whitney.

16

C am knocked on Whitney's office door five minutes later.

"Come in."

She was standing behind her desk, her arms crossed.

He shut the door behind him. "You wanted to talk?"

"If there's something about the new product idea that you don't like, you can tell me to my face."

That wasn't what he'd been expected at all. "I like everything about the new product idea."

"Then why didn't you say *one* word about it during the meeting and then kick me out of the conference room to talk to the guys about it without me?"

Cam crossed the room, coming to stand opposite her across her wide desk. "That's not what happened."

"You kicked me out of the conference room to talk to the guys about something," she said.

"I didn't mean for that to come off as me kicking you out."

She rolled her eyes and dropped her arms. "Seriously? How did you think it would come off?"

Okay, that was fair. "Sorry," he said honestly. "I was..."

Did he want her to know that he'd been coming to her defense with his friends?

"You were...?"

Fuck. Honesty. That's what he and Whitney needed a lot of. Open communication. "I was telling them how I expect them to treat you."

She opened her mouth, but seemed to process his words and shut it again, simply frowning.

"I didn't like how Grant wasn't giving you immediate feedback and how Dax was getting distracted with the website idea."

"You can't do that."

"Yes, I can."

She blew out a breath. "I need to handle all of that on my own, Cam. Grant doesn't need to treat me any differently than he does anyone else. Dax is just Dax and—"

"And while we're talking about how people are acting, you have to stop giving them passes," Cam interrupted.

She looked surprised. "Excuse me?"

"If Grant isn't communicating his thoughts about a project, you need to *ask* him for input and feedback. Don't let him just sit there with that infuriating nonexpression on his face."

She lifted her chin. "I will deal with—"

Cam was around the corner of her desk, his thumb on her chin before she even finished the word *with*. He pressed on the center of her chin, tipping it back down.

"Don't," he said softly.

Her eyes were wide as she stared up at him. "Don't what?"

"Don't lift your chin with me, Whit."

"What?"

"This." He pressed gently again. "You lift your chin whenever you're getting pissed but are trying not to yell at me. You don't have to act tough. You don't have to gather your... fortitude. Or whatever that is." He ran the pad of his thumb back and forth over the soft skin under her bottom lip. "Just talk. Tell me off. Tell me what you're really thinking."

She wet her bottom lip with the tip of her tongue and his gaze followed the movement.

"You find the way Grant sits there and doesn't say anything infuriating?" she asked.

Cam met her eyes again. "Not until today. When he did it to you."

The corner of her mouth twitched. "I don't find it infuriating."

"No?"

She shook her head slightly, causing his thumb to slide over her chin again. "No. He's just taking it all in. I know he'll tell me what he thinks eventually."

Cam thought about that. So it was all *his* problem. That didn't surprise him, actually. "Guess I'm feeling a little protective of you."

That corner of her mouth fully curled now. "You don't need to."

"I do. Those guys are used to working together only. And with Piper. They don't know how to be gentlemen with a woman who doesn't know them and their quirks and how to read them. I want you to know that they all think you're amazing and they're completely impressed with you and what you're doing."

Something in her expression softened and she fully smiled. "And all this time I expected *you* to be the one that wasn't a gentleman when we worked together."

He nodded. "I expected that too. I guess..." He swallowed. "I didn't expect soft feelings. I expected fighting and fireworks. Especially when it came to this company." He felt himself smile. "Who would have guessed that the thing I'd want most would be for you to be successful and happy at Hot Cakes?"

She gave a soft, surprised laugh. "Crazy."

"Yeah." His voice was gruff and his eyes were on her lips again.

"What did you think of the new ideas?" she asked.

He looked up. "I love it. All of it."

"Really?"

"Of course."

"You didn't say that. You didn't say *anything*."

"I knew you wanted to hear from Aiden and Grant," he said.

A slight frown pulled her eyebrows together. "I did. But I certainly wanted to hear it from you too."

"But..." He shrugged. "You know I think you're amazing."

She stared at him. Slowly she shook her head. "No. I don't." She leaned in slightly. "I don't even know if you want to kiss me anymore."

"Liar," he chided softly. "You know very well that I want to kiss you."

"You're the one who said we don't know each other anymore. I don't assume anything about how you're feeling or what you're thinking," she said. Now her gaze dropped to his mouth.

Damn. He really had assumed they'd be arguing a lot more. Fighting. Hashing the past out. Maybe angry fucking in the kitchen. Instead, every time he was with her he felt soft. Protective. Proud. Amazed. Happy.

"You're right," he said, moving his thumb from her chin to her bottom lip and stroking back and forth. "We both need to be *very* clear about what we're thinking and feeling. And wanting. And needing."

The tip of her tongue darted out to wet her lip, but touching his thumb in the process. He felt the jolt to the soles of his feet.

"You first," she said.

"Okay." He looked into her eyes. "I think you are completely different from the girl I was in love with in high school. That girl was confident and daring and knew who she was and where she fit."

She sucked in a little breath and almost pulled back, but Cam caught her upper arm, holding her in place.

"Now you're a grown woman who's a little broken, a little hurt, but even if she's not sure where she fits, she knows what she wants and is willing to work her *ass* off for it. You're creative and sweet and a little too humble and you've never been more beautiful. Seeing you keep trying, keep working, keep *wanting* in spite of years of being taken for granted and overlooked kills me and inspires me and makes me want you so much more than I ever did when you were sure of yourself."

He saw the shock in her eyes but knew he had to keep going.

"I thought I could encourage you to yell and argue and push and fight but... instead, *you* make *me*... softer. I'm quieter and more patient and more open just since being around you. I've been knocking heads and fighting and being a pain in people's asses for the last ten years. I thought I liked that. It made me strong. No one overlooked me or got away with anything. I thought I was tough."

He gave a soft huff of laughter and shook his head.

"But I had no idea what tough was. Tough is being ignored but not leaving. Tough is being overlooked, but knowing you have something to contribute. Tough is being able to see long term in spite of the short-term shit you have to plow through. Tough is... you."

Whitney pressed her lips together and blinked rapidly, but she didn't say anything. He was glad she wasn't arguing with him. He wanted her to hear this. All of it.

"You've been knocked around, emotionally, by people you loved and trusted and looked up to, but you're still here. Most people would have said fuck it and walked out by now. That's sure as hell what I would have done. Making a lot of noise and trouble as I went out. That's what I *have* done in some situations. But you believe in something deeper and bigger—this town or these people or your family legacy or... something—and you're still here."

Her eyes were shiny now and Cam thought maybe she was on the verge of tears. But he knew she wasn't sad.

He shook his head. "After just a few weeks being around you, I just want to be quiet and hear old stories and watch TV reruns and bake cookies." He gave a short laugh as the words came out without him really planning them. "I don't know how you're doing it, exactly, but you are showing me how to be a fighter in a whole new way. Just by being there and taking care of things behind the scenes, quietly, being supportive and letting someone else... you... do the ass-kicking. I'm shocked but, I like it. I really do."

She took a shaky breath. "The stories and reruns and cookies are Didi," she finally said, her voice husky.

"No. Those are all the by-products of the things you're making me feel," he said, not letting her make light of it. "You're showing me how to be in for the long haul and how to be a part of something bigger by being the guy behind the tough girl."

She swallowed hard.

"Even back in high school you understood that. I was ready to give up my scholarship and even college to stay here with you, but you understood the big picture, even then. You knew I had to leave. You realized that putting up with things sucking in the short term would matter for the long term."

"You make me sound a lot more insightful and smarter than I am," she said softly.

"Maybe you don't *think* you're those things, but that's just because your brain isn't recognizing it. Because it comes from your heart," he said.

She just looked at him for several ticks from the clock on her desk. Cam let her look. He hadn't planned on saying any of this. He hadn't put most of this to words even in his own head before this. But it was all true. He'd spent the past ten years fighting and being hardheaded and driven. Now he felt... content. With her. Not because Whitney was content. She clearly wasn't. She had a lot of unfinished business here. But because he now knew that what he needed to do was be here so she could finish that business.

That didn't seem as strange as it maybe should.

"How you feel about me and my ideas here matter more than anyone else's," she finally said.

"Really?"

"Yes."

"Why?" He sincerely wanted to know. He wasn't the CEO or CFO of the company and he was already a huge fan of hers. "You've already won me over," he told her with a smile.

"I think because..." Her brow furrowed. "Well..." She was clearly thinking it through.

Cam grinned. "That's what I thought."

"No. Honestly." She pressed her lips together, then said, "Okay, it's sad, but, there's not a lot of difference between my personal life and my work life. Hot Cakes has always been a family business, so it's always been a part of my home life too. But it's also because I'm a workaholic and don't have a lot of friends. I simply can't separate Hot Cakes into any kind of compartment. It's a part of everything."

She drew a breath. "But with you, I suppose I want you to feel like all the extra time you're putting in helping with Didi and everything is worth it. That believing in me is worth it. That makes this personal in a way it's never been before."

She pulled her bottom lip between her teeth as she waited for him to respond. He couldn't for a second as his heart actually kicked painfully against his ribs.

Finally he moved his hands to hold her face. "Well, then, it's very important for you to hear me say that it's *all* fucking amazing," he said gruffly.

Her smile was bright even as her eyes were shiny with tears again. "Yeah?"

"Very much so. It's very worth it to me to see you happy and proud of yourself and feeling fulfilled."

She looked legitimately touched by that. "Thank you, Cam."

"You're welcome."

She gave a soft laugh. "I can't believe this."

"What?"

"This. Us. The fact that you're helping me do more at Hot Cakes, of all places, and you're involved with my family and..." She shook her head. "Just all of it."

"We couldn't have been here ten years ago," he said. "I realize that. I had to grow up to get past the company and your family and the details to see the big picture of you and me. You were right."

She smiled sadly. "I had no idea that we'd end up here, Cam. I'm glad we did, but I had no way of knowing that it would work out. It wasn't about you and me. Me breaking things off was just about you."

"You sent me away for me."

Whitney nodded. "You couldn't have stayed here. That was a ridiculous idea."

"You did it because you wanted me to be happy."

She pressed her lips together and nodded.

"Because you loved me."

She swallowed hard. But nodded again.

"I totally get that now." His voice was thick and he hoped she could see what all he meant by that.

Suddenly she leaned in, putting her lips against his and wrapping her arms around his neck.

His hands went to her waist, squeezing and bringing her up against him more fully. Nothing had ever felt as right as this woman did in his arms. Resisting her was getting more and more difficult every day and when *she* touched *him*... he was a goner.

Whitney opened her mouth with a little sigh and Cam immediately swept his tongue against hers. His hands moved down to cup her ass and press her against his growing erection.

She gripped the front of his shirt, arching closer, making a frustrated sound at the back of her throat when it wasn't close *enough*. She turned, tugging him with her, until the backs of her thighs were against her desk. Then she pulled her mouth from his.

But only long enough to give him a sexy, mischievous smile, and to slide her skirt up her thighs.

His heart thundered and his cock hardened as she wiggled the navy blue skirt up high enough that he could see her panties.

Yellow. Bright freaking sunshine yellow. That was what his girl wore under her boring freaking skirt.

Then she pushed herself up onto her desk and spread her knees.

He was there immediately, stepping between them, pulling her ass to the edge of the desk, and cupping the back of her head, his fingers gripping her hair with just a slight tug as he tipped her head back.

He pressed his aching hard-on against the hot, wet center of those cheery-as-fuck panties and ground into her as he kissed her deeply, making her gasp and moan into his mouth.

The vision of knocking her day planner and the boring black pencil holder and matching lamp to the floor so he could lay her back and fuck her on her desk was vivid in his mind. He wanted to do things to her that she would think about during *every single* conference call and meeting she had in this office from now on.

Cam reached out and sent the pencil holder skittering over the surface of the desk, pens scattering, before it *thunked* to the floor.

Whitney jerked her head to look at it, then back to him.

"What was that?"

"I'm going to—"

His phone started ringing.

And he was jerked back to reality and how this was all *way* friendlier than he'd intended to be.

The phone kept ringing.

He sighed.

He thought about ignoring it, but he couldn't. The ring tone was the theme song for *Magnum, P.I.* The original, of course.

Whitney started laughing. "You gave her her own ring tone?"

Yeah, the moment was gone.

He grinned as he reached for his back pocket. "Of course." He swiped to answer and lifted the phone to his ear. "Hey, Didi."

"I'm ready to go," she announced. "It's almost time for yoga."

It was, indeed. He looked at Whitney. Then at Whitney's lips. Then at Whitney's yellow panties. Then at the pencil holder on the floor. Then back to the panties. Dammit.

"We need to stop at the store on the way home too," she said. "I told Maggie I'd bring salad and I need lemons for my lemon vinaigrette. Don't forget."

He grinned in spite of being cock-blocked by a seventy-two-year-old. "Got it." Didi might have her times mixed up and she might forget things once in a while, but she didn't forget everything. She and Maggie had talked about that salad three days ago. "I'm on my way."

"Hurry up." Then she hung up on him.

Grinning, he looked at Whitney. Holy hell, she looked so

hot with her blouse pulled loose from her skirt and her hair mussed and her cheeks flushed. "I need to go."

Whitney was watching him with a strange expression. It was part amused and part puzzled and part affectionate, if he wasn't mistaken.

"This is all so... weird," she said.

It was. And a little terrible, he thought, as she slid off the desk and smoothed her skirt down.

"It's all good," he told her.

"Yeah." She nodded. "It seems to be."

"So go, kick some more ass and I'm going to go... relax and meditate with some kittens." He grinned and stepped back.

Immediately he missed the feel of her body heat and her scent.

"Okay." She stood watching him for a moment. Then she stepped close and pressed her lips to his again.

The high heels put her at the perfect height.

Screw it.

He cupped the back of her head and tasted her deeply for a moment.

When they separated they were both breathing a little harder again.

Whitney licked her lips. "See you later."

"Yeah." He glanced at the pens scattered over her desk. "Sorry about the pencil holder."

She let out a little sigh. "Worth. It."

He grinned. He didn't know what was going on with them *exactly*. But he knew that his feelings were real and they were growing and he fucking liked everything about how things were between them.

Except there wasn't nearly enough naked time.

That was his fault. Well, maybe not *fault*. That was his *doing*. And he didn't regret it. If he'd been sleeping with Whitney this whole time, it would have been hard to separate loving having

her in his bed and making her want him again and just...
loving her.

It hit him hard.

It had been teasing around the edges of his consciousness
for a while now. Like when he'd realized that she maybe really
had loved him even as an eighteen-year-old kid and that he
maybe hadn't *actually* felt the same way. But now it was clear.
He'd fallen back in love with her. In the midst of 3 a.m. view-
ings of *Magnum, P.I.* and baking cookies and watching her
bloom and seeing her have quiet, happy moments with her
grandmother because she wasn't stressed and pressed for time
and weighed down by a million other things. Like guilt.

It was ironic that it was Hot Cakes that had brought them
back together, but here they were and it felt good. Right.

Giving into the urge, he leaned in and kissed Whitney once
more. Just a quick, sweet kiss on the lips, then he looked at her
with the knowledge that he'd see her at home later. And maybe
they could sneak in some quiet time before *Magnum, P.I.*

———

Whitney took a deep breath as she pulled her phone out
and stared at the screen.

She never did this.

Never.

It was completely foreign territory.

Her phone was used for emails and the occasional call
when she was away from her desk and pulling up her boarding
pass when she was traveling.

She almost never texted.

And she never texted like *this.*

She wasn't even sure she was going to do it right.

She swallowed. But she really wanted to.

Opening her contacts, she scrolled to the one she needed

and pulled up the number. Then she typed, *I got done early today and I'd love to just have some fun tonight. Are you up for something?*

She stared at the words.

Then she frowned.

And typed, *This is Whitney, by the way.*

Then she sat and waited. And wondered if she should have said something else. Or said it differently. Was that enticing at all? Was it stupid? Is this how people started this stuff?

Finally, after about four years—or maybe about two minutes—she saw the little dots dancing, indicating she was going to get a response.

LOL. I know it's you! And dammit! I'm so sorry! I've got plans.

Whitney felt her heart drop to her stomach. But she forced herself to actually smile, even though Piper couldn't see it, as she typed back. *No worries! Of course you do. This is really last minute. Sorry!*

Don't be sorry! Piper replied. *I love that you're done early! That's awesome! I would love to do something but I'm... out at the alpaca farm.*

Whitney paused with her thumbs over the keys and reread that. Piper was at the alpaca farm? As in Drew Ryan's farm? Uh-oh.

We were going to talk about all of this, she finally typed back, suddenly feeling less silly about texting Piper for an impromptu girl's night. Her nerves about asking a girlfriend out for drinks—something she'd literally never done before—disappearing in light of her concern over Piper getting cozy with Drew. Drew Ryan was a great guy. Good looking, kind, funny, successful. But... he wasn't Ollie.

Whitney couldn't explain it any better than that.

Ollie was a handful. She knew that. Especially for Piper. But he seemed to be *Piper's* handful. He was Cam and Grant and Aiden and Dax's handful too, but there was something about

Ollie and Piper that just seemed to click. And Whitney knew that Ollie had feelings for Piper. He just wasn't good at showing that. Or maybe even admitting it.

But she was rooting for them. And Drew Ryan would be fine. He could have just about any woman in Appleby. Drew wasn't lonely, that was for sure. He didn't need Piper.

We were going to talk about it, Piper replied. *And we will. Promise.*

Whitney felt terrible suddenly.

She and Piper had had a moment in the conference room earlier. A moment Whitney never had with other women. That moment of silent understanding that said *I've got you, girl*. Piper was like the little sister at Fluke and the guys all cared about her. It was obvious. But they were *guys*. And Piper had moved here from Chicago with them. Or because of them. She wasn't from here and probably didn't know many people. Piper maybe needed a girlfriend as much as Whitney did.

But what had Whitney done? She'd gone back to her office and gotten immersed in her work. Of course she had. That's what she did. Today had been almost worse than usual. She'd flown through her to-do list, high from the meeting and knowing that the guys were excited about the new bars and then her talk with Cam.

Her heart flipped even now thinking about *that*.

It had been so much more than a *talk*. The way he'd looked at her. And cupped her face in his big hands. And looked into her eyes. The intensity in his voice when he'd told her that she was amazing and creative and sweet. And a little broken and hurt.

Her heart twinged now remembering that.

Cam saw her. He saw her now in a way he hadn't in the past.

Maybe because there was more to see now. Maybe because he was more mature and more *able* to see it. She wasn't sure. But they were not the same people they'd been ten years ago.

This man she had very much had a huge crush on was *not* the same guy she'd crushed on in high school.

It all felt new and exciting and scary.

Scary because now they were adults and it could actually mean something now.

She took a deep breath and focused on her phone and Piper.

This was something else she needed to work on. If she wanted to have friends, she had to *be* a friend. That meant paying attention when people needed her.

Are you sure you can't get away for a drink? Whitney asked. *We should talk now. I'm concerned.*

Don't be concerned, Piper texted back almost immediately. *This isn't about Ollie.*

Whitney took a breath. Something she knew even less about than girlfriends was romantic relationships. Cam had been her only one. And they'd been kids. And now, in retrospect, it was clear that a lot of that excitement had been about a whole series of firsts—her first boyfriend, her first kiss, first sex, first defying her parents—and the rush of sneaking around and breaking her family's rules.

She hadn't done that. Not before Cam. And not really since.

Her parents had been married for thirty years. They'd been high school sweethearts and, well, they'd just done what they'd been expected to do—go to college, get married, take over the family business, have kids.

Her grandparents had been married for fifty-one years. But she knew it hadn't been all that happy. Her grandpa hadn't been abusive. At least not physically. She was realizing now that both her grandfather and father had been emotionally abusive, and her grandfather had been financially abusive toward her grandmother, making all of the money decisions and doling money out to her like she was a child, requiring her to get his "permission" for the things she bought. And he'd taken over *her* company. The thing she'd first taken a chance on. The thing she'd lost her best friend over.

Yeah, Whitney didn't know much about strong relationships. Except with her grandmother. And she wasn't going to win any granddaughter of the year awards over the past couple of years.

I can come over to your house, Whitney finally typed to Piper. Piper was a woman she wanted to be friends with. Because she had a feeling Piper could *teach* Whitney how to be a good friend. Piper would tell Whitney when she was falling down on the job and she'd tell her exactly what she wanted Whitney to do to make her feel better. *I can bring cookies or liquor. Your call.*

The cookies were ones Cam had made but she didn't think he'd mind if she swiped them for this.

In fact, she smiled thinking about telling him that she was "borrowing" the caramel-and-toffee oatmeal cookies he'd made last night to have some girl talk with Piper.

He'd approve. He'd like that she and Piper were getting close. He'd like that she was developing a friendship. He'd like that his cookies were a part of that.

Whitney felt a wave of heat sweep through her.

He was so damned sweet. And she wanted him so damned much.

She'd always been attracted to him and they'd had some hot moments over the past few weeks. But it was the freaking cookies and the dusting and the way he was caring for Didi and —more than any of that—the way he seemed so *happy* to be doing it all. He truly seemed to be happy to be doing all of it with the knowledge that Whitney could then focus better on work.

It was the weirdest turn of events.

And it made her want to strip his clothes off of him and cover him in cookie dough and lick every swirl of every tattoo on his body.

She *really* hoped he had some she hadn't seen yet because they'd been covered by his jeans and shorts and...

Her phone pinged, pulling her attention back to her texting conversation with Piper.

The woman she wanted to be *friends* with.

Man, she really sucked at this.

Cookies and liquor both sound awesome. But honestly, it's not like that. I'm out here talking to Drew about a project. It's truly about alpacas. It's not a date. Rain check on the drink? And the cookies?

Whitney sighed. A project with Drew? About alpacas? Okay, well, she was launching a new snack bar with fox footprints on them and she'd had alpacas *and* goats at her dessert tasting. Who was she to judge?

Deal, she texted back. *Soon.*

Definitely.

Whitney sat back in her chair. Well, that had not gone the way she'd expected. She chewed her bottom lip. There was one other woman who she would like to have drinks—or cookies—with. It was more of a longshot than Piper, who she saw every day and had gotten to know better over the past few months the guys had been in town. They at least had Hot Cakes and the guys in common. But there was one other option, and she really was in the mood to go out and be social.

She could just go home, of course. She always wanted to go home and see Didi. And take her heels and bra off. And now Cam was there and that made it even more enticing. Plus the house always smelled amazing now. A combination of cleaning products, which she knew were homemade by his mother because she'd overheard the guys joking about it one day, and food. Usually baked goods, but he also made casseroles and he'd talked Didi into burgers at an actual decent dinnertime the other night. They ate at Maggie's most nights, but they ate at home every once in a while. And they always saved Whitney some food. They either brought her a plate from Maggie's or they saved her some of whatever they made. So the house always smelled very *homey* when she walked in.

She was *really* getting used to having Cam around.

Not just because of the housekeeping/cooking/caregiving tasks.

But not *not* because of those.

Throw in some naked baking and/or orgasms and she'd never let him leave.

Hell, she'd be okay with him just walking around without his shirt on a regular basis.

Huh, it seemingly took just a few minutes of free time with her to-do list crossed off and her brain immediately, happily, shifted into another gear all together.

But she couldn't just go home and throw herself at Cam.

Probably.

Until later. When Didi was in bed.

No, she scolded herself. Not even then.

She'd made a big deal out of the fact that she didn't want to do the relationship thing, and then he'd made a big deal out of supporting her in that and she should really let him. And respect that. And stuff.

Free time was obviously a problem. If she had too much time to think about things other than Hot Cakes, she got into trouble. She needed to keep busy.

She took a breath and pulled up Paige's number in her phone.

Paige was quite a bit younger but she was very... Whitney wasn't sure of the word. Mature sounded dumb. She was, of course, but there was something else about Paige that made her seem older than her just-turned-twenty-two years. It was her calm spirituality. Or something. Paige was just very sure of herself, who she was, what she wanted. She did yoga and collected cats and was a vegetarian in a little town in Iowa where that was regarded as a bit strange. But she did it all with a smile and a general disregard for what others thought of her.

She was just... calm. She was very soothing.

It was why Whitney loved her yoga classes and just enjoyed talking with Paige whenever she had the chance.

Whitney probably needed more soothing in her life.

So she should definitely invite Paige for drinks and a girls' night out with her.

Whitney typed and hit send quickly before she could think about it too hard.

Hi! It's Whitney. Wondering if you'd be up for having a drink tonight?

Again, the two-minute lag time between sending and receiving a response felt like years.

Hi! I'm so sorry, Whitney! I have plans tonight. I would love to do it another time.

Oh, no problem. It's last minute, I know, Whitney typed back quickly.

I can't believe you're asking me to go out on the ONE night that my friend is back in town from Louisiana and can get together! Paige texted back.

It's fine! Whitney assured her. *You should see your friend.*

She moved to Louisiana because she fell in love a few months ago. Paige sent an eye-rolling emoji at that.

Whitney had to laugh. Paige was really not into falling in love and people upending their lives to be with Their One True Love.

Paige loved to date and didn't sit home on the weekends unless she wanted to. But she did *not* get serious. Every time someone asked her when she was going to settle down, or worse, get married, she got another cat.

We can do it another time, Whitney replied. Maybe Paige would talk her out of all these mushy, semi-in-love feelings she was having for Cam.

Would that be a good thing? Or not?

Tori is a vet, Paige went on. *She's the one who took care of all my cats. Lol! So she's looking at my new stray for me. She's here to collect her own animals and take them back to Louisiana with her.*

Whitney smiled. *Seriously, no problem.*

Well, she did bring her boyfriend and his HOT cousin with her. Paige sent a smiley face emoji with the tongue hanging out and then a fire emoji. *So I'm not exactly upset.* She included a winking emoji.

Whitney laughed. *Have fun!*

Oh, I will! This Louisiana drawl is doing it for me. Paige sent a grinning emoji. *But I really want to go out with you sometime soon, okay?*

Whitney nodded. She wanted to do this too. She had rain checks for two girls' nights out now. That was a lot more than she'd had an hour ago. *For sure. And then I can hear all about how things went with this guy.* She hesitated before sending that, but that was the kind of stuff women talked about on girls' nights out, right? She finally pushed the button.

Sounds good! Paige sent a GIF of a girl fanning her face. Then she added *And then I can hear all about you and Cam.*

Oh.

Well... if Paige was going to spill about this guy and whatever happened, then Whitney probably had to tell her *something* too. She just didn't have much to tell. Well, nothing physical anyway. She had a whole lot of emotional stuff she could spill.

And suddenly having someone to bounce all of that off of sounded kind of great. She could use some advice.

Okay.

She sent the response, feeling like she was making a huge commitment.

The heart emoji she got back from Paige made her feel good though and she put her phone down smiling.

A second later though, she blew out a breath as she looked at her especially clean desk. She really was done for the day.

Well... fuck. She'd finally gotten her nerve up to reach out to potential new friends and they both, of course, already had plans. Normal people probably did make plans ahead of time. Whitney never really made plans because she worked all the time. But if she were going to do something other than work, she probably wouldn't be able to plan it too far ahead. She never knew how long she'd be at the office.

But she sighed as she thought that.

It wasn't entirely true.

She was in control, to an extent at least, of how long she stayed at the office. She worked a lot, yes, but she did it intentionally.

And she'd been realizing more and more over the past few days that it was, in part, because she'd been trying to prove herself. First to her family. Then to the Fluke guys. But it was also because she hadn't really liked going home. Because she'd felt pretty damned useless there.

She wasn't a cook or a baker. She didn't enjoy keeping house. Not that anyone probably *loved* cleaning toilets, but she knew people liked decorating their homes for different holidays and changing up the little touches like throw pillows and centerpieces. She got the impression that Maggie McCaffery enjoyed things like making the little sachets Whitney had found in her drawer the other day. There was no way Cam had *made* those and she would bet half her salary he'd gotten them from his mother. Just like he'd surely gotten the hand soaps in the powder room on the first floor from Maggie.

Some people enjoyed that stuff. Cam even, clearly, enjoyed baking.

That wasn't Whitney.

And she hadn't known what to do for Didi, to make her happy and to help her. She'd struggled with things like the little parties at 3 a.m. and knowing if it was right or wrong. She'd struggled with juggling those things with work. She'd struggled with feeling that she was really doing a good job with *any* of it.

At work, at least she'd known what she was doing. Her dad and grandfather hadn't *let* her do much, but she understood what was going on and enjoyed the atmosphere at Hot Cakes. It was more familiar. Her grandmother and mom had always had people cooking and cleaning for them, so she hadn't seen that as a nurturing, happy thing people did.

Until Cam.

Cam had been raised with a mother who clearly loved to cook and have her family and their friends around in big groups, feeding and taking care of them.

It made Whitney wonder about Letty. Had she been like that too? She'd certainly been a baker. And she'd apparently staunchly stood by the idea that fresh-baked, homemade baked goods were superior to mass-produced snack cakes.

And that made Whitney wonder if Didi had missed that part of Letty too. Cam had told her that Didi said she missed Letty's baked goods. But Whitney wondered if Letty had had that nurturing spirit too and if Didi missed that as well. Or more. She was certainly soaking that up from Cam. And his family.

Which gave her an idea.

A crazy, maybe-I-shouldn't-do-this idea.

But as she pushed away from her desk, she felt a little flip in her stomach that told her she *was* going to do it.

And she couldn't wait to see how Cam reacted.

17

Wanting to tell his parents and friends and little brother that they needed to get the hell out of the house so he could put Whitney Lancaster up on his mother's kitchen counter and do very, very dirty things to her where he'd just helped make a chicken and ham casserole was probably not appropriate.

That was still his reaction when his mother came back into the kitchen with Whitney in tow.

Maggie had gone to answer the doorbell because Steve had been taking corn on the cob out of the pot on the stove, Grant, Aiden and Dax were setting the table, Zoe, Jane and Josie were out on the back patio, and Henry and Didi were in the middle of a quest in *Warriors of Easton* and couldn't stop according to Henry's shout from the family room.

No one came to the front door anyway, so they'd all assumed it wasn't anyone all that important.

They'd been wrong.

Cam was literally standing in the middle of the kitchen, holding a hot casserole dish, his mouth hanging open, staring at Whitney.

She looked shy and unsure and completely gorgeous.

Her hair was down, falling in loose waves around her shoulders. She wasn't wearing any of her usual "office" makeup. No eye shadow or lipstick. She also, thank you Lord, was not wearing one of her office skirts. She wore a pink sundress and cock-hardening scuffed brown boots. She looked every bit the girl next door in a small Iowa town and he wanted her with every fiber of his being.

"I knew better than to bring food, and especially dessert," she said with a little smile. "So I brought liquor." She held up a bottle of lemon vodka in one hand and a bottle of red wine in the other.

Maggie laughed and took both bottles. "Brilliant girl," she praised. Then she nudged Whitney toward Cam. "We're so happy you're here."

Someone—he wasn't sure who—took the casserole dish from Cam, then slipped the oven mitts off his hands, and nudged him toward Whitney.

They met partway across the kitchen.

"Is this okay?" she asked him softly.

Right. He still hadn't said a fucking word. Like how happy he was to see her. Here. At his parents' house. On a weeknight. For one of their big group dinners.

"This is..." He couldn't properly express himself here in the middle of the kitchen with people around. "Come on." He took her hand and tugged her toward the hallway and into the bathroom just past the stairs that led up to the bedrooms.

He pushed her into the tiny room in front of him then stepped in behind her and kicked the door shut.

They wouldn't be able to hide out in here long. And they weren't *alone*. At least not enough to do all the things he wanted to do to her. But he needed a few minutes without eyes on them.

"Cam, is every—"

She didn't finish that thought because his mouth was on hers a moment later. He slid his fingers into her hair, holding her head still, and stepped her back until she was against the wall by the sink. Then he *kissed* her. Hard, deep. With tongue and moans and his fingers curling into her scalp and her hands gripping his shirt at his waist.

She arched into him. She moaned too. She opened her mouth and let his tongue stroke deep.

He heard footsteps in the hallway outside of the door and knew their time was running short, but he couldn't let her go just yet. He dropped his hand to her hip and skimmed it down to where the hem of the dress hit her thigh, then he dragged his hand up the silky smooth skin, bunching the skirt as he went.

She shuddered under his touch. He didn't stop until he hit the skin-warmed silk of her panties. He slid his hand over the slick fabric to cup her ass and then dragged his mouth along her jaw to her ear.

"*This* skirt is so much better than the others."

She gave a soft laugh and nodded. "I agree."

He squeezed her ass, then reluctantly let her go. He leaned back, looking down at her. "I'm so happy you're here."

"You are?"

"Surprised, but yes."

"I got done early and... realized I wanted to do something." She lifted a shoulder, then admitted, a little sheepishly, "I actually invited both Piper and Paige out for drinks first. But they were busy."

Cam felt his grin. She'd reached out for a girls' night. He loved that.

"I've got you," he said. He took her hand and turned toward the door.

"Wait." She grabbed his forearm with her other hand.

"What?"

"What was *this*?" she asked, looking around the bathroom and then at him, her gaze dropping to his mouth.

He immediately turned back and leaned in. "This was holy-shit-you-look-gorgeous-and-I'm-so-fucking-happy-to-see-you-and-I-love-that-you-came-over-here greeting."

"Really?" She looked happy. "I know your mom is too polite to turn me away but—"

He laughed. "She is. But I promise that's not what this is. I'm so glad you're here. I would have been bringing you over here every night if you'd been at home and..." He cupped her cheek again. "I love that you knew you could show up here with all of us."

She frowned slightly but then nodded. "Yeah. I guess... I didn't even think about it. I was focused on surprising you. But it didn't occur to me to be nervous that the other guys would think it was weird that I was here." She looked like she'd just had a realization. "That's new."

He smiled, his heart expanding. "It is. You know you belong with us."

Her smile grew and, damn, the brightness in her face almost brought him to his knees.

"And you can still have your girls' night," he said, starting for the door again, tugging on her hand. "Zoe and Jane and Josie are out back."

Whitney immediately stopped moving, jerking him to a stop.

He looked back.

She wasn't smiling. *Now* she looked nervous.

"Whit?"

"I... oh my God, how did I not think of that? Of course they're here."

"Of course they are," he agreed. Dax and Grant were good friends of his but they hadn't started showing up at Maggie's dinners until they'd fallen for Jane and Josie. Well, Grant had come once... and he'd then been officially ass over nose for Josie after that. Jane and Josie, however, had been coming to dinner here for years.

"I can't crash their girl time," Whitney said, frowning at him. "I can't just show up at their regular thing and expect them to include me."

"They won't see it like that."

"You don't know that."

"Whitney—Jane and Josie are two of the nicest women I know."

"You didn't say Zoe too," she pointed out.

He shrugged. "My little sister is sassy," he said. "But she'll be sweet to you."

"I'm the granddaughter of her grandmother's arch nemesis. I'm the daughter of the family that owned the business she's always thought of as her primary rival."

"She's over that," Cam said. And she was. Mostly. Aiden had helped Zoe see that they were just two completely different businesses, on two completely different levels. Though, yes, Zoe could hold a grudge almost as well as Letty had.

"But she's felt that way for a long time. It's easier for her to not think of Aiden as her competitor because they're in love," Whitney said. "And you're her brother and Grant and Ollie are your friends. But I'm..."

"The woman I'm crazy about."

Whitney stopped, her mouth open, ready to keep going. But then she snapped it shut.

He couldn't help but grin. "You know that."

She took a deep breath.

"Whitney," he said. "You know that." He wanted to hear her admit it. He hadn't told her how he was feeling, but he hoped that when she really thought about it, that she would know.

He thought he knew how she was feeling about him.

Of course... yeah, it would be nice to hear.

"I know that we've been getting along well," she finally said.

He grinned and pulled her in close, resting his forehead against hers. "We have been. Things have been great. But for the record, I'm crazy about you. And I'm so fucking happy that you're here. And I'd really love it if you spent some time with the girls. That would feel really good. I want my family and my friends to know you better."

She swallowed and nodded her head against his. "Okay."

"Okay." Well, she wasn't saying she was crazy about him too, but that could come later. She was stubborn and proud and she'd been hurt in the past by people she loved. He could give her time. Some time. A little bit of time.

"Cam?" she said softly when he leaned back.

"Yeah?"

"Thanks."

He lifted a brow. "For?"

"Being crazy about me. I know it's not easy."

He gave a soft laugh. "It's stupid easy, Whit. It's like I can't even help it."

She gave him a smile that he could have sworn he'd never seen. She seemed touched and maybe a little surprised and turned on and maybe a little bit in love.

He wanted her feeling that, whatever it was exactly, for the rest of the night.

With a lingering look at *that* expression, he finally led them out of the bathroom and back to the kitchen.

All the guys and Cam's parents were in the kitchen and they all jerked to action as he and Whitney came around the corner, clearly attempting to look busy.

Cam rolled his eyes, but he was grinning and he was certain that his best friends and parents—people who had known him very well for a very long time—would be able to read that grin as *stupidly in love*. That was okay.

"Dinner is ready," Maggie said, handing Cam a plate of chicken and Whitney a bowl of salad.

No one said anything about him pulling her off to the bathroom immediately or even about her being here in the first place. They just all gathered food and drink and headed for the dining room.

Aiden went to the back door and pulled it open. "Dinner!"

Soon the dining room was full. Henry and Didi came in from the family room. Zoe, Josie and Jane joined them from the back patio. There was already an extra chair for Whitney— Cam gave his mom a quick smile for that—and Didi greeted Whitney as if she'd been expecting her granddaughter to show up tonight.

Even Zoe and the girls didn't seem shocked to see her.

Henry was the only one who said anything other than "Hi" and "Welcome."

"Didi says you should play *Warriors,* but that it will be tough for you," Henry told her, scooping cheesy potatoes onto his plate.

He was seated between Whitney and Didi, a move that Cam knew was not random but that he wondered about. Why had Maggie chosen that seating arrangement?

Henry added potatoes to Didi's plate and then passed the dish to his father. The last time they'd been at dinner and Henry had dished up for Didi and they'd asked him why, he'd said that the casserole dishes were too heavy for her to hold, so he did it for her. He'd said it so matter-of-factly that they'd all just nodded and later agreed that, even though they were playing video games together, spending time with Didi had matured Henry. As the baby of the family, by a lot, there just weren't many chances for him to care for others. Didi had changed that and it was pretty cool to see his baby brother stepping up to help someone out.

"She said *Warriors* will be tough for me?" Whitney asked him, bemused. "Why is that?"

Henry was only eleven, but he'd grown up with much older siblings and a constant houseful of people older than himself so he wasn't shy and he could hold a conversation with nearly anyone. "She said you don't sit still very well," he told Whitney.

Whitney nodded. "She's right."

"But she said no one needs a chance to kick bad-guy ass more than you," Henry said.

"Henry!" Maggie admonished.

He looked at her. "What? Didi said it."

Didi nodded. "I did. And it's true."

Didi thought Whitney needed a chance to kick bad-guy ass? Cam looked at Whitney and thought about that. Didi saw how Whitney tamped down her urges to yell and fight, he realized. He wondered if she noticed the little chin lift Whit always did when she was swallowing back sharp words. He'd bet good money that she did.

So Didi thought Whitney would enjoy swinging a virtual sword and chopping off some troll heads, huh? She might have a point. He'd have to introduce Whitney to the game. He could let Henry do it, but he had the sudden inkling that seeing Whitney glaring at the screen, her hair wild from not doing it for a couple of days because she was engrossed in the game, growling softly as she chased down trolls and ogres and monsters and kicked their asses in the name of saving the kingdom and freeing the people would be pretty hot. *He* wanted to see that.

"Can we use the word *butt* instead?" Maggie asked, but her expression said she knew the answer to that.

Didi looked at Henry. "*You* need to remember to use the word *butt* when you're repeating this stuff to your mother."

He nodded. "You're right."

Maggie sighed, but didn't say anything more.

Cam grinned and took a bite of cheesy potatoes—which were the best thing to ever come out of his mother's kitchen. He loved that Henry and Didi were coconspirators.

"You don't want salad?" Henry asked Didi when she shook her head as he held the bowl out to her.

"No."

"But you made it," Henry said, slightly exasperated.

"So?" Didi asked.

"You made something you don't like?"

"I put cucumbers in it."

"You don't like cucumbers?"

"No."

"Why'd you put them in then?"

"You said you like them."

Henry grinned at her. "I do."

"So that's why."

"You can pick them out of yours and give them to me," Henry offered.

Didi shook her head. "I cut them up really small."

He sighed. "Okay." He passed the bowl to his dad. "But next time, make them big so we can pick them out."

"Okay."

Cam grinned and took the basket of rolls from his sister, but when he glanced at Zoe, he could see tears in her eyes. He frowned. She smiled and shook her head. Then he looked at his mother. She had a wobbly smile and shiny eyes too. He glanced at Whitney. Her eyes were wet and she was watching Henry and Didi with a look of wonder.

Cam shook his head. But couldn't help smiling. It was sweet. And he was glad Whitney was here to see it.

They ate and chatted comfortably and casually, but Cam couldn't stop from glancing at Whitney over and over. She didn't say much but she had a happy look on her face as she absorbed the conversation.

"So we have an announcement," Josie said as Maggie started to push her chair back at the end of the meal.

Maggie had mentioned cinnamon roll cheesecake and Dax's mouth had fallen open in amazement.

Maggie paused.

Dax looked from Maggie to Josie to Maggie and then back to Josie. "But... can you make the announcement over dessert?"

Josie shook her head and looked at Grant.

"You can't wait two more minutes?" Grant asked Dax.

"You heard what she said, right?" Dax asked. "*Cinnamon roll cheesecake.* There's not one word in that name that says I can wait two more minutes."

"What if it's something that's really important to two of your best friends?" Josie asked.

Dax gave her a look, one eyebrow up. "*Cinnamon. Roll. Cheesecake.* You better be getting married or something if I'm waiting on that."

Josie's amused smile curved into a wide grin.

It took a second, but Dax's eyes narrowed. Then he sat forward. Then he looked from Josie to Grant and back. "Are you getting *married*?"

Josie's grin grew even wider; she nodded and held up her left hand. A gorgeous diamond ring twinkled under the light that hung over the dining room table.

There was a beat of silence and then all at once, everyone erupted into gasps and squeals and laughter and congratulations.

Except Cam and Whitney.

They looked at one another and grinned. They had a shared secret. Grant and Josie were already married. They'd gotten married when Josie had needed her gall bladder removed and hadn't had the health insurance to cover it. They'd both thought it was a simple favor, a temporary marriage of convenience. Cam and Whitney had realized early on that it wasn't simple and it shouldn't be temporary.

Grant had asked Cam to act as his attorney to make sure the insurance claims went through smoothly. And to draw up the divorce papers.

He'd done both.

But he hadn't wanted to draw up the divorce papers. He'd seen that Josie was exactly what Grant needed—and vice versa—and so he'd gone to Whitney to ask her what he should do.

It had been an impulse, but he hadn't regretted it.

She'd been shocked. Then she'd been pleased. And inspired. Together, they'd come up with the idea to make the divorce papers only mostly official.

And it had worked. Once Grant and Josie thought they were officially divorced, they'd immediately realized they didn't want to be. They'd been relieved, if surprised, to find out that Cam had kept them married.

Things had shifted between him and Whitney then. Things had gotten easier. They'd been a team. One small thing. Not about them. About two people they cared about. But they'd both recognized the love and that Josie and Grant needed each other, and that had felt like a particularly important bond for them to share.

Now, smiling about it across the table made him feel like he'd love a lot more *bonding* with her.

Yep, across his mother's dining room table with cheesy potato remnants between them.

"This definitely calls for cinnamon roll cheesecake!" Dax announced.

They all laughed.

"What do you see in me?" Jane asked. "I don't bake, and with your sweet tooth, I don't know why you're with me."

"Well, honey, there's sweets and then there are *sweets*," Dax told her, sliding his arm over the back of her chair and leaning in to nuzzle her neck.

Grant and Josie were beaming about their engagement, Dax and Jane were nuzzling, Zoe and Aiden were whispering about something and... Cam wanted that. All of that. Looking across the table at Whitney gave him a sense of anticipation and nostalgia at the same time. Nostalgia didn't completely make sense. They'd never had this. They hadn't been a couple in public. They'd never sat at his mother's table together. They'd never hung out with friends together. But he'd wanted to. He'd imagined it. *This.* He'd wanted and imagined this.

And now he had it.

And he wanted so much more.

———

Whitney couldn't believe how nervous she was to step out onto that back patio. She trailed behind the other women as they headed outside with glasses of lemonade. Spiked lemonade. Apparently it was the drink of choice with the girls of the group, and when they'd heard Whitney had brought lemon vodka they'd declared they *had* to try it.

She swallowed hard and thought about chugging the drink in her hand. She wasn't sure why Zoe, Jane, and Josie made her nervous. They were nice women. Jane and Josie were in love with two men that Whitney liked a lot. Men who were on their way to being her friends. That felt strange to think about, but it was true. She and Dax and Grant were getting to be friends. And Cam liked and cared about Jane and Josie. That was a big plus. Surely Whitney would like them too.

But that wasn't the problem. She wanted *them* to like *her.*

And then there was Zoe. She was Cam's sister. She was the sister to the man that Whitney was falling for. If she and Cam were involved, if they really tried to make this happen, it would mean more dinners around that very table in that very dining room in this very house and...

She felt her heart start racing. She was so glad that she'd been caught up in Didi and Henry and watching everyone interact and then the excitement of Josie and Grant announcing their *engagement*. The shared smile with Cam when they announced they were getting married had made her heart race too, but not in the panicky, I-need-*a-lot*-more-vodka way she was experiencing at the moment. It had been a very intimate and strangely hot moment between them. Having a shared memory, a shared secret had made her want to have a lot more of those. Secrets like the sound he made when she ran her tongue over the ridges of his abs and down the V on either side that she'd been fantasizing about since seeing him in the hallway in only a towel the other day.

But also secrets like what they'd gotten Maggie for Christmas. *They*. Not him, but they. As in they were giving her a gift from both of them. As a couple.

Or secrets like that they'd let Henry stay up extra late and have brownies for breakfast when he spent the weekend with them. Secrets like that they were going to sneak out of town for a romantic getaway and were only going to text to say they were fine and they'd see everyone on Monday morning. Secrets like a new idea for Hot Cakes that Cam was in on before any of the other partners because he'd sat up at the kitchen table with her designing the presentation and helping her brainstorm. Secrets like that they were engaged for a few days, or even hours, before telling anyone else. Or that the pregnancy test had been positive.

Her heart squeezed hard. She was getting *way* ahead of herself here. They weren't even dating. They were... friends. Good friends. Friends who wanted to get naked together.

"Hey."

She felt Cam move in behind her, his voice low as he spoke just to her.

"Hey," she said softly, still looking at the back door that had closed behind Josie a couple of minutes ago.

"You okay?" he asked.

She nodded.

He laughed lightly. "Liar."

He knew her. She loved that. "I don't know if I'm a hang-out-with-the-girls girl," she admitted.

"Well, you don't have to be," he said. He turned her to face him. "You can do dishes with us guys. You can go play *Warriors* with Didi and Henry. You can go talk to my mom and dad. You can slip upstairs and hang out in my room and I'll join you as soon as I can. Or you can head home."

She looked into his eyes, feeling her heart rate slowing. "Really?"

"Of course. I want you comfortable being here. I want you to come back. A lot. I want dinner here with all of us to be something you look forward to, not that you dread. Whatever you want."

She believed him. And she felt a strange mix of gratitude and affection and silly suddenly. "I'm making a big deal out of lemonade on the patio, aren't I?"

He shrugged.

She was. Not because those women would automatically like her because she was charming and funny and they had a lot in common. Those things weren't really true. But they would like her because Cam liked her. They loved Cam and Cam cared about Whitney and so those women would care about her because of Cam if nothing else.

That was friendship. That was love. That was acceptance.

She was catching on. She could learn this.

Those women were important to Cam and he would like

nothing more than to see Whitney hanging out and getting along with them. So she could do this. For him.

She lifted on tiptoe and pressed her lips to his quickly. "I'll be okay," she said as she pulled back.

He nodded. "You will."

"But thanks for giving me the option not to be."

Something flickered in his gaze. She thought for a second he was going to grin and say something flirtatious.

Instead, he said, "You can always be not-okay with me, Whit."

Her heart squeezed hard and for a second she couldn't take a deep breath. But she knew exactly what to give him in return. She nodded and said, "I know."

His gaze intensified and she knew she'd said the right thing. He leaned in and kissed her again, then set her back from him. "Go hang out. We'll head home in a bit."

Home. Together. She was shocked by how good that sounded.

They were friends. Hell, he might be her *best* friend. Yes, she realized a moment later, he *was* her best friend. He knew her, well, and he liked her anyway. She could be herself with him. She could be raw and real.

But they were more than friends. Already. Without getting naked. Without it being official.

But she definitely wanted to get naked with him. More now than before.

They needed to do that soon.

"Heading home sounds nice," she told him. "So yeah, give me a little bit with the girls, but I'll be ready whenever."

He looked at her a moment longer, then nodded. "Good."

Yeah, it was good. It was all good.

Or, it would be after this patio thing anyway.

18

Whitney took a breath, then turned and opened the back door. She stepped out onto the patio, pulling the door shut behind her, closing her off from Cam. Her lifeline.

No, that was stupid. She wasn't *scared* to be out here. She wasn't in danger. Except of making an ass of herself.

Zoe, Jane, and Josie all looked over. With smiles. Whitney felt some of the tension in her shoulders ease. These were Cam's friends. Family. Even the two that weren't his blood relations. She could spend time with them.

"Here, sit with me." Josie reached out and snagged Whitney's hand, tugging her down onto the love seat she was occupying.

Zoe and Jane each had a chair. The patio furniture was gathered around the stone firepit on the back patio. There was a fire but it was turned low and giving off little to no heat. Clearly it was for ambience as the night was warm.

The women all seemed relaxed, their drinks still mostly full.

"We were just talking about how amazing it is that Josie kept this engagement a secret from us," Jane said to Whitney.

"She's the romantic of the group and I cannot believe she didn't call us *immediately*."

"She was just about to tell us how Grant proposed," Zoe said.

Josie cast Whitney a look, then smiled.

Jane's eyes narrowed. "Hey, what was that?"

"What was what?" Josie asked, her eyes round with innocence. She lifted her glass for a sip of lemonade. Or to hide her expression.

Whitney also took a drink. Did Josie know that she and Cam had known about their marriage and "divorce"? She assumed that Josie knew about Cam's involvement, since he'd been the attorney to draw up the papers, but did she know Whitney had been in on it?

"That look you gave Whitney," Jane said. She sat forward, looking at them both with suspicion. "What do you know?" she asked Whitney. "You two have a secret."

Whitney's eyes widened. "Um."

Josie shook her head. "You don't know what you're talking about," she told Jane.

But Jane focused on Whitney. "Did you know they were engaged before you came to dinner tonight?"

Whitney thought fast. Had she known they were *engaged* before she came to dinner tonight? No. Because they weren't engaged. In her mind. Because she knew they were already married.

"No," she said truthfully.

But she made the mistake of taking a beat too long. And glancing at Josie right after answering.

Now Zoe sat forward too. "Nuh-uh. There's something going on." She wiggled a finger back and forth between Josie and Whitney. "What's up?"

Whitney *really* wanted Josie to take the lead here. This was *completely* Josie and Grant's secret. They should tell—or not tell

—whoever they wanted to *when* they wanted to. Oh, man, she could not screw this up.

"Nothing is up," Whitney said. "I had no idea that Josie and Grant were going to announce they were engaged at dinner tonight." Totally true.

"But you showed up tonight for the first time," Zoe said, her expression suspicious. "That's just a coincidence?"

Whitney nodded quickly. "Absolute coincidence."

"So you know *nothing* about Josie and Grant being engaged and planning to get married?" Jane asked.

Whitney lifted her chin, in that way that Cam called her on. Yes, it was the way she summoned her moxie. He'd told her not to do it with him and no, she knew she didn't need to anymore. But with these ladies? Oh yeah, she needed all the spunk she could muster to hold her own.

"I know that Josie and Grant are perfect for each other and I'm thrilled they're together." She glanced at Josie. "No matter how it happened."

Josie gave her a big grin and Zoe and Jane looked at one another. Then Jane nodded. "Nicely done."

Whitney lifted a brow. "What do you mean?"

"I mean, we know that you already knew they got married. And you managed to keep their secret *and* not flat-out lie to us. I'm impressed."

Whitney felt surprise course through her. "Wait, you know they're married?"

"I confessed earlier before we came inside," Josie said.

Whitney slumped back against the cushion behind her. "Thank God."

They laughed and Whitney felt a funny feeling of accomplishment. "You were testing me?" she asked.

"Of course," Zoe said. "If you're going to be a part of the group, we have to know you can keep secrets."

Another emotion surged through Whitney. Was she going

to be a part of the group? That sounded so nice. At her age, she should *not* want to be included and liked this much. It was pathetic. But it was still real.

"But not flat-out lie," Whitney said. "That could be complicated sometimes."

"Oh, you might have to lie sometimes," Zoe said.

Jane nodded. "Sometimes."

"Really? Like when?" Whitney asked. She needed to understand these rules if she was going to be a part of the group.

She lifted her glass to hide the smile that thought brought to her lips. She wasn't twelve and being asked to sit at the cool-kid table in the cafeteria.

But it felt like she was.

She'd *been* one of the cool kids for God's sake. She'd been fine in high school. Which meant she was one of those sad women who'd peaked in high school, stayed in her home town, and never quite gotten past those years. Ugh. She really hated that. These women had all stayed in their home town—the same one incidentally—but they'd changed and gotten better.

Whitney regarded them as she thought about that. Zoe and Josie still worked at the same bakery they'd always worked at. They were still best friends, just like they'd been in first grade. Zoe lived a block away from her parents and was now involved with a guy who had been a part of her life as her brother's best friend forever.

Josie lived in her grandparents' house, worked in the bakery she'd started working in after school as a a teen, and saw her family every day.

Jane worked in the factory, where she'd worked since she'd been sixteen, and, again, saw her family all the time.

Still, they were content. Happy. Had grown and changed and didn't see the things that *hadn't* changed as failures. They actually protected them. Jane was a huge advocate at Hot Cakes and continued to work there even though she was engaged to a millionaire. Zoe had always fiercely protected her bakery and its reputation. Josie, too, took Buttered Up and its place in the community very seriously, guarding its recipes as if they were her own.

Whitney could learn a lot from these women, she realized.

"Okay, times for lies," Jane said. "Like, if I say, 'is it time for strawberry pie yet?' The answer is always yes. Even if it's four a.m."

"But," Whitney said, pretending to be confused, "that isn't a lie. It's always time for strawberry pie, but *especially* if you're asking at four a.m."

Jane grinned and lifted her glass. "Exactly."

Whitney took a deep breath. This was going well.

"So we know that you already knew Josie and Grant were married. But I want to know *how* you knew," Zoe said, glancing between Josie and Whitney. "Have you been baking for her on the side?" Zoe asked Josie.

Josie worked for Zoe but she also had a side baking business. One that she'd kept from Zoe for a long time. It had never been anything that competed with the bakery. Josie only made things that Buttered Up didn't offer. Zoe had been a stickler for following in her grandmother's footsteps right down to every single recipe and every single product on the menu, so that hadn't been difficult.

But Josie had come clean about a month ago and now worked part-time for Buttered Up and part-time for herself.

Whitney shook her head. "No, nothing like that. Grant was in my office discussing the launch of the new snack cake when Cam came in and told him the insurance claims had all been paid and handed him the divorce papers."

"Insurance claims?" Jane asked.

"For her gall bladder surgery," Whitney said. "Since they'd just gotten married for the health insurance, Cam was letting Grant know it was all covered and over with. Cam handled all of that paperwork and drew up the divorce papers." She smiled. "Well, kind of."

Then she realized the other women weren't smiling. She looked from Jane to Zoe and then to Josie.

Josie was draining her glass of lemonade.

"What did you need health insurance for?" Zoe demanded.

Oh. Crap.

Whitney grimaced. "You hadn't told them that part?" she asked Josie.

Josie swallowed her lemonade and vodka. "Nope."

"Shit." Well, it *had* been going well.

"It's fine." Josie took a breath and quickly explained that she'd needed to have her gall bladder removed and had been worried about it because she didn't have health insurance through Buttered Up. Grant had stepped up and offered the idea of getting married, temporarily, so she'd be covered under his.

"But we fell in love and it all worked out wonderfully," she said. "So the gall bladder thing doesn't matter."

"But you were going to get *divorced*?" Zoe asked. "Cam even drew up the papers?"

"Well, they were really just cat adoption papers," Whitney jumped in, hoping to help the situation. "They weren't real divorce papers."

Zoe and Jane both looked at her with confusion. "Cat adoption papers?"

Whitney nodded quickly. "He came to me upset because Grant thought he wanted to go ahead with the divorce." Dammit, that didn't sound right either. She swung toward Josie. "I mean, he *didn't* want to get divorced, but he did because he wanted to give you the chance to date him and fall for him for real." She grimaced. "I mean, not that you didn't have real feelings for him... he wanted to be *sure* that you were together because of real feelings rather than because of the insurance."

Dammit, she wasn't saying this right. She grabbed Josie's hand. "He *knew* that he was in love with you," she said. "When I talked to him he was really torn up about it all. He just wanted a fresh start. To have the relationship develop from the beginning without the money and everything in the way. He didn't want you to *need* him. He just wanted you to want him." *Fuck.* This still sounded wrong. "I mean... Dammit," she finally said out loud. "I'm messing this up." She took a deep breath. "Grant was in love with you and he just wanted to be sure that he was doing the right thing."

She finally stopped, pressing her lips together.

No one said anything.

She lifted her glass and took a huge gulp, welcoming the feeling of warmth from the vodka spreading down her limbs. And hopefully stopping her runaway tongue.

Finally Zoe spoke. "Wow."

Yeah. Well, that wasn't a terrible summary.

"So these cat adoption papers," Jane said. "Is this why you have Melody, Val, and Alan?"

"Melody, Val, and Alan?" Whitney asked.

"The cats. Two girls and a boy," Jane said. She grinned. "They're named after characters from *Josie and the Pussycats*. Of course."

Whitney laughed out loud. "Of course. That's awesome."

Josie looked pleased. "Grant's idea, but I think it's hilarious. Was the cat adoption your idea?"

Whitney shook her head. "Cam. He knew he needed to give you papers for you to both sign, but didn't want them to be divorce papers." She looked at Zoe and Jane. "He knew that as soon as Grant and Josie thought they were officially divorced, they'd realize they didn't want to be. But I agreed. And I helped get them back together by keeping Grant busy at work while Josie planned their romantic dinner." She looked back to Josie. "And I'll admit that the *three* cats might have been me."

Josie grinned. "Good call."

"Wait."

They all looked at Zoe.

"So you're telling me that my brother, Camden asshole-extraordinaire-never-met-a-fight-he-didn't-want-to-have-will-argue-with-anyone-about-anything McCaffery recognized that Grant and Josie should be together and worked to keep them married?"

Josie and Whitney both nodded.

"But... asshole extraordinaire is a little harsh isn't it?" Whitney asked.

Zoe shook her head as if still processing what they'd told her. "Are you trying to tell me that Cam might be... romantic?" She wrinkled her nose as she said it, as if it were just too hard to believe.

But no one answered her. Instead they all looked at Whitney.

She lifted her glass for another drink.

Her last.

There was no lemonade and vodka left when she lowered the glass.

"Well?" Jane asked, lifting a brow. "Is Cam romantic?"

"And why are you assuming I would know?" Whitney asked. Asking a question rather than answering a question turned out to be a great way to avoid lying. She would have to remember that.

The three women snorted.

"Sure, no reason," Josie said.

"He's been... sweet. Very supportive. Helpful," Whitney hedged. Was that romantic? He'd been hot and dirty a couple of times. Sweet and charming several times. But romantic? That she wasn't so sure of.

"He's been making you cookies and cake and bars," Josie pointed out.

"Yeah, Aiden told me about the apron and everything," Zoe said.

"Oh, Dax told me too," Jane said. "The housekeeping too. And of course, Didi's been singing his praises every time we see her."

Whitney couldn't help but smile. "Like I said, sweet, and supportive, and helpful."

"And romantic," Josie said.

"Dusting my house and sitting up late with my grand-mother is *very* nice," Whitney said. "He's been a good friend. That's what we've been working on. But I'm not sure I'd call doing laundry and taking my grandma to yoga *romantic*."

But suddenly she wanted these women to tell her it was romantic.

The things Cam had said, the way he'd looked at her, the way he'd kissed her—even tonight when she'd showed up here —the way he wanted her to succeed, the way he wanted her to have girlfriends and feel supported at work... those were all... something. Was that romance?

Hell if she knew. Just like she didn't know how to do girl talk, she really knew nothing about romance.

"It is," Zoe said. "It's how he loves people. He takes care of things. He gets things done. He takes care of their problems so they can do the things they want and need to do. It's why he's the company's attorney. He does the messy legal shit so the other guys can do the creative stuff. Or, in Aiden's case, the leadership stuff he loves. Or so Grant can just play with his spreadsheets and calculator all day and not worry about the contracts and stuff."

"He doesn't like the legal stuff?" Whitney asked, realizing that had never occurred to her.

"He does," Zoe said. "Because, like I said, he loves confrontations and fights. He likes the legal stuff. But what he *loves* is being a part of something with his friends. Taking care of stuff for them. Making their jobs and lives a little easier. I'll bet he loved doing the insurance paperwork and the divorce-slash-cat-adoption-paperwork for Grant and Josie. That way Grant could just concentrate on what was making him happy... Josie." Zoe gave her friend a soft smile.

Whitney thought about all of that. The way Cam had been happy to stay at the house with Didi, not caring about not being in the office, fine with some of the other in-house attorneys doing some of the legwork so he could be with Didi.

So it wasn't the actual legal work he liked. It was the taking care of the people he cared about that he liked.

That fit, she realized. Of course. The guys had met in college when they'd been undergraduates. He and Aiden had started in business classes together and they'd met Grant and Dax and Ollie in their second year. Dax and Ollie had already created the beginnings of *Warriors of Easton*. They hadn't known the game would take off like it had, but she could imagine they'd all sat around and dreamed of turning it into something big and talked about what each of them could contribute. It had been clear, she was sure, that Dax and Ollie were the creative parts of the team. Grant was older and was clearly the financial mind of the group. Aiden was a natural leader and CEO type. Cam had possibly chosen law as the piece that was still needed and that he could fill in order to contribute and be an integral part of the team.

She was fascinated by this.

"So him dusting her end tables *is* romantic," Jane said. She said "dusting her end tables" with innuendo that her fiancé would have been very proud of. Clearly Dax was rubbing off on her.

Zoe laughed. "For sure."

Josie shook her head. "There's more."

Whitney looked at her. "There is?"

Josie gave her a smug smile. "The baking."

"He does that for Didi," Whitney said. "She told him she's missed Letty's recipes all these years, so he's making them for her."

"Oh," Zoe said, her voice soft and her expression touched. "That's so nice. That she's missed them and that he's doing that."

Whitney agreed. "It is. She loves it."

"But," Josie said. "He's been doing more cookies and bars lately, right?"

Whitney looked at her suspiciously. "How did you know that?"

"Because you haven't gotten any from me in a while," Josie said with a grin.

"Well, he's..." Whitney thought about what Josie was clearly implying.

"He's been baking the ones *you* like." Josie sighed. "You're getting them from home and don't need me anymore."

"Hold *on*," Zoe said, scooting forward in her chair. "You bake for her on the side?"

"No. We've been secretly selling her Buttered Up products for a long time."

Zoe frowned, then her eyes widened. "What?"

Whitney's eyes were also wide. "You knew?" She'd always been so careful. She'd paid two little girls to go into the bakery for her.

Josie laughed. "I knew. The Swanson girls spilled the beans the second time they ever came in for you."

Whitney groaned. "You must have thought I was an idiot."

Josie shook her head and looked at Zoe. "No. I always thought the feud between your families was ridiculous, but I respected it."

Whitney nodded her agreement over the ridiculous part. "But you never told Zoe?" She looked at the other woman.

"I would have forbidden her from selling them to you," Zoe said with a little frown.

"And no one should go without our sugar cookies, and caramel bars, and cinnamon rolls," Josie said. "So I kept quiet."

Whitney gave her a smile, but she focused on Zoe again. "You would have forbidden her to sell to me?"

Zoe nodded. Then shrugged. "I was pretty stubborn and bitchy about your family and Hot Cakes. Until Aiden."

Whitney saw the softness in Zoe's expression when she mentioned her fiancé. "I'm glad that's changed."

"Me too."

"Really?"

"Really. It makes having you and your grandma here for dinner a lot less awkward."

They all laughed lightly, but Whitney couldn't help but ask, "Do you think Cam would have brought Didi here if you still felt the same way about Hot Cakes?"

Zoe snorted. "For sure. Cam's never shied away from something just because it's awkward or tense. He loves a good confrontation." She grew quiet, regarding Whitney for a long moment, then said, "Until recently."

Whitney wet her lips, but didn't say anything. The attention shifted fully to her.

"Yeah," Jane said softly. "*That's* romantic."

"What is?" Whitney asked.

"When a man changes because of how he feels about a woman. Not that he becomes an entirely new man, but when he becomes... a better version of himself."

Whitney felt her throat and chest tighten. Had she done that for Cam? He'd definitely done it for her. She was more confident, more willing to speak up, more willing to believe she was valued.

He'd said that she made him softer. She'd really thought

that was Didi but... maybe not. Maybe she was influencing him for the better too.

Josie, the hopeful romantic, sighed happily next to Whitney. "This is nice," she said, settling back in her seat. "I'm so glad I have you girls."

And damn if Whitney didn't believe she was a part of that.

19

They were home and Didi was upstairs listening to an audiobook forty-five minutes later.

Whitney joined Cam in the kitchen after settling her grandmother. She slid up onto the tall stool at the breakfast bar and watched him put the leftovers from Maggie in the fridge.

"I had fun tonight."

He looked over his shoulder at her with a smile. "I could tell when you came back in that the patio time was good. I'm glad."

She nodded and ran a finger over the swirl pattern in the marble of the counter top. "So I guess the point of girl talk is to get advice, compare notes, or rant," Whitney said.

He came to stand across from her. "Makes sense."

"I didn't really have any work notes to compare. I do that with you guys."

"Okay."

"And I didn't have anything to rant about. My new bosses are pretty great and things are good with my grandma and my mom and dad are in Dallas and I've barely talked to them and they don't have anything to really do with my stuff anymore."

"That's all good."

She nodded. It was good. Very good.

"And I only need advice on one thing. And I think I have another friend who can give even *better* advice about that than they could."

Cam braced his hands on the counter, his muscles flexing, distracting her for a moment. "You got something you need to ask Piper about?"

"Nope."

"Paige?"

She shook her head. "No."

"Then who?"

"You."

He seemed to have been expecting that. One corner of his mouth curled. "You know I'm here for whatever you need."

That made her heart *thunk* at the same time it made heat curl through her lower stomach. She nodded. "I know that."

"So what do you need advice on?"

"Well, there's this guy."

That curl to his lip turned into more of a smirk. "I do know something about guys."

She nodded. "Yeah. I would very much like to know what you think I should do with this one."

"I think I can come up with a few suggestions."

The curl of heat turned into more of a swoop. She smiled. "Good."

"So is he hot?" Cam asked.

She laughed lightly. "Very. Though he knows it so there's this cockiness about him too."

"Is that a turn-off?"

She shook her head slowly. "Not exactly."

He was still smiling but his gaze was more intense. "Have you told him how you feel?"

Her heart *thunked* again but there was a swirl of nerves

along with this one. "Not in so many words. Not lately. But we have history."

"Good or bad history?"

That was a great question. A year ago she would have said bad. Their time together had been wonderful but it had ended so painfully that the bad had colored the rest for a long time. "Good," she finally answered. "There were some hard times, but they were important."

"Yeah?"

"For sure." She said it with surprising confidence. "I think we both realize that all of that had to happen to get us to where we are now. It's a part of both of us."

He gripped the edge of the counter, making his forearms bunch. He nodded. "That's probably true. But it's made things better now? Now that you're back... together?" He met her eyes. "Or are you back together?"

"I think we're coming back together," she said softly but with an assurance that swept through her as she said the words out loud. "It's interesting though... I think we both keep thinking our past has something to do with all this, but I'm not sure it does. We're different people than we were before. It's been a long time. A lot has happened to us both. It's almost like we've met for the first time and have gotten to know each other and have... started falling for each other for the first time."

He looked at her, saying nothing for long seconds, then suddenly pushed back from the counter top, straightening. "You're falling for him?"

She nodded.

"And you think he's falling for you?"

She nodded again.

That should have felt scary. He'd said he was crazy about her, but that wasn't love. Still... she *felt* it. She felt it in the way he encouraged her with work, the way he took care of her from the little things like the way her room smelled to the way he made her grandmother smile to the way he called her grandmother out when she was being mean. It was in the way he looked at her. Strangely, it was in the way he *hadn't* gotten them both naked yet.

"So what advice do you need?" he asked. His voice was gruff now and his gaze was burning into hers. Even across the granite countertop she could feel the heat.

"I guess I just want to know if you think he'll be annoyed that I've changed my mind."

He arched a brow. "About?"

"I made a big deal about not wanting to get involved because I wanted to focus on work, but... I've changed my mind. I'm still very focused on work, and I'm really proud of what I'm doing there, but"—she took a deep breath—"I want him."

Cam's eyes flared, and Whitney felt her reaction deep in her belly and between her legs.

She went on before he said anything. Or did anything. Because once he *did* something, she wasn't going to want to talk much anymore.

"I want to be with him. And it's amazing because he gets it. He wants me to be successful at work. He knows how important that is to me. But he's fully supportive of it. Not just that, but he's helping me make it work. He's a part of all of that success. It feels like we're a team and he's totally behind me. I'm feeling like I—we—can have it all and I guess..." She took another breath. "I want to know how to let him know that."

A muscle ticked along Cam's jaw and he just stood looking at her, not saying a word.

She finally asked. "Do you think he's going to be annoyed that I changed my mind?"

He cleared his throat. "No. I don't think annoyed is how he's going to feel about that."

Then he stepped back and bent to open the cupboard

under the breakfast bar. He pulled out a mixing bowl and the hand mixer. He got a spoon and a spatula from a drawer, then the measuring cups and spoons from another drawer. He set them all out on the counter between them. Without a word, he went into the pantry and came back with an armful of ingredients. He put them down before going to the refrigerator for butter and eggs.

She watched him measure everything out, melt the butter, and cream the eggs, butter and sugar before saying, "What are you doing?"

"Making chocolate chip cookie dough," he said without looking up.

O-kay. She wasn't worried here. At all. He wasn't ignoring her. He hadn't missed what she'd said. This wasn't him blowing her off or changing the subject.

This was, somehow, part of the subject.

So she just watched him mix. Until he got to the point of adding the chips.

"No semisweet chips?" she asked.

He looked up. "No."

"You use two kinds instead?"

He nodded. "Milk chocolate. The super sweet ones. And dark chocolate. A little more bitter and stronger. Together they make the overall semisweet flavor. But this way each bite has both distinct flavors."

"That's your secret with these cookies?"

"Part of it. Yeah."

"From your grandma?"

"Nope. This is all mine. She liked mine better than her own."

"Why do you like it this way better?" She somehow knew there was a reason.

"The semisweet chips aren't really anything in particular. They're kind of sweet and kind of dark. I think that if you're going to be something you just *be* it. Be sweet. Be dark. But really *be* it."

"People can't be both? They can't have times they feel sweet and times they feel dark?"

"Of course. But too often we try to cover the sweet times with a little self-deprecation or nonchalance because we don't want to be too sweet. Or we try to cover our dark with more sugar because we don't want to be too sad or too scary."

"Like when we're suddenly working from home and baking cookies with a friend's grandma all day?"

He nodded without a smile. "We should embrace that. There's nothing wrong with a soft, sweet side."

There wasn't. At all. It was hot as hell that this tough guy who loved to fight big corporations in court, who had tattoos and muscles and a smirk that wouldn't quit and sarcasm that was as natural as breathing, had a secret to his chocolate chip cookies and had learned to love lemon drop martinis and liked looking at photo albums with his grandmother's best childhood friend.

"And there's nothing wrong with having a dark side sometimes," he told her. "You don't have to cover it up with sweetness. Sugar isn't the answer to everything. It's okay to be a little bitter, to have a little bite. It just makes the sweet stuff sweeter when it's time for that."

She nodded. He was right. Her being bitter about her family and the business and how things had been at Hot Cakes for the past ten years was okay. It wasn't perfect. It wasn't how she would have chosen it to be maybe. But it made everything now—her new bosses who were more like partners and were becoming friends, and their new ideas, and the new successes —even sweeter.

And the same was true with her and Cam. The little bit of bitterness between them was making *this* now sweeter.

"How long will those cookies for Didi take?" she asked. She

ERIN NICHOLAS

assumed he was making them up now so they were done for when Didi woke up later. So that maybe he and Whitney could steal some time together before that happened.

"These aren't for Didi," he said. He met her eyes. "They're your favorite, right?"

She swallowed. There was a heat in his eyes that she'd seen before, but there was something else there now. Something new.

Intention.

This wasn't going to end with him pulling back and telling her that they couldn't keep going.

"Yes," she said. "Those are my favorite." She wasn't even going to ask how he knew that. She didn't know if he remembered it from years ago or if Didi had told him or if he'd noticed that she'd eaten nearly a dozen of these when he'd made them before, whereas she'd only swiped maybe half a dozen of the others.

It didn't matter. He'd been making cookies and bars for her. And, yes, Josie was right, that was romantic.

"You asked me what you should do with this guy you're falling for," he said.

She nodded.

"Take off your clothes."

———

It was time.

He'd wanted to give her a chance to feel secure, to know he was here for her as a friend first, to figure out what she really wanted.

But... It. Was. Time.

Cam watched her take a deep breath and braced himself for her to lift her chin, gathering her nerve.

But she didn't.

She slipped off the stool, stepped around the corner of the counter so she was facing him fully, and stripped her dress off.

The sweet little sundress that was nothing like those fucking corporate pencil skirts she wore that made him nuts.

His heart was thundering and he felt everything in his body tighten almost painfully. He wanted her. So much. She was gorgeous. Physically. Any man would think so. He'd always wanted her.

But now he wanted *her*. This woman. Not the girl he'd been missing for the past ten years, not the woman he'd run into here and there over the years when visiting Appleby, not the woman he'd thought he was sparring with in the offices at Hot Cakes. *This* woman.

The one he'd gotten to know better and watched grow and who now stood in front of him naked. Literally, but also figuratively. She was letting him in again and this time there was even more on the line than their parents finding out about them back in high school and making them break up.

It would have felt like the end of the world. It *had* felt that way when it had ended. But what they'd lost were stolen kisses and some messing around in the dark and some laughter and, yes, friendship. But kid friendship.

Now... if they messed this up it was so much more.

Now their hearts and their futures were wrapped up in all of this.

Now they really would lose a true friendship. With each other.

Yeah. That was true.

But if they did this... they could have all of this forever.

"You didn't have panties on? This whole time?" he asked, his voice gruff, but trying to lighten the mood. Trying to make things playful and dirty. Because if he didn't, he was going to propose to her and *that* might have been too much.

She also didn't have a bra on so when she propped her hands on her hips, he could see everything.

Every-fucking-thing.

"I wore panties to your mother's house for dinner with your family and my grandmother, of course," she said, one eyebrow up. "I took them off upstairs when I brushed my teeth."

He smirked. She'd been classy enough to have underwear on while having dinner with their families. Of course she had. Whitney Lancaster wouldn't go to a family dinner without underwear on.

But she'd also taken them off—and brushed her teeth—before coming back down here to talk to him in the kitchen while he made cookies. Gee, what had she thought might happen? Maybe the *take your clothes off* hadn't just been his idea. Maybe she'd been on her way to seduce him. He really liked that thought.

Proposing *might* have been too much tonight.

But maybe not.

"Well, maybe you're more prepared than I am here," he said. "I had no idea we were having pantyless kitchen time tonight."

She came forward, her hips swaying, her breasts bouncing softly, completely distracting him as she moved.

"You had *no* idea that we were having pantyless kitchen time tonight?" she asked, stopping right in front of him.

Yes, he very much loved this more confident side of Whitney.

"I might have *hoped* for pantyless time tonight," he said. "But the room doesn't really matter."

She reached for the bowl of cookie dough and scooped up a spoonful, lifting it to her mouth and then sucked it from her finger.

Cam's body heated and hardened.

She looked up at him. "So you have underwear on under those jeans?"

"I do."

"Guess that makes *me* the optimist here."

"Makes me damned grateful."

She smiled. "Good."

"Can you do that thing with the cookie dough again?" he asked.

She took another dab on her fingertip and lifted it to her lips, but he caught her wrist at the last moment and brought it to his mouth. He slid it past his lips, over his tongue, then closed around it and sucked.

Her eyes darkened and she swallowed hard.

"I was actually going to bake these for you," he said.

"Let's see if there's any left for that." She took his hand, dipped his finger into the dough and lifted it to her lips, licking, then sucking as he had.

The feel of her hot, wet mouth around his finger made his cock ache and press insistently against his zipper. He wanted her mouth around his cock. She could coat it in cookie dough if she wanted to. He didn't care if he could get her lips around him.

"Whit—"

She dipped more cookie dough out of the bowl and then painted it over one nipple.

Or they could do this.

Without a word, he bent his knees, placed a hand on her back to hold her steady, and licked the dough off her nipple, sucking to be sure it was completely clean.

Her hand cupped the back of his head as she arched closer. "Oh my...*Cam*."

He wanted to hear a *lot* more of that. "Fuck." He straightened and reached for the bowl.

She reached for his pants.

He let her.

She unzipped his jeans, shoving them and his boxers just low enough to free his erection. She sucked in a quick breath as she took in the sight, then circled him with her hand.

Cam gripped the counter and locked his knees as lust and heat coursed through him. "Whitney," he said, his jaw tight. "Babe."

She stroked up and down his length, not taking her eyes from the action, or saying a thing.

"Whit."

"Just give me a minute," she told him.

He huffed out a laugh, then a groan as she squeezed and stroked.

"I need more tattoos," she said, suddenly, pulling her hand from his cock and sliding both palms under his shirt. She pushed the cotton up his torso and he lifted his arms, letting her strip it up over his head. When she got it higher than she could reach, he grabbed the shirt and pulled it the rest of the way off, tossing it over his shoulder.

"Yes," she said softly, almost reverently, as she slid her palms back down his body, over his shoulders, chest, and down his sides.

He watched her looking at him. She ran her hands over his tattoos, her fingertips tracking the lines, her eyes studying them all. She had him turn so she could see them all. His ink covered one arm from shoulder to wrist, his other arm elbow to wrist, his left shoulder blade, his right ribs, and his right abs.

"This is all so beautiful. You'll have to tell me what they all mean."

"Okay." His voice was thick. He would do this however she wanted. But he really didn't want to talk about his tattoos at the moment. "This one is—"

"Oh, later." She laughed lightly, running her hands up his

ribs on either side and lifting her eyes to his, leaning in to press her breasts against his chest. "Much later."

He bent and captured her lips with his, cupping her face and taking the kiss deep immediately. Their tongues stroked, their groans mingled, their bodies pressed skin to skin. Mostly.

Growling, he pulled away and dropped his hands to his jeans, pulling his wallet out and tossing it on the counter, then shoving them down. He went back to kissing her, but her hands went back to stroking him and before he could reach for the condom in his wallet she'd reached for the cookie dough.

And gone to her knees.

Again he gripped the edge of the counter as she smeared the cookie dough down his length then dragged her tongue along the hard shaft, licking it clean. Cam worked on breathing, cupping the back of her head, not pulling her hair, not thrusting, just breathing. And watching. Absorbing it all.

It was clear she was no expert, and that thrilled him more than anything else she could have done with her mouth. Of course, any blow job was a great blow job. He let her lick and suck, loving her little moans and the feel of her hot mouth and hands on him until he simply couldn't take it anymore.

He pulled back and stared down at her, breathing hard.

I love you and *marry me* were both on the tip of his tongue but immediately after having her greedy mouth on his cock wasn't the right time for either of those. He'd thought them both prior to her licking cookie dough from his dick, but it might be hard to convince her of that.

Besides, he didn't want to talk. And he didn't need to in order to show her how he felt.

He pulled her to her feet, then lifted her onto the counter, shoving the bowl of dough back and stepping between her knees. She spread her thighs, welcoming him against her with her arms going around his neck and her legs going around his waist.

They kissed, long and deep. He ran his hands up and down her back. She gripped his back and arched close. Her pussy was hot and wet against his cock and he rocked against her gently.

She was moaning softly and saying his name as he dragged his mouth down her neck and then bit down where it curved into her shoulder.

"*Cam.*"

"You want to do this here?"

The kitchen seemed appropriate, but they were sleeping together tonight. All night. In a bed. They could move this show upstairs right now.

"Yes. Here. Now."

Didi wasn't going to be coming down. He'd told her that he needed to talk to Whitney—Didi had agreed—and asked if she'd stay upstairs tonight until her alarm went off on her phone. She'd thought that was a great idea. So he had until 3 a.m. to worship every inch of Whitney Lorraine Lancaster.

That was five hours.

That wouldn't be enough time for him to come even close to getting enough of her. But it would be a very good start.

He reached for his wallet, pulling the condom from between the bills. He kept kissing her as he ripped it open and rolled it on. Then he pulled her butt forward on the counter.

"I've missed you so fucking much," he said.

"This feels like the first time," she told him softly, running her hand over the side of his face and into his hair.

She was right. It did.

"I'm in love with you, Whit."

Okay maybe *immediately* after having her mouth on his cock hadn't been the right time but this felt good.

He hoped.

Her eyes widened for a moment. But then she smiled and breathed out. "I'm in love with you too."

Neither of them said *again*.

Because this was different than before. This was new.

But when he pulled her forward and she wrapped herself around him and he slid into her hot, tight body, it felt like they'd been doing it forever.

"Oh yes Cam," she half whispered, half moaned.

"Whit. Damn. Yes," he answered. Sort-of. It was more of a grunt-groan honestly.

He pulled out and thrust again. And again. She clung to him, her body—from her arms to her pussy—tight around him, not letting him go far. But he had to move. The friction, the push and pull, the heat and wetness everything he needed.

He gripped her ass, felt her hot breath on his neck, her silky hair against his chest.

"Please," she whimpered.

"Anything."

"Just... more. Harder."

Well, that he could do. "Lean back."

She shifted, looking up at him.

He kissed her and then pressed her back until she was leaning on her elbows.

"Gorgeous." He ran a hand up one thigh to her stomach then up to one breast, playing with a nipple and feeling the resultant tightening around his cock.

The angle was gorgeous too. He could see everything where they were joined.

"You're incredible," he told her, pulling out and sliding back in, watching her body take him then lifting his eyes to her face.

She was breathing hard, her eyes on him, her cheeks pink.

"Ditto," she told him breathlessly.

He pulled back then thrust forward again, sinking into her welcoming sweet, wet heat. "I will never get over this," he told her sincerely.

"Good. I'm already addicted." She ended that on a gasp as he hit a particularly good spot.

"Oh, like that?" he asked.

"Yes. Please. Again."

He complied.

And again.

"Harder." She tightened around him. "Faster."

He did. Both. He watched her breasts bounce. Watched her head fall back, her hair trailing over the countertop. He watched the flush climb up her chest.

"Yes! Cam," she gasped.

He gripped her thighs where he held her and picked up the pace even more. He was pumping into her hard and deep and he felt his climax building. He moved a hand, pressing his thumb against her clit, then rubbing.

"Oh! Yes!"

He circled the spot, feeling the beginnings of her orgasm, watching her mouth fall open as she panted and the way she gripped the edge of the counter.

"Cam!"

He circled and thrust faster and then she clamped down on him, one hand gripping his wrist as her pussy milked him and she cried out.

He let himself go, thrusting three times, and coming hard, calling her name.

"Whitney! Yes! Yes!"

She immediately pulled herself up and wrapped her arms and legs around him. He held her tightly, feeling the goose-bumps pebbling her skin. Then he yanked his pants up, scooped her up with his hands under her ass, and turned toward the hallway, heading for the stairs.

"Our clothes. And the cookie dough," she protested weakly, her face against his neck.

"I'll take care of it all later," he promised.

She reached out and flipped off the light as they passed it, leaving only the soft glow of the light over the sink.

He loved that she just let him take care of things. He hadn't realized how important that was to him until he'd moved in here. His mom had always taken care of things in their home. His grandmother had single-mindedly taken care of their family business. He absolutely contributed to Fluke, Inc. and now Hot Cakes, but... he was an attorney. He was easily the most replaceable of any of the guys. He knew they never *would* replace him, but what he contributed was much more in the category of friendship than it was anything legal that another lawyer couldn't handle.

But here with Didi and Whitney it was different. He was doing something here that he truly felt no one else could do as well. It was very domestic and very full of fat and sugar at times but it was important.

He turned to climb the stairs, loving the feel of her in his arms.

"You can't carry me all the way up," she said.

"Watch me."

He started up the steps.

"This is so hot," she murmured.

"You like being carried?"

"Yeah, but don't tell anyone."

"No one would believe me anyway," he said against her head with a smile.

It made him feel stupidly manly. And he would never tell anyone *that* either. Probably not even her. She wasn't some "little lady" who needed a big strong man to take care of her.

But she liked when he did. And so did he. So, yeah... no one else needed to know.

He turned down the hall heading for her room. He could take her to his, of course, but his room was a guest room. He wanted to be with her in *her* room, in a permanent place. And, yes, a place where she'd think of him every time she lay down.

He hoped to be in there with her every time she lay down

from now on but... they still had some talking to do. They were absolutely on their way to permanently lying down together though.

He got it. That's what she'd said earlier. He knew what she wanted and needed. She was falling for him because he understood her needs with her career.

Cam frowned as he put her down on the bed.

"Come here." She pulled him down with her.

He went willingly. Of course.

She turned her back and snuggled her body right into his, spooning like they'd done it every night forever.

And it felt right.

But he was still frowning.

No. She wasn't falling for him *just* because he was supportive of her career and made it one-thousand times easier on her to pursue it. But he'd helped her see that she could have it all. Him and Hot Cakes.

And... she could. It had stung a little to realize that part of what she needed was for him to *not* need her. Not need her there for regular family dinners or even every night by a certain time. To not need her to remember appointments or to meal plan or dust.

But she did need him for orgasms, dammit.

And cookies.

She sighed and snuggled closer and pulled Cam's arm around her body and he sighed too.

Orgasms and cookies. Yeah, he could work with that.

20

Something woke them up at 4 a.m.

But it wasn't an alarm. Or the theme song to *Magnum, P.I.*—on TV or on Cam's phone.

But it was Didi. Shaking them awake.

She was at the bottom of Whitney's bed, shaking the entire mattress. "Whitney! Camden! Wake up! Wake up! It's bad!"

They both sat bolt upright.

"Grandma! What's wrong? Are you okay?" Whitney started to get out of bed, realized she was naked, realized Cam was beside her weighing down the other side of the sheet, yanked it hard, then realized that would leave *him* naked.

She grabbed for a pillow and tossed it over his lap and then yanked the sheet again, pulling it over her body and sliding out of the bed.

"Henry called. It's Maggie," Didi said.

Still half-asleep, Whitney stood at the side of the bed, blinking.

Henry? That name was familiar...

"What did he say?" Cam was off the mattress, the pillow clutched against his midsection, moving toward Didi.

Henry. Cam. Right, Cam's little brother.

"Why did he call you?" she asked.

Okay, maybe at 4 a.m. that wasn't the most important part of the situation. And it was 4 a.m.? She blinked at the clock. Why hadn't Didi gotten up to watch *Magnum, P.I.*?

"He said Maggie got sick and they took her to the hospital," Didi told Cam.

He reached her and put a hand on her shoulder, the other still holding the pillow in place. "Maggie is at the hospital?"

Whitney felt her stomach tighten as her grandmother nodded.

Then Whitney realized that Didi was dressed. Fully. She had on pants and a blouse and shoes. She even wore a necklace and had her purse in one hand. She had her hair brushed and —Whitney blinked—Didi was also wearing lipstick.

"We need to go," Didi told him. "Right now."

"I need to call Henry. Or Dad. Or Zoe." Cam looked around for his phone, turning to face the bedside table.

Didi's gaze dropped to his backside. "I already told you what he said," she replied.

Whitney rounded the bed quickly, turning Didi by the shoulders and pulling her grandmother's attention away from Cam getting dressed.

"Did Henry say what happened?"

"Maggie got sick and they called the ambulance and to tell Cam."

"Fuck," Cam swore.

Whitney glanced at him as her stomach roiled. This was not good.

"Can I see your phone?" she asked Didi.

She was praying that Didi had imagined the call, she could admit. It was 4 a.m. Usually Didi would have been up for a few hours by now and downstairs watching TV. Maybe Didi was sleep walking? Or just confused since it was the middle of the night. Why would Henry, of all the McCafferys, call Didi of all the people?

"Okay." Didi dug her phone out of her purse.

There was, indeed, a recent call from a number that was labeled HENRY. About thirty minutes ago.

She decided not to tell Cam about the time since the call. Clearly Didi had taken that time to get ready to go before coming in to tell Cam what was going on.

"My phone is down in the kitchen," Cam said, now with his jeans on and the pillow back on the bed.

Whitney assumed hers was as well. She'd laid it and her keys and purse down when they'd first gotten home. Typically she brought it upstairs with her when she came to bed but, nothing about coming to bed last night had been typical.

She watched Cam stomp toward the door and listened to his steps on the staircase.

"We need to go," Didi said again, taking her phone back. "Henry is really scared. He wanted to know when I'd be there."

Whitney looked at her grandmother. "We can't go. Cam will go and let us know what's happening."

The last thing the family needed was extra people around to take care of. And that's what Cam would do. He'd try to take care of everyone. It was better if she and Didi stayed behind.

But... Whitney blew out a breath. She had a huge meeting today. Hot Cakes' biggest account was going to be the first to see the plans for the new bars. It was a perk of being loyal and long-term customers. They were flattered and excited, but the CEO, Gordon Perkins, a long-time friend of her father's, was skeptical. The new ownership, particularly with no one with the last name of Lancaster and no one over the age of thirty-five was making him nervous.

The Perkins family owned the largest chain of convenience stores in the Midwest. They'd been in business with the Lancasters, carrying Hot Cakes products, since Gordon had taken over from his father about the time Whitney's father, Eric, had taken over Hot Cakes from *his* father.

She had to convince Gordon that everything would be fine. That new didn't mean bad, that change didn't mean that quality would go down or prices would go up or that he wouldn't be able to enjoy a good relationship with the new owners. He was already frustrated that there were four men to contend with instead of one. And that none of the four particularly liked to golf.

Grant and Aiden had decided she should lead the meeting since Gordon knew her. They would be there too, to meet him and his team and to reassure them that everything was going to be even better going forward. But she had to be there. She was a Lancaster. Gordon would not be as friendly with anyone else.

She supposed that meant Didi would be coming with her to the meeting.

On one hand, that could be amazing. Didi was, after all, the founder of Hot Cakes. The original Lancaster behind it all.

As long as she was having a good day and didn't start telling Gordon about cat yoga or *Magnum, P.I.* or her kicking ass at *Warriors of Easton* or anything else that would make Gordon question the validity of the other things she might say about how well the company was doing.

"Didi!" Cam called up the stairs. "Come on!"

Didi turned and started out of the room.

"Wait!" Whitney went to follow her, but tripped on the bottom of the sheet. She yanked on it, gathering it up above her feet, wadding it in her hands and ran after Didi.

Cam was standing at the bottom of the staircase texting and Didi was a third of the way down.

"She can't go with you."

He looked up from his phone. "Why not?"

"To the hospital? Where your family is with your mother?" Whitney shook her head. "No, she can stay with me."

"Do you want to come later?" Cam asked Didi as she got to the bottom. "You're all dressed up like you were coming now."

"Oh, I'm coming now. I told Henry I'd be right there." She held up her purse. "I have books."

Whitney couldn't help but smile at that. She would guess *Alice in Wonderland* was in there. And that was a great choice. It would maybe help keep Henry's mind off of what was going on with his mom. It would also be comforting to Didi.

Cam nodded at Didi as if that made perfect sense. He looked up at Whitney. "She can come with me now since she's ready. I need to get right over there."

Whitney wasn't going to argue with him. He was right that he needed to get there as soon as possible and Didi was already crossing the foyer to the front door. "Okay. Is... what's going on?"

"They think a heart attack." His voice was thick. "They're doing tests now. I talked to Aiden. He and Zoe are there."

"Oh, good." That did make her feel better. Aiden was a natural leader. He'd take charge and make sure they got the answers they needed.

Except... this was his mother too. Not biologically, but he was a part of the McCaffery family. He wasn't just there supporting his fiancé and best friend. He was probably scared to death too.

"So..." Cam glanced at the front door.

"Go," she said quickly. "Of course. Go. Let me know what's going on when you can. And if you need me to come get Didi."

"I—" He frowned. Then nodded. "Okay."

She watched them leave. The door shutting behind them made her heart ache. She wanted to be there for him. With him. She wanted to go to the hospital and sit and hold his hand. She wanted to... help.

But Cam would be the helpful one. He was the one that

took care of everyone. He'd take care of their dad and Henry and Zoe and... Didi.

And he'd have help taking care of Zoe. Aiden was there. He and Cam could support each other. The way brothers would.

Then she realized that Grant and Josie would be there too. Josie had been close to Zoe their entire lives. She'd be scared about Maggie and would want to be there. Which meant Grant would be there to support her. And Cam, who was one of his best friends and like a brother.

Jane and Dax would be there too. Jane was close to the McCafferys and Dax would want to support her and Cam.

Yes, Cam had plenty of people around him for support and help. He didn't need her. Especially when she would be no help there. She had no experience with this. Her grandfather had died of a massive stroke. He'd been there one minute and gone the next. There had been no medical testing or procedures, or hospital stays. If there had been, her family wouldn't have looked to her for coordinating anything anyway. She knew nothing about heart attacks and procedures and tests for that. She'd be no help there at all.

But staring at the front door, she realized that there *was* something she could do. She *would* be helpful at Hot Cakes.

She could run this meeting with Gordon Perkins for the company.

That was what she could contribute. She could manage things at Hot Cakes while they were all out of the office and focusing on Maggie.

She could reassure Gordon that everything was fine and that he not only wanted to continue working with them, but that he wanted to be the first to introduce the new snack bar to the public in *his* stores. He'd want to put up huge displays in *all* his stores and do big promotions and really push this out to the public.

That was exactly what Hot Cakes needed as the next step

with this new product. A big partner in their public launch. Gordon Perkins would be perfect.

Whitney could make this happen. For her bosses.

For her *friends*.

————

Three hours later, Whitney strode into the executive office suites of Hot Cakes in a bright, cherry red pencil skirt. The red color was out of the ordinary for her. She'd ordered it online on a whim last week. She'd been waiting for the right moment to show it off to Cam.

Today was the right moment to wear it though. She was ready to be in charge. That was what the skirt said to her. That's what mattered. She didn't need to say that, or show it, to Cam.

The red heels made her happy as well. Rather than getting them for the extra inches they'd add, she'd gotten them because of the sassy straps and the big red bow on the toe. Those were also for her.

The crowning touch was the black blouse with white polka dots. She'd seen it on the webpage and immediately wanted it.

No, none of this was the red wiggle dress of Piper's Whitney had tried on in her office the night Cam had said her tits looked amazing. But this was her. This made her feel confident, like she was bold and confident and stretching her wings.

Dammit, she *liked* the pencil skirts and how they made her look and feel.

Yes, she also liked the color red.

"Hang on. Ollie's on his way." Piper rose to her feet as Whitney approached. Then she stopped and looked Whitney up and down. "Wow. You look amazing."

Whitney smiled. "Thanks." Then she tipped her head. "Ollie's coming?"

"He's going into the meeting with you. We both are."

"You... are?"

Piper smiled, but she looked like it was a bit of an effort. "Of course. We're the only ones here, but we're here for you while everyone else is at the hospital with Maggie."

Whitney felt her heart squeeze hard in her chest. She'd been trying to concentrate on the meeting and not on what was happening in Dubuque.

Gordon Perkins, his son Matt, and his business partner, Stephen McDonald, were driving in. They were from Minneapolis but had been doing a tour of their stores throughout Minnesota and Iowa and were planning to go on into Indiana. They'd visited their Iowa stores, finishing with the six in Dubuque yesterday. They didn't have a store in little Appleby but had been willing to stop by for this meeting while in the area. She had to focus here and make it worth their stop.

"And everyone thought I needed help?" Whitney asked. Ollie and Piper both knew the basics about the new snack bar, of course, but the details that Gordon and his team would need would come from Grant and Aiden. Or Whitney.

"Oh, we're purely moral support," Piper said, shaking her head. "Mr. Perkins and his team should be here in about thirty minutes. I made coffee here and ran over to Cedarville for muffins since the bakery is closed this morning."

Whitney took a deep breath. She hadn't even thought about that. *How* had she not thought about that? Of course, Buttered Up hadn't opened this morning. Zoe and Josie were both at the hospital. The main person who filled in when they couldn't be there was Maggie.

She felt a pang in her heart. *God, please let her be okay.*

She focused on the bakery. Not only was that a problem for them business-wise—obviously they couldn't make money if they didn't sell anything today—though that was less of an issue with both Zoe and Josie being engaged to millionaires—but it was a problem for the waste of the food inside the bakery and, well, it was a problem for the town. Not a horrible, natural disaster type of problem, of course, but if there were a way to have the bakery open, it would be best for everyone.

She thought quickly. "Can you check with Paige?" she asked Piper. "Maybe she could go over and open the bakery. At least for a little bit?"

Paige also filled in once in a while for her sister and Zoe. She liked to add zucchini and carob chips and almond flour and other healthy things to the recipes which drove Zoe a little nuts, but Paige wouldn't be baking today. She could just run the register.

Piper nodded. "Oh, that's a good idea. I'm sure she would. It's a little later than they usually open, but we could put something up on the town Facebook page and send out a text to the community list."

Whitney frowned. "There's a community text list?"

"Yeah, Drew told me about it. It's for announcements like the school closing because of snow. Things like that. But they also use it for things like announcing retirement parties for people. Funeral services. Birth announcements."

See, that was why small towns were so great. "Do you think this qualifies?" Whitney asked.

"I think everyone will want to know that Maggie is in the hospital and that the bakery is open so people can go support the McCafferys," Piper said, already typing into her phone.

Whitney thought about that too. The McCafferys were beloved in Appleby. That was just a fact. *Her* family had feuded with them for half a century, but that didn't mean the rest of the town didn't realize how loving and sweet and generous they all were.

She sighed. Wow, things had really been messed up for a really long time. She was so grateful that Aiden had started breaking those walls down and that now she and Cam could maybe help further the healing.

"You know what?" Whitney said. "I'm good here. If Ollie stays and represents the new partners with Gordon Perkins and his team, I think we can handle this. Could you go help Paige at Buttered Up? Then I could come over and help after this meeting."

"You would help at Buttered Up?" Piper asked.

She nodded. "I actually did once before. When Aiden proposed to Zoe and swept her off her feet, literally, I got behind the counter and waited on customers. It was a great way to show the town that things were changing between the two businesses."

"And this is all about the two *businesses*?" Piper asked.

Whitney blew out a breath. "No. Not anymore. This is about me supporting the McCafferys. But there are only so many ways I can do that. I can be here and make this meeting successful and I can then go help at the bakery and make that work."

Piper hesitated. She opened her mouth. Shut it again. Frowned. Then said, "You could also just... be there. At the hospital."

Whitney shook her head. "There are plenty of people at the hospital. But if I'm not *here*, there's no one who can do this meeting and if we don't go to the bakery, there's no one there."

"But *being there* for people... it's about *being there*, Whit," Piper said. "You don't always have to *do* stuff or be accomplishing things or working."

Whitney felt a shiver of... something... go through her. She was pretty sure it was that she wanted to believe Piper. But that she didn't quite.

Cam took care of her by taking things off her plate, making it so she didn't have to worry. That's what she was doing here. Or trying to do here. She wanted to take care of Cam.

"It's a work in progress," she finally said.

Piper nodded. "Okay. Well then, I can go to the bakery with

Paige and Ollie will be in there with you and... when it's over we can go from there."

Whitney nodded and looked down at the files in her arms. This she knew. This she was comfortable with. *This* she could pull off.

Ollie joined her in the conference room a few minutes later. "'Mornin'," he greeted. His smile was a lot less bright than usual.

She understood. "Morning."

He took a chair as his phone chimed. He pulled it out and opened the message. Whitney felt her heart kick. Was it news about Maggie? How was she? How was everyone else?

"They found a blockage in three vessels," Ollie read. He scrubbed a hand over his face. "She's going in for surgery."

Whitney felt her throat tighten and she forced herself to swallow.

"Dammit." He laid his phone on the table and took a deep breath. "Poor Cam and Aiden." He looked up. "And Zoe, of course. And Steve and Henry."

Whitney nodded. She knew he hadn't meant to leave the rest of the family out. But Cam and Aiden were two of his best friends. Of course they were in the front of his mind.

"Who's—" She had to clear her throat and try again. "Who's texting you?"

"Grant."

Her air swooshed out. She'd hoped it was Cam. That would mean, in her mind anyway, that he was taking some control by relaying the information and keeping people informed. But of course it was Grant. He was the calm, cool one. Of course Cam wouldn't be calm and cool right now.

She imagined him pacing the waiting room, growling at everyone, and snapping at staff when they couldn't give him the answers he wanted *right now*. Then again, she could also picture him sitting with his arm around his dad or holding his sister's hand or taking Didi and Henry to the cafeteria for brownies at 8 a.m. as a distraction.

She would *really* love to know for sure how he was and what he was doing.

"Has Cam said anything more to you?" Ollie asked, leaning forward. His eyes were tired. He looked worried. Very worried. And Ollie never looked worried.

She shook her head. "I haven't heard from him."

Ollie was clearly surprised by that. "Oh. I just assumed he'd be wanting to talk to you."

Yeah. Well, he was surrounded by people who could support him and make him feel better. Who had been a part of his life over the past nine years and knew Maggie well and loved his mother as much as he did.

"He knew I was covering this meeting," she said, lifting a shoulder. "Maybe he didn't want to distract me."

Or maybe he figured you wouldn't want to be distracted.

The little voice that whispered through her mind surprised her. She wasn't here because she wanted to have this meeting. Not exactly. She was here because she was trying to help her partners... well, her bosses. Her *friends* with something they couldn't handle themselves right now.

But it was something she would have done in the past too. For different reasons. To prove herself. To take the chance to make a business contact without her bosses breathing down her neck. To further the business just to, well, further the business.

Her throat tightened again and she felt the backs of her eyes sting. She blinked rapidly.

Ollie's phone dinged again and he looked at it. "Dax," he said, swiping the message open. "They're doing a bypass. Surgery could take four to five hours. And she won't be awake for another two or three after that." He shook his head. "This is going to be a long fucking day."

Whitney agreed. And watching Ollie now made her chest ache. No doubt Dax and Grant looked much the same. Maybe worse. Their girls were worried and emotional too so they'd be supporting them as well as Cam. And then, of course, there were Cam and Aiden. Their mother was going into a major surgery. It would be hours before they knew how things were going to turn out.

Whitney had to blink again as her eyes stung and her throat got scratchy.

She didn't know exactly what Cam was doing but he was at the hospital and surrounded by people who loved him, who would make him feel stronger by being there and would make sure he had whatever he needed.

She trusted that.

No matter how much it hurt to not be one of those people.

"Did Grant or Dax say—"

Her question was cut off by the conference room door opening.

She took a breath and forced a smile as Gordon, Matt, and Stephen came in. She glanced at Ollie as she stood. He was also smiling and pushing to his feet. But she knew him. Oliver Caprinelli was upset. He wasn't the business meeting type in the first place and it was clear it was bothering him a lot to not be at the hospital with his friends.

"Good morning, Gordon," she greeted, pulling her attention from Ollie.

"Hello, Whitney. Good to see you again," the older Perkins greeted her with a handshake.

"Hello, Matt," she said, turning to his son.

"Hi, Whitney." Matt Perkins was good looking, charming, and sophisticated. And knew it. He gave her a grin and a glance that went from the top of her head to the flower on the toe of her shoe.

She ignored him. She turned to Stephen. "Mr. McDonald."

"Hello, Whitney."

She should probably ask them to call her Ms. Lancaster. Or they should just call her that without her having to ask. But they'd known her since Gordon and her father golfed together and she and Matt hung out at the country club swimming pool.

"This is Oliver Caprinelli, one of the new owners. Oliver, this is Gordon and Matt Perkins and Stephen McDonald."

"Nice to meet you all," Ollie said, shaking each man's hand. "Thanks for stopping by."

"Nice to meet you too," Gordon said, taking in Ollie's disheveled hair from where he'd been running his hand.

Ollie had put a tie on for the meeting and Whitney smiled to herself. That was a huge gesture and she appreciated it. But it was loose at the neck and his shirt wasn't tucked into his pants tightly and his pants were, well, jeans. He was also wearing Converse tennis shoes.

It didn't matter. Ollie was an owner of Hot Cakes and had as much, if not more, money than the Perkins men did. And he didn't really care what they thought. In fact, Whitney would have bet her month's salary that Ollie didn't even notice the way Gordon had looked him over.

"Please have a seat, everyone," Whitney said, pulling her own chair out. "Help yourself to coffee. We won't keep you long. I know you made a special stop here today." Whitney took her seat at the head of the table where Aiden usually sat.

She glanced at Ollie out of the corner of her eye. He was looking at his phone again.

It wasn't rude. She knew he wasn't ignoring her. He was checking in at the hospital. And she really wanted to know what the text said. He also wasn't going to be presenting here today. She was fully in charge. He was here as a face for the new owners only.

Piper slipped in just then. She gave everyone a bright smile and asked, "Just seeing if you need anything, Ms. Lancaster."

Whitney fought her grin. She loved Piper.

"This is Piper Barry," Whitney introduced. "She's our executive assistant."

"Hello, Piper," Matt said, sitting forward in his chair and giving her a big grin.

Ollie looked up at that. He frowned at Matt and looked over at Piper. He also sat forward in his chair. "Thought you were going down to Buttered Up?"

"Paige is getting things opened up. I thought I'd see if I can help Ms. Lancaster with anything before I go."

Ollie looked at Whitney, then back to Piper. "I've got Ms. Lancaster covered."

Piper didn't *quite* roll her eyes at him, but it was definitely implied. "Ms. Lancaster?" she asked, dismissing Ollie.

"I'm fine, actually," Whitney said. "But thank you."

"Absolutely. We'll talk later."

"Of course." Whitney watched as Piper slipped back out.

She was relieved to know that Paige was already at Buttered Up and that Piper was on her way.

She still wanted to get this meeting over with.

That was new. She never wanted to rush through meetings. She always wanted to be sure every T was crossed. Twenty-four hours ago, she'd been excited about this meeting and showing business associates of her father's and her bosses what she could do. Now she just really wanted to get these men out of here and on the road to Indiana.

"Why don't we get started?" she said. "In front of you, you'll see the information I'd like to go over today."

For the next twenty minutes, she filled them in on the details of the new product and her ideas for the launch and how Perkins Foods could be a part of it. But her mind was only partially on the presentation. She couldn't stop looking at Ollie who couldn't seem to stop looking at his phone. What was going on at the hospital? How was everyone?

She wrapped things up without going over the details for the television commercials in local markets or the Facebook ad plan.

"I'd love to hear your thoughts," she said, closing the folder in front of her.

But just then she noticed Ollie scowling at his phone.

Dammit. What had happened?

Gordon opened his mouth, but Whitney put up a finger. "But if you could just give us one minute, Gordon?" she asked. "I need to speak with Oliver about something pressing. Why don't we take a short break? You can refill your coffees." She pushed her chair back and stood. "Please help yourself to more muffins. The restrooms are just down the hall to the left," she spoke as she moved toward Ollie's chair. She snagged the sleeve of his shirt and tugged. "Can I see you in my office for a moment?"

He looked confused and it was clear that he hadn't been paying attention. "Uh, yeah. Sure." He got to his feet and followed her out the door and to the right.

Once they were in her office she faced him. "What's wrong?"

"They were going to do a bypass for two blockages. Now it's three."

"Dammit."

He nodded. "Yeah."

"You should go over there."

"What?" He frowned. "No. I'll wait until you're done."

"No. Go. You're worried sick and they would want you there with them. I've got this."

"But—"

"Ollie, what are the in-store displays going to look like?"

"Uh..."

"Come on. Are they going to have alpacas or bobcats on them?"

"Alpacas."

"Wrong." She smiled. "Neither."

He sighed. "I'm sorry. I'm just distracted."

"I know. And I get it. But I don't need you in there. I can answer all of their questions. I promise."

He was thinking about it, she could tell. So she pressed.

"Do you trust me?"

"Of course."

"Then please go. Take care of your friends. And send me an update as soon as you get there."

He finally breathed out. "Okay. I know you've got this. You'll be fine without me. I just wanted you to know you were supported."

She felt her chest warm as she realized that she already knew that. "I do know. The people who need your in-person support right this minute are in Dubuque."

She wanted those people—all of them but, yes, one in particular—to have everything, and everyone, they needed to feel supported. Ollie being there would make them feel better. He'd make Cam feel better. Piper would too.

"Go get Piper from the bakery. If it's too busy for Paige on her own, just close it up again. I think Piper needs to be at the hospital too."

Ollie nodded. "She's worried."

"I know."

Ollie reached out and squeezed her arm. "Go kick ass. I'll text you."

"Thanks."

He left and she stood staring at a door through which someone had left her again. But this was okay. She was where she needed to be.

She rejoined the other men in the conference room. They'd just settled back in with fresh coffee. She smiled as she took her seat.

"Where's Oliver?" Gordon asked.

"A friend's mother is in the hospital," Whitney said. "He left to be with him."

"Oh, I'm sorry to hear that."

It sounded like he said it more because he felt it was the right thing to say, but Whitney nodded.

"What questions do you have?" she asked.

"I'm curious what your father thinks of the plan."

She blinked, then stared at Gordon. Then frowned. Then blinked again. "My father?" she finally asked.

"Yes. I haven't spoken to him in a while but he didn't mention anything about a new product the last time we did talk."

"I'm sure he didn't," Whitney said, confused. "He doesn't know anything about it."

Gordon seemed confused now. "He doesn't?"

"No." Whitney leaned in. "My father doesn't own Hot Cakes anymore, Gordon. He's not a part of any new plans or products anymore."

"Well, yes, I know that's technically true," Gordon said. "But surely you're talking with him about decisions and turning to him for advice."

Whitney felt her eyebrows rise. "Actually, no, I'm not. There are four men who are making the decisions now and who I get advice from. And give it to, incidentally. Aiden Anderson, Grant Lorre, Oliver Caprinelli, and Camden McCaffery. The new owners."

"All young men with no previous experience in the food industry," Gordon said.

She nodded. "Which is why I'm here."

"Also young and inexperienced."

"Young, perhaps, but I've been involved with Hot Cakes all my life. It's been my family's business for almost fifty-two years."

"I'm aware of that." Gordon gave her a placating smile. "But I meant inexperienced in *actual* business."

Whitney expected to feel the typical frustration welling up. The anger at being dismissed. The exasperation.

Then... she started to laugh.

Gordon's eyes widened. He looked at Matt and Stephen.

Whitney glanced at them as well, laughing and shaking her head. She was actually... amused. These men were misogynistic fools. They were treating her the way her own father, grandfather, and brother always had. They wouldn't get it, no matter how she explained it to them.

And it didn't matter.

It didn't matter who they thought had come up with the ideas or who thought they were great. It didn't matter if Gordon Fucking Perkins thought she could handle this.

All that mattered was that Aiden, Grant, Ollie, and Cam thought she could handle this.

And they did.

All Gordon Perkins needed to know was that Hot Cakes was no longer a Lancaster family business.

She was the idiot. She'd put time and energy into this. She'd worn her new skirt for this. She'd stayed here instead of going to Dubuque, where she *really* wanted to be.

For these jackasses. Who would never get it. And whose opinions didn't matter.

"What's so funny?" Gordon finally asked.

"That you think my father, who nearly put this company out of business, is someone that any of these men would listen to," she said. Honestly. "Look, Gordon, your choice is simple—do you want to continue working with Hot Cakes or not. If yes, then you'll be a major partner in helping us launch our new product. If no, then..." She pushed her chair back and stood. "You're an idiot. You will never find four men more dedicated to doing the right thing and making their business successful then these four. But they will do it their way. You can come on board or you can miss out." She gathered her folder and stepped out from behind the table. "Now, if you'll excuse me, I've already given you enough of my time today. There's someplace else I need to be.

Someplace else she should have been a long time ago.

"Now wait," Gordon protested, coming to his feet. "I didn't say I wasn't interested."

She looked back. "Like I said, I've already given you enough time. We can schedule another meeting after you've thought about everything."

"I'd like to do this now. We can hash out the launch plan for our stores in Iowa right now."

"I want more than Iowa."

"Fine. All of our stores," Gordon said.

Whitney smiled. "Great. I'll have Piper put that on our agenda. For our *next* meeting."

As she walked out of the conference room, she thought about the fact that she'd maybe just ruined the relationship with the biggest account Hot Cakes had.

She might have just let her bosses down. Her friends down.

But as she put her folder on her desk and grabbed her purse so she could head to the hospital, she knew that wasn't true.

She was going to Dubuque. To the hospital to be a friend. Finally.

21

I t had been a shit day.

A really shit day.

Right on the heels of the best night of his life.

Whitney was in love with him. They'd reconnected, in every way.

And now his mother was on an operating table and a surgeon was cutting into her chest.

He rolled his neck and shoulders and looked around.

Aiden was holding Zoe. Grant was holding Josie. Dax was holding Jane. Didi was holding Henry. Or maybe Henry was holding Didi. The only two people without someone holding their hand or someone's arm around them were Cam and his dad.

That was because the person his dad wanted to be holding was the one with her chest split open right now.

And because the person Cam wanted to be holding was in Appleby in a fucking business meeting.

"Wow, you really look like crap."

He turned to find Piper handing him a muffin and a bottle of water.

"Hey." He was surprised to see her. Then he shook his head. "You can't bring a McCaffery a muffin. Buttered Up or home-made are the only kind we're allowed to eat."

She nodded. "That's from Buttered Up."

He frowned. "But—"

"Paige opened the bakery and I went in to help her. Stayed open until we ran out of stuff. Well, besides the stuff I swiped for you guys."

He looked around again and noticed that everyone now had food.

Cam looked at Piper. "Wow," he finally said. "Thank you. For the muffin and for managing the bakery this morning for Zoe and Josie."

"It was Whitney's idea."

His chest tightened painfully. "Oh." That was... nice. Awesome even. She'd been thinking of him and his family. She'd come up with a way to help.

In Appleby. From a distance.

It wasn't as if he believed she *hadn't* been thinking of him. Or them.

But she wasn't *here*.

She'd stood on those steps, wrapped in a sheet, probably still smelling like him and cookie dough, and she'd let him leave without her.

There was a big meeting today. A big meeting that mattered a lot to her. A big account, one she had history with. One she wanted to impress.

And of course it mattered to Hot Cakes, too. But it hadn't even occurred to her to reschedule.

"You okay?" Piper asked.

"Sure. I mean..." He gave a soft, humorless laugh. "No. Fuck no, even." He took a breath. "My mom's in surgery, my dad's a mess, my sister and brother are scared, and there's nothing I can do."

Piper nodded. "And Whitney's not here."

He thought about asking what she meant. Or maybe even denying that was on his mind. But Piper had been helping him nurse his hangovers after seeing Whitney for ten years now. She knew him and the other guys better than they knew themselves sometimes.

He finally nodded. "Yeah. And Whitney's not here."

Piper sighed and turned to lean on the windowsill next to him.

He twisted the top off the water bottle and took a drink, preparing to hear her say that he should have specifically asked Whitney to come. Or that Whitney was doing what she thought she needed to do by keeping the meeting. Or that Whitney thought she was helping by having the meeting and keeping things going so the guys could all be here with him and his family.

But instead, Piper said, "You're going to have to decide if you can handle having only part of her."

Cam frowned. "What do you mean?"

"I mean... I get it. I get how it feels to be in love with someone who can only give you *part* of themselves. And, the thing is, that's not their fault. We know who they are, Cam. They've been honest about it. It's our stupid fault for still wanting to be with them. So—" She looked at him. "You have to decide if you can be happy with only having part of her. Having her be gone, sometimes physically, a lot of the time mentally. Giving her heart and time and energy to something else."

"That's how you feel about Ollie?"

"Tell me I'm wrong."

Cam sighed. "Yeah. Okay. But..." He looked at the floor and thought about what she'd said. "I think you're wrong."

Piper snorted. "I've been in the front row for five years, Cam."

"Right. But... they can learn. They can change. They're not

doing it because they don't care. They're doing it because they don't think they'll be good at the love thing."

Piper studied him. "You think that's what's going on with Whitney?"

He nodded, realizing it was true. "She's not *here* because she doesn't know what to *do* here. She doesn't know how this works. She's in Appleby because she does understand all of that. She can do that right."

Piper nodded. "Doing things right is a big thing with her."

"It is."

"But, ironically, she's doing it wrong."

He nodded. "I know." But he felt the bitterness and hurt fading as he understood what he was explaining to Piper. "She's still figuring out the unconditional thing. It's only been a couple weeks. She'll get there."

"Only been a couple of weeks of what?" Piper asked.

"Of being loved like that," Cam said. "Didi's the only one who's ever done it. And I think the unconditional part just kind of takes time to learn and understand."

Could he give her time? Could he wait while she figured out that when he said "no matter what" he meant it?

Yes. For sure.

"That's what's going on with Ollie too?" Piper asked, her eyes finding Ollie across the room.

"I think Ollie is very used to doing things and trusting the rest of us to tell him when he's off track."

She nodded.

"And he's especially used to *you* telling him when he's off track," Cam said.

Piper looked up at him.

He nodded. "Yeah. I think you need to talk to him. Tell him how he's screwing this up with you."

She pulled in a deep breath and then looked back at Ollie, blowing it out. "Huh."

Cam grinned.

The door to the waiting room opened and he turned, hoping it was the doctor.

But it wasn't.

It was Whitney.

He actually felt a little light-headed as relief coursed through him.

He felt Piper's hand on his back. "Well, I'll be damned. Maybe they *can* learn how to do this."

He huffed out a laugh and then headed straight for Whitney.

Her eyes were wide and she was chewing on her bottom lip.

"Hi," she said as he came to stand in front of her.

"Hi."

She gave him a wobbly smile. "I knew better than to bring food, and especially dessert. And I thought liquor was probably not the right call this time. So..." She shrugged. "I'm empty-handed here."

He reached out and pulled her into his arms, hugging her close, and burying his face in her neck, breathing in her scent.

She wrapped her arms around him, holding him. "I could have brought—"

"Shh," he said against her ear. "This is all I need."

"But—"

"Nope," he interrupted again. "Just this. You. Here. With me."

Her arms tightened around him and they just stood, holding each other like that. And it really was exactly what he needed.

Long moments later—two minutes, thirty, a week, he didn't know—the door opened again.

This time it *was* the doctor.

Cam unwrapped himself from Whitney as everyone stood and came to cluster in the middle of the room to hear the news.

He kept her tucked tightly against his side though. He'd been getting okay with her *not* coming but now that she was here, he wasn't sure he was going to be able to let her go.

Aiden and Zoe hugged each other. Dax had Jane tucked securely under his arm. Grant stood behind Josie with his arms wrapped around her. Didi and Henry stood holding hands. Even Piper and Ollie were standing together. He had a hand on the back of her neck and she was leaning into him slightly. Cam's dad, Steve, stood at the front of the group.

The doctor focused on him. "It went well," he said.

The room let out a collective sigh. Cam felt his knees actually weaken. Whitney's arm tightened around him as if she sensed that.

"We got all the blockages taken care of," the doctor went on. "Her vitals were strong throughout and are strong now. It will be another hour or so until she's awake. She'll be in the ICU for a day or two. She will need cardiac rehab after she goes home. But I expect she'll do well with all of it."

A tear slipped down Steve's face as he let out a breath and extended his hand to the surgeon. "Thank you so much."

"Delivering good news is my favorite thing to do." The doctor smiled at them all. "She clearly has a wonderful support system here. But, let's limit the visitors to just a couple tonight."

He answered a couple of questions and then left them.

Steve turned to face everyone. "Thank you all so much for being here."

They all nodded. There was nowhere else any of them would have been.

"I'm going to go in and see her when she's awake," he said. "But maybe the rest of you should head home for now. You can come back later when she's a little stronger."

"But I want to see Mom," Henry protested. He looked scared.

Cam felt his chest tighten. The last time someone Henry loved had gone to the hospital, she hadn't come home.

"Oh, you know what Whitney did for me when I was in the hospital?" Didi asked him.

He looked up at her. "You were in the hospital?"

"Oh sure, a few times," Didi told him, waving her hand as if it was no big deal.

Cam smiled. That was perfect. She was reassuring Henry by letting him know that people *did* come out of the hospital.

"I had my tonsils out," Didi said. "And my appendix out. And three babies. And, the time I was going to tell you about with Whitney, I had a broken leg that needed surgery to put it back together."

"What?" Henry asked.

"Yep. They put metal pins and screws into my bones."

Henry's eyes were wide. "No way."

"Seriously. I can show you the x-rays."

"Yes," Henry said emphatically. "For sure."

Everyone laughed.

"Anyway," Didi went on. "When I was in the hospital that time, Whitney was about eight and she made me decorations for my room. Hospital rooms are so plain and boring. So Whitney drew pictures and got balloons and streamers and stuff. I think we should do that before we go see your mom."

Henry thought about that. "That would be nice."

"And the sooner we get home and make that stuff, the less time she'll spend looking at plain old white walls," Didi said.

Henry nodded. "We could do it while she's still asleep."

"Good plan."

Cam smiled and looked down at Whitney. She was doing that smiling-with-shiny-eyes thing she did when she watched Henry and Didi together.

"I can't believe she remembers that," Whitney said softly.

"It obviously mattered a lot to her."

She nodded. "And now she's taking care of Henry instead of the other way around."

"That's what friends do," Cam agreed.

Whitney looked up at him and gave him the sweetest, most loving smile he'd ever seen. "I love you, Cam."

He was surprised, but inordinately pleased. "I love you too."

"And I think you should stay here with your dad."

He nodded. He should. But that meant Whitney was going to take Didi and Henry home. Which was fine. It really was.

"And I'll see who can take Didi and Henry home."

"Wait, not you?"

"I not going anywhere," she told him, squeezing his arm. "I finally figured out *this* is where I want to be. No matter what."

He couldn't believe how those words affected him. "Whit—"

"We're going to head out," Grant said, stopping with Josie. "I'm so glad she's going to be okay."

"Thanks for being here," Cam told him.

They shared a quick hug and then Cam hugged Josie. "We'll tell her you were here and that you'll be back when she's feeling better."

Josie wiped at her eye. "Thank you. My God, I was so scared."

Aiden and Zoe came up beside them.

"We're going to stay," Zoe said. She looked at Whitney. "Piper told me about what you guys figured out for the bakery. Thank you so much." She reached out and pulled Whitney into a hug. "That was... amazing."

Whitney squeezed her back and Cam felt his throat tighten at the sight.

"Of course," Whitney told her. "Anytime you need anything, I'm here."

Zoe gave her a wobbly smile. "That's so weird. Great," she added quickly. "But weird."

Whitney laughed. "I know."

"Okay, so we'll all hang out with Steve," Aiden said. "You guys able to take Didi and Henry?" he asked Grant and Josie.

"Of course." Grant looked at Whitney. "We can stay at your house with them. If that's okay."

Cam braced for her to decline their offer or to realize that if she didn't go with them someone *would* need to stay with them, which meant she'd probably decide to leave.

He was shocked when she said, "That would be so great. Thank you. If she can't find her keys, there's a spare under the cherub just to the left of the porch. And help yourself to anything."

He wanted to kiss her so badly.

"Hey, how did the meeting go?" Grant asked her as he was turning to leave.

She winced. "Oh. Well..." She looked up at Cam, then at Aiden, then at Grant. "I might have ruined that entire relationship. I wanted to get out of there so I could get over here and Gordon started asking what my dad thought of everything—"

"Wait, your dad?" Aiden asked with a frown.

Cam was scowling too.

She sighed. "Yeah. He was shocked to learn that I hadn't consulted him and was concerned that we didn't know what we were doing. So I told him he'd be an idiot to not want to work with us and he could take the offer on the table or not but I didn't care and I was leaving and I walked out."

"Well, good," Grant said, also frowning. "Fuck him."

Whitney smiled. "I'm glad you feel that way."

Aiden was studying her. "You already have another idea anyway, don't you?"

She glanced up at Cam. "No. I just—"

Wow. She did already have a new idea. He was really going to just have to accept that it was always going to be like that. He grinned. "Go ahead," Cam said, nudging her.

"I... it wasn't like I was thinking about it on purpose," she said. "It just came to me as I was driving over."

"What is it, Whit?" Aiden asked with a smile.

"Well, okay. We don't *need* Perkins Foods. I mean, yes, they're the biggest chain, of course. But we're *Hot Cakes*," she said. "We're one of the biggest snack cake companies out there and we're the best. So... what if we only put our products in small stores. Family owned, independent grocery stores and gas stations. We wouldn't have as many locations, *but* if people want a Hot Cakes snack cake, they'll be willing to go looking for them. That would bring business to those smaller stores *and* make Hot Cakes a more exclusive item."

Grant seemed to be thinking about that. But he did not, for once, keep an unreadable expression on his face. He nodded, then smiled, then said, "I like it. Let's talk more about that."

"Yep, and if Gordon Perkins comes crawling back," Aiden said, "we'll let *you* decide if we work with him or not."

"I might tell him to fuck off."

"That's your call," Aiden said with a wink.

Whitney turned a huge grin up to Cam.

He gave in then and bent to kiss her.

It was just a quick, sweet one, but it seeped into his bones and made him, quite simply, *happy*.

"Mr. McCaffery?" a nurse asked from the doorway.

Cam turned, but he knew she was talking to his father.

"You can come with me now," she said.

Steve was clearly relieved. Cam, Zoe, Aiden, Josie, and Jane gave him hugs. He knelt before Henry to give him instructions to be a good listener and to text him if he needed anything.

"I'll call you later and you can talk to your mom if she's up to it," Steve told him.

Henry nodded. "Okay. But I'll be all right."

Steve looked up at Didi, then stretched to his feet. "I know you will, son," he said. He met Didi's gaze. "Thank you."

"It's my pleasure," she told him. Then she reached up and put a hand on Steve's cheek. "I wish I could have known you sooner."

Steve looked a little choked up. Letty had been his mother. This was her childhood best friend. What wounds Letty and Didi hadn't been able to heal, *he* was able to heal with Didi. At least a little.

He put his hand over hers on his face and said, "We have time for that."

She smiled. "I look forward to it."

Then Steve turned and left with the nurse.

Everyone else just stood quietly for a moment.

Until Didi asked Josie, "If we're riding back with you, does that mean we can stop at the bakery for pie?"

The mood officially lightened, everyone laughed and Josie slipped her arm through Didi's—the one that wasn't holding Henry's hand—and said, "Absolutely. Pie makes everything better."

"We will be right behind you," Jane, the ultimate pie lover, announced.

She and Dax stopped and hugged Cam and Whitney and Zoe and Aiden. So did Ollie and Piper.

And then it was just the four of them.

Cam settled on one of the waiting room couches near the far wall and pulled Whitney down beside him, while Aiden and Zoe took the couch closer to the door. They were together, but this way the couples could chat in private.

"So you know," he said as Whitney snuggled into him. "I'd really love to have your grandma stay at the house and not move into Sunny Orchard yet."

Whitney stiffened in surprise and looked up at him. "Really?"

"Really. Things are going great. She's doing well. I love being with her. I know we haven't had any really bad days yet and I know things will get worse. There may be a time when Sunny Orchard is the right place for her but..." He'd been thinking about it a lot over the past week as the end of his month with Didi had been getting closer. "I think we could keep her at home longer."

Whitney didn't say anything. She just studied him, a soft smile on her face.

"What?" he asked finally.

"I really like hearing you say *we* and *home* and talk about the future like that."

His heart kicked hard in his chest. "Me too."

"And, yes," she said. "I mean, I love having her there. If that's what she wants. And you're up for it."

"Turns out that Hot Cakes needs *a lot* less legal work than Fluke did and, well, I'm damned good at being a stay-at-home grandson."

Whitney's expression softened. "Oh, man. You really are sweet. Those tattoos and muscles are a total cover-up."

He laughed. "Just with you. And Didi."

"And your mom. And Henry. And your sister. And Piper. And—"

"Okay, so my badass reputation is trashed." He grinned down at her.

"Totally trashed," she said with a nod. "But... at least you still have the tattoos."

"You like those, don't you?"

"So much," she said in a lusty sigh.

He kissed the top of her head. "Maybe we should get you some."

She didn't say no. He looked down at her.

"Whit?"

"Just thinking about what I would get and where," she said. "Especially if you would want to lick them as much as I like licking yours."

Predictably, hospital waiting room or not, his body responded to that. "I would," he said. "Very much. And I have some very specific ideas about what and where if *that* is part of the criteria."

She grinned up at him. "Oh good."

Yeah, he was definitely in love with her.

O*ne month later...*
   "A toast!" Dax announced.

Everyone quieted and turned to face him. Except Maggie and Steve. They were sitting in the chaise lounge chairs off to one side. Still, they were facing Dax.

Maggie was doing great, but it was late and she still got tired easily, especially at these big group gatherings. Though she loved them more than anything.

Of course, anymore, *all* of their gatherings seemed to be big group gatherings.

Whitney had been amazed to find out over the past month that she was actually an extrovert. She'd thought so in high school, but the last few years, she'd been *fine* at home alone or just with Didi. Now though, with this group, she loved getting everyone together and talking and laughing and joking and encouraging each other.

"I don't know what the hell we were thinking, but I'm sure glad we bought Hot Cakes," Dax said.

Everyone laughed and raised their cups.

"Lord knows there were about a million ways we could have screwed that up," Dax went on. "*But*, thankfully, we had Whitney."

Everyone turned to hoist their cups toward her.

Whitney felt her eyes stinging.

"You are our fearless leader, our cheerleader, our visionary and... our friend." Dax's voice got softer on that last word and he gave her an affectionate smile. "You've also made our most ornery partner into a freaking teddy bear."

Everyone looked at Cam who was, of course, right beside Whitney. She grinned at him.

"And for that we do truly believe you are magical," Dax said.

Whitney gave a little curtsy.

Cam pinched her ass when she straightened.

She giggled.

He always acted growly when they teased about how *nice* and *sweet* and *cuddly* he was now, but the truth was, he freely admitted it. He was downright domestic. Not only was Didi still living with them, but they were now also fostering kittens. Or Cam was, anyway. Whitney still wasn't entirely sure how Paige had talked him into that, but honestly, seeing the big guy with the bulging, tattooed biceps bottle-feeding a kitten was even hotter than watching him bake cookies. And that was saying something.

"So it is long past time for us to finally make you, Whitney Lancaster, an official *partner* at Hot Cakes," Dax said. "Thank you for saying yes when we asked you."

Her eyes were stinging again but she smiled widely. "I'm thrilled."

"To Whitney," Dax said.

Everyone repeated, "To Whitney!"

"Now can we jump in?" Henry called as everyone drank.

Whitney laughed.

"Yes, now you can jump in," Cam said. "But stay in the—"

Didi and Henry jumped into the swimming pool at the same time, throwing water up onto the patio and making Dax and Jane jump back, laughing.

"Shallow end," Cam finished, as he watched them head for the slide. In the deep end. "Guess I'm going in for lifeguard duty."

Yes. The party was at Whitney and Didi, and Cam's, house. On the back patio. At 3 a.m.

And they were grilling burgers and drinking hard root beer.

No one was going into work tomorrow.

Whitney kissed him quickly. "You're the best."

"If you *really* loved me, you'd join us. In that red bikini I got you."

"I thought that was for swimming when it was just the two of us."

"Okay, sunrise swim. Just the two of us. And the red bikini."

"Deal."

She watched him head for the pool and her grandmother and his little brother. He stripped his shirt off, tossed it to the side, and then gave her one more look over his shoulder before diving in.

Yeah, those tattoos and muscles were all hers. As were the cookies he'd made just for her, hidden inside where the friends and family who they loved—just not enough to share *every single* cookie with—would never find them. She was in a really good place.

Speaking of really good places... Whitney looked around the patio. Everyone was here. Even Paige and Piper and Ollie. She sighed a happy sigh.

She'd spent time with her own mother and father and brothers on this patio over the years.

But she'd never actually been with *family* here.

Until now.

———

Thank you so much for reading *Semi-Sweet On You!* I hope you loved Cam and Whitney's story!

Next up is Paige and Mitch's story in

Oh, Fudge!

It's a Hot Cakes story with a hint of the Boys of the Bayou series! You do not have to have read that series *at all* to enjoy this story! But it might make you want to take a trip down south to Louisiana when you're done!

A sassy, small town Iowa girl.
A hot, rugged Louisiana boy.
A surprise visit. A nosy family. A winter festival.
Dang, is this was falling in love feels like?
Oh, fu...fudge.

———

The Hot Cakes Series
Sugar Rush (prequel)
Sugarcoated
Forking Around
Making Whoopie
Semi-Sweet On You
Oh, Fudge
Gimme S'more

———

If you want to check out the Boys of the Bayou series before Oh, Fudge releases (and figure out who the heck Mitch is...and meet the rest of his big, crazy, fun family...) you can do that now!

Small town, hot-country-boys-with-Louisiana-drawls, crazy-falling-in-love fun!

My Best Friend's Mardi Gras Wedding
A fake relationship, small town, rom com

Sweet Home Louisiana
A sexy second chance, small town rom com

Beauty and the Bayou
A beauty and the beast, wounded hero,
small town rom com

Crazy Rich Cajuns
A sexy opposites attract, nerdy hero,
small town, rom com

Must Love Alligators
A fish-out-of-water, nerd heroine, small town rom com

————

And join in on all the FAN FUN!

Join my email list!
http://bit.ly/ErinNicholasEmails

And be the first to hear about my news, sales, freebies, behind-the-scenes, and more!

Or for even more fun, join my **Super Fan page** on Facebook and chat with me and other super fans every day! Just search Facebook for Erin Nicholas Super Fans!

————

If you love sexy, funny, small town romance and, well, hot

kitchens and baked goods ;) you should also check out my
Billionaires in Blue Jeans series!
Triplet billionaire sisters find themselves in small town Kansas
for a year running a pie shop...and falling in love!

Diamonds and Dirt Roads
High Heels and Haystacks
Cashmere and Camo

Find all my books, including a printable book list, at
www.ErinNicholas.com

ABOUT ERIN

Erin Nicholas is the New York Times and USA Today bestselling author of over thirty sexy contemporary romances. Her stories have been described as toe-curling, enchanting, steamy and fun. She loves to write about reluctant heroes, imperfect heroines and happily ever afters. She lives in the Midwest with her husband who only wants to read the sex scenes in her books, her kids who will never read the sex scenes in her books, and family and friends who say they're shocked by the sex scenes in her books (yeah, right!).

Find her and all her books at
www.ErinNicholas.com

And find her on Facebook, Goodreads, BookBub, and Instagram!

CPSIA information can be obtained
at www.ICGtesting.com
Printed in the USA
FSHW012248170920
73840FS